THE WILD SEED

Also by Iris Gower

THE LOVES OF CATRIN
COPPER KINGDOM
PROUD MARY
SPINNERS' WHARF
MORGAN'S WOMAN
FIDDLER'S FERRY
BLACK GOLD
SINS OF EDEN
THE SHOEMAKER'S DAUGHTER
THE OYSTER CATCHERS
HONEY'S FARM
ARIAN
SEA MISTRESS

IRIS GOWER
THE WILD SEED

BANTAM PRESS

LONDON · NEW YORK · TORONTO · SYDNEY · AUCKLAND

TRANSWORLD PUBLISHERS LTD
61–63 Uxbridge Road, London W5 5SA

TRANSWORLD PUBLISHERS (AUSTRALIA) PTY LTD
15–23 Helles Avenue, Moorebank, NSW 2170

TRANSWORLD PUBLISHERS (NZ) LTD
3 William Pickering Drive, Albany, Auckland

Published 1996 by Bantam Press
a division of Transworld Publishers Ltd
Copyright © Iris Gower 1996

The right of Iris Gower to be identified
as the author of this work has been asserted in accordance
with sections 77 and 78 of the Copyright Designs and Patents
Act 1988.

A catalogue record for this book is available
from the British Library.

ISBN 0593 033558

Typeset in 11/13pt Plantin by
Falcon Oast Graphic Art
Printed in Great Britain by
Mackays of Chatham plc, Chatham, Kent.

To Emma, Anna and Adam with love.

CHAPTER ONE

The girl in the bed looked gloriously abandoned, her long, fiery hair rippled over her shoulders, partly covering the curve of her creamy breasts. Her eyes were closed, she was rosy in the glow from the gas lamp; content beneath the thickness of the satin quilt.

It was quiet in the room except for the rumble of wheels on the cobbled street outside the Swansea Hotel and the hiss of the coals shifting in the grate.

'It's getting dark, *cochen*; time to go home.'

She stirred, her eyes opening; wide, green, mysterious eyes that seemed to look into his soul. God in heaven, how he loved her. Perhaps he had always loved her and had never recognized the feeling until now.

'Oh, Boyo, don't say that, it's so cold and wet outside and it's so wonderful having you here; so homely, so comfortable, so *right*.'

He knew exactly what she meant. He sat on the bed beside her and took her hand. His own was smooth, the nails clean, well-manicured; it was the hand of a gentleman. Except that Boyo Hopkins had been born in sin, brought up in a workhouse, given the name of 'Boyo' because he had known no other. Now he was called Boyo Jubilee Hopkins after his grandfather, he was a man of substance, of standing in the community.

'I *must* go.' He spoke regretfully, his once rough accent barely noticeable now. He rose and stood before the long oval mirror that graced the huge bedroom. He was, to all intents and purposes, a man of refinement and if now and again the rough edges of his origins were revealed, they were more than compensated for by the sizeable fortune he possessed.

'Boyo, why can't we be open about our love? Why are

7

we here in some strange hotel? You should come to see Mam and Dad. We are so isolated on the farm that a visit from you would be like a breath of fresh air. Are you ashamed of me now you've come into money?'

He turned and looked at her. Her skin was fresh and dewy, she was everything that was young and beautiful and she had been a virgin until he had taken her to his bed.

'Of course I'm not ashamed of you,' he said, and he meant it. He would like nothing better than to take her out, to flaunt her openly, to have the envy of other men.

'It's time you were married, time you were showing a wife off to the world,' Catherine said. It was as though she had picked up the thread of his thoughts. 'I know you are only a few years older than me, love, but you don't need to make your way in the world, do you? It isn't as if you can't afford a wife. Perhaps you don't want to marry me, is that it?'

He rose to his feet. '*Duw*, don't be silly, girl.' He was slipping into the Welsh, an indication that he was agitated.

'We must get to know each other, catch up on the past.' He knew he sounded defensive.

'Would things have been different, I mean, if you and I had remained friends, if we hadn't lost touch, lost some years when we should have been together?' Her voice trailed away wistfully.

Boyo shook his head and remained silent. He should tell her the truth, say the words he was afraid to say, that he was married already. He thought back to his wedding, a quiet affair, conducted in a small church in the tiny village of Ilston. Bethan Llewellyn had been a spinster, a mature woman. She was a lady from good farming stock, she possessed what he'd never had: breeding. On their marriage, Bethan's father had given Boyo a gift: a fine hotel situated near the coast. A gold-mine which Boyo did not need or want. Shortly after their marriage, he had returned the deeds to Bethan.

'Penny for them.'

8

He turned and looked at the girl, now sitting on the edge of the bed, her feet, bare and pink, not quite reaching the carpet, and his heart melted. Six short days ago they had met again, brought together on the cold spring breeze of the beach at Swansea. They had stared at each other, recognition dawning with a sense of wonderment and joy.

He smiled, 'I was thinking of you, of our meeting on the beach.' He touched her hair, red in the firelight, glowing, alive.

'Nice thoughts?'

'Of course.'

She came to him and wound her arms around his waist, putting her head against his heart.

'Tell me something, Boyo, why do you call me *cochen*? Why don't you use my proper name?'

He sighed. 'You don't seem like the Catherine I once knew. I remember the child running wild on Honey's Farm. Now you are a woman, a flame, a glorious redhead, that's what *cochen* means.'

'Oh?'

He bent and kissed her. Her lips parted invitingly, he felt his blood stir; would she always have this effect on him, however many times he lay with her? He disentangled himself.

'We have to go, love.'

'I know, but I miss you already. Will I see you, tomorrow?'

'Yes, tomorrow.'

Outside the hotel, he waited for the man to bring his horse around and then he lifted Catherine and set her on the saddle.

'It's not a fine carriage,' he apologized, 'but old Jason here will serve us better on the rough ground.'

He took her home to the farmlands above Swansea. Honey's Farm stretched for miles across the hillside, the rich earth planted now with seed which the summer sun would bring to fruition. Boyo felt a pain within him as he thought of the days of his youth. He had spent a great deal of his spare time at the farm, eating with Fon and Jamie O'Conner, sharing their warmth and hospitality. Now, he would be ashamed to face them.

He kissed the sweetness of Catherine's mouth and released her, feeling suddenly cold. 'Go in, your parents will be worrying about you.'

'They wouldn't be if they knew I was with you. They always liked you, even when you were Boyo the tannery worker.'

'Hush, go on now, I'll watch until you are safely indoors.'

He stood for a long time, looking at the darkness of the farmhouse against the rising moon. His heart ached suddenly for the boy he had been, he had worked hard but he had been happy, without responsibilities; free.

Across the dip of the valley was *Glyn Hir*, the tannery Catherine had spoken of. It had been his home. Ellie Hopkins, old Jubilee's beautiful young widow, had made sure that he did not work too hard and that the other men treated him fairly. For a long time, Ellie had worked alongside him in the mill, grinding the oak bark for tanning the leather.

It was on his sixteenth birthday that the voluptuous Rosie, Ellie's maid, had taken him to her bosom, literally, teaching him all he needed to know about love, the pure and the carnal. He remembered it as if it were yesterday, the smell of the wood fire, the sound of a fiddle playing in the distance and Rosie, soft and warm and so willing in his arms.

And then, unexpectedly, he owned a fortune. Ellie had learned that Boyo was Jubilee's grandson. The money and land she had inherited from Jubilee, she felt, was rightfully Boyo's. She had been generous, had signed it all over to him. He wondered now if he would have been happier had he remained a working boy.

He sighed and turned away from the warmth of the light in the farmhouse windows. Bethan would be waiting and Bethan was his wife, his friend.

He was betraying her, reneging on their pact of trust

and mutual respect, but he was not betraying her love; he reassured himself on that point. They had both known from the start that theirs was not a marriage made in heaven but a marriage of friendship, as well as the merging of two great fortunes.

By the time Boyo reached the large house on the hillside overlooking the sweep of the bay, he felt the peace that coming home always gave him.

He rode around the building to the stables and dismounted from his horse, experiencing the sense of pride that settled on him whenever he returned to the house he had made his own.

It was poised like an eagle's nest over the fine bay of Rhosilli, with the sound of the sea and the wind and the calling of the birds.

The groom took the reins, tipping his cap before throwing a blanket over the animal's heaving flanks. 'Wet evening, sir, getting misty, too. The fireside's the best place on a night like this.'

'You're right, Roberts, I'll be glad to get indoors out of it.'

He walked through the back of the house, past the kitchens where a fire blazed in the blackleaded range and where the cook and the kitchen maids were working in the cheerfully spotless room; the low hum of their voices was somehow welcome and soothing. The inviting smell of roasting meat made him realize, suddenly, how hungry he was.

He opened the doors of the large drawing-room and Bethan rose to greet him, smiling at him over her spectacles. She was by no means a pretty woman but her elegant bearing and the dignity in the way she held her head, facing the world fearlessly, had the strangest ability to bring out all that was best in Boyo.

He leaned forward and kissed her, she was as tall as he was and large of bone. She was angular, with no soft curves and yet she was regal; awesome. A wave of affection washed over him. It was followed swiftly by feelings of guilt. He had no intention of hurting Bethan, of

11

breaking the vows he'd made at the altar; he could never leave her and yet how could he bear to deny the fate that had brought Catherine O'Conner back into his life?

'Darling, you're cold and look at the mud on your boots! Boyo, are you aware that you stink of horses? Go upstairs and get washed and changed, supper is almost ready.'

He tweaked her nose, 'Hush, you sound like an old hen.' As soon as the words were spoken he wished he could snatch them back. Had they been put there by Catherine or had the thought been with him since he'd first set eyes on Bethan?

She was not one jot aggrieved. 'Get on with it you big fool! Have you forgotten that my father is joining us this evening?'

He had forgotten and his mouth twisted into a rueful smile.

'You idiot!' Bethan made a mock sweep at him with her hand and he caught her to him, holding her close, his face buried in the warmth of her neck.

'See how I am abused and in my own home too?' He appealed to the empty room behind him and Bethan twisted out of his arms, her eyes full of laughter.

'Poor old soul, is his evil harridan of a wife being unkind yet again?'

'Yet again,' he agreed, his tone sombre.

'Anyway,' Bethan moved from him towards the fire, settling her spectacles on her nose, 'what kept you so late?'

Boyo knew it was an inquiry made out of genuine interest with no hint of suspicion behind the words. He swallowed hard, 'I went over to Honey's Farm.' It was easier to tell the truth or part of it. 'I looked down on my past, on the sweeping fields and across the valley to where the tannery once stood.' He felt inexplicably sad. 'It's just a ruin now.'

'You grow, you move on,' Bethan said reasonably.

'You are right, of course. Well, no more brooding over the past, I'm going to make myself presentable for my father-in-law.' Boyo moved to the door, determined to shake off the strange feelings that were haunting him.

He stood in the bathroom and looked round at the black-and-white-tiled walls and the large bath that would have dominated a lesser room. All this luxury still gave him a sense of pride, a feeling of achievement. Until he was seventeen years old he'd never possessed anything except the clothes he stood up in.

As for love, he'd lost the only girl he could ever love when April had died, or so he'd believed then. Her young life had been extinguished by the epidemic that had swept through Swansea some years before and he had been devastated.

Boyo's life had been empty until he met Bethan. She had offered him warmth, kindness and he had clung to her like a drowning man clings to a spar. He had married in haste, was he to repent at leisure? For now there was Catherine.

His heart had turned over when he'd first seen her again, April's sister, grown into a lovely woman. He had never given her a thought, not in the seven or so years since he'd last seen her. But now, he could not imagine life without her.

It was not fair, of course not, Catherine was young, much younger than he was in every way. As she'd pointed out, there were not that many years between them, but life had made Boyo old before his time. As for Catherine, she had her whole future before her, she should be free to find a good husband and bear him children. The thought was almost a physical pain.

He rose from the steaming water and stood looking at his naked frame in the mirror. He was taller than average, well-built, muscular; the hard work he'd done as a boy had seen to that. He wondered if he was handsome; his jaw was firm, his eyes clear but there was an almost brooding quality about him that he recognized as his need to conceal his thoughts and feelings from others. It was a way he had developed of protecting himself. Sometimes, when at a fine soirée peopled by the rich and successful of

13

the town, Boyo would think ruefully of the ragged tannery worker he had once been. He would have been given short shrift by these same people who now accepted that he was one of them.

Later, dressed in a pristine shirt and immaculate suit, he made his way downstairs to the dining-room. The candles were lit on the long table. Silver and glass gleamed in the flame and across the room a fire burned brightly in the ornate grate. His was a comfortable life, a life in which he had become content. Why then was he jeopardizing everything by falling in love so suddenly and so devastatingly with Catherine O'Conner?

'Daddy will be here any minute,' Bethan bustled into the room bringing with her the clean scent of lavender. She came to him and he kissed her cheek in the usual familiar gesture that had become a habit.

'The peach room is made up for him, he likes it in there with the curtains open. He likes to sit up in bed and watch the moon over the sea.'

'Your father is a man of impeccable taste,' Boyo said and meant it.

Dafydd Llewellyn was from old Welsh stock, reputed to be linked to Welsh princes somewhere in the distant past. It was easy to believe; he was a man of regal bearing, he spoke Welsh as he spoke English, without blemish. That he was learned became obvious as soon as he opened his mouth and yet Dafydd patronized no-one.

The great brass bell outside the door jangled loudly and Bethan's face lit up. 'There he is, I can't wait to see him again.'

Within a few minutes, Bethan returned, her arm linked with her father's. The man had such presence that Boyo was filled with the urge to bow over the man's hand as if he were a saint, or indeed of royal blood. Instead, he smiled and went forward holding out his hand. The handshake was warm, firm, in spite of Dafydd's advanced age.

Supper was a pleasant, leisurely business. The first course was soup, rich and hot with pepper and leeks. The fish fell from the bone, whole turbot decorated with nuts

14

on a bed of sliced boiled eggs. The beef was braised in a dark gravy and served with cabbage and carrots and the very first of the new potatoes grown in the Gower farmlands.

Dafydd declined the pudding filled with sultanas and currants and covered in steaming custard. His eyes under their heavy lids were difficult to read; Boyo saw his father-in-law as some ancient Merlin, mysterious, wise and invincible.

'How is business?' Dafydd relaxed in his high-backed chair and regarded his son-in-law carefully. 'Leather still bringing good prices?'

'Very good,' Boyo said. 'It seems that large manu-facturers are buying skins in great quantities for huge suites of furniture for hotels.'

Both men knew that Boyo need never worry about business again. His fortune, once great, was now, by dint of clever investments, bringing in enough money to keep Boyo in luxury for the rest of his life. Combined with Bethan's profits from the Gomerian Inn, the couple were among the wealthiest in the Principality.

'Not tired of the leather trade yet, Boyo?' Dafydd held out his pipe waiting for his daughter's nod of consent before lighting it.

'I don't think I'll ever be tired of it,' Boyo said honestly. 'It's part of my heritage, part of me.'

Dafydd eyed him thoughtfully. 'Your grandfather must have been a clever man.'

Boyo was surprised, his origins were scarcely ever referred to. The mists that surrounded his birth were rarely drawn aside and yet, even now, it was a mark of pride to Boyo that he had not been the nameless, penni-less foundling he had so long believed himself to be.

Dafydd's next question brought a wary feeling of tension, though Boyo made every effort not to show it.

'Were you in town today?'

'Yes, I was.'

'Business or pleasure?'

Boyo wondered if the questions were loaded. 'Bit of both,' he replied.

15

Bethan, as though sensing a tension she could not quite understand, leaned forward and rang the bell. 'Time we had some coffee.' She looked at her father. 'Boyo was reliving his past, going back over his old haunts.' She put her hand over Boyo's. 'Honey's Farm still has the power to hurt you, doesn't it, love?'

He felt tenderness rising within him. 'The things that happened there, yes, sometimes.'

'The past is best left alone,' Dafydd spoke in an easy tone but his words seemed filled with meaning. 'Turning over old stones can be a mistake.'

Was there a warning in his words? Boyo could not be sure. He remained silent and the silence lengthened. Bethan was looking from one to the other of them.

'Is there something going on I'm not aware of?' She smiled a little uncertainly. Boyo held his breath, not sure how much his father-in-law knew about his activities, or indeed, if he knew anything at all.

The taut lines of Dafydd's thin face seemed to relax. 'Just being an old fool, airing my home-spun philosophy and turning into a bore. Forgive me, I think I'm tired. The trip from Swansea seemed to take for ever, those dreadful, twisting lanes are a hazard for any self-respecting carriage driver, not to mention the passenger.'

He rose and Bethan too. She kissed her father on both cheeks. 'We can talk more in the morning, when you are feeling more rested.'

He smiled down at her, the long lines around his aquiline nose deepening. 'I want to know when you are going to give me a grandson.' He touched his daughter's shoulder. 'I do hope you are being a good wife, we men are such pathetic creatures when it comes to moral fibre. If we don't have what we need on our own hearth we tend to look for it elsewhere.'

He glanced towards Boyo. 'Good night, son-in-law, take care of my daughter, your wife is an extraordinary woman, as I'm sure you realize.' Again the old man's words seemed loaded.

Bethan accompanied her father upstairs and Boyo

moved to the drawing-room, helping himself to a liberal measure of port from the gleaming decanter which had been strategically placed on an occasional table near the fire. Bethan thought of everything.

As he sat and waited for his wife, Boyo felt a spirit of gloom descend on him. He had gone headlong into this affair with Catherine, snatching eagerly at the thrill and the passion and yes, the love that burned within him like a fire suddenly ignited. He had not stopped to consider the consequences: what the outcome of such a liaison could mean should his infidelity be discovered. And Catherine, how long would she put up with a part-time lover?

He should give up this foolishness at once, he should never have started the affair in the first place. But now Catherine had become, in a few short days, like a drug to his senses, a drug he had no wish to do without.

'That's Daddy settled.' Bethan entered the room and sat down in the chair at the opposite side of the fire. She took off her glasses and folded them with studied care.

'Boyo, is anything wrong?' She was looking at him but he could not meet her gaze. He rose and poured himself more port. 'You would tell me if something was troubling you, wouldn't you, love?'

He forced himself to smile down at her. 'Bethan, you are an old worrier, stop fretting, I'm perfectly all right.'

'You seem, well, not yourself. I don't know how to explain it but you even look different these past few days, more alive somehow.'

'Silly fancies, Bethan, I am the same boring old Boyo I always was.'

Bethan's hands twisted together. 'You are so young and yet in many ways so much older than I am. There's a darkness about your past. I wish you would discuss it with me, Boyo, it might help.'

Suddenly her questions irritated him. 'Bethan,' his voice was quiet, 'leave well alone, there's a good girl.'

Bethan's mood changed. She smiled at him in her old teasing way. 'Big buffoon! Spoiled boy! I should take the

17

broom from the kitchen to you, give you a good hiding.'

He wasn't to be jollied. He filled his glass once more and moved to the door. 'Excuse me, Bethan, I'm going into the den, I have work to do.'

It was a thin excuse and they both knew it. The administration of his many business affairs was handled by experts, by men specializing in their field. Boyo Hopkins employed only the best.

In the den the fire was burning low in the grate. Boyo knelt on the carpet staring into the flickering embers. He felt tired, no, perhaps jaded was the word. Suddenly he was out of sorts with himself. He lifted lumps of coal from the scuttle with his hands, taking a strange satisfaction in the gritty feel of the fuel against his skin. He studied his grimy fingers, that was how they should look, how they *had* looked – once. He was becoming soft, if he did not take care he would become flabby, inept. He would lose his muscle tone, the hardness would leave his body, he would develop a paunch from overindulgence. He smiled, if he did not take care he would lose his sense of proportion.

The flames brightened, leaping upward into the chimney. He was reminded at once of Catherine's hair, falling red and gold in the lamplight across her ivory skin.

It was no casual affair, he wished it was, he could cope with that. No, this bond between himself and Catherine had been there since childhood. Now it was forged again and it would not be easy to disentangle himself.

He didn't know how long he sat staring into the fire but his eyes felt filled with grit, he needed to get some sleep. He heard Bethan in the hall, she opened his door and peered in.

'I'm going up to bed, now, don't be long Boyo, you look all washed out.'

He left it for an hour, hoping that by the time he joined Bethan in the big four-poster she would be asleep. It was a false hope.

She turned to him at once and wound her arms around his neck. 'Boyo, hold me, I feel lonely and cold.' She snuggled against him and he breathed in her familiar scent; a wash of affection made his response much warmer than he'd intended and Bethan lifted her head, drawing his mouth down on hers.

Her kiss was not one of passion, but then passion had never been part of their relationship, yet he felt touched by the warmth of his wife's embrace.

Her arms wound around his waist, she pressed herself closer to him, her breasts soft against his chest. He was a normal red-blooded man, usually he responded to her as any healthy young man would to his wife, but not tonight. Tonight he had been with the woman who aroused the demons of hell in him by her passion.

Gently, he eased her away from him. 'As you said, Bethan, I'm washed out tonight, not very good for anything.'

He kissed her brow and turned away from her; he could feel the depths of her rejection by the rigid line of her body. He didn't want to hurt her, perhaps it would be as well to talk it over, to bring everything out into the open, to ask her what she wished to do about it.

He sat up and pushed back the sheets. 'Bethan. . .' he spoke softly almost in a whisper. She did not reply and tentatively he put his hand on her shoulder.

'Not now, Boyo,' she said in a hard, dry voice, 'we'll talk in the morning.'

Somehow, he knew from the way she spoke that Bethan was afraid, afraid she might hear something she didn't want to hear. Pity overwhelmed him; how could he burden his wife, a good, kind, generous woman, with his own conflict of conscience?

He put his head on the pillow and closed his eyes, knowing he could not sacrifice Bethan's peace of mind for his own. What he had done, was doing, was wrong, but he could no more stop it than he could turn back the tide in Swansea Bay.

CHAPTER TWO

Catherine awoke to feel the sun slanting across her face. She lifted her head and saw the curtains lift gently in the breeze. Outside, the birds were singing, it seemed that even nature was conspiring to enhance the happiness that was sweeping through her.

She turned over on her side, her hand beneath her cheek, the heavy weight of her braided hair fell across her neck like a lover's caress. Excitement flared through her, she, Catherine O'Conner, had a lover.

From the kitchen she heard the muted sounds of morning; the ashes being riddled in the fireplace, the chink of crockery, and realized that she had overslept. She smiled softly, it was just like her parents to allow her to lie in bed until she chose to rise.

That they indulged their only child was a fact of which Catherine was well aware. A great deal of her mother's protectiveness and her father's gentle kindness stemmed from fear, for they had lost their sons at an early age. April too; beautiful April, tragic April. Catherine pushed the thought away, she did not want to think about April, not now when she was so happy. Light steps approached her room and her mother peered around the door. 'Awake then? About time, too, *cariad*.'

Catherine sat up and stretched her arms, closing her eyes against the bright sunlight and the feeling of happiness that rose within her.

'Come on, I can't hold this hot tea by here for ever, I've got the breakfast to cook.'

'Right, Mam, I'll take the tea, I could do with it, I'm parched.'

'You're looking very pleased with yourself this morning.' Her mother handed her the cup. 'Were you out with a boy last night by any chance?'

Catherine bent her face over the steaming tea. 'Don't be soft, Mam. Just because you and Dad are so much in love you think everyone wants to be the same as you.'

'And don't they?' Fon O'Conner was still a very beautiful woman. Her hair swept away from her face, revealed fine cheek-bones and a clear, direct gaze that was sometimes disconcerting.

She sat on the thick patchwork quilt. 'Don't be in too much of a hurry, love, there's plenty of fish in the sea, mind.'

'Please, Mam,' Catherine said softly. 'It's all so new, I don't want to spoil anything by talking about it.'

'Fair enough, I should have expected this sooner but your dad and I have plans for you, you must know that, love?'

'I have to live my own life, Mam, and if I am going out with a boy, you will just have to trust me, won't you?'

'I do, but he *is* a good boy, a respectable boy, isn't he? I mean he wouldn't . . . do anything wrong, would he?'

'He's very respectable, Mam, so don't worry.'

Fon took her hand. 'You see, love, some men take advantage, they are not all gentlemen, do you know what I mean? I would prefer you to go out with someone we know and approve of. We wouldn't try to run your life but we do want to protect you from someone unscrupulous, out just for a bit of foolishness with the first girl who's willing.'

'I'm not a child, Mam. Anyway, he isn't like that.'

'Hasn't he got a name?'

'Mam, please!'

'All right.' Fon rose to her feet. 'Get up soon, mind, I'll have breakfast on the table in ten minutes.'

Catherine sighed with relief as her mother left her alone. Fon was too sharp for her own good. What would she think if she knew her daughter had lost her virginity to the man who had once been betrothed to her sister? Catherine bit her lip. Her mother would think she was second best, an echo of the past for Boyo, and was she?

21

She pictured Boyo's face as he made love to her. There was passion, oh, yes, there was passion, flaring like a white-hot flame between them, but there was more, much more, she need never question that.

Downstairs, the appetizing smell of bacon filled the kitchen. Catherine kissed her father's unshaven cheek and sat next to him at the table.

'So you were out courting last night, darlin' girl?' Jamie leaned forward, his big arms brown beneath the rolled up shirtsleeves. Catherine looked at her mother who avoided her gaze.

'Yes, Dad, and he is very respectable and no, he won't take advantage of me; I'm a big girl now, mind.'

'That's what your dad is afraid of,' Fon said drily. She placed a plate before her husband and Jamie took up his knife and fork.

'These eggs look good, the new mash I'm giving the hens must be suiting them.'

Catherine sighed with relief, Jamie was not going to pursue the subject of her 'courting' as he called it. She looked down at her own plate, the bacon still sizzled hot from the pan and the eggs were done to perfection.

'You girls coming into town with me today?' Jamie asked, cutting into a slice of curling bacon.

'Got work to do here, love,' Fon said easily. 'You go and take Catherine, buy her some pretty ribbons or something.'

'Well?' Jamie pulled at his daughter's hair. 'Going to keep your old dad company are you?'

'I suppose I'd better, there's no telling what trouble you'll get into on your own.'

'I don't know what you mean.' Jamie leaned back in his chair pretending to be indignant but there was laughter in his eyes.

'You know what I mean. If I don't come with you you'll have all the women of Swansea aflutter with your Irish blarney.'

Fon smiled, 'He'd better behave himself if he knows what's good for him, I'm not the sort of woman to put up with any nonsense, mind.'

'Sure an' did I not speak only of going into town for supplies? No mention was made of roaming the bars and chasing women.' Jamie rose to his feet. 'I'll be ready in about half an hour, if you are coming along to protect your dad, you'd best hurry up.'

Jamie left the kitchen and Fon began to gather the crockery together. 'It will do you good, both of you,' she said. 'You don't see enough of each other these days.'

'But Mam, I work on the farm most days, I'm as good as a son any day, ask Dad.'

'I know that,' Fon took the tablecloth in both hands and carried it to the back door, shaking the crumbs onto the yard outside, 'but Jamie's down the fields and you're in the hen-house or milking the beasts; you're not exactly *together*, are you?'

She put the cloth away in the dresser drawer and turned to face her daughter. 'Dad's done the milking and I've fed the hens and there's labourers enough for the lambing so make the most of it.'

'Mam, this isn't a conspiracy, is it?' Catherine was suddenly suspicious. Fon avoided her gaze.

'I don't know what you are talking about. I want you to keep Dad company, that's all, he hasn't quite been himself lately.'

'Mam, he's not sick, is he?'

'Hush girl, all this fuss just because your dad wants you to go to town with him, what next?' Fon did not look at her and Catherine was suddenly afraid.

'You would tell me, Mam, if something was wrong, I mean?'

'Aye, I would tell you, if there was something to tell. Now get off out, will you and leave me to have some peace.'

Half an hour later, Catherine sat up in the front seat of the trap beside Jamie, watching his strong hands gently direct the horses over the uneven ground of the lane leading away from the farm. And yet, she could not help studying him covertly, looking for any sign that he was not in his usual robust health. He appeared relaxed, his skin was lightly tanned by the sun and weather, he looked just the same as he had always done. A little older, perhaps, with a few more lines around his eyes and mouth but that was only to be expected.

'Sure it's a lovely spring day, all right.' Jamie sighed, lifting his face to the pale sun. 'I love the spring with the new buds shaking the trees and the lambs leaping everywhere as though pleased to be alive. It's a time of new beginnings, sure it is.'

Catherine thought so too but not in a way of which her father would approve. For her, life had blossomed since Boyo had come back into her life, she had freely given her virginity and in six short days she had fallen hopelessly in love.

Catherine was quiet, hugging her secret to her and Jamie seemed content with the silence as he easily lifted the reins to encourage the animals to go faster.

Over the crest of the hill, leading away from Honey's Farm, the land fell away revealing the valley of huddled buildings and twisting streets and beyond the town perimeter, the wide shimmering band of sea stretched as far as the eye could see. It was a sight which never failed to take Catherine's breath away.

'Isn't it beautiful, Dad?' She leaned against her father's broad shoulder, breathing in the salt of the breeze drifting in from the sea. He glanced down at her fondly.

'Aye, but then so is Ireland, darlin', it's not called the Emerald Isle for nothing. And the water runs clear up golden sands and the hills are so lush and green. I'll take you there one day, and then you can see for yourself.'

Catherine had Irish blood in her veins from her father's side of the family but her mother was Welsh and Catherine had been born on the farm on the Welsh hillsides, she could imagine nothing as lovely as the scene before her anywhere else in the world.

Instead of driving to the store as he usually did, Jamie halted the horses outside the Grand Hotel, looping the reins around a post and clucking softly to the animals.

'What are we doing here, Dad?' Catherine looked

24

down at her father as he held up his hands to lift her into the roadway. She noticed then, for the first time, that he was smartly dressed in a crisp linen shirt, good trousers, waistcoat and a jacket.

'What's all this about, what's going on, Dad?'

'All in good time, girl.'

Catherine hung back, suddenly suspicious. 'What is going on, Dad?' she repeated more forcefully.

'It's just a little surprise, nothing to get all agitated about. Would I do anything to hurt you?'

She followed him in silence through the double doors and into the lobby which smelled of polish that did not quite cover the stale smell of beer.

Catherine wrinkled her nose. 'Dad, it's much nicer out there in the sunshine, what do we have to come in here for? Not going to become a drinking man at your age, are you?'

'Watch that tongue of yours, madam,' Jamie said, ushering her through another set of doors and into a small back room.

As her eyes became accustomed to the gloom, Catherine saw that two men and a very old lady were seated in the corner on plush but uncomfortable-looking chairs.

'Top of the mornin' to you all.' Jamie moved forward, hand extended and a babble of greetings rang in Catherine's ears.

Then Jamie drew her forward. 'This is my daughter, Catherine O'Conner, a good girl and born to the farm life.' He ushered her into a seat and began to introduce his friends.

'Three generations of Cullens, relatives from Ireland, you see before you Catherine. Maeve Cullen,' Jamie paused and Catherine awkwardly took the gloved hand the old lady held towards her. 'Brad Cullen and his son Liam.' He said the last name as though he was a conjurer producing something precious out of a hat.

The two men murmured a greeting and Liam held onto her hand slightly longer than was necessary. She looked at him closely; he was a little older than she was and very handsome, a fine man and she might have taken more interest in him if Boyo had not burst into her life like a shaft of lightning.

Liam engaged her in polite conversation while the others talked quietly together. Catherine tried her best to listen to what was being said but the conversation was rapid, heavy with the Irish lilt and she found it difficult to follow.

Drinks were ordered and the morning wore on slowly for Catherine. She would have preferred to be outside in the sunshine, she did not want to sit in the gloom of a hotel with people she didn't know.

'Well, I think we've come to an amicable enough arrangement.' Jamie was leaning back in his chair, a satisfied smile on his face. The three strangers were staring at her now, sizing her up, assessing her as though she was a prize heifer.

A strange prickling sensation raised the hair on the back of her neck. She sat up straighter in her chair, knowing, with sudden clarity, what this meeting was all about. Jamie, her father, the dear father who had loved and protected her all her life was trying to arrange a marriage for her with Liam Cullen. Jamie had no son, Liam Cullen, it seemed, would be a substitute, a man who could run the farm when Jamie was too old.

She must decide what to do. Should she make a scene and storm out of the hotel? The thought was tempting but Catherine was reluctant to embarrass her father. And yet she could not continue to sit there, allowing the Cullens to think that she was agreeable, that she would meekly marry a man she had never met until this morning.

She rose to her feet with sudden resolve. 'If you will excuse me, Dad, I have things I must do in town.' She nodded with dignity to the Cullens. 'It was charming to meet you, may you have a pleasant journey home to Ireland.'

Before anyone could speak, Catherine was hurrying away from the table. She pushed through both sets of doors and once in the street began to run, before turning into a lane leading from the High Street into the Strand. She glanced back, fearful that her father had followed her but he was nowhere to be seen.

He would be angry, she didn't doubt it for one moment, but once she was home, she would talk to him, reason with him, explain that she could not fall in love at will with any man he chose for her. This was the twentieth century and she was a modern girl with a will of her own. She would tell him about Boyo and he would just have to understand that what was between them was nothing to do with April, nothing to do with the past at all. Jamie would not approve of her becoming Boyo's mistress but at least he would have to accept it.

She found herself entering into the bustle of Swansea market. At the gates women sat selling shellfish. Catherine paused for a moment to catch her breath. As she watched, one of the women dipped an oyster shell into one of the baskets and measured out a cupful of cockles, salted and ready to eat.

'Want some, *cariad*?' Her voice was loud, friendly, her face round and beatific beneath her black straw hat.

Catherine shook her head and moved on, not sure where she was going but feeling the need to put as much space between the Grand Hotel and herself as she could.

She left the market at the rear and decided to walk on towards the beach. If she turned west, she would shortly come to the slip where she could cross the railway lines on to the beach.

Catherine hardly noticed the hardness of the streets beneath her feet. Her head was full of questions. Why had her father done this to her? What did he think she was, a piece of his stock to be sold off to the highest bidder? And what part had her mother played in all this?

The sand was soft and cool and golden as Catherine crouched against the shelter of the wall running beside the railway track. The tide was full in, lapping the shore with gentle, almost timid waves edged with white like finest lace.

The sun was warm on her face and she leaned back and closed her eyes, wondering at the way her life had been turned upside down in a few short days.

Anger mingled with the panic within her. How dare her father embarrass her the way he'd done? How dare he think he could chose her partner? Was the plan that she would meekly go off to Ireland, to a strange land with a man she didn't know? How could her parents say they loved her and yet treat her this way? Surely her father could not, would not, force her into marriage?

A gull cried raucously overhead and, on the horizon, an oyster skiff skimmed the water. Soon, now, the boats would lay up for the summer, give the oysters a chance to grow. Not that there were many oysters left in the bay these days. Now the sailors went out to deeper water searching for whiting or bass.

Catherine looked around her, the beach was deserted and she suddenly felt very much alone. She longed to be with Boyo, to talk to him, tell him what had happened, ask his advice. But Boyo lived miles away, perhaps twenty miles down the coast, though Catherine wasn't quite sure how far Rhosilli was from Swansea, but it was certainly too far to walk.

Catherine bit her fingernail, what if she hitched a lift with a farmer, there must be quite a few of them returning home from town? And if Boyo was a little annoyed with her for turning up at his door, she could tell him that she needed his advice, desperately. Once she had told him what had taken place, he would understand her panic. He would come home with her, explain how things were between them and then Jamie and Fon would understand.

Catherine rose and brushed the sand from her skirts, her heart beating swiftly. Did she have the courage to actually go to Boyo's home unasked? He was a rich, influential businessman now by all accounts but he loved her, she knew he did. Surely he would want to help her, to give her advice?

She stood on the Mumbles road and watched the

28

wagons roll past, some laden, some empty and wondered at the risk she was about to take. She had never travelled so far from Swansea. What if she were to lose her way?

The choice was made for her. A wagon containing a few sacks pulled up beside her, a man in clerics' clothes, a stiff white collar at his throat, looked down at her from the driving seat.

'Want any help?'

'Are you going anywhere near Rhosilli?' she asked breathlessly.

'Aye, I am that, come on, climb up, you'll have to sit with the groceries I'm afraid. I've been sent to Swansea to stock up the larder you see, and I dare not disobey my wife.' He smiled and she looked at him more closely.

He turned and smiled. 'I remember you now, you are April O'Conner from Honey's Farm, aren't you?' He did not wait for her to reply. 'I am Daniel Bennett, I married Ellie Hopkins who used to own the tannery. Where might I ask are you going so far from home?'

For one frantic moment, she almost called out for the man to stop the cart. She felt foolish, like an impulsive child but she imagined herself in Boyo's arms and her courage returned.

'I'm April's younger sister, Catherine,' she said, 'and I'm visiting Boyo. We used to be friends when he worked at the tannery, before he owned it, that is.'

'Ah, Boyo, a fine man now, he's done well, all credit to him.' Daniel clucked to the horse, encouraging the creature to move faster and Catherine bit her lips wondering what madness was possessing her. Her parents would be angry, worried when she did not return home. Should she turn back now, before it was too late?

Once outside the town the hill curved upwards leading on to the common land and from there to the lanes that wound along the coast to the Gower Peninsular. The land was flatter now and the horse broke into a trot, doubtless knowing that home and fodder were drawing nearer.

'Still a farming girl, aren't you?' He turned to look at her. 'Even if I had not remembered you, I would know by

29

the fine clear skin and the beautiful blush in your cheeks.'

Catherine smiled. 'Yes, I was born to the land, grew up knowing how to milk a cow before I could walk properly. I could never imagine any other way of life.'

'Your parents keeping well, are they?' Daniel asked and Catherine nodded.

'Aye, both of them are fine, thank you.' They made the rest of the journey in a companionable silence except for an occasional desultory remark from Daniel Bennett which required no answer.

The vicar drew the cart to a halt on the rise of land high above Rhosilli. The bay curved in a vast expanse of gold around a blue sea capped with white.

'It's so beautiful,' Catherine exclaimed and Daniel smiled proudly as he helped her down from the cart.

'It's very beautiful; Ellie and I have come to love it. You know that strangers come from all over the country to see such a sight as Rhosilli on a day like this.'

He paused, looking down at her. 'Will you be all right now, you know where you're going don't you?'

Catherine hesitated, not sure what to say, and then she decided there was no harm telling some of the truth. 'I'm not quite sure where Boyo Hopkins's house is, he's not expecting me, you see, it's a surprise. Do you know where he lives?'

'His house is just across the fields there, you can see the tall chimneys, very distinctive they are.' He pointed, 'See, the big house above the bay, you can't miss it. Just carry on along the road, you'll be there in two minutes.'

Catherine pushed aside a feeling of apprehension. 'Thank you for the lift, it was very kind of you.'

As the cart pulled away, Catherine resisted the urge to call Mr Bennett and beg him to take her back to town. The words died on her lips, the vicar had a home to go to, a wife waiting for him.

Catherine straightened her shoulders and began to walk purposefully towards the house. It was further away than it had first appeared and she began to wonder just how she was going to get back home to Swansea, it would be dark by then with hardly any traffic on the road. But then Boyo would take her, he would never allow her to travel alone, not at night. The thought warmed her and she broke into a run, covering the uneven grassland of the hill.

Close to, the building was imposing, almost frightening in its grandeur. Catherine hesitated at the gates, staring along the tree-lined avenue to the big arched door. Her feelings of apprehension returned and she had to force herself to continue to walk towards the house.

She pulled at the bell before she could lose her nerve and the sound echoed hollowly within the house. She had imagined it would be grand but when the door was opened by a tall, stern-faced butler, Catherine caught her breath, astounded by the sheer size of the hallway. Marble statues graced the airy room, the floor too was marble, covered in huge, rich rugs.

'How may I help you?' The man was looking down at her with barely concealed curiosity. Catherine swallowed hard, she realized now how great a mistake it had been to come here. She glanced over her shoulder uncertainly and heard the man speak again. 'Is it the mistress you wish to see on some charitable matter?' he prompted not unkindly.

'Mistress?' she wondered who he could be referring to. 'No, it's Boyo I have to see.' The words came out in a rush. 'Boyo Hopkins, he is here, isn't he?'

'I'm afraid the master is in Swansea on business. In any case, you should make an appointment if you wish to see Mr Hopkins, he is a very busy man.'

Catherine bit her lip and looked down at her dusty shoes, there seemed nothing for it but to try to make her way back to Swansea at once.

'What is it, Richard?' The voice was light, seemingly disembodied as it echoed through the hall. A woman came into the range of Catherine's vision, a tall woman, a woman with a large-boned face and a touch of grey in her hair.

'This young lady wishes to see the master, madam.'

The man glanced at Catherine almost with pity. 'She didn't realize she should have made an appointment.'

'I'm sorry you've had a wasted journey, have you come far, dear?' the woman asked pleasantly. Catherine felt a sinking sensation within her, this elegant woman must be the housekeeper.

'From Swansea.' She didn't know how she managed to speak but the woman smiled kindly, encouragingly.

'Bring the young lady in, Richard, and have Gladys serve a glass of something refreshing.'

Catherine wanted to run and never look back but she found herself inside the house, breathing in the scents of flowers and polish and richness. So this was how Boyo lived now. He had come a long way from the boy who had worked in the tannery and who had attended church in a suit several sizes too small for him.

'Was it very important?' The woman had led the way into a large room with huge windows that looked out on to the beach below. Catherine took a deep breath. 'No, I'm sorry, I shouldn't have come.' She looked down at her hands, guilt swamping her. This woman was a lady, a kind, dignified lady; if she knew the truth she would think of Catherine as nothing but a fancy piece to a rich man.

'What is it, dear? I won't bite, don't worry.' There was a hint of laughter in the woman's voice, she was very kind and Catherine took her courage in both hands.

'I knew Boyo when I was a child, he was walking out with April, my big sister.'

'I see.' The woman sat quietly, hands folded in her lap while a maid brought a tray of drinks into the room. The door closed behind the girl and Catherine felt the silence weigh heavily upon her.

'I'm sorry, I'm not explaining very well, it's just that I wanted to talk to Boyo, to ask his advice about something. I was silly to come all this way, I realize that now.'

'It must be something very important.' The woman was being patient and kind and Catherine stumbled into speech once more.

'They want to marry me off to a stranger!' The outrage and pain came pouring out and Catherine was amazed at the way she was revealing herself to this woman who was nothing but a servant.

'They?' The word was put softly and Catherine shook back her hair, making an effort to control her trembling hands.

'My mother and father. They think they know what's best for me but how can they?'

'I'm sure they both have your best interests at heart but can't they be persuaded to give you time to get to know this young man?'

'I don't love him, I could never love him,' Catherine said hotly.

'You are very sure; are you in love with someone else?'

Catherine hung her head, trying desperately to think of a reply that would not compromise Boyo in any way. Perhaps he did not like the servants, however gracious, to know too much about his private life.

Before she could speak, the door opened and Catherine felt shock waves run through her as she saw Boyo framed in the doorway. She smiled up at him happily, rising to her feet, her heart suddenly beating rapidly within her at the sight of him.

'Catherine!' He looked at her in concern, 'What's wrong?'

Suddenly she began to cry and Boyo crossed the room and took her in his arms. 'It's all right, everything will be all right, just tell me what's happened.'

Catherine lifted her head and saw Boyo's housekeeper leave the room. She was being kind, tactful and Catherine felt ashamed, wondering what the woman must be thinking of her foolishness. 'I shouldn't have come,' she said, 'but I didn't know what else to do.'

'All right, you are here now, dry your eyes and tell me what you are so upset about.'

Catherine told him about the way her father had taken her into town, had introduced her to the strangers who had, without any discussion, arranged affairs to suit

33

themselves. 'They want me to marry this Liam,' she said at last. 'I can't marry him, Boyo, tell me they won't make me.'

'Look, I'll have a bed made up for you here,' he said gently. 'I'll send a man to Honey's Farm to tell them you are safe, we'll talk about this in the morning.'

'But your servants, what will they think?'

'What have you told them?' Boyo held her hands in his, his expression was concerned and Catherine felt a pang of jealousy.

'I told your housekeeper that we were old friends, I didn't say too much about . . . about us. I just said I wanted your advice.'

'Catherine, I have to talk to you, right now. Sit down.' He held onto her hands and she stared at him in bewilderment, he looked so serious, so guilty.

'That lady you spoke to, she's not my housekeeper, she is my wife.'

She felt waves of pain run through her, from the tips of her toes up into her chest so that she could not breathe. 'It's not true, you can't be married, Boyo, you just can't!'

'I am, I should have told you. I am sorry, Catherine, I was afraid I would lose you if you knew the truth.'

'Boyo!' She stared at him, her hands on her cheeks, her eyes suddenly hot and dry. 'You are married and yet you made love to me. No, I don't believe it.'

'Believe it.' The voice came from the doorway, Catherine looked up to see the woman she had imagined to be the housekeeper entering the room, slamming the door shut behind her, a look of burning anger on her face. Her whole demeanour had changed from that of a kindly, caring woman to that of an outraged wife.

'So this . . . this child is your strumpet, Boyo?' She spoke fiercely, her eyes gleaming. 'And she dares to come into my house, sullying my home, has she no shame? Throw her out at once, do you hear me?'

'No, I will not throw her out; be reasonable, Bethan. You just called her a child, would you turn a child from your door?'

34

'This . . . this piece of rubbish has no place in a decent household, she belongs in the streets.'

'Hush, Bethan, do you want your father to know all our business? Be quiet, let us sort this out reasonably.'

She seemed to grow calm suddenly, the heat left her cheeks and she sighed heavily. 'I suppose I might have expected this, I have had enough experience of the double dealings of men while running my hotel. Sort it out, Boyo, and at once.'

'She will stay the night, tomorrow I will take her back to Swansea,' Boyo said firmly. 'Now she must have something to eat, she can take it in one of the bedrooms.'

Catherine was bewildered, she allowed Boyo to take charge. He took her up the gracious staircase and opened one of the many doors from the landing.

Catherine did not see the elegantly proportioned room, nor the silken drapes, she sagged against Boyo and closed her eyes against the warmth of his shoulder.

'Don't you worry about a thing,' he said. 'Bethan is angry and shocked, of course she is, but at heart she's a good, kind woman, she wouldn't want me to turn away an old friend.'

His words hurt. 'So that's all I mean to you?' she said in a strangled voice. 'You have hurt me, deceived me, Boyo, how can I ever forgive you?'

'Of course you are hurt and bewildered but for now, let us be calm, think all this through, see clearly what must be done. Look, it might be that you should follow your father's wishes, make a decent marriage, I just don't know.' He ran his fingers through his hair and her heart twisted at the look on his face.

'I could not marry Liam, you must know that I love you, Boyo. I love you still even though I know you've lied to me.'

'We will talk in the morning. I can't think clearly just now,' he said. 'I'll have a tray brought up to you and then you must try to get some rest.' He left the room and Catherine fell onto her knees on the thick carpet and wept.

35

Later, as she lay in the soft luxurious bed in the strangely large room with the moonlight slanting across the silk quilt, Catherine thought of Boyo in bed with his wife. She bit her lip, wondering if he loved her, this wife of his. Wondered if all his words had been false, if he had lied to her about his feelings from the first day they met. It was growing light by the time she had cried herself to sleep.

Ellie Bennett looked out at the squat church buildings nestling against the green of the countryside. Ilston was a beautiful place, an ideal parish for a young vicar and his wife. The community, sparse and scattered, had viewed them at first with reserve; the vicar was young, inexperienced in the ways of the Church and in the ways of the world, but now the people of Ilston treated Daniel as though he had lived in the village all his life.

Ellie looked up from her chair as Daniel entered the room. He looked so solemn in his dark suit with the white collar that declared his calling. He was so decent, so earnest, so dear to her. He was carrying his Bible and a sheaf of papers and she could see he was having difficulty with his Sunday sermon.

He bent over her and kissed her mouth lightly but he was clearly preoccupied. He sat opposite her and scribbled a few words on his notes. She felt love flow through her. As if sensing her thoughts, Daniel looked up and met her eyes. He smiled and she pouted at him.

'About time you paid your wife a little attention.' She pretended to be aggrieved and he immediately put down his papers and came to kneel before her. He took her face gently in his hands and kissed her with passion.

'That's much better.' She put her arms around his neck and nuzzled her mouth against his cheek. 'You grow more handsome by the day, do you know that, Reverend Bennett?'

'Flatterer!' He kissed her again, his hand straying to her breast. Laughing, she pushed him away.

'Later, vicar, the servants might catch us and then what would they say?'

He made a wry face. 'They would say what is true, that the vicar loves his wife. But all right, I'll accept that my advances have been rejected.' He resumed his seat and picked up his notes again. 'By the way, I gave a lift from Swansea to a young lady last evening.'

Ellie looked at him archly. 'I see, dallying with young women already, are you? Was she good-looking?'

'Very, she was one of the O'Conners from Honey's Farm, making her way down here to see Boyo Hopkins. She looked a little distressed I'd say.'

'Oh, dear, I wonder what Bethan Hopkins had to say about an uninvited guest, you know what a stickler she is for what she calls "proper manners".'

'It's none of our business but I must say, I felt responsible for the girl, she was little more than a child really.'

'Well, Dan, you showed her Christian charity, there was not a lot more you could do without downright interfering.' She frowned thoughtfully.

'Boyo used to go to the farm quite a lot, he was walking out with the older girl, April, remember?'

Daniel nodded, 'I remember.' He smiled, 'Those days seem so far away now, don't they? Such a lot happened while we were in Swansea, so many dramas, so much upheaval, I'm so grateful for the peace we have here.'

'Me too.' Ellie smiled, 'You know, I have never, even for one second, regretted handing over the tannery to Boyo. Although Jubilee was my husband and left me everything he owned, he was more like a father to me. If he had known that Boyo was his grandson, he would have wanted him to have the tannery, I'm sure of that.'

'You did the right thing, Ellie,' Daniel said softly. 'You are far too wise to set store by worldly goods.'

Ellie sighed. 'I have all I'll ever want in these four walls with you, my love.' They exchanged a smile and Ellie's mouth curved a little. 'Might I have second thoughts? There is something else I want.'

'Like what?' Daniel asked, rising to his feet and holding out his arms. Ellie went into them.

'I don't think I need answer that, do I, Vicar?' Her smile vanished as his mouth, hot and ardent, came down on hers.

CHAPTER THREE

'We've lost it all, even Summer Lodge?' Hari Grenfell stood near the window of her home, the home she had entered as a happy bride many years before and tried to suppress the panic that was rising within her.

'It looks that way.' She heard her husband's voice crack with fatigue and despair and turning swiftly, she went to him and held him close.

'Craig, don't look like that, we still have each other, that's what's important.'

He buried his face in her neck and she clung to him, loving him more deeply than she had ever done in the first flush of romance.

'All I can say is thank God our children are out of it, making a good life for themselves in a new country. At least they won't have to suffer for my failures.'

'You are not a failure.' Hari pushed him away and looked into his face, his forehead was furrowed, his eyes shadowed and etched with tired lines.

'Come, sit by here then, lovely.' She slipped into the Welsh, emotion overcoming her as she drew her husband towards the fire. Outside, the rain began to fall, beating against the high windows as though to emphasize the misery that was growing in Hari.

'Tell me, exactly what has happened?' She sat beside him on the deep, cushioned sofa and held his hands. His shoulders were bent in an attitude of defeat and Hari felt tears well in her eyes.

'I've made a bad mistake, Hari, I put my money, *our* money into shares.' He glanced up at her. 'Solid gold, that's what everyone said, well now the shares have dropped like a stone.' His eyes were red with weariness. 'There's more bad news, I'm afraid. I've overextended

39

myself, taken on too many properties, branched out when I should have been drawing tight the purse strings. It will take every penny we have left to simply pay off the debts I've accrued.'

Hari swallowed hard. She looked around her, seeing with fresh eyes the house where she had brought up her children. The ceilings were high and gracious, the windows sweeping down to the floor allowing in the misty light. She saw the dog-eared books which Craig had flung down in fury; the books that contained the accounting for all the years of their joint business ventures.

She forced herself to look away from the proof of the disaster that had overtaken them. She stared at the furniture, good solid furniture, polished by loving hands; servants' hands. She looked down at her own hands, white and small, unused now to hard work. A feeling of strength rose within her, a sense of power. She had been taught the skills of shoemaking, her father had instilled in her, his only child, the knowledge that she could make her own way in the world, earn her own living by her hands.

She had not worked at patterns for some years, neither had she done any designing, for these days boots and shoes were made mostly by machines. Gone were the days when bespoke boots were a sought-after commodity. Or were they? Could she not find a place in the market for new concepts in shoemaking? She had done it once, built up a great emporium from virtually nothing. She had made the name of Hari Grenfell synonymous with style and class and excellence.

She stared into the fire, watching the leaping flames without really seeing the cheerful glow behind the ornate façade of the grate. Could she do it again, could she, in her middle years, find the energy she had known in her youth? Would the skill still be there, in her mind, in her fingers? Questions ran riot through her head.

'We will go through everything together.' She rose to her feet with a sudden sense of purpose. 'We will sift through our assets, see what we can salvage.'

'It's no use,' Craig put his head in his hands, 'I have failed you, there is nothing left.'

Hari touched his cheek, refusing to be daunted, yet understanding Craig's despair. 'You must rest, you have ridden a long way, you are very tired. I don't want you falling sick, not now when I need you so much.'

'You would be better off without me, I have bankrupted us.'

'Come on, Craig, this is not like you.' Hari allowed her anger to show in her tone. 'Where is your fighting spirit? We can face this thing together, Craig. We must fight.'

'I have been fighting, all night,' Craig said. 'I have reasoned with my debtors until I have almost lost my mind. I have gone over and over the problems we face and can find no solution.'

'Go up to bed.' Hari's tone softened, 'I will fetch you something to help you sleep. When you are rested we will talk again.'

She took his arm and urged him up the winding gracious stairway towards the master bedroom. She was concerned about his pallor, he was so subdued, so unlike the forceful, almost arrogant man she knew that she was frightened.

She gave him a glass of hot milk and sat with him smoothing his hand until, finally, he slept. She bent and kissed his forehead, gently touching the white in his hair with her lips. Her heart was full of love, tears burned behind her lids. Resolutely, she swallowed her fear and moved quietly away from the bedroom.

Once downstairs, she picked up the set of accounting books and hugging them against her bodice, took them into the study.

How long she spent working over the books she did not afterwards remember. The daylight hours passed unnoticed, she drank the cups of tea and coffee brought by a succession of maids but left the trays of food untouched. The light faded and she lit the gas lamps, the whitening light making her blink a little with fatigue.

When she lifted her head from the books, it was

41

morning, the dawn, pale and grey, was lightening the sky outside. Hari fell back in the chair, the red captain's chair that had been in Craig's family for generations. She rubbed at her eyes wearily. The amount of money owed was more than they could raise, even by selling the house; much more. She looked at her notes and the figures swam before her eyes.

'Thousands of pounds.' Her voice echoed inside her head even though she had whispered the words. The bank would foreclose, they would take the house and the Grenfells would still be in debt.

'No!' She rose to her feet, she would not let it happen. But how could she prevent it? She had escaped poverty once, how on earth had she done it? She thought back to her younger days, days before her marriage when she had courage enough for anything. She had taken on a building even though she had no money, had asked for a month's grace with the rent and then had gone out and sublet the place in small units, making an immediate profit. It was with such scant assets that she had begun her business. Could she do it again?

She moved to the small window in the study and looked out; below her was the sea, pewter now beneath the intermittent rain-clouds. She could think about renting the rooms of Summer Lodge to retired gentlefolk in diminished circumstances. Perhaps that way she could keep the house and begin to pay back the huge debt that was owed.

As she stared into the rain-swept day sudden hope filled her, she could make Summer Lodge into an emporium. The bigger rooms could be converted quite easily into showrooms and workshops and the upper rooms would serve as living quarters.

She rubbed at her eyes again and sank wearily into the cold leather of the captain's chair, facing facts coldly. She had no knowledge of how quickly the house could be converted into a business premises but she could imagine the cost. Wages would have to be paid, shop girls expected to live in, they would need food and heating and lighting. All that would require money she did not have.

She leaned forward, resting her head on her arms, her hands tracing the leather top of the desk. What if she employed married women, women only too glad to go home at nights? That might be the solution. It was a radical idea, but it might just work. Her mind closed in, she was too weary to think any more and she slept.

She woke some time in the afternoon and as the concerned maid placed yet another tray on the desk, Hari smiled, knowing she had her solution.

'It won't work, love, just accept that it's over. The good life is finished for us, we'll be lucky if we can afford a cottage somewhere.' Craig was sitting at the dining table, the candles were lit, shimmering on the crystal and silver, reflecting against the polished surface.

'It will work.' Hari spoke doggedly. 'I can design again, I can make boots and shoes that will be sought after in the town and beyond, just as I did before. We'll have a repair shop where we can tap working boots, that's a service that's always necessary.'

'But love,' Craig could scarcely conceal his exasperation, 'that was before machinery became so sophisticated that anything in leather could be produced to perfection.'

'Yes, *mass*-produced.' Hari leaned forward, 'There are still a great many people in Swansea who go to London for handmade footwear, made to measure on the customer's own last. These shoes are a perfect fit which the machine-made shoes are not.'

'Look,' she spoke again when Craig shook his head. 'Don't dismiss my ideas out of hand. We have some stocks of leather left in the storeroom.' She held up her hand. 'I know the store warehouses will be sold off but we can shift the stock before the bailiffs move in.' Even as she spoke, the word 'bailiff' brought a chill to her spine. She remembered her childhood spent in the slums of World's End, when the visit of the bailiff to one of the houses was a time for fist fights and abuse, when poor sticks of furniture would be put out on the pavement for everyone to see and then carted off to be sold or dumped. It had seemed to Hari then that the poor were being punished because they *were* poor. If the people had money they would pay their debts. Well, she was in the same position now as the poor from World's End and the thought was frightening.

She rose to her feet. 'You see, Craig, I could bring in a milliner and a glove maker, there are many women with talent who are unemployed, women who will take a chance on me.'

Craig lifted his head, swayed against his better judgement by her enthusiasm.

'The kitchens are huge and there are several unused storerooms, we shall have tearooms with *Bara brith* made to my own recipe and Welsh cakes and *Tiesen lap*. What the Clarks have done for Street in Somerset I can do for Swansea. I will make Summer Lodge into a new kind of emporium, you'll see, Craig. We can do it, I know we can. What do you think, Craig?'

Craig looked at her with a glimmer of a smile in his eyes. 'I can see you are fired with the old enthusiasm, Hari. I think you, if anybody, can make this mad scheme work.'

'I'll make it work, you can depend on it.' Hari swept around the table and hugged him. 'Have faith in me, my lovely.' She sobered suddenly. 'Convincing you was the easy part, now I have to convince the bank that it would be worth their while to give us a bit more time.'

Craig nodded, 'Aye, that's the first step and perhaps the most difficult but you have given me hope, you know. I believe in you, you have to make the people at the bank believe in you now.'

It was two days later when Mrs Hari Grenfell stepped out of the cab onto the pavement outside the Hammet Bank. She looked up at the elegant façade and bit her lip, feeling fear turn her blood to ice. It was a long time since she had needed to beg for anything but if necessary she would go down on her knees, even shed a few tears, if it would get her what she wanted.

Less than fifteen minutes later, she left the bank with nothing but a faint hope in her heart. The edict of the great man of banking had been that she had two weeks to get backing for her scheme from outside. The bank would hold off for a little while, but in no way could the bank advance Mrs Grenfell any further funds.

Hari breathed in the freshness of the air, the rain that had beaten down on the town for days had stopped and a pale sun shone from between the clouds. She moved along the street almost in a daze, searching her mind for a way out of her dilemma. If the banks would not lend her money, then who would? Who could? In her mind she compiled a list of people to whom she could appeal for financial backing. One by one she discarded them until it came down to just two names: Arian Smale, owner of the highly profitable *Swansea Times* and Boyo Jubilee Hopkins, a fellow dealer in the leather trade and by all accounts a very rich man.

With courage born of desperation, Hari Grenfell walked towards the offices of *The Swansea Times*. The clatter of typewriting machines hit her like a stone wall and she hesitated for a moment, unsure what to do next. She had expected to see Arian Smale in person but the room was full of men and just one or two girls tapping away at machines with the confidence of the young. An elderly man with fine eyes and a slightly sardonic twist to his mouth looked up at her.

'I would like to see Miss Smale, if it is at all possible.' Why was she so diffident? Why did she not act like the grand lady everyone thought her? But then, it had never been her way to feel superior to anyone.

The man inclined his head. 'Mrs Grenfell, isn't it?' His mouth widened into a smile and she responded, liking him.

'That's right, how sharp of you to recognize me.'

'Not really, I've been reporting on the doings of the gentry for so many years now that I know most of the town's élite by sight if not by name.'

'I am not one of the élite, I assure you,' Hari said

quickly. 'I began life as a shoemaker's daughter and I'm proud of it.'

'I know. I'm Mac. Wait here, I'll go and find Miss Smale.'

Hari tried to compose herself, she was very nervous, wondering how she was going to approach Arian Smale, how she was going to bring herself to ask for money. She thought of Craig waiting for her at home and lifted her chin high, knowing that she needed to summon all her resolve.

'Hari Grenfell, how nice to see you!' Arian was a beautiful woman, her hair was fine and silver in colour, swept up from a gracious, swan-like neck. Her smile was warm but would that warmth fade when she knew what Hari wanted?

In the office, Hari clasped her hands together as though the gesture could give her strength. 'I might as well come straight to the point,' she said breathlessly. 'I am here to ask you to invest money in my new business venture.'

'Sit down, Hari.' Arian seated herself behind the desk but leaned forward on her elbows, smiling her encouragement. 'I must say I'm intrigued. What scheme are you up to now, haven't you proved yourself a success many times over?'

'I thought so until the day before yesterday.' Hari swallowed hard trying to find the right words.

'Some disaster has occurred, of a financial kind, I suspect; am I right?' Arian was a perceptive woman and Hari met her eyes knowing that there was no need to prevaricate, Arian was quick-witted enough to grasp the essentials without detailed explanations.

'Everything has gone,' she spoke with more confidence now, 'I have no money at all. Worse, my company is in debt to the bank and to cap it all I'm in danger of losing Summer Lodge. However, I do have an idea that might just save the day if only I can get someone to back me.'

'What can I do to help?' Arian leaned back in her chair, 'I am willing to put money into any scheme run personally by you, Hari.'

46

'I want to turn the house into a new kind of emporium, I want to design new-style shoes, I want to make gloves and hats on the premises and serve teas, anything to promote the interest in handmade leather goods and footwear. I think it will work, I know there is a corner of the market that needs filling, people are growing tired of the machine-made shoes that are two a penny.' Hari paused for breath and saw that Arian was nodding.

'How much do you need?'

'Whatever you can spare.'

'You shall have my cheque for 1,000 guineas by tomorrow.'

Hari was overcome at the ease with which Arian had agreed to invest money in what was a risky concern at best and a total failure at worst.

'Thank you, Arian, I won't let you down.' She had to swallow hard to prevent herself from shedding tears. Arian touched her shoulder.

'I know you won't.' She accompanied Hari to the door of *The Swansea Times* and took her hand in a firm grip. 'I have every confidence in you; I know your strengths and more importantly, so do you. Good luck to you, Hari Grenfell.'

Hari was trembling as she left the newspaper offices. For a time she walked without purpose, unable to believe her luck; Arian Smale had faith in her, she had said so. The thought gave Hari renewed courage as she turned into College Street towards Gower Place where Boyo Jubilee Hopkins kept a small office.

To Hari's disappointment, Mr Hopkins was not there. '*Duw*, don't get into town much do Mr Hopkins, no need, like, his business runs itself.' The young woman seated at the desk had large blue eyes, before her was a typewriting machine but it was covered in dust, testifying to the truth of her words.

'I see, well thank you.' Hari left the office and stepped out into the sunshine. To her right was a farrier's stable and the sound of hooves against cobbles rang out in the fresh morning air. She glanced around and saw, with a leap of her heart, that Boyo Hopkins was leading an animal towards the roadway.

'Mr Hopkins, may I talk with you?' She stepped forward and he smiled down at her, a tall young man with a shock of hair that jutted out from beneath his cap.

'Mrs Grenfell, good day to you.' He spoke in beautiful accents, he was reputed to be one of the richest men in Swansea and yet his origins were something of a mystery.

'I need help with a business venture,' she said quickly, 'I know this is neither the time nor the place but I understand that you do not come in to work at your office very often, so please forgive me for accosting you in the street.'

'Please, don't worry about that, Mrs Grenfell. Tell me how I can help.'

'Money, investment,' Hari said quickly. 'I have one backer, Miss Smale of *The Swansea Times*, but I need another.'

'I see.' Boyo Hopkins was clearly puzzled. 'Why have you approached me?' He smiled to soften his words. 'Not that I am adverse to having a business flutter, mind you.'

'This will be more than a flutter, I assure you. I am talking to you because you have been in the leather business since you were young, you know good leather, you know the best way to tan the hides and where to buy the best skins; I know how to make the skins into fine footwear. I believe we share a kinship for the leather we work. To come to the point, what I need first and foremost is at least 3,000 guineas.'

'You are very direct,' Boyo said. He glanced around him. 'The street is not the best place to do business, however. Would you like to call on me at my home and discuss this further?'

Hari felt her spirits begin to fall. 'It's urgent, I need an answer now.' She looked up at him earnestly. 'I must be honest with you. I have no funds of my own, I am ruined; I need to take drastic measures if I am to survive but I promise you that I will make the business work, I have the skill, believe me.'

'I know, your reputation is solid gold in the town.'

Boyo Hopkins seemed to reach a decision. 'I'll take a chance, it's a long time since I acted on gut instinct alone. I'll fund your venture to the tune of 2,000 guineas. Tell me the name of your bank and I will deposit the money as soon as I can.'

'Within the next few days?' Hari was appalled at her own daring but Boyo smiled.

'Very well, will tomorrow do?'

Hari gave him the name of her bank and he nodded. 'Right, Mrs Grenfell, if our business is concluded, I'll wish you good day.' Hari was jubilant as she turned towards home; she decided to walk up to Summer Lodge, it would do her good to walk, she would enjoy the fresh air, clear her mind and make her plans. She had at her disposal 3,000 guineas, far more money than she had dared to hope for. Fear clutched at her, cramping her stomach. Had she taken on too much responsibility? It could be that she would still lose and end up owing more money than she had to start with. She looked up at the sky and stood, for a moment, with the pale sun shining on her face. She felt a surge of strength, she would not lose, she had not lost her touch, she had been a success once and she would be again.

CHAPTER FOUR

The morning sun illuminated the silk hangings on the walls of the dining-room. An appetizing smell of hot food rose from the plethora of silver dishes gracing the sideboard but Bethan did not feel like eating. Catherine O'Conner had stayed only one night but her visit had caused ripples that had not yet died down.

'Do you want to talk about it?' She had not been alone with Boyo these past few days, since the night of Catherine's visit, and she'd had the absurd idea that her husband was avoiding her. Her throat was dry as she waited for his reply. He appeared absurdly young in his silk robe, carelessly thrown over his bare torso. Normally she would have chastized him with easy humour, admonishing him to dress properly before appearing at the table but this morning such matters seemed trivial.

'What?' He looked up at her across the expanse of table and she shook her head with rare impatience, 'The girl, of course.' Any moment now, Father would be joining them, there would be little opportunity to talk then.

'What is there to say?' He was prevaricating and they both knew it. He helped himself to coffee from the silver pot. 'Catherine is an old friend, she needed help and she came to me, that's all there is to it.'

'An old friend you took to bed. Don't treat me like a fool, Boyo. Are you in love with her?' She looked at Boyo with clear eyes, daring him to tell her the truth whatever it was.

He did not answer, she saw the tightening of his lips but she was compelled to go on questioning him. 'Have you got this girl into trouble, is that it?'

He shook his head almost wearily. 'No, I haven't, as you so quaintly put it, got the girl into trouble'.

50

The door opened and Bethan rose quickly to greet her father, she flashed Boyo a warning glance but he was looking down at his cup and did not see her.

'*Bore da.*' Dafydd came towards the table, his gaze sliding over his son-in-law's state of undress, with nothing to show his disapproval except a slight tightening of his lips.

'Daddy, what do you want, tea, coffee?' Bethan took her father's arm, leading him to the table. Almost immediately, Boyo rose and smiled apologetically.

'I shall take my tea to my room and I won't return until I am properly shaved and dressed. Please excuse me.'

Bethan watched him with worried eyes and her father rested his hand on her shoulder. 'What is it, Bethan?'

'I don't know what you mean, Daddy.'

'I mean there is a feeling of unrest about the house since the rude O'Conner girl's visit and it is a feeling I do not much like.'

'I'm sorry, Father.' Bethan was aware she sounded abrupt but she felt no remorse, whatever might be wrong was between herself and her husband, nothing to do with her father.

Breakfast seemed to go on interminably, her father ate slowly, his teeth after all were old. Bethan felt like screaming at him to hurry.

At last, when he rose from the table, dropping his immaculate napkin beside his plate, she rose too, sighing in relief. 'I shan't be long, Daddy, I have things to do.' She hurried from the dining-room, aware that her behaviour was very much removed from her usual placid calm.

Upstairs, the sun slanted fingers along the huge landing, lighting the faces of the portraits on the walls: Bethan's ancestors. She looked at the painting of Elizabeth Llewellyn who died tragically at an early age, she might almost be looking at her own image, except that Elizabeth had a beauty, a grace of feature that Bethan knew she lacked.

Bethan entered her bedroom and sank onto an ornately upholstered chair in the window, staring down at the sea far below. What was between her husband and the young girl with the red hair? What secrets did they share from their past, the past that had nothing to do with Bethan, Boyo's wife.

It was an absurd revelation, but in that moment Bethan knew what she'd suspected for some time. She had believed she had married Boyo out of friendship, out of mutual admiration and trust and because they were both lonely people who felt each could give the other a great deal. Oh, yes, she had married him for all those reasons but underneath it all, she had married Boyo Hopkins because she loved him.

The farmhouse came into sight, the building dark against the light of the sky. Across the valley the jagged teeth of the ruined tannery buildings sent shadows across the ground that appeared, from this distance, to be gaping holes.

Boyo had been thinking about business as he rode into Swansea, pondering on the problems that had forced Hari Grenfell to come to him cap in hand, so to speak. He had been happy to assist her, her reputation in Swansea as a fine and honest businesswoman was unsurpassed. Even if he was throwing good money away on a hopeless enterprise, he could well afford it, he would not miss the money he had paid into the Hammet Bank. Still, that was not the point, it was perhaps foolish to hand such sums willy-nilly to anyone who asked him for help.

As he approached the farmhouse and saw Catherine run towards him, her skirts lifting in the breeze, thoughts of business went out of his head.

'Boyo,' she paused, breathless, her colour high, her mouth, that sweet, kissable mouth, trembling. 'I'm glad you came; my father won't speak to me, he's ashamed of me, the way I stayed out all night. He thinks the worst, you must talk to him for me.'

Boyo dismounted from his horse and resisted the longing to take Catherine in his arms. When he had taken her home, a few days ago, he had not waited to talk to her parents, it had seemed tactful to keep out of it, but now he was troubled, feeling he had avoided his responsibilities.

'And you must be in trouble, too, with your wife. I shouldn't have come to your house, I'm sorry, Boyo, but I didn't know . . .' Her voice trailed away and guilt gripped him. Catherine looked up at him, her silky hair streaming about her face as she stood close to him.

'Let's worry about your problems, solve those before we talk of mine, shall we?'

'Boyo,' she leaned against him and he could smell the perfume of her skin; desire flamed through him and such love that he hadn't believed possible. With sudden clarity, he realized that Catherine was everything to him. He was glad that their affair was out in the open; now perhaps Bethan would agree to giving him a divorce. The thought was not without pain, he hated the idea of hurting Bethan, divorce brought scandalmongers out from the woodwork, however innocent the injured party.

'Mam and Dad are angry with me but they will listen when you explain what happened; that I stayed at your house with you, that we love each other . . . You do love me, don't you Boyo?'

He kissed her then, pressing her sweetness against him. 'I do love you, Catherine and we will be together, I promise you.'

She touched his face. 'You must tell my father that I can't marry this Liam Cullen; it's out of the question. I would die if Dad made me go to Ireland, away from you.'

Boyo took Catherine's hand and approached the farmhouse door with some trepidation; from what he remembered of Jamie O'Conner the man was independent, fiercely proud, a man who would not be lightly swayed.

As he drew nearer the farmhouse, he saw Jamie himself come to the door. He felt Catherine stiffen and eased his arm over her shoulder. 'It's going to be all right, no-one can force you into a marriage that you do not want.'

'So, it's Boyo, the tannery worker, the one who took my hospitality, who courted my stepdaughter. Now, sure

53

enough, you are after my youngest, my only surviving child, ruining her reputation along the way. I think you have a great deal of explaining to do.'

'Dad,' Catherine interrupted, 'just listen, let Boyo talk.'

Jamie took Catherine by the shoulders. 'Go inside, I'll talk to you later.'

Boyo looped the reins of his horse over a post. He moved towards the door but Jamie barred his way. 'I never invited you to step over my threshold and I would be obliged if you would give me your explanation, if there is one, and then leave me and my family in peace.'

'I can't do that, Mr O'Conner.' Boyo suddenly felt all the old insecurities swamp him. Once, many summers ago, when he had been just above sixteen years of age he had come to this very farmhouse with nothing and had been made welcome. Now, he was no longer welcome.

He had come a long way from those penniless days but not in the eyes of Jamie O'Conner. To the Irishman he was still Boyo, the labourer, the boy who owned nothing.

'If Boyo can't come inside then I won't either,' Catherine said firmly.

'Go indoors when I tell you.' Jamie's eyes blazed and he took a step towards Boyo. 'Get on with you, back where you belong.'

'No,' Fon had come outside, drying her hands on a cloth, her fair hair escaping from the pins that held it away from her face. 'Come in, Boyo, I once said you would always be welcome here and I meant it.'

She gave her husband a hard look and, after a moment, Jamie stepped aside. 'Very well,' he said, 'since you have made my family's business your own you might as well come and hear what I have to say.'

Inside the kitchen it was bright and cheerful, just as Boyo remembered it. He was taken back, as though swept by an unseen wave. He saw again April's sweet face, her eyes looking into his; felt a pang of pain for the love that had been between them.

'You have seen fit to hide yourself away from me since

54

your night of sin with my girl and I am waiting for an explanation.' Jamie stood proudly before the fireplace, his arms folded across his chest, his eyes hostile.

'Catherine came and stayed the night with me and my family,' Boyo said. 'We were not alone in the house, I assure you.' He smiled encouragingly at Catherine.

'So you have not taken her to bed then, is that what you are saying?'

'At least I am not trying to sell her off into a marriage with a stranger.' Boyo heard the anger in his voice and knew he must control his temper, shouting would get him nowhere.

'It wasn't like that at all, colleen!' Jamie looked at Catherine. 'The Cullens are kinsfolk, I wanted you to meet them, I hoped you'd come to realize that Liam Cullen would be a fine catch.' He softened a little. 'But there was no thought of forcing you into anything.'

'You wanted me to go off to Ireland and marry Liam, don't try to get out of it, Dad.'

'Liam and his family are well set up, a wealthy family; you would have been treated like a queen, given everything you ever wanted. All I was doing was paving the way.' His voice was gentle. 'Don't you know I want the best for you, always?'

'Everything I ever wanted is here in this kitchen.' She looked meaningfully at Boyo and his heart seemed to melt within him.

'Explain yourself, Catherine! Do you mean to marry this man then?' Jamie had caught the look, his voice had grown harsh. Fon put the teapot on the table with a thud.

'No need for words, these two are in love with each other,' she said softly. 'And isn't it natural enough; knew each other as children, didn't they? We can all talk of marriage in good time, no need to rush into anything, is there?'

'Well, I'll be damned!' Jamie sank into a chair and ran his hand through his dark curls. 'Is this the lad you've been courting, then, Cath?'

Catherine hung her head and Jamie leaned over and

touched her shoulder. 'Catherine, answer me.'

'I love him, Dad, I can't ever love another man, please try to understand.'

Jamie looked at Boyo, took in his good clothes, his riding crop with the silver top, his good, handmade riding boots. 'Well, it should have been done right, you should have called to see me before this, discussed matters with me. As to rushing, Fon, my darlin', it seems these two have been bedded before being wedded and that I do not approve of. Still, it can all be mended, I dare say. And you, Boyo, what do you say about all this?'

'I love Catherine,' Boyo answered sharply. He was suddenly, tinglingly aware that the Irishman did not know he was married.

'And your prospects?' Jamie bristled at Boyo's tone.

'I think you could say that I don't need prospects, I am already one of the richest men in the county.' Boyo did not understand why he felt the need to impress Jamie, perhaps it was the patronizing way the older man was looking at him, assessing him.

'Well then, why did you not come calling like a proper suitor?' Jamie crossed his big arms, the muscles bulging beneath the flannel of his shirt.

It was pointless prevaricating and Boyo knew it. 'Because I couldn't, I'm a married man.'

'Holy Mary Mother of God!' Jamie crossed himself almost as though he had come up against a devil. He rose to his feet and thumped his fist on the table.

'You fool, Catherine, you have thrown yourself away on a married man, a man who will only use you for his pleasure.' He stood before his daughter. 'And you went to his bed like a strumpet, how could you?'

Catherine lowered her eyes. She didn't answer but her shoulders began to shake; it was clear she was crying. Boyo hurriedly knelt beside her, his arm around her as though to protect her from her father's anger.

'So, you have shamed my daughter, taken from her the one thing that would bring her a good match, her innocence.'

Jamie snatched the crop from Boyo's hand and raised it high. It swished through the air and then whistled down across Boyo's back.

Slowly, Boyo rose to his feet and faced the other man, his expression cold. 'If you were not Catherine's father and if I did not have so much regard for this family I would take you apart for what you have just done.'

Jamie turned away in disgust. 'Get out of here, the both of you,' he said, his voice thick.

'No!' Fon's voice was thin with fear. 'No, Jamie, I will not have you to send our daughter away like a leper.'

'She is no longer my daughter,' Jamie said bitterly. 'She has made her bed with a married man and if he is as wealthy as he boasts then he is well able to support her and any bastards he might father on her, too.'

He turned and looked at his wife. 'She goes, Fon, or I do.'

Catherine rose to her feet slowly. 'I'll go, don't worry; I wouldn't stay here now, not in the house where I could be sold to the highest bidder like a piece of meat. Is that your morality, Father? Is that what your faith teaches you, to peddle your daughter's virginity for the best price you can get?'

Jamie's hand lashed out and caught Catherine across her face. She staggered back and Boyo moved swiftly, catching her before she could fall to the ground. He took her up in his arms and stared at her father with cold eyes.

'I could kill you for what you have done today,' he said slowly.

'And I could kill you, too, you bastard from the work-house,' Jamie said, his eyes suspiciously bright. 'Go on, get out of my sight before I take the shotgun to you.'

As Boyo carried Catherine outside and set her upon the saddle, he could hear Fon crying bitterly. A great sadness came over him; all this, it was so far removed from the wonderful days of the summer when he had come here as a young boy and had fallen in love with April.

Catherine huddled against him. 'I'm sorry, Boyo, I never thought it would come to this.'

'Hush, it's going to be all right, I'll take care of everything.' His mind was racing, he would have to take her to a hotel for a few days, just until he could find her a house.

'What do you mean to do with me?' Her voice was small, uncertain.

'I shall buy you a pretty cottage, with roses around the door,' he said in an attempt to cheer her; 'it will have a garden and it shall be near the sea.'

'So I shall be your kept woman, is that it, Boyo?'

His heart lurched. 'My love, if I was a free man I would marry you tomorrow. I will tell Bethan I want a divorce, it will be a terrible shock to her, I must try and break it gently, when the time is right. The best I can offer you for now is a home and all my love. Will that be enough for you?'

She leaned back against his shoulder and sighed as though she was very weary. 'It will have to be, Boyo, it will have to be.'

Bethan was relieved when her father had returned home to Ty Craig, the big gaunt house where she had been born. The last few days had been a strain with all of them keeping up the pretence that nothing was wrong.

Boyo had studiously avoided intimate contact with her and it was only for appearance's sake that he had shared her bed, she knew that well enough. Passionate response there had never been but, now, his indifference to her was like a huge wall that split the ground between them into a chasm. The moment her father had gone, Boyo had moved to another room without any explanation at all.

Bethan felt fear grow within her, she wondered if it was best to remain silent, to keep the marriage, from the outside at least, a stable one.

He was out a great deal but she was used to that. Previously, his absences had not bothered her, but now, suspecting he was with that other woman, every moment apart was torture.

And then everything changed. Bethan discovered that at thirty-eight years old, she was pregnant with her first child, she must have conceived on the very last night she had slept with her husband. It was ironic.

It was almost unbelievable. She sat in the big drawing-room and stared unseeingly out of the window. She rested her hand on her stomach and a feeling of peace came over her. Whatever happened, she would always have a part of Boyo to call her own.

'I love it, Boyo, it's like a dream house.' Catherine clung to his arm as they stood in the sun-splashed kitchen of the house. He had told her he would buy her a cottage but this gabled building was far more than that. It had eleven bedrooms, most of them facing the sea. The living-room ran the length of the house, with one wall almost completely taken up by the huge window. The kitchen where they stood was airy, filled with the most modern of fixtures and fittings, it was a place out of a fairy tale.

'I hope you won't feel too cut off down here.' Boyo put his arms around her from the back and drew her against him so that her head rested against his shoulder. 'I know Caswell is a quiet spot but it's conveniently placed between Swansea and Rhossili and so lovely, I couldn't resist it.'

'I love it, I told you that, Boyo, but I would have been happy with you in the smallest cottage. I mean it, you don't have to buy me fancy things to prove how much you love me, mind.'

'I know.' He kissed the top of her head. Catherine twisted around so that she was looking up at him.

'I only wish Mam and Dad would come and see me but I don't think my father will ever forgive me for spoiling his plans.'

'Don't worry, *cochen*, I'm here to look after you now.'

She smiled up at him. 'Boyo, my love, my sweetheart, my darling, please don't call me that.'

'*Cochen*? Why?'

'I don't know, it sounds impersonal, somehow. Call me Cathie, anything, but use my name.'

He kissed the tip of her nose. 'Right then, I shall call

you Cat because you are like a little kitten.' He paused and leaned away from her, laughter in his eyes. 'A little kitten with red fur!'

She pretended to slap him but he caught her hand and then he was kissing her passionately. She responded to him with joy and abandon and when he lifted her and carried her to the master bedroom with its floral drapes and silken sheets, she sighed softly.

'I love you so much, Boyo Hopkins, I was only half alive until you came back into my life.'

He slowly undressed her, kissing her eyes, her throat, her breasts, her belly. She shuddered in anticipation, she wanted him inside her, possessing her, setting his seal upon her. But he made her wait, he made her quiver with expectation and excitement. She heard small moans come from her throat and wondered why, so quickly, she'd changed from an untried girl into a passionate woman.

'Please, Boyo, love me, love me now.'

He came to her then, smoothly, gently taking possession of her. She cried out, clutching at his shoulders, wanting the sensations to go on and on.

His hands were beneath her, lifting her towards him so that he could possess her more fully. And then a fury began within her, a flame of ecstasy that was almost pain. It shuddered from her toes through her thighs and belly, encompassed her breasts and stole her voice from her. It was a rainbow fragmenting within her, washing her with brightness and colour and joy. She began to cry, tears of release, tears of wonder that such sensation could be hers. He held her close, still within her and they clung together for a long time, their breaths mingling, their limbs entwined.

At last she stirred and touched his cheek. 'Boyo, I didn't know such feelings existed.' Her voice was little more than a croak. 'I could never have imagined such . . . such . . .' she stopped, lost for words. He kissed her mouth gently.

'I love you, Cat, never doubt that, never.'

She closed her eyes, a feeling of drowsiness creeping over her. 'Boyo, what a wonderful beginning to our new life together,' she whispered.

Later, they ate dinner in the small dining-room. It was a meal prepared by Catherine, a simple meal of cold meat and pickles and fresh bread spread with thick salt butter.

'I'm sorry it's not very much, I'll have to learn to cook.' Catherine was apologetic. 'If it wasn't for your thoughtfulness there would be no food in the pantry at all.'

'No need for you to learn to cook, Cat, I have advertised for some staff for you, I'll be interviewing candidates at the beginning of next week.'

'You are so good at taking charge, it's wonderful to be cared for this way.'

'It's only what you deserve. In any case, I'm sure that Fon did everything she could for you, spoiled you rotten.'

'Aye, that's true but I had to work in the fields, mind, help my father whenever I could.' A shadow fell across her happiness, now Jamie would be working alone. If only her parents had responded differently. Their blessing she did not expect but she was entitled to their understanding, wasn't she?

It was growing dark by the time the meal was finished. Boyo rose and lit the lamps, going around the house closing windows, locking doors. With a sinking feeling inside her, Catherine realized he was not staying with her for the night.

'Do you have to go, love?' She looked up at him, her eyes pleading. He rested his hand on her shoulder.

'It's only for tonight, I have to prepare Bethan. Now that her father has returned home, I can talk to her about the divorce, that's what we both want, isn't it?'

She held onto his hand. 'Of course it is, Boyo, but I'm going to miss you so much. You'll be here tomorrow, won't you?'

He smiled and touched her cheek. 'Try keeping me away.'

It was silent in the house when he had gone and Catherine wandered around picking up books and

61

ornaments and replacing them almost at once. She sighed, it was so quiet. She moved the curtain aside and looked through the window. The moonlight fell across the sea in a silver pathway and she shivered, she didn't think she could bear to be alone like this too often.

She might as well go to bed, at least there she could breathe the scent of him, remember him holding her in his arms, kissing her, loving her, making her aware of her body as she had never been before.

She crouched beneath the covers, hearing every creak of the boards, every rustle of the trees outside, telling herself it would be better once the staff had been employed. She looked at the empty pillow beside her and somehow she wasn't convinced.

'You shouldn't have waited up for me, Bethan.' Boyo kissed his wife's cheek feeling like a Judas. 'I told you I might be late.'

She regarded him steadily and it was as though she could read his thoughts. She sighed heavily.

'I have something important to say to you.' She didn't shift her gaze from his face, not even when he filled his glass with brandy and sat opposite her. The last thing Boyo wanted was for Bethan to be hurt but the sooner he told her his plans the better.

'I want to talk to you, too, Bethan,' he said slowly. She nodded.

'I know about your little love-nest, there's no need to tell me, news travels fast, especially gossip of that sort.' She spoke softly without censure.

'Please, hear me out,' she said as he made to speak. 'Then you can have your say.' She paused as if to gather her strength. 'I realize that our marriage was not one made in heaven; we married because it suited us, both of us. But you are well aware that I will not, under any circumstances, consider divorce, not now.'

'It is not altogether your decision.' Boyo felt compelled to return the challenge in her eyes. He noticed that she was very pale, even sweating a little and he was concerned. He made a move to rise to his feet.

'Bethan, can't we leave all this until the morning? You look very tired.'

'I have waited patiently for you to come home, Boyo,' Bethan said. 'I have to speak now, so please, just be quiet and listen to what I have to say.'

He subsided in his chair and raised his glass to his lips, waiting with a sense of apprehension to hear what was on his wife's mind. Whatever it was, he had the feeling he was not going to like it.

'You have taken a woman, you have set her up in a house in Caswell, that is a situation which I cannot change and so am prepared to put up with.' She held up her hand again to stop him speaking.

'That affair is not important, what is important is that you are still my husband and you will do me the courtesy of being discreet, do you understand?'

He rose to his feet and stood looking down at her. 'Bethan, I have a great deal of regard for you, you know that.' She flinched visibly at his words. 'I feel a great deal of affection for you,' he added hastily. 'But please don't try to treat me like a recalcitrant schoolboy.'

'You are behaving like one,' Bethan said, her tone curt. 'You are running around like a boy who has never had a woman before.'

'I haven't, not like Catherine.' He saw her turn away. 'I'm sorry to hurt you but there is no way to say it other than right out; I love her, Bethan.'

'Love; to a man it is such a transient thing. Well, you might change your mind about your "love" when you hear what I have to say, so please listen. I learned something today that is wonderful news to me and I hope to you, too.'

'What news could that be, Bethan? That your hotel has made you even richer than you are already?'

'I'm going to have our child.'

At first he thought he couldn't have heard correctly. 'But Bethan, you are too . . .' The words trailed away but she knew what he had intended to say.

'I am too old? Apparently not.'

He stared down at her, trying to assimilate this new idea; a child, perhaps a son and heir. He shook his head. 'You are sure of this, Bethan, it's not some trick?'

She looked at him scathingly. 'Since when have I needed to resort to tricks, Boyo? Just listen to yourself, will you?'

'I'm sorry, that was unnecessary. Do you feel well, are you strong enough to bear a child?'

She laughed without humour. 'Well, I'm not a delicate little doll, am I? It seems to me I have no choice in the matter; I am having this child and that's all there is to it, I'll have to be strong.'

He put his head in his hands, he was filled with a confusion of sensations: pride, joy, despair, he didn't know what to feel. Bethan, sensing something of his dilemma, took pity on him.

'Look, Boyo, you can see her, you can stay with her sometimes, but for the sake of our child, if not for me, can you act with discretion and pretend to the world that all is well with our marriage?'

He looked at her, he had never seen her ask for anything before; she had been self-sufficient, in charge of her emotions, but now Bethan was vulnerable, she needed him. Wearily, he rose to his feet.

'Don't worry, we'll work something out.' He suddenly felt he must get out of the room, he must be alone to think. 'We'll talk more in the morning,' he said and Bethan inclined her head without replying.

In his room, Boyo went towards the window and stared out at the moonlit night. In the huge gardens, the trees were tipped with silver, the lily pond just beyond the terrace looked like a fairy ring. They would have to fence that in when the baby came.

It hit him then, he was going to be a father. He sank onto the bed and covered his eyes with his hands, he didn't know what he should think or feel, all he was aware of now in the darkness of the night was what a mess he had made of his life.

CHAPTER FIVE

'My love, you've borrowed 3,000 guineas! Do you know what you are taking on?' Craig was seated at the window of Summer Lodge, his eyes resting on the manicured lawns and the carefully situated flower-beds which gave apparently random splashes of colour to the garden. He did not look at his wife, he felt ashamed, he had betrayed her, not with his body but with his lack of business acumen.

'Don't worry, Craig, it will work, it has to work.' Hari placed her hands on his shoulders and kissed him lightly. He closed his eyes in sudden pain, he loved her so much and he had brought her from the heights of wealth to the depths of poverty with a few foolish moves.

'The money has given the bank a little more faith in me.' Her voice was soft and yet edged with excitement. 'I'll use it well, don't you doubt it.' She moved away from him and stood at the centre of the room looking around her. 'I intend to begin by making the necessary alterations to the house. I'm sorry, my love, but Summer Lodge will shortly be unrecognizable.' She kissed the top of his head. 'But then anything is better than losing our home, isn't it?'

He heard the hint of uncertainty in her voice and knew he should be reassuring her. How could he? He had no faith in himself any more, anything he had to say would be worthless. 'The leather,' he forced himself to speak, 'has it been taken away from the warehouse by the bailiff yet?'

'No and it won't be, not now that the bank has agreed to wait. I have had the stock moved to the old tannery; I have Mr Hopkins's permission to use it as a store for the time being at no charge. And with the help of Mr Hopkins, I have let the warehouse at a very satisfactory figure, so it will not be draining us of any money but bringing us income instead.'

'You seem to have everything under control, Hari.' He turned to face her and she crossed the room swiftly and sat on his knee, her arms around him hugging him to her.

'I'm doing it for us, Craig, please don't be hostile to me, I'm trying my best.'

He buried his face in her neck. 'I'm sorry, Hari, I'm so afraid, afraid that we'll just sink deeper into the mire.'

She turned his face up to hers and kissed his mouth. 'I promise you, my darling, we are going to succeed. What I did once, I can do again, please believe me.'

He felt tears burn behind his lids, he who had been the strong one, master in his own home was brought to this, depending on his wife to bail him out of problems he alone had created.

'Don't let pride stand in our way, Craig,' she said and he knew she could read him like a book, 'help me, don't hinder me and we'll make it, I know we will.'

He drew her mouth down to his again and tasted her lips, as sweet now as they had been when she was little more than a young girl. Hari, the shoemaker's daughter, a woman of spirit and fire, the love of his life. 'I think I want to make love to my wife.' He spoke softly and his heart lifted as he saw the happiness in his Hari's eyes. She rose to her feet and clung on to his hand.

'That's a very good idea.'

It was some time later when Hari was asked to come to the drawing-room by the flustered maid.

'Sorry, Mrs Grenfell, but there's the vicar and his wife called to see you, was it all right to let them in?'

'Of course, Phoebe,' Hari smiled at the young maid in amusement, the girl's eyes were large in her pale face as she looked towards the bed where Craig still lay beneath the sheets. It did not take a quick mind to assess the situation.

Hari finished buttoning her blouse, ushering the girl to the door at the same time. 'Tell my visitors I will be with them in a few minutes.'

When the door closed behind the maid, Hari moved back to the bed and sank down next to Craig. 'She's shocked,' she said, laughter bubbling within her, 'Phoebe probably thinks we are far too old to be doing this sort of thing.'

'You are an insatiable, demanding woman,' Craig said smiling. 'I swear your plan is to wear me out with pleasure so that you can inherit my vast fortune.'

Hari touched his cheek. 'That's more like the man I married, I'm glad your sense of humour has returned.'

'Aye, when you are down, the only way is onward and upward and thanks to you, Hari, that's where we're going.'

Hari rose to her feet. 'Now, make yourself respectable, you can't take tea with the vicar looking like the cat who got the cream.'

'Why, do you think the dried up old stick will be jealous?'

Hari threw a pillow at him and moved to the door. 'Show some respect, old Reverend Jones is a fine preacher even if his sermons are far too long.'

She made her way downstairs to the drawing-room and, as she entered the sun-splashed room, she saw with surprise not the old vicar of Swansea as she had expected but Daniel Bennett and Ellie, his beautiful wife.

'Ellie, Daniel, how nice to see you again.'

Hari saw that tea had already been served to the guests and with a sigh of relief, she sank into a chair. She was getting rather old for mad passion in the middle of the day.

'We heard of your misfortune,' Daniel said without preliminaries. 'Don't look so surprised, news does travel as far as the village of Ilston, believe it or not.' He smiled. 'Why we have come is because we want to offer our help.'

Hari looked at Daniel Bennett in surprise. 'What sort of help?'

'Well, I have no fortune,' Daniel smiled his charming smile. 'I do, however, travel a great deal around the various parishes in my domain. If I could take samples, say, of your new designs to the outlying areas it might be of some help. What do you think?'

Hari felt tears burn against her closed lids as she fought for control. 'That's very kind, a very generous offer, but how did you know that I was starting up again on my own?'

It was Ellie who replied. 'There isn't much goes on that Daniel doesn't hear about, I think it's something to do with his earlier training as a newspaper reporter.' She paused, 'On this occasion, though, it was our old friend Boyo who told us about your situation. Please let us help, we would be so happy to do all we can.'

A ray of sunlight reached across the room like long fingers and touched Hari's face. It felt like a benediction, an omen that everything was going to go right for her.

'I'll accept your generous offer,' she said softly. 'Please spread the news that Hari Grenfell is still in business.'

Daniel smiled again, his eyes were twinkling. 'Well, I've had a word with Him up there.' He pointed to the ceiling. 'He helps those who helps themselves, if you'll forgive the cliché.'

Hari felt tears constrict her throat, she felt strong and humbled all at once, she had the good will of fine people on her side, how could she fail? She looked at Daniel and briefly touched his hand. 'Keep talking to Him upstairs, I am going to need all the help I can get.'

CHAPTER SIX

Catherine O'Conner sat in the kitchen of Honey's Farm staring doggedly before her. Boyo's revelation that his wife was pregnant had come as a devastating blow. She had cried for days. She had sat in the house in Caswell, staring out at the rain coming down in torrents outside, greying the landscape so that the sea was no longer visible. Then she had received her mother's letter begging her to come and visit them. Catherine had been impatient, Fon's desperate plea to see her had been ill-timed and unwelcome.

But now, sitting with her mother, who appeared white-faced and worried, Catherine was concerned in spite of herself. Fon's eyes were red-rimmed, deeply shadowed and Catherine felt somehow threatened by her mother's emotion.

'I had to send for you, *cariad*.' Fon rubbed at her eyes. 'Your father's ill and he's been asking to see you; please, please go upstairs and talk to him.'

Catherine shook her head slowly. 'There's no point, Mam, he'll just shout at me again, tell me I'm living a life of sin.'

Fon closed her eyes for a moment as though in pain. 'No, love, he's past that, he just wants to tell you how much he loves you before . . . before it's too late.'

'Too late?' A prickle of fear touched Catherine's spine as though cold fingers had reached out for her. 'Mam, what do you mean?'

Fon breathed in slowly. 'Catherine, your father is sick, very sick.'

'But he can't be. When I left home he was a fine healthy man, how could he suddenly fall ill?'

'He didn't, fall ill, not suddenly, anyway.' Fon's words

were disjointed, she had to force herself to speak because tears obstructed her throat.

'It's his heart, the sickness has been coming on him for a long time but he wouldn't admit to it. Can't you understand? That's why he wanted to see you married to a tidy man who would look after you and the farm.'

'Dad should know better than anyone that I couldn't do what he wanted. I have to make my own way in life, Mam, just as you did. In any case, how do you know that Liam would want to live here?'

'He said he would, it's not so far from Ireland, mind. Look, just try to humour your dad, will you, Cath? You surely owe him that much.'

'But can't the doctors, can't they do anything for him?'

'They've tried, don't you think I would have insisted on trying harder if there was anything to cure your father? Go on, go to see him, tell him you love him, make him feel better.'

Reluctantly Catherine rose to her feet and, slowly, she made her way up the familiar stairs, hearing the third stair creak as it had every night since her childhood, remembering the sweetness of honeysuckle drifting in from outside the landing window.

Her father lay beneath the blankets, already he seemed diminished, as though sickness had robbed him of his will. He looked up at her, a spark in his eyes.

'Holy Mother be praised, you've come to see me, Catherine.' He held up his hand. 'I'm sorry, darlin' girl, for what I tried to do and it was wrong of me to cast you from my door. Do you forgive me, Catherine?'

'There's nothing to forgive, Dad, don't be silly.' He took her hand and held it and his grip was still firm. He had colour in his cheeks and it was difficult to believe that he was sick.

It was as though he read her mind. 'I'm going to die, Catherine, I don't know if it will be this week, next week or next month even, but sure enough my days on God's earth are numbered.'

'Don't Dad!' She clung tighter to his hand.

70

'Hush, Catherine, it's the truth, no good hiding from it like a child.' He paused, he was very short of breath, something Catherine had never noticed before.

'I have to ask you a favour.' He looked at her pleadingly and she felt her heart contract, she knew what he wanted and she shrank from hearing the words out loud.

'Come home, love.' He had spoken and Catherine swallowed hard trying to push the words away from her conscious mind. 'It won't be for long, I promise.'

Tears burned painfully behind her eyes, he was begging her to come home, promising her that his life would be ended shortly as though he was inconveniencing her by living.

'Oh, Dad!' She bent over him and rested her cheek against his. 'Of course I'll come home. You should have told me all this before, I wouldn't have been so horrible to you then.'

'It's for your mother's sake, darlin'; Fon has never been alone in her life and I don't want her to be alone when I . . .'

Catherine gently put her hand over his mouth. 'Hush, Dad, don't try to talk any more, you'll only upset yourself.' She rose from the bed. 'I'll fetch my things, I'll be back by nightfall, I promise.'

When she returned to the kitchen, it seemed to be full of people. A man turned to look at her and she saw with a shock that it was Liam Cullen. Slowly he walked towards her, unnoticed by his father and grandmother who were talking earnestly to Fon.

'Look, about that first meeting, sure an' I'm that sorry for the upset it caused. No offence was intended.'

She stared up at him, he was handsome in a rugged sort of way and with a shock of red hair the same colour as her own. He smiled and his cheeks dimpled and she felt herself relaxing a little.

'I don't think any of that matters now, does it?' She forced herself to hold back the tears. 'I understand why Dad did it but you, why were you party to such an arrangement? Can't you find a girl of your own to love in Ireland?'

He made a wry face. 'I confess to my sins, girls I have known, lovely girls, sweet colleens, maidens who would have made my life easy and happy.'

'Well then?'

'Well then I was shown a picture of you, Catherine O'Conner, and I fell in love.'

'That's daft.' She spoke bluntly.

He shrugged, 'Maybe it is daft but there it is.'

'Well, you can see that in person I'm not as sweet and nice as you might have believed me to be. I'm a scarlet woman, I'm living with a married man, living a life of sin. What do you say to that, Liam Cullen?'

He shook his head. ''Tis sad, sure enough, to see a good girl, a beautiful girl, throw herself away on a man who will not put a ring on her finger and make an honest woman out of her.'

'It's not like that! Oh, why am I bothering to even talk to you?' She moved towards her mother, 'Mam, I'm going to collect my things, I'll be back before dark.'

Fon looked up at her, eyes limpid with gratitude. 'I'll be waiting, love, take care on the journey.'

It was a long walk back into town to the hotel where Boyo was waiting for her. On the way she thought about her father, about the way his eyes had pleaded with her. It shamed her that he had to beg for her to come home when he knew that he was so ill. That he was dying, she would not, could not, accept; her father was a strong man, he was not so old, surely he could get over this sickness and be well again?

Boyo was pacing the room, the richly furnished but impersonal hotel room. 'Cat,' he took her in his arms. 'It's bad news isn't it?'

She clung to him, wanting the comfort of his arms around her. He pressed her close, his lips to her hair.

'My father,' her voice was muffled against his chest, 'he's sick, very sick.'

Boyo held her away from him and looked into her face. 'Who says so?'

'The doctor has told him it's his heart.'

'The doctor! Who is he, some local quack? Look, I'll get the best doctors from London, we'll have a second opinion, there's probably nothing wrong with him that a good rest won't cure.'

Catherine looked up at him, her eyes full of tears. 'I can see it in his face, hear it in his voice, he is very ill, there's no getting away from it.' She paused, 'He wants me to go home.'

'No!' Boyo clasped her more tightly. 'Cat, I can't do without you, I love you desperately, you know that.'

Suddenly she was impatient with him. 'You can't think only of yourself in this,' she said quickly.

She thought of Liam's words that she was throwing herself away on a man who wouldn't make an honest woman of her. Perhaps she had believed he would leave his wife, even now, take her away somewhere far from Swansea so that they could live openly together. She'd had dreams of them spending the rest of their lives together, but those dreams had been cruelly dashed by Bethan's news of the coming child.

'You have your wife and soon you'll have your child to comfort you.' She turned away from him. 'Now, I can't think of you, I have to think about Dad, give him my love while I can.'

'I'm sorry, you are right, of course.' Boyo sank onto the bed. 'I'm being selfish, your father needs you, of course you must be with him.'

Suddenly uncertain, Catherine turned to him. 'Boyo, my life is going to be so empty without you.'

He drew her towards him and kissed her throat and her breasts and then her mouth. She sighed softly and surrendered herself to his embrace and it seemed that both of them knew their lovemaking was born of despair rather than passion. It was a farewell gesture and they both knew it.

Jamie was seated on a chair near the open door of the kitchen. He stared out at the lands of Honey's Farm falling away before him. He loved this land, had given it

73

his sweat and blood, had forced it into yielding him and his family a good living. And now, he was saying goodbye to it all.

He was much weaker, Fon and Catherine between them had half carried him downstairs. It was for the last time, he could not face the effort and pain of it again.

Outside, he saw the brightness of his daughter's skirt against the green of the fields. She was carrying a pail of milk and even as Jamie watched, he saw Liam Cullen take it from Catherine's hands and carry it with ease.

He allowed himself a small smile. Once a long time ago, his first wife, Katherine, sick unto death as she'd been, had chosen Fon to take her place. It had been a stroke of genius, for he and Fon could not have been happier together. Now, Jamie was of a mind to match his child with a good Irishman. If the plan of throwing a couple together had worked once, he could not see why it should not work again.

As they came closer, he saw that Catherine was smiling up at Liam, her red hair was escaping from the confines of its ribbon and as Liam leaned towards her, the figures seemed to merge, both red-haired, both with good Irish blood flowing in their veins.

Liam was a fine man, a man who would not let one mistake on Catherine's part unduly influence him. That he was falling in love with Catherine was obvious to anyone who had eyes to see.

Catherine waved and ran the rest of the way towards him. 'Dad, you've got a lovely colour in your cheeks.' She bent to kiss him and Jamie revelled for a moment in the feel of her petal-soft skin against his own. Of the children he had sired she was the only one left and he wanted everything that was good for her.

Fon came and stood behind his chair, her arms around his neck, her lips touching his hair. Tears came to Jamie's eyes; his two girls, his loves, they were here with him, would be with him until the end, that was all he could ever ask of God.

★

'You'll come with me to the fair on Saturday, then?' Liam was leaning on the fence, his sun-freckled arms bare beneath the rolled-up sleeves of his shirt.

'I suppose so, it seems to be what Dad wants.'

'Is that the only reason you're going to come with me, then?'

Catherine looked at him carefully; over the past two weeks she had grown used to him being around. His presence on the farm was welcome and very necessary; some of the work was too heavy for Catherine to do alone. The labourers had gone, money was short, most of the savings her parents had made over the years had been spent on doctor's bills.

'No,' she conceded slowly, 'I'm coming with you because I enjoy your company.' It was true, she liked being with Liam, he was fun, easy to get along with and, if it hadn't been for the unfortunate circumstances of their first meeting, she would have liked him unreservedly.

'Well, that's a start, then.' He smiled down at her, his eyes dark beneath the heavy thatch of red hair. That was where Liam differed in appearance from Catherine: his eyes were brown, dark and unfathomable and hers were green, flecked with amber.

She felt a lift of excitement that had nothing to do with Liam or the proposed visit to the fair. Tomorrow she would be meeting Boyo. She would wait for him in the park opposite the beach and then they would drive in Boyo's carriage to their home in Caswell. The fires would be lit by the caretaker Boyo had hired, the house would be cared for by the man's wife. It would all appear normal and homely. They would have only a few short hours together but, for a time, she could pretend that everything was all right, that she and Boyo were entitled to be living this way.

She never asked about his wife and he didn't volunteer any information. Sometimes he was troubled and moody and she could not bring herself to ask outright if anything was wrong. In any case, she had her own problems to worry about.

Her father was growing weaker by the day and Catherine felt she was under as much pressure as she could endure without taking on Boyo's troubles as well.

'I've lost you.' Liam's voice, heavy with the lilt of his Irish accent, broke into her thoughts.

'I was thinking about my father.' It was partly the truth. 'He's growing weaker, I can see it and I don't feel I'm doing enough to help him.'

'There, there, colleen, nature will take her course whatever we do or don't do.'

'Colleen', that was the endearment used by Jamie when he spoke to Fon. Tears misted Catherine's eyes. For the first time she wished she had never seen Boyo Hopkins again, that she could fall in love with Liam, do what her father wanted her to do.

She glanced at Liam, would marriage to him be so bad? He was young, vigorous, handsome. He had his own property in Ireland but he was more than willing to remain on Honey's Farm and make it thrive with the innovations he employed on his own lands. So well were his farms organized that they needed only a manager to keep things in order. If Dad and Liam had their way, Honey's Farm would be run along the same lucrative lines.

She was probably being selfish holding out against her father's wishes, but to marry Liam was to put Boyo out of her life and that was unthinkable.

Her meeting the next day with Boyo did not bring the unadulterated joy she had been expecting. He had greeted her by saying he couldn't stay long. Bethan, it seemed, was not coping with her pregnancy very well.

'Serve her right for getting pregnant at her age.' The words had come out of their own volition and she had seen the frown that had crossed Boyo's face before she had flung herself into his arms and begged him to forgive her.

Now, he was making ready to leave. Their coupling had been swift, a release for Boyo, but for her it left a feeling of being used.

'Don't forget to leave the money before you go,' she said with sarcasm. He looked at her quickly.

'Cat, what do you mean?' He came and knelt beside her and took her hands.

'Well, I'm behaving like a whore, I can't blame you if you treat me like one, can I?'

He held her close and suddenly she was crying. 'Oh, Boyo, you don't know how unhappy I am.'

He gave her his handkerchief and she mopped her eyes. 'Dad's so sick and you can hardly spare me five minutes of your time, can't you see what it does to me to have you take me and then run home to your wife?'

'Cat, my love, I've been thoughtless and I apologize.' He kissed her fingertips. 'Perhaps when the baby is born and when . . .' his words trailed away for a moment. 'Perhaps we can take up residence together again when the time is right.'

'When you have your son and I lose my father, you mean? How kind of you, Boyo!'

He rose to his feet. 'I can't seem to say anything right, I'd better go.' He took up his coat. 'I'll send my man to bring you a cab.' He stood in the doorway. 'I'll be in touch, Catherine. I'm sorry to prove such a disappointment to you but perhaps your cousin, the Cullen fellow, is offering you the comfort that I, apparently, singularly fail to do.'

She looked at him sharply. 'Liam, what has he to do with anything?'

'Well, he is staying at Honey's Farm, I understand, acting as lord of the manor from all I hear.'

'So you have your spies out watching me, have you?' Catherine was angry. 'Yes, Liam *is* a comfort and a strong arm to lean on. As you say, in that way *you* are a disappointment.'

His face blanched and Catherine moved slowly towards him, touching his arm. 'Boyo! I didn't mean it, I'm overwrought, that's all.' She buried her face in his neck and the tears came fast and hot, bitter tears of frustration and anger.

He patted her shoulder. 'I know, I understand, we are both under strain. It will all work out for the best, you'll see. Everything passes in time, difficulties, unhappiness, even sorrow. We have our lives before us, we don't need to grasp at them, we can take everything one step at a time.'

Later, the rest of her clothes in a bag, she drove home to Honey's Farm, tears she could not shed, hot beneath her lids. Catherine thought over the heated words that had passed between her and Boyo and she knew that he was right; they were both young and healthy, their lives stretched out before them, no need to take their happiness at the expense of others.

She asked the driver to stop at the end of the lane; she didn't want to answer awkward questions by turning up at the door in a hired cab. She listened to the clip clop of the horses' hooves dying away in the distance before she began to walk towards home.

Liam was standing at the top of the lane and from his easy stance as he leaned against the gate, it appeared he had been waiting for her.

'Been shopping?'

'No, visiting an old friend.' Catherine knew she sounded defensive but she felt irritated, Liam had no right to question her movements. 'I do have to get away from here from time to time just to keep myself sane.'

He put out his hand and touched her shoulder in a comforting gesture. 'I know, it's an unhappy time for you. Let's have your bag. Lord, 'tis heavy enough, what have you got in here?'

She smiled up at him wanly. 'Just a few clothes. Liam, I'm sorry for being so sharp, you mustn't mind me, I'm like a bear with a sore head. I don't know why you should put up with my moods.'

'I put up with you because you are the loveliest thing I've ever seen in my life.'

In a moment of weakness she leaned against him. He held her close, not taking any liberties for which she was grateful. He held her for a long time until at last she freed herself.

'I'd better go in, my mother will be worried about me.'

Upstairs, in the bedroom where Jamie lay sick, Fon stood at the window holding back the curtain.

'If you could see what I've just seen you would be very pleased.' She turned to her husband, her tone soft. 'Liam was just holding our Cath in his arms, just holding her, not trying to kiss her or anything. He's a good man, I hope our girl sees sense before it's too late.'

Jamie was too weak to answer but Fon was rewarded by a faint smile. She forced back the tears and bent to kiss her husband's forehead.

'If young Liam is half as good a man as you then our Catherine will be a very lucky girl indeed.'

He took her hand and held it close to his cheek. There was a glint of tears in his eyes.

'I'll go down and get the supper.' Fon fought the pain within her, how could she bear to live her life without Jamie? 'I'll bring you a little bit of *cawl*, you can eat that, can't you, love?'

Jamie opened his eyes as though with a great effort. 'I'll try, colleen, I'll try.'

Fon swallowed hard and once outside the door, she leaned against it, the tears running salt into her mouth. How it hurt her to see Jamie brought to this. It wasn't fair! What had they done to deserve such troubles? Soon she would lose him, she had tried to prepare herself for it but in her heart she knew, once her husband was gone, life for her would be over.

Downstairs, Catherine and Liam were laughing to-gether. It cheered Fon, a small oasis of normality in the sea of dread that was gripping her. She pushed away the waves of fear and forced herself to speak normally.

'Cut some bread for supper, there's a good girl.' As she sat there with her daughter who was bright-eyed, chatter-ing easily to Liam, Fon felt her spirits lift a little. Here was youth and health and happiness and she drank in the atmosphere eagerly.

Watching Catherine, it was clear to Fon that her daughter was unaware of how sick her father really was.

Would it be kinder to try to prepare her? But no, let her remain in happy ignorance until the truth was forced upon her.

'Are you tired, Mam?' Catherine leaned forward solicitously. 'You are looking so pale, shall we have an early night?'

'No!' Fon shook her head emphatically. 'No, I'd much rather stay here by the fire and listen to you two chattering.'

She subsided in her chair knowing that deep within her she was afraid, afraid to go upstairs to the bedroom she'd shared for so long with her husband, afraid that in her absence he would have slipped away from her into a world which she could not reach.

CHAPTER SEVEN

Bethan stared at her reflection in the long oval mirror in the bathroom and smiled wryly to herself. She had never been a beautiful woman, she could not even be described as pretty but impending motherhood seemed to suit her. Her cheeks had a bloom, her eyes were bright and even her hair had taken on a glossy sheen.

She was approaching the sixth month of her pregnancy and now, feeling the tiny movements of her child, she wondered that she had not realized her condition sooner. She rested her hand on the swell of her stomach and amidst her delight in her condition, she felt an icicle of fear. She was old for motherhood, how would she manage at her confinement, would there be complications? And the child when it came, would she be able to care for it properly? And above all her anxieties was the overriding knowledge that she was married to a man who didn't love her.

Boyo cared, of course he did, but love, the love a man gave to his wife, that was missing. It was no-one's fault. Boyo had made no pretence of being in love with her and, in the beginning, she thought she did not love him. Or did she? Had she known all the while that love had been there underneath the friendship and the companionship and the liking that she felt for her husband? Had it been lurking, afraid to declare itself all this time?

So many questions. Impatiently, she turned away from the mirror, such introspection did little good. She had made her bed and now she must lie in it.

Bethan grimaced at the triteness of her thoughts but then she had never pretended to be an original thinker. She was a moderately intelligent woman, a pleasant if not spectacular conversationalist, but what she had to offer was, obviously, not enough.

She heard the front door slam and with a lifting of her heart, she realized Boyo had come home. Where he had been she didn't know and she didn't want to know. Bethan made her way along the landing towards the graciously curving staircase, below her she could see her husband handing his coat to the maid.

He looked up and smiled and even from this distance she could see the hint of anxiety in his eyes. 'Come down to the drawing-room, Bethan, I have something I wish to discuss with you.'

Her heart dipped in fear, her mouth was dry but her head was high as she descended the stairs. In the drawing-room, Boyo was standing with his back to the ornate mantelpiece. Behind him, the fire glowed and flickered and Bethan fixed her gaze on it as a source of warmth and comfort and normality.

She took a seat. 'Are you going to leave me, Boyo?' Her voice was shaky, desperate and Bethan hated herself for the weakness that revealed her dependence on her husband.

'Bethan! Of course I'm not going to leave you, not now when you need me so much. What kind of a bastard do you think I am?'

She felt weak with relief. She clasped her hands together in her lap and risked a glance at Boyo. 'What's on your mind, then?'

He paced across the room towards the small round table where a tray of decanters stood and helped himself to a brandy.

'I must settle some money on Catherine, it's only fair.' He didn't look at her so he didn't see the fleeting look of relief cross her face.

'Is that all? It's your money, Boyo, you must do what you wish with it.'

'But it's yours, too and our child's.' He turned to look at her. 'So you don't mind, then?'

She minded, of course she minded, the gesture meant that this girl was still a large part of his life and would continue to be so for some time to come.

'I don't object.' She spoke in measured tones. 'There is enough money between the two of us to keep half the county. If you chose to give some of it away then that is your right.'

'Her father is sick, very sick, he needs specialist care.' He sat down opposite her and leaned forward, looking into his glass. 'Jamie O'Conner was very good to me when I . . . well, a long time ago. I feel I owe it to him and to the family to do my best for him now.'

The feeling of relief spread into a glow, this she could understand, it was no more than the repaying of a debt. She smiled at him.

'You are a good, kind man, Boyo Hopkins.'

He shook his head. '*Duw*, don't talk such rubbish.'

Bethan concealed a smile, he was touched by her praise, that was evident by the way he slipped into the Welsh tongue. She realized suddenly that his gaze was fixed upon her, she looked up and met his eyes.

'I'm sorry for the mess I've made of things, Bethan.' He took a drink. 'Are people gossiping about me, about my "love-nest" with a farm girl?'

Bethan answered him honestly. 'There has been gossip but then people are quite used to the notion of a wealthy gentleman taking a mistress from the lower orders.'

She saw him flinch. 'I'm from "the lower orders" myself, or have you forgotten?'

'Yes, I had forgotten, you were a rich man when I met you, Boyo, a successful businessman and that's how I think of you. I was not looking down on such people, I do assure you, I was just stating the facts as the people of our good town would see them.'

'I know.' He rose to his feet and she knew that he was about to take refuge in his den. She held out her hand.

'Boyo, I have felt him move, our child.' She took his hand and drew it towards her stomach. 'There, feel him kick.'

An expression of amazement appeared on Boyo's face. 'That's miraculous!' He smiled down at her. 'He's going to be a good strong chap, this son of ours.'

Bethan felt a feeling of euphoria settle over her, she was going to give Boyo what no-one else in the world could give him: a legitimate heir. It was a tenuous thread, she was wise enough to know that when a man is young and the sap is rising, passion takes precedence over all, but passion had a habit of fading. All she had to do was be patient and, one day, Boyo would be all hers again.

Catherine lay in the warmth of Boyo's arms and breathed in the scent of him. Her heart ached with love even as her body responded to his touch. She had not realized that she could feel such depth of emotion. It was more than passion, more than love even, it was the sense of belonging with this man that was so strong a bond between them.

'Cat, my lovely girl.' He kissed her eyelids, her cheeks, her throat and then his mouth moved to her breasts. Her nipples were proud, pressing against the heat of his mouth. He swung her round so that she was above him, his hardness deep within her. 'I'm your slave, Cat, I'll always be your slave.'

She closed her eyes, her head thrown back as she moved softly at first and then with growing passion. Beneath her hands were the firm contours of his chest, she felt his heart beat and then she was riding on the moon; the stars were within her head, within her senses, driving her on desperately to reach the glittering peak of her excitement. The explosion of sensations shuddered through her, tingling in her belly and up to her head. She bent over him, making little sounds of pleasure, kissing his mouth, her hair hanging over his face.

He turned her over onto her back and then he was bringing her fresh delights; she cried out, feeling she would die from the rush of joy that seemed almost painful in its intensity. 'Boyo, Boyo, I love you so much.'

Afterwards, they lay quietly side by side in the great bed, the hours passing in dreaming and whispers and sometimes in snatches of sleep. Catherine's limbs remained twined around his, her face against Boyo's heart. The beating was rapid, loud in her ears. She felt privileged to enjoy such happiness, such fulfilment and yet she knew the magic must end, he would rise, go to the bathroom and then he would be making for home and for his wife.

'Cat,' he said softly and it was as if he sensed her thoughts. 'I must go soon but there's something I want to say first. Now, don't be angry or offended but I've opened a bank account in your name. Please don't say anything, I have so much money that I don't know what to do with it. Your father, he was good to me once – a long time ago, this is perhaps the only way I can repay him.'

Catherine was silent, was this his way of telling her it was over, of paying her off? 'Are you saying goodbye, Boyo?' She asked, her voice suddenly hard. He sat up and looked down at her in exasperation.

'Why is it that I am misunderstood at every turn?'

'What do you mean?'

'Look, I told Bethan what I was going to do, to give you some money of your own. She thought I was going to leave her. Now this from you. Women! I'll never understand them.'

Catherine suddenly saw the funny side of it. Boyo sitting up in bed naked, his hair tangled over his forehead like that of a small boy and a bewildered look on his face, trying to do his best in what must be a very difficult situation.

'If you'll never understand women, how is it you have two in your life?' She fell back on the pillow and tears rolled down her cheeks and she wasn't sure if she was laughing or crying.

'You vixen, I ought to give you a good spanking.' He held her close and kissed her mouth gently. 'I love you, Cat, I'll never say goodbye to you, I promise. But I cannot abdicate my responsibilities at home either, not now. All I can do is my best and the two women in my life will have to take it or leave it.'

'I know.' She nuzzled close to him. 'I'm a harridan and a nag. Thank you for the money, it's a kind thought.'

'But you won't use it, not even to try to cure your father?' He read her well.

'No, I won't use it. As for curing Dad, I accept now that it isn't possible. He's sick unto death, he has had enough and he's ready to die, he's told me so. Mam thinks I don't realize how bad Dad is but I realize, oh, I realize only too well.' There was a catch in her throat and suddenly her happiness had evaporated. She clung to Boyo.

'How am I going to face it? I can't imagine life without my father.' She caught her breath. 'And Mam, she will be lost and alone. We both have more than our share of responsibility and, like you, I feel all I can do is my best, to share myself out between you all.'

'What we mustn't do is quarrel between ourselves,' Boyo said softly. 'I do not want to add to your troubles. My only worry is that I can't spend as much time as I want to with the only woman I will ever love.'

Catherine clung to him feeling warmed and comforted by his words. He loved her, that was a knowledge she must hold to her in the dark days that were to come.

Liam was standing near the gate when Catherine returned to Honey's Farm, waiting for her seemed to have become a habit with him. She looked into his face anxiously.

'Dad, is he worse?'

'He's just the same, colleen, no change at all.' He began to walk beside her along the path. 'It's just the feeling in the house, the oppression, it gets to me sometimes, all the pain of it.'

She took his hand. 'You are a very nice, very sensitive man, Liam,' she said softly. He gripped her hand tightly.

'Sure and don't I know that without you telling me? I'm a handsome buck into the bargain and you should be glad to be seen with a fine fellow like me.'

'Seen with you?' Catherine asked unable to resist a smile at his cheek.

'Yes, seen with me, have you forgotten we are going to the fair tomorrow?'

She looked at him doubtfully. 'Do you think we should, Liam? I mean perhaps it would be better if we stayed with Mam.'

'Positively not,' Liam said. 'Uncle Jamie was on to me about it only this evening. "Taking my girl to the fair tomorrow, aren't you, giving her a bit of a break?" That's what he said.'

Catherine could well believe it, her dad was the sort of man who thought about the feelings of others, he probably realized she needed to laugh a little now and again to lighten the burden his sickness placed on her.

'Yes, then, we shall go to the fair. Satisfied?' She smiled up at him and behind him the sun was going down, highlighting the red of his hair. He really was a handsome man, why couldn't she have fallen in love with him she asked herself not for the first time.

'I could grow on you.' Liam spoke as if he had heard her thoughts. 'We could make a good marriage and in time you would come to love me. What girl could resist me for long?'

She shook her head. 'No, Liam, I am in love with Boyo Hopkins, I am his mistress whether you like it or not. I know I can't be his wife but then I have something his wife does not have, his love.'

Liam stopped walking and put his hands on her arms. 'Are you sure, love?' He asked softly and there was no censure in his voice. 'Men say all sorts of things, make promises, will do anything when they want a woman as beautiful as you.'

'Liam, I know you mean well but don't worry about me. I'm not a child, I know what I'm doing and I know Boyo loves me. I don't have to prove that to anyone else.'

He sighed and drew her against his shoulder and held her gently, his chin resting on her hair.

'Well, I'm in love with you, Catherine O'Conner, and I can't help that. I think I've loved you from the first moment I saw you, first your photograph had me spellbound and then the sight of you in that hotel; so fresh, so lovely, how could I help loving you? I believe we are meant to be together.' He held up his hand as she made to protest.

'I won't put any pressure on you but I will be here if ever you need me. Come on, give me a hug.'

She was happy to rest in his arms for a few moments, gathering her strength to go into the house. 'Liam,' her voice was muffled, 'I'm glad to have you for a friend but that is all that can ever be between us.'

When Catherine made her way into the kitchen, Fon was dozing in her chair, the pages of *The Swansea Times* strewn on the floor around her feet. She looked so young suddenly, so defenceless, that Catherine had the strangest feeling that they had changed places, she had become the strong one, the mother figure, and Fon the child.

She knelt on the floor and put her arms around her mother holding her close. 'Mam,' she said softly, 'come on, let me take you up to bed, you're exhausted.'

Fon leaned sleepily against her shoulder and Catherine felt a wave of protective love sweep over her. Fon needed her, needed her more than anyone in the world right now.

'I'll have a cup of tea first, love.' Fon stirred and leaned away from Catherine. She looked up, her eyes were brimming with tears. 'Oh, Catherine, I'm so afraid.'

'I know, I know.' Catherine rocked her mother to and fro, her eyes closed, a sense of despair and inadequacy rising within her.

She heard Liam build up the fire and then the scrape of the kettle against the coals. He was a good man and she was grateful to him but that was all she could offer him, her gratitude.

The water in the kettle, already warmed on the hob came swiftly to the boil. Liam moved about the kitchen quietly and efficiently and then Catherine heard the scrape of a chair on the flags.

'Right, you two idle women,' he said cheerfully, 'come and have this cup of tea before it goes cold.'

Fon looked up and smiled through her tears. 'You are a good boy, Liam. I'm so glad you're here, I don't know what we would do without you, love.'

'I know, as I keep telling Catherine here, I'm indispensable and a fine handsome man to boot and tomorrow I am taking Catherine to the fair in town. I think I deserve a kiss from my Auntie Fon for such devotion to duty.'

Fon rose from her chair and crossed to where Liam was sitting and hugged him warmly. 'I'd have known anywhere that you came from the same stock as Jamie, you are so like him.'

'And that's the highest praise any man could ask for.' Liam reached up and touched Fon's hair and for a moment, their eyes locked. It was, Catherine thought, as if the two of them were drawn together in a conspiracy and she knew full well what that conspiracy was.

Well, they could plan and plot but much as she loved her mam, she could not marry Liam, ever. The both of them would have to accept that sooner or later.

'Drink your tea.' Liam nodded towards Catherine as Fon released him, 'Come on, both you girls could do with a bit of warming up, you are as pale as little day-old chicks the pair of you.'

There was silence in the kitchen except for the ticking of the clock on the mantelpiece and the shifting of coals in the grate. Catherine became aware that Fon was reluctant to go to the bed she shared with Jamie, fearing he would die in the night and leave her alone.

'I'll go and see to Dad.' She rose with a sense of purpose, 'I'll make sure he's comfortable and settled for the night.'

Fon glanced at her gratefully. 'There's a good girl.' The relief in her voice was almost tangible. Catherine squared her shoulders and moved to the door and Liam's quietly spoken words followed her.

'If you need any help, colleen, just call me.'

It was dark in her father's room and Catherine lit the lamp and watched as the soft light spilled over the bed. Jamie's eyes were open and he forced a smile as he looked at her. She sat carefully on the bed beside him. 'Do you need anything, Dad?' She touched his hand, his skin was dry and hot.

'I need the privie, Catherine.' He sounded apologetic. She smiled.

'You don't need to worry, Dad, there's a chamber under the bed, I'll get it for you.' She scrambled on her knees beneath the bed and drew out the china chamber-pot. She helped her father swing his trembling legs over the side of the bed and then attempted to draw him to his feet.

He looked up at her, his face suddenly covered in a sheen of sweat. 'It's no good, Cathie, we are not going to manage it.' He bent his head. 'Oh, God, let me die in dignity, don't make this torture go on.'

'Wait here, Dad.' Catherine left him propped against the iron bedpost and hurried to the top of the stairs. 'Liam, could you give me a hand up here?' She kept her voice calm so as not to worry her mother. The door downstairs opened and Liam was taking the stairs two steps at a time.

Together, they accomplished the difficult task and afterwards, as Liam carried the chamber away, Catherine fetched warm water and bathed her father as though he was a baby.

'You shouldn't be doing this, my little love,' Jamie was exhausted, his face grey; 'you are a child, it's not fair on you.'

'Don't talk rubbish, Dad!' Catherine tweaked his nightshirt into place and covered him with the blankets. 'I'm a big, strong farm girl and if I can't give my father a helping hand with what comes naturally then there's something wrong with me.'

'Now,' she looked down at him, 'I shall bring you a nice hot cup of tea with plenty of sugar, just as you like it.'

'Forget tea,' Jamie said with a show of his old spirit, 'I think I deserve a drink of something stronger after what you and that nephew of mine have just put me through.'

'What about a little drop of brandy then, Dad?' she winked at him. 'But don't go telling Mam and getting me into trouble, mind.'

Downstairs, she washed her hands in the water from the kettle and then poured her father a liberal measure from the brandy bottle.

'What's that?' Fon asked without any real curiosity.

'Never you mind, it's a little treat for my dad, he'll sleep tonight, have a good rest.' She paused, her hand on her mother's shoulder, 'A little drop of brandy can't do him any harm now, Mam.'

Later, when Fon had gone to bed, Catherine sat in the kitchen with Liam and she was grateful to him for the companionable silence they shared. The coals shifted and sparks shot up from the cinders in the pan beneath the fire.

'Time to go to bed, I suppose,' Catherine said softly. She looked at Liam. 'Mam is right, I don't know what we'd do without you.'

'It's the least I can do.' Liam smiled his slow smile and rose to his feet. 'Right then, bed it is and don't worry about your dad's ablutions in the morning, from now on, I'll see to that.'

He knelt and riddled the coals in the fire. 'I'll be out of bed early, I always am, it's the way of farm life, it becomes a habit, so don't worry.' He glanced at her over his shoulder. 'Go on, get your rest, you've got shadows under your eyes as deep as the folds in the mountains of Mourne.'

But when she was lying in bed with the moon stretching fingers of light across the floor and bed, Catherine was unable to sleep. She thought of Boyo and, for the first time since their relationship began, she felt a tinge of resentment against him; she was hurt and angry that he couldn't be with her at this time when she most needed him. It was a long time before she closed her eyes.

The day of the fair dawned bright and sunny. Catherine rose from bed feeling a lifting of her spirits, Liam was taking her to town. For an hour or two, she could forget her father's sickness, forget her mother's haunted eyes and just enjoy being young and healthy.

Liam and Fon were already in the kitchen when she

descended the stairs. Liam was sitting at the table and Fon was serving the breakfast, she was actually smiling. 'Liam's seen to your dad,' she said eagerly, 'and we both think he looks a little better today.'

Catherine felt pity drag at her. She met Liam's eyes and she knew they shared the knowledge that Jamie O'Conner would never get better.

'I'm glad he's having a good day.' She kissed her mother's cheek. 'Anything I can do?'

'Aye, pour some more tea, I'm parched.'

'So am I,' Liam said. 'I thought you'd never get out of bed and do some work down here in the kitchen.'

'Work, that's all I ever do,' Catherine returned his banter. 'Put upon by my cruel family I am.'

'My heart bleeds for you,' Liam said dryly and Catherine smiled at him. She was growing fond of this cousin of hers.

The morning was a busy one, the usual chores had to be done and though Liam had hired four labourers to work the farm, he was still needed to supervise. It was late afternoon by the time Catherine climbed into the trap beside him and headed towards Swansea.

The sun was high above, warm and comforting, it was good to be alive. Catherine had become very much aware of her own mortality lately, her father's sickness had made her realize how uncertain life could be. She breathed deeply, how lucky she was to be able to enjoy the sunshine.

'Was Dad really feeling better this morning? Is he having a good day?'

'He is.' Liam smiled down at her. 'He's got the fighting spirit of the Irish in him, hasn't he?'

'I know but last night he was so sad, so weary, he just wanted to die.'

'Well today is a new day,' Liam said emphatically, 'and right now, you and me are going to enjoy it.'

'I feel as excited as a child.' Ellie smiled up at her husband and Daniel bent and kissed the tip of her nose. 'It's so long since I've been to a fairground and more importantly, so long since I've visited Swansea.'

'And we are going to ride in a grand carriage,' Daniel said, with a gleam in his eye. 'It's a fine thing when your wife knows so many influential people.'

'It's only Boyo and Bethan we're going with,' Ellie said reproachfully, 'and Boyo is an old friend, isn't he? Anyone would think I was a social climber.'

'Ah, but Boyo's wife is county, you know.' Daniel adopted a heavy attitude and stared down at her with a long face. 'It is not often that a poor cleric and his wife have the pleasure of travelling in style with the toffs.'

Ellie laughed. 'I suppose I was considered a toff, once before . . . well, it's a long time ago now.'

'I was forgetting', Daniel teased, 'that my wife was born to a rich family herself and was once owner of *Glyn Hir* tannery, a woman of great fortune.' He drew her close. ' A woman who gave it all up for me and into the bargain made a young man very rich and very happy.'

'The tannery was rightfully his,' Ellie said, touching her husband's cheek. 'Boyo has done well with what I gave him, he has made himself a much bigger fortune than he started with; all credit to him.'

The bell rang sharply and Ellie heard the maid cross the hall and swing back the arched door of the vicarage. Then the room seemed full with Boyo's tall frame blotting out the light from the window and Bethan coming forward to kiss Ellie's cheek.

'You are looking well,' Ellie said admiringly, 'approaching motherhood seems to suit you.'

Bethan's face was suddenly transformed, filled with light. She ran her hand over the curve of her belly and her eyes filled with tears. 'I know, I'm so happy. I can't believe it has happened, after all I'm not a young woman any more.'

'Nonsense!' Ellie protested. 'You are a woman in your prime, you look beautiful.'

Boyo hugged Ellie and she looked closely into his face, realizing that he was not as happy as a man about to become a father should be. Had the shadow in the back of his eyes anything to do with the O'Conner girl? Rumour had it that the pair were lovers, still, it was none of her business.

'Come along then,' Daniel said, 'let's get to this fair before it closes, shall we?'

'Forgive my husband's sarcasm.' Ellie would have liked to link arms with Bethan but there was something about the older woman that forbade familiarity.

As the grand, gleaming carriage bounced along the lanes towards Swansea, Ellie felt a renewed sense of excitement. It was so long ago that she had lived there, had laughed and cried as she sat on the sands of Swansea Bay and looked out at Mumbles Head. She had known many joys and many sorrows while she lived at Swansea and there, she reminded herself, she had met Daniel. She glanced at him, resisting the urge to touch his cheek. Daniel had loved her in spite of her strange past, loved her even though she had been a mistress to one rich man and then a wife to another. And he had made her so happy. She reached out her hand and slipped it into his and he looked down at her and smiled. Ellie became aware that Bethan was looking at her with something like envy in her face and, quickly, she withdrew her hand as though she was a child caught out doing something wrong. Once at the fair, Ellie would make sure that she and Daniel had time to wander around on their own, for somehow, something about Bethan Hopkins made her feel uneasy.

The fairground was opposite the beach and the crowds milled across from one side of the road to the other, enjoying the salt breezes on the shore as well as the crowded sideshows of the fair.

'Let me buy you some ribbons.' Liam thrust his hand into his pocket and took out some coins. A man standing listlessly against the side of one of the booths snapped to attention, a smile crossing his toothless mouth as he held out a handful of brightly coloured ribbons.

'A green one, I think.' Liam selected a colour and when

he had paid the man he smiled down at Catherine. 'Turn around then, let's fasten this in your red curls. It will make you look very fetching, better than the smart ladies from the big houses.'

Catherine indulged him and felt him lift the thickness of her hair from her neck. She was about to ask him to be quick when suddenly, coming towards her, was Boyo with his wife clinging to his arm. It was easy to see the soft swell of her stomach and suddenly Catherine felt sick with jealousy. Until now she had not thought of Boyo lying with his wife, making love to her. She knew it happened, of course, but now she was faced with the proof of it and she wanted to cry.

Liam, whether by design or accident, bent at that moment to touch his lips to her neck. Catherine didn't move but she saw Boyo's face darken with anger.

It was as though some devil had taken hold of Catherine as she faced her lover, she wanted to hit out at him, to hurt him as she was hurt. He looked down at her and then at Liam, but it was Bethan who spoke.

'Miss O'Conner, isn't it? I remember you arriving at my house that time, mud-stained and dishevelled, I felt so sorry for you.' She smiled and it was clear her words were calculated to embarrass Catherine.

'No need to feel sorry for me,' she said, 'I'm young and strong, you see.' She saw Bethan flush at the intended insult to her age.

'This is my cousin Liam from Ireland.' Catherine hugged Liam's arm to her side and stared Boyo in the face defiantly. 'He's handsome, don't you agree, Boyo?'

There was an awkward silence and then Bethan's face seemed to change, her eyes glittered and her mouth was twisted. 'I hate you!' The words came out so low Catherine wondered if she had heard aright.

'You could have any man you wanted,' Bethan said, her voice harsh, 'couldn't you leave me with the only one I will ever want?'

The two women looked at each other and it was Catherine who looked away first.

'Come on, Liam,' she said, her head high, 'we are here to enjoy ourselves after all.' She glanced at Boyo, his face was set and expressionless.

She felt her cheeks burn as she turned away from the raucous noise of the fair and half-stumbled across the road, stepping blindly over the tracks of the Mumbles railway before falling onto the soft sand.

'That was a nasty encounter.' Liam sank down beside her. 'I felt almost sorry for Hopkins back there. Two she-cats spitting over him, how he must have burned with embarrassment.'

'Liam!' Catherine said aghast. 'Is that what it seemed like to you? Was I that awful?' She covered her face with her hands. 'I know I was, I'm a bitch, Boyo will never forgive me.'

Liam drew Catherine against him. 'There, the man loves you, anyone with half an eye can see that. But then, so do I and I, my dear Catherine, am free, I have no wife and child hanging on my coat-tails.'

Catherine felt tears burn her eyes, what a mess she was in, how unhappy she was. And all the time she was playing the fool with a married man, her father was lying sick unto death wanting only a respectable marriage for her.

'Take me home, Liam, will you?' He held her hand as he led her away from the bay and towards the place where he had tethered the horse. He lifted her into the trap and climbed into the seat beside her.

'Right, madam, home it is.' He clucked softly and the horse jerked the trap into motion. Catherine closed her eyes and then opened them quickly again as the picture of Boyo with Bethan on his arm came into her mind.

As the horse and trap moved through the streets of town and out towards Honey's Farm, Catherine felt a sense of despair. This had been a bad day and somehow, she felt, it could only get worse.

CHAPTER EIGHT

Hari Grenfell walked slowly across the road towards the beach. The sun was high in an azure sky, the sea lapped the shore with sparkling fingers of foam. It was a day to rejoice in being alive.

She had just taken tea with Boyo Hopkins's wife; the invitation had come as a surprise but Hari was glad she had accepted it. Bethan had shown an insight into Hari's financial problems that was remarkable. She had made very good suggestions for cost-cutting and she had volunteered additional funding should Hari need it. Bethan Hopkins was an astute woman, she ran her own business very successfully: an old coaching inn now turned into a hotel with a splendid view over the sea.

Hari stood at the slip and looked out across the bay, enjoying the sound of the sea washing the shore and the seagulls calling overhead. Behind her, near the park, waited the cab to take her home but Hari had felt the need to be alone for a while.

Careless of her good worsted skirt, she sank onto the sand. The salt air was crisp, clean, the sky was a blue arc which met the sea on the horizon and merged into shimmering gold where the sun touched the water. Had she missed all this beauty before? She had certainly never seen it with the painful clarity she did now. Perhaps being in the same circumstances as she'd been at the start of her career gave her a clearer vision.

But she was not really beginning again. Now she had a fine reputation, a supportive husband and the backing of reliable business people, such help had been beyond her in her early days. Now she had resources she did not have when young, a property that would bring her in money, friends who were with her all the way in this new enterprise.

She rose and shook the sand from her skirts and took in a deep breath of the salt air, knowing she was going to need all her determination and all her strength to make her new venture succeed.

She glanced up at the skies, so wide, so huge above her and she was aware of her own insignificance in the scheme of things. Doubt swept over her; could she rise again? Clear the debts and get on with her life? What had she achieved for all the hard work she had put in through the early years?

'Stop feeling sorry for yourself!' She listed her blessings: she had married a fine man, borne his children and, perhaps, with her shoemaking skills, she had brought a little happiness to children with deformities of the foot. Not an earth-shattering list of achievements but enough to make her realize how lucky she had been; some women never found fulfilment. It was about time she returned home and stopped thinking such foolish thoughts.

She returned to the cab and, nodding to the driver, climbed inside. She sank back in the leather seat and sighed, soon she would be home, she would be seated at her own fireside and now, with her efforts, it would remain her own.

A small smile curved her lips, she knew in that moment that her doubts and indecision had passed. She felt more alive than she had done in a long time, she had a challenge to face and she would face it with courage.

Excitement filled her, ideas raced through her head. She could devise new designs for the re-launch of the latest collection of her Welsh leather footwear. She would fit women out from head to foot with the best leather: coats, hats, gloves, as well as shoes. Perhaps she could specialize in bridal footwear as a sideline, velvet and satin slippers and millinery and gloves to match. Hari felt a moment of sheer happiness, she was alive, she still had Craig as her strength and her support, she would fight to her last breath to make their future secure.

'I took tea with Mrs Grenfell the other day,' Bethan was

seated in her chair, a tapestry on the frame before her, her needle poised, her glasses slipping to the end of her nose. 'She is such a fine person, I never thought I would enjoy the company of another woman but indeed, I had a very pleasant afternoon.' Bethan paused and bit a thread with her fine white teeth.

'She seemed willing to listen to my suggestions and I think I might have given her some fresh ideas. She has such courage, facing poverty and debt the way she is, I am so pleased you decided to help her.'

Boyo was hidden behind *The Swansea Times*, he grunted, as though he had no interest in the matter.

'Think the business will pull through, Boyo?' She refused to be ignored, she wanted his attention; if she could not have his love, could they not at least resurrect the easy friendship that had been between them?

Her husband shook his head. 'I expect she will do her damnedest to make it pull through, she has a fine spirit, as you say.'

'And you, do you mean to help her with further funds should she need them? I myself have volunteered extra cash, I'm sure the woman will make a good try to save her business.'

'I agree.' He was not in the mood to talk and yet Bethan could not let him rest, she needed him to take notice of her at least once in a while.

'She's very fortunate, is Hari Grenfell, she enjoys a happy and stable marriage.'

He looked at her then. 'Not like some, is that what you mean?'

Bethan shrugged. 'I was just making an observation.'

Boyo threw down the paper and rose to pour himself a drink from the decanter, the liquid shimmered in the glass as he swirled it around before tasting the ruby wine. He returned to his seat and sat down, he was frowning.

Bethan knew what the problem was, Boyo had been in a foul mood ever since the day at the fair when he had seen Catherine O'Conner with her handsome Irish cousin. Since then, he had kept away from the girl, no doubt wishing to air his disapproval of her actions, which was rich considering he was a married man with responsibilities himself.

'Are you being fair to Catherine, do you think?' Bethan blurted out the words before she had time to evaluate them. 'I mean you are keeping her away from young society. She's at an age when she should be making a good marriage, having children. That cousin of hers seems a very suitable match, don't you agree?'

'Keep out of this, Bethan.' There was a warning in Boyo's tone that she chose to ignore.

Bethan's patience snapped. 'Just think what you are doing to her, you are ruining the girl's chances of a normal life, is that what you want? She needs a husband, children, she is a young healthy woman, what good is a part-time lover? That is not going to be enough for her, she'll grow tired of the situation and of you, believe me.'

Boyo rose without another word and left the room and, shortly afterwards, Bethan heard the front door slam behind him. She sighed and put down her sewing; well, the seeds of doubt had been planted in Boyo's mind. He was a fair man and if he really loved this girl it was best he gave her up now before there were even more complications.

In her heart Bethan knew just what sort of complications she was afraid of; the girl was young, healthy, she could provide a brood of fine sons for Boyo. She sighed, her hand moving across her stomach; well, whatever happened, it was *her* child who had first claim on Boyo, for this son or daughter would be his legitimate heir, one he could proudly show off to his friends. She closed her eyes, she must just bide her time, be patient and everything would fall into place.

Boyo rode the animal hard, the big hoofs kicked up soil and grass as the horse negotiated the rugged land of Honey's Farm. He must see Catherine, he had to know she was still his. He burned to hold her and his mind was tortured by pictures of her with Liam, of the man bending and kissing the white nape of Catherine's neck. He gripped the reins tightly, if he had the man here now he would cheerfully strangle him.

As he crested the hill, he saw her, her skirt bright against the green of the fields. Her hair gleamed in the sunlight, red streaked with gold, spun gold that held the light like a halo around her head.

'Cat!' He dismounted and flung the reins around a branch. She turned towards him and he could see that her face was pale. 'Catherine, my little darling.' He moved to take her in his arms but she spun away.

'Don't touch me.' She spoke in a soft voice, her face turned away from him.

'But Cat, I love you, I want to be with you, I long to hold you close and make you mine.'

'You haven't come near me for days, how can you say you love me? You haven't asked me about Dad, do you care about anyone other than yourself?'

'Cat, I'm sorry . . .'

'Sorry!' she glared at him. 'Sorry's such a pathetic word.' She took a deep breath. 'Seeing you at the fair with her, realizing that all the while you are sharing your wife's bed as well as mine. Don't you think it hurt, seeing her like that, full with your child?'

'But my love, that was before we found each other again, I have not touched her in passion since then, I promise you.'

She looked at him then from under the corners of her long fair lashes. 'Is that the truth?'

'It is the truth, I swear. I have my own room, my own bed and Bethan knows that I love you, how can she not know?'

'But she is willing to have what little you can spare of yourself, is that it?'

It sounded so selfish the way Catherine said it. Damn it! It was selfish. He sighed. 'I have been honest with both of you, I don't know what else I can do.'

'You could leave your wife, couldn't you?' She stared at him, her heart beating swiftly.

'And would you be in a position to stay in our house in

Caswell with me if I did?' he challenged in return.

'Not at the moment.' She spoke reluctantly, 'I need to be with my father, he is very sick, not that you give a fig for that.'

'I have offered help, Catherine, I can do no more. And as for Bethan, she is an older woman who is expecting her first child, she needs a husband to give her support and comfort which I feel obliged to give. I have a duty to do just as you have, or is there one rule for you and another for me?'

Catherine sank onto the ground, the basket she was carrying spilling eggs onto the grass. On the edge of the field he could hear the gurgling of the brook over the stones, the day smelt of summer. He sat beside her and took her in his arms, closing his eyes as he breathed the scent of her.

'My darling girl, I love you so much all I want is to be with you every moment of the night and day. Can you understand how difficult it is for me being trapped in that house, held prisoner by my own conscience?'

Catherine looked at him with big eyes. 'Boyo, why did we start this affair? It's such a mess.' She paused. 'I know you love me but you do . . . have feelings for your wife, don't you?'

'Of course, but there are times, like today, when I could almost hate her for coming between us.'

'Oh, Boyo, I'm sorry! I'm a scold, I'm making life more difficult for you when what you need, what we both need, is comfort and love.'

She drew him down so that they were lying in the sweet grass. He smelled the freshness of her, breathed in her scent and he knew he wanted this woman more than he had ever wanted anything in his whole life. He would give away his house, his fortune, everything he possessed, if he could marry her and make her his own.

They made love with renewed passion and with great tenderness and when it was over, they lay twined in each other's arms, the sun on their faces, the freshness of the grass all around them. He felt he would never forget this day, ever, not if he lived to be a hundred.

Later, he watched as Catherine bathed in the stream, her feet bare, her slender legs pale against the sun. Her hair gleamed like fire and he melted with love for her.

She came and stood beside him, carrying her shoes in her hand and he touched one of her small, exquisite feet with his fingertips. 'So lovely, all of you from your head to your toes. I love you, Catherine.'

She looked up and away from him, her head tipped to one side in an attitude of listening. He heard it then, the voice calling her.

'Something is wrong.' She was pale, her eyes had taken on a haunted expression. 'It's Liam, he's come for me, Dad must be worse.'

The young Irishman bounded across the fields towards them and, ignoring Boyo, he took Catherine by the shoulders. Before Boyo had time to digest the fact that Catherine accepted the man's touch, the boy was speaking rapidly in strong Irish tones.

'I've been looking everywhere for you, come home, it's your father, he wants to see you.' She clutched his arms, her knuckles white.

'Is it . . . is it the end?'

'Sure an' only the good Lord in His heaven knows that, my colleen, but the priest has given your father the last rites so you'd better come now, there's no time to waste.'

Catherine looked back at Boyo as he rose to his feet. 'I have to go.' She licked her lips. 'I'll see you when I can.'

He watched as she hurried over the fields, her arm through that of the young Irishman and a pain burned within him. He looked down at the grass, at the place where they had lain together, at the eggs, brown, white and speckled, lying broken on the ground and somehow it seemed like an ill omen and he was afraid.

Catherine crept into the darkened bedroom and bit her lip, hesitating a moment, almost afraid to move towards the bed. Her father was not alone, Fon sat beside him, her face pale and anguished, her pain and fear too deep for tears.

When he saw her, Jamie lifted his hand, it trembled as Catherine took it.

'Cath, my little girl,' he patted the bed, 'sit by me.' His voice was threadlike. She obeyed him and felt the presence of Liam behind her and knew she was glad he was there.

'Dad.' She touched his cheek tenderly, the skin rustled beneath her fingers, parchment thin. He had sunken into himself, he was not the father she'd known only a few weeks ago. Jamie had always been a big hearty man but now the disease had taken its toll and he was sinking beneath the burden of it.

'Make me a promise, Cath.' It was clearly difficult for him to speak. 'Give him up, he's married, he's no good for you.'

'Dad!' Her voice was thin with fear. 'Don't ask that of me, please don't.'

'It's for your own good, Cath, you know it in your heart. You need a man who will work the farm, look after you and your mam, give you a brood of children. Please, Catherine, won't you promise me this, even on my deathbed?'

Guilt clutched at Catherine with cruel claws, while her father lay dying she had been out in the fields, rolling around like a whore.

'Cath . . .' His voice failed and Catherine leaned close to him, tears streaming down her face. He closed his eyes for a moment and then, with a supreme effort, spoke again. 'I wouldn't ask it of you but I know it's for the best. I love you so much, I don't want to see you live out your days as the mistress of a married man. He will never leave his wife, you know that.'

'Hush now, Dad,' Catherine's voice was hard with tears, 'don't talk any more.'

'I must . . .' Jamie broke off, his eyes moving beyond Catherine to where Fon was standing, her face white, her eyes overlarge in her drawn face.

'Promise him, for God's sake.' Fon spoke in a strangled

voice. 'He only wants what's best for you.' Her hand squeezed Catherine's shoulder.

Jamie stared into her eyes as though he would draw her soul from her. 'Quickly,' he whispered, 'there's no time left.'

'I promise, Dad!' The words spilled from her in a torrent of love and fear and pain. How could she deny her father when he was dying before her eyes?

Fon knelt beside the bed and touched Jamie's face and on the other side of the bed, Liam stood silent and yet staunch in his strength.

Jamie smiled briefly and then, gently, his head rolled to one side and the breath slid from between his lips like a sigh. There was silence for a moment and then Fon was weeping, her head on the bedclothes, her hands stretched out before her as though in prayer.

Liam took Catherine's arm and led her from the room. 'Come away, colleen, let them be together this one last time.'

Downstairs, he held her to him and rocked her as she cried. She rested her wet face against the sweet clean smell of his shirt-front. She was so grateful to him; he was here, Boyo was not.

In contrast to Catherine's mood of despondency, the day of the funeral was bright and warm, with the spring flowers in full bloom. Beyond the sloping ground of the cemetery, the panoply of the docks was spread out like jewels flung to the ground, sparkling with sunlight. Catherine stared at the water, wishing she was anywhere but here.

She had not seen Boyo since her father's death more than a week ago. He had written to tell her that Bethan was poorly and he would be in touch as soon as he could. Catherine had held the letter to her breast, kissing the writing, imagining his hand on the paper, and then she had thrown it into the fire. That part of her life was over and done with, for ever. How could she love him when he was failing her, now when she most needed him?

She swayed a little as the coffin was being lowered into the dark earth. Her hands clenched into fists as she realized the finality of death. She would never see her father again, not on this earth.

She felt a warm arm around her and looked up into Liam's face. He looked sombre in his good dark suit and she realized how much his presence meant to her.

Fon was standing close to the open grave, her face was covered by a dark veil. She was upright, dignified in her grief and Catherine felt a surge of protective love for her mother.

She glanced up at the sky, it was blue with a scattering of fluffy white clouds and Catherine tried to envisage pictures in the shapes. Was that the face of an old man, of God come to take Jamie's soul? Perhaps the thought was blasphemy but she didn't think so. She hoped that God was looking down on her, she would need strength from somewhere if she was to keep her promise to her father to stay away from Boyo.

The return to Honey's Farm in the hired coach was a silent one. Fon had refused to consider the Catholic ritual of a wake and instead had opted for the Welsh tradition of a tea of ham and pickle and fresh bread.

Catherine had become separated from her mother and from Liam in the crowd. She took one look at the hoards of visitors who were making their way towards the farmhouse and was spurred into action, running across the fields as if the hounds of hell were after her. She ran until she was breathless and then she fell onto her knees. The tears ran unchecked as she cried out her pain. He was gone, her father was lost to her for ever and so was Boyo, that was something she must face sooner or later. It was over, her childhood was gone, it was time to grow up.

At last, she returned to the farmhouse, knowing she could put off the evil moment no longer. She dreaded facing her mother, so stricken, so silent in her grief, but Fon needed her.

Liam was alone in the kitchen, clearing away the dishes, for the tea had been over some time. Ham curled dryly on large platters and butter melted in the dish. He looked up at her and seeing her face, put down the stack of plates and took her in his arms.

She leaned against him gratefully. He smoothed her hair, making soft noises to soothe her, swaying to and fro as though he was rocking a child. And she had been acting like a child, Catherine thought with self-loathing; a selfish, grasping child, wanting what was not hers, could never be hers.

She clung to Liam, sobs racked her body with a violence that almost tore her apart. Liam lifted her in his arms and carried her to the rocking-chair and sat there with her in his lap, gentling her as though she was a creature from the fields. From the parlour came the low murmur of voices. Someone laughed and Catherine wondered how anyone could laugh today of all days.

At last, the tears ceased. 'I'm all right now.' She made an effort to control herself and Liam rose and set her in the chair and fetched a bowl of water to wash her blotched face and burning eyes.

'How's Mam?' she asked and Liam smiled reassuringly.

'Don't worry, she's bearing up well, putting on a show for the friends and relatives. Later I'll see she goes to bed for an hour, it will do her good.'

He left her side and sat near the table looking at her in compassion. 'I know what your father made you promise was the hardest decision you've ever had to make,' he said. 'I admire you for giving him what he wanted so badly for you.' He paused and leaned forward earnestly. 'I know Uncle Jamie wanted you to marry me but I wouldn't hold you to anything, sure you must know that Catherine?'

She looked down at her hands without replying, she did not know what to say to him. Her mind was numb, she felt dead inside, it did not matter one way or another what she did with her life now, it was over for her before it had begun.

'Why don't you get away for a while?' Liam said. 'Have a change of scene. Go back to Ireland with Dad and Maeve, sort out your problems in the peace and quiet of my country.'

107

'And what about Mam?' Catherine asked softly. 'I can't leave her, can I?'

'Take her with you,' Liam smiled. 'I'll be here for a while yet; if Fon doesn't want to go away, I'll take care of her. I don't have to go back to the farm for a few weeks yet, the manager is taking care of everything very well, according to Dad.'

It was as if a cold splash of water had hit her face. 'You will be going back then?'

'Of course, I'll have to. But it won't be for ever, Catherine, not if you need me here.'

'How can you be so nice to me, how could you stay here when you knew my dad was trying to push us into marriage?'

'Catherine, I love you, that's why I've been here all this time. And I love you too much to try to tie you down to something you might regret. Anyway, you have enough to deal with for the time being. You'll be happy again, in time, I'm sure.'

'How can you be sure?'

'I can be sure because I know the sort of girl you are; a girl with courage, with fire in her belly, a girl who will get up and fight her corner.'

Catherine sighed heavily, 'You are a very nice man, Liam, I'm only sorry I didn't meet you before . . .' her words trailed away. 'Anyway, you wouldn't want me, not now. You deserve a wife who is pure and good, not a scarlet woman like me.'

He smiled and then he shrugged. 'That's just the way of the world, colleen. It's not easy for anyone in this life and a man or a woman must take a little bit of happiness where they can find it and while they may. That's what you were doing so don't feel too bad.'

He moved towards the fire. 'Sounds like the last of the guests are leaving. My father and Maeve are staying at the Swan Inn, you remember that they're taking Fon with them, don't you? I'll say good night for you when I go down there later, if that's what you'd like.'

Catherine was grateful to him, she could not face anyone at the moment and certainly not her mother with her haunted, haggard face.

At the door he turned and looked at her. 'I'll riddle the ashes before I go. Why don't you get off to your bed?'

She stared at him for a long moment and then spoke timidly. 'I'm frightened to be alone, will you stay in my room with me till morning?'

He hesitated and then nodded briskly. 'I'll be back as soon as I can, no-one need ever know I've come back here.'

She waited for what seemed an eternity but, at last, he returned. Holding her round the waist, he led her upstairs.

Catherine lay in his arms, a great weariness overtaking her. She must have drifted off to sleep because she was at the graveside, staring down into the earthy darkness. A shape was emerging from the open ground, rising up, confronting her, a skull with a hideous grin. She cried out and sat up and then Liam was beside her. He took her in his arms and rocked her gently.

'It's all right, I'm here, you're not alone.'

She looked beyond his shoulder fearfully, the bedroom was as it had always been, a dull fire glowed in the grate and on a chair was a pillow and a blanket, Liam had kept his word and stayed with her.

She was shivering and he held her close in his arms. She leaned wearily against his shoulder and slowly, softly, she drifted into sleep again. When she woke again it was morning, sunlight spilled into the room and a breeze lifted the curtains in a gentle billow. Outside, the birds were singing. Of Liam there was no sign.

When Catherine went downstairs to the kitchen it was to find the room empty. The fire burned cheerfully behind the blackleaded bars and on the hob the kettle simmered, gently issuing forth steam.

Liam would not leave her alone for long. She must cook breakfast for when he came in. Catherine made a pot of tea and looked in the pantry for something to cook for breakfast. She had been utterly spoilt by her mother she realized suddenly, she didn't even know how to cook a simple meal of bacon and eggs, but she must try, for Liam's sake. Working on the farm gave a man a healthy appetite. It was about time she grew up, she reminded herself, as she took the side of bacon from the hook on the beam above her.

It was difficult to cut but at last she had some ragged pieces of bacon ready to fry. Soon, the bacon was sizzling reassuringly in the large pan and she felt an absurd sense of achievement.

Catherine had seen Fon wait until the bacon was almost cooked and then break half a dozen eggs into the spluttering fat, surely that couldn't be difficult?

The first egg she cracked spilt into the fire, the yellow yolk running over the bars, sizzling as it solidified. Catherine looked round guiltily as though she was going to be given a dressing-down for her carelessness and then she smiled. For the first time in days, there was no-one to witness her awkwardness and there were eggs by the basketful; she would try again.

She made another careful attempt to crack an egg and this time most of it landed in the pan. She added several other eggs, becoming more adept with each one and watched as the egg-whites turned from transparent to opaque, feeling a tiny glow of achievement. She carefully lifted the eggs onto a plate, breaking them in the process so that the yolks spread in a yellow flood over the pieces of bacon.

'Damn!' The word fell from her lips in a moment of exasperation just as the kitchen door opened behind her.

'Cursing and so early in the morning, who got out of bed the wrong side then?'

Liam smelt of grass and beasts and chickens and Catherine was reminded of her father. Pain caught her and she took a deep breath, determined to put a cheerful face on things.

'Hey, look at that then, bacon and eggs, I'm famished.' He sat down at the table and then looked up at her. 'And where's your breakfast, madam?'

110

'I'll just have some toast.' Catherine forced herself to eat a little. The tea she drank eagerly, it was hot and comforting.

'You'll make a farmer's wife yet,' Liam said, 'though I would have liked a bit of fried bread with the eggs.'

The latch of the door lifted and Fon came into the kitchen. She was like a sleepwalker, there was a dullness in her eyes and tired lines on her face and for the first time she looked old to Catherine.

'Mam! Have you walked all the way up from town then? Come and sit down, have some breakfast.'

Fon shook her head. 'Just a cup of tea, love.' She sank into a chair and looked round her, almost as though she did not recognize the room.

Catherine touched her mother's cheek. 'Come on, Mam, you must eat something to keep up your strength, there's a lot of work to do here, mind, can't neglect the farm, can we? Have something to eat, if it's only a bit of toast. See, have this piece, it's lovely and brown with salt butter on it.' She pushed her own plate across the table.

If she had hoped to bring a little normality into her mother's face, she was disappointed. Fon looked distantly into the fire and then, as though the words had just sunk in, shook her head. 'I can't eat, not now he's not here with me. Oh, Cath, how can I bear life without him?'

Catherine swallowed her own tears. 'I need you, Mam, I made an awful mess cooking the eggs, see, yolk all over your lovely grate and I'm dying for some breakfast.' She wasn't, she felt food would choke her, but her words had the desired effect.

'All right,' Fon shrugged off her hat and coat. 'Fetch me my pinny and I'll cook you something nice.'

Catherine looked at Liam and he nodded encouragingly, it seemed she had done the right thing. She went up to the room her mother and father had shared for so long. Without looking at the empty bed, she took an apron from the drawer and then stood for a moment staring out at the fields beyond the small glass panes of the window. She felt shackled, there was no way she could make a new

111

life for herself, not now; Mam needed her, badly.

Without someone to live and work for, Fon would fade away and die. Catherine was trapped, here on this land, in this house; she would just have to face it, there was no alternative.

Slowly, she descended the stairs, clutching her mother's apron to her face, smelling the fresh ironed scent of the cloth, trying hard not to cry.

She should be ashamed of feeling sorry for herself and thinking only of her own happiness. Well, she would make it up to her mother: she would run the farm for Fon, make it flourish. It was too late to make up to her father for all the grief she had caused him, all she could do for him now was to keep the promise she had made him never to see Boyo Hopkins again.

As she made her way towards the kitchen, she forced herself to look calm, composed; she must care for Fon now, forget herself and her own needs. She swallowed hard, the future suddenly seemed bleak.

CHAPTER NINE

Bethan had been sick for over a month; she rested in her bed in the huge room overlooking the gardens and the sea, looking as though she was facing the end of the world. She was pale and drawn and Boyo's heart ached for her.

He was sitting now at the window staring outwards but he didn't see the magnificent view spread beneath him; in his mind's eye, he was with Catherine, touching her red hair, her pale skin, making love to her, feeling the freshness of her body respond to his.

'Boyo.' His wife's voice penetrated his thoughts and he rose hastily.

'What is it, are you feeling worse?' He moved to her side and took her hand and her forced smile tugged at his heartstrings. She was a brave woman, this wife of his.

'I think the baby is coming early,' she was clearly making an effort to be calm. 'You had better send someone for the doctor.'

He felt a surge of something that was a mingling of excitement and fear and, even as he rang the bell for the maid, he knew that it was relief that his enforced imprisonment was almost over.

The bedroom became an area of bustle, of the midwife and doctor talking quickly, speaking words Boyo did not understand. The smell of soap and disinfectant made him feel ill and finally, the midwife ushered him from the room.

'Fathers are best out of it,' she said cheerfully as she closed the door in his face. Boyo was relieved, he had felt it his duty to be with Bethan through her ordeal, because ordeal it was. The pain, judging by the contorted expressions on Bethan's face, was almost unbearable but it appeared that husbands were a hindrance not a help in such situations.

The business of bringing a child into the world was an enigma to Boyo. He heard an occasional strangled cry from Bethan and closed his eyes as guilt raged through him. How could a man put a woman through such pain, time after time? It did not seem right and yet some couples had huge families of eight or nine children without the mother suffering any harm. But then perhaps Bethan was a particularly delicate woman and she was rather old for child-bearing.

He paced the room downstairs, poured a drink from the brandy bottle and put the glass down untouched. He tried to force away the treacherous thoughts that plagued him but there was a joy in him, that soon he would be able to go to Catherine with an easy conscience because Bethan would have her child to occupy her days.

He must have dozed in a chair for some time because it was dark when the door opened and Cara, the young maid, came into the room bobbing a curtsey. 'If it please, sir, you are wanted upstairs.'

He rose and took a deep breath trying to clear his thoughts. 'Light the lamps, there's a good girl.'

With a strange feeling of reluctance, he moved upwards, his hand caressing the smoothness of the curved banister, his eyes resting briefly on the portraits of Bethan's ancestors. Now there was another branch to the old family: the Hopkins branch. Boyo's heart swelled with sudden, unexpected pride; he had a child. He felt that, at last, he had become a whole person.

There was an eerie silence in the bedroom. The doctor, who was engrossed in closing his bag, didn't meet Boyo's eyes. It was the midwife who brought the small bundle wrapped in a pristine shawl across the room towards him.

'This is your son, sir, perhaps you should hold him in your arms, it might be best.'

Puzzled, Boyo took the child and looked down into the perfect face. The skin was waxen, the eyes of the baby closed. This was Boyo's son and he was dead.

Afterwards, he was ashamed of his reaction, he handed the child back to the nurse and, turning, left the room. He had to breathe fresh air, he had to ride until he dropped, he must do anything but remain in the room where his wife lay silent and suffering.

He rode his unsaddled horse as though demons were chasing him. Once away from the lanes of Gower, he guided the animal out of town and uphill towards Honey's Farm. It was not conscious thought but a reflex action that led him to the farmhouse. It was only when he was outside the door and saw that the place was in darkness that he realized the lateness of the hour.

Defeated, racked with guilt, he turned his sweating animal and headed back home. He must face what had happened, there was no running away from the fact of his son's death. From somewhere he must find the strength to comfort Bethan.

The days passed darkly; the funeral of the baby was a swift affair and when the small coffin was lowered into the ground, Boyo felt a sense of relief, because now the tragedy could be stored away somewhere in the deep recesses of his mind and he could get on with his life.

Even amid the grief and pain of losing his son, Boyo thought constantly about Catherine. He wanted her and needed her more than he had ever done. He needed the reassurance of her young body, he wanted to revel in her health and strength. He ached to hold her, to hear her laugh. He felt he could not bear it that his wife, diminished by grief, had become a silent stranger.

He rose one morning to a clear day and stared out towards the hugeness of the sky above the sea. Clouds raced across the heavens, the wind was high, driving still-green leaves over the lawns below him. He made up his mind with no hesitation, he would go to Honey's Farm again, try to see Catherine, talk to her, ask her to return to their house in Caswell.

It was a brisk morning, late roses were blooming in the garden of Honey's Farm and the back door stood open. Boyo moved into the slant of sun and, blinded for a moment by the sudden dimness of the kitchen, did not see Catherine run quickly from the room. It was Fon who came towards him.

'She does not want to see you.' Fon did not meet his eyes. There was a vagueness about her he had not noticed before.

'Can't I just talk to her, please, Fon?' He was almost begging, he hated the note of pleading in his voice but he could not help himself. Fon shook her head.

'No. Just leave, please, Boyo.' She looked past him into the open valley that dipped away from the farm. 'It was summer madness, that's all, forget it.'

Summer madness, it was that and more. He had taken Catherine under the skies, in the sweet grass, he had poured his soul into her and he loved her, she was part of him. Fon continued speaking without realizing the memories she had aroused in him.

'Please leave us in peace.' She was on the point of tears.

He tried to see beyond Fon into the house. 'Is the Irishman still here?' He hated himself for probing but he felt compelled to ask.

'Go away, can't you?' Her voice rose. 'They'll make a future together if you leave them alone. My husband is dead, do you understand? It was his dying wish they marry, one Catherine will honour.'

The rush of shock and bewilderment at her words, her assumption he would just go away, was swiftly followed by anger. 'We love each other,' Boyo said. 'Fon, you should understand that better than anyone.'

'I don't understand anything. Go away, you are a married man. You spare her a little bit of your time when you want a roll in the hay.' She looked at him with tears in her eyes.

'Where were you when Catherine needed you, when her dear father lay dying? What sort of man are you to say you love her and then to use her and to ignore her when her life is torn apart?' Fon was growing hysterical but it was her grief as much as anything that made her turn on him. How could he tell Fon that he had his own sorrow to deal with? It would just sound like another excuse.

'You took my daughter and made her into a kept woman.' She began to cry. 'Well she's too good for that, don't you think so? Get out of my sight, you are no longer welcome here on Honey's Farm, is that plain enough for you?'

'Fon, I'm sorry, I didn't mean to upset you, it's just that I love Catherine so much.'

'Would you divorce your wife for her?'

He shook his head, he was defeated and he knew it. How could he leave his Bethan now when she walked the house like a ghost of her former self, grieving for her lost baby?

Fon was calmer now. 'Just go away, Boyo, you can only cause both Catherine and me heartache if you persist in coming up here. Go back where you belong, with your wife. Don't ruin the lives of two women.' She closed the door firmly in his face.

He turned away and if there were tears in his eyes, there was only the breeze and the sun and the softness of the roses to see them.

Catherine stood at the window in her room and stared at Boyo's retreating figure. She watched him mount his horse, watched as he rode away without looking back. Her hands clutched the sill as she forced herself to remain still. Her entire being was urging her to run after him, to fling herself into his arms, to beg him to love her, but she had made a promise to her father, a promise she could not break. She knew it made sense to keep away from Boyo, there was no future in the affair for either of them. The parting was for the best, why then did she feel so awful, so cut off from the living?

Ever since Liam had returned to Ireland over a week ago, Catherine had felt lost, alone with her grief. Worse than her own sense of loss was seeing the pain that her mother was feeling. Fon had become thinner, she had lost the lustre of love that had always made her so beautiful. Fon seemed to be fading away before Catherine's eyes.

117

When she had her feelings under control, she hurried down the stairs into the kitchen.

'Give us a kiss, Mam.' She hugged Fon tightly. 'Thank you for speaking to . . . to Boyo for me.' Her mother looked at her with a dullness of expression that had become habitual since the death of her husband.

'What, thanking me for sending away the only man you will ever love? I suppose it was the only thing to do but he looked so hurt.' Catherine saw that tears were streaming down Fon's cheeks.

'It's for the best, Mam, you're right, he'll never leave his wife. He never came to me when Dad died, he was too wrapped up in his own life; how can I waste myself on a man like that?'

'Oh, dear God in heaven, how can I bear to live now he's dead?' Fon put her hands over her face and Catherine rubbed at her eyes as her mother sank into the old rocking-chair.

'I've got to get away, Cath,' she said in a low voice. 'I will never get over Jamie's death while I'm here in this house.'

'But where will you go?' Catherine asked, fear running through her in waves.

'I'll go to Ireland, just for a little while. You stay here on the farm. There are the labourers to help you and Liam will be back soon. You won't be alone.'

Fon shook her head. 'Ever since your father died I've been going mad, I can't think straight, not here, not now.' She paused briefly, 'When I was young, my family used to say I was too good for this life, always reading the Bible and such. Well, I'm not good but—' she paused to take a breath, holding up her hand to prevent Catherine from speaking. 'Maeve has asked me to go and stay with her for a while. I need to find peace and I can't find it here. Can you understand that, Cath?'

Catherine sank into a kitchen chair and shook her head. 'Mam, you can't go away from me, not now, you can't, I need you. Mam, I'm feeling grief too, mind.'

'I know, love, but I can't help you, I just can't, I'm sorry. I can't help myself.'

Catherine sighed. 'I can see you are not yourself, per-haps you do need a break away from the farm. When will you leave?'

'I don't know. Liam is making arrangements for the journey. He'll tell me when the time's right.'

'So Liam knows what you want to do, you told him before you told me?'

'I couldn't talk to you, Cath.' Fon rose and Catherine could see she was trembling from head to foot. Her mother was sick, sick with grief. That was normal enough, wasn't it? Given time, her mother would come to terms with her pain and loss and then she would come home.

Fon spoke again, dashing her hopes. 'I think I might enter a convent, or a retreat, I've had enough of this world and if it wasn't a sin in the eyes of God I'd kill myself. The next best thing is to shut myself away.'

'Mam! Don't talk like that.' Catherine caught her mother's thin frame and held her close, trying to stop the terrible trembling of Fon's limbs.

'You must do what you think right, Mam,' she said, her voice almost a whisper.

'I don't know what is right, not any more but I must find peace if I'm to save my sanity. Won't you give me your blessing, Cath?'

Catherine closed her eyes for a moment, forcing herself to be strong. 'Of course I'll give you my blessing, but come back as soon as you're better. I'll miss you, Mam.'

Fon stroked her hair. 'There, there, Catherine, you are young, you are a strong, determined woman. You will make a good wife and a good mother and then you'll see what life is really all about.' She kissed Catherine's silky hair.

'You'll have your work cut out to make the farm pay, Dad let things go here in the last few years, I see now that he wasn't up to the work.' She met Catherine's eyes. 'Liam will be here with you soon. Can you manage till then Cath? Please tell me you can.' She swallowed hard. 'I'm sorry, I'm not strong like you, Cath, I know I should

119

help you on the farm but I can't stand it any more; the empty rooms, the bed where your father died, it all haunts me until I feel I'm going mad. You'll be all right, won't you, Catherine?'

'Yes, of course I'll be all right, Mam.' She would have to be all right. Her future stretched out bleakly before her. She would live her life alone working the farm with only casual labourers to help. She would grow into a lonely old maid, in all probability, for she doubted that Liam and she would ever be married.

'Mam, I'm so confused.' Her voice was muffled but she knew her mother had heard her by the way her arms tightened around her.

'We are all filled with confusion, Catherine, and we must each find a way out of it on our own terms. No-one can solve your problems but you, no-one can tell you what you want from life; it's experience that will teach you that.'

Catherine looked up into her mother's face. 'And by the time I have enough experience to be even halfway wise, it will be too late to do anything about my life.'

'We'll see. Go on and check the hens, I don't think I've fed them today.'

Catherine rose to her feet and stared down at her mother. Fon was pale and there were circles of blue beneath her eyes, her clothes were untidy, her hair escaping from the pins. She did need to get away, desperately, Catherine could see that now.

It was one of the last days of summer, a bright, gleaming day, when Catherine said goodbye to her mother. Fon, with a small bag of possessions, took her leave of Swansea and began the first leg of her journey to Ireland. Liam would meet her at the port in Cork and take her to his farm. Then, when he could, he would return to Wales and to Honey's Farm.

Catherine felt bereft as she wandered aimlessly through the streets of the town. She felt suddenly alone and unloved, little better than an orphan.

Boyo had been an orphan. He had come to *Glyn Hir*

tannery as a child with nothing, not even a name, and he had left it as the proud owner, wealthy and influential, and had married an equally rich wife.

Catherine walked to the beach and sat on the promenade staring across the bay to Oystermouth. There, her mother had lived as a child, brought up in the small fishing community, loved and cared for until the day she had chosen to move to Honey's Farm.

Catherine rose impatiently, she must stop feeling sorry for herself, it was merely self-indulgent and did no-one any good. She had lands and money enough to live on, she had her health and strength and it was about time she got on with her life and stopped moaning about her lot.

'We must try again for another child.' Bethan lifted her chin and stared into Boyo's face, trying to read his expression. 'You want an heir, I know that and I, well, I want a baby to hold close in my arms, a live baby to suckle at my breast . . .' Her voice broke for a moment, 'I know I can't replace our first son but another child would do much to alleviate the pain of our loss, don't you agree?'

She watched his face carefully, she knew that he had been sent packing from Honey's Farm, knew that somehow something had gone wrong in the relationship he had shared with Catherine O'Conner and she could not help but rejoice, for now he would stay with her. Boyo would be true to his vows, he would protect her and care for her and if he did not love her, well, hadn't she known that all along?

'I don't know,' he said at last, 'your age is against you, Bethan, I don't want you to risk your life for what might end in another tragedy.'

'It's because of my age that I want us to try again as soon as possible, Boyo.' She spoke softly, 'I'm not asking you to forget your love for the young O'Conner girl, I know that it's impossible, at least for the time being. All I'm asking is that we try for another chance at happiness. Please, Boyo, I need a child so very badly.'

121

He rubbed his forehead and she could see the mixture of expressions flit across his face.

'Boyo, I'm not so repulsive to you that you cannot come to my bed am I?'

'Of course not.' He took her in his arms and held her close. She could hear his heart beating and tears rose to her eyes. If only she could have his love, she would be the happiest woman in the world.

'All right.' He spoke the words on a sigh. 'If your heart is set on it then we shall try for a baby.'

It was only a beginning but suddenly Bethan felt as though she was lit from within with happiness. She clung to him, feeling the crispness of his hair beneath her fingers, her heart bursting with love for him. She closed her eyes and sent up a small prayer of gratitude to the heavens. Boyo would again hold her in his arms and perhaps, just perhaps, they could recapture the old easy relationship they had once enjoyed.

Boyo moved upstairs to the master bedroom with an air of a man attending his own funeral. He felt he was about to be unfaithful to Catherine, which was absurd, he was going to bed with his lawful wife, how could that be wrong? And yet it felt wrong. Every instinct within him urged him to move on past the open door to his own room. He stopped for a moment on the landing and closed his eyes. In a moment he was transported from his home to the house he had shared with Catherine. He could picture her stretched across the bed, her hair like fire around the whiteness of her shoulders. A great surge of need drove through him, followed quickly by a feeling of loss. How could he make love to Bethan feeling as he did?

Purposefully he moved into the room and stood for a moment as his eyes became accustomed to the gloom. The lamps were turned down low, the curtains open, revealing a fine moonlit night, a night for lovers.

He saw Bethan stretch a pale arm towards him and he went to her, closing his eyes, trying to warm himself into a feeling of love for her.

Once he was beneath the sheets, he held her close and her arms clung to him, her breasts soft against his chest. He caressed her gently and she pressed closer; he could feel the tears on her cheeks, they tasted of salt beneath his lips.

His body refused to respond and then, unbidden, there came to his mind the image of Catherine. With a groan he turned away from his wife, burying his face in the pillow, as though hoping that by hiding his face, he could quench the misery that rose within him.

He felt Bethan's hurt as she turned her back on him, dragging the bedclothes with her and yet he could do nothing to help her, his own pain was too much to bear.

'It's over, then.' Her voice was muffled but he could hear the hardness that was an attempt to hide her feeling of rejection.

'Oh, Bethan, leave me alone, I don't want to hurt you, I'm so sorry.'

'She has ruined our lives, hasn't she?' The harshness was still there but now it was tempered by sorrow. 'What we had is gone for ever and I do not even have the consolation of a baby to care for.'

Bethan began to sob quietly and Boyo knew he should turn to her, take her in his arms and comfort her and yet he could not. He had never heard his wife cry, she was a woman of immense control but he had broken her with his love for another woman. In that moment he wondered what perverse fate had brought Catherine back into his life only to snatch her away from him again.

CHAPTER TEN

Summer Lodge was almost unrecognizable. Rooms once elegant and gracious were becoming a desolate waste, empty of furniture. Carpenters worked tirelessly, the sound of hammers and saws echoing through the hallways. Servants cowered in the kitchen, dreading the day when work would begin on the place that had been their own, a sanctuary from the whims of the ruling classes.

Hari was appalled at the way the money was being eroded on the alterations, materials cost the earth and the labour of the men employed ate into her money at a frightening rate. She worried constantly about the future, her's and Craig's, but outwardly she was the collected Hari Grenfell everyone knew.

The stocks of leather from the warehouse had been lodged at the tannery belonging to Boyo Hopkins. The warehouse was bringing in a good regular rent which Hari used to eat away at her debts.

Hari was seated now in the office which had once been Craig's den. The room had required very little by way of alteration, at least structurally, but the furnishings had been changed. A gleaming typewriter held pride of place on the leather-topped desk. A cupboard to hold files had been crammed into a corner. The soft, comfortable old sofa had been stored in the attic and in its place stood a drawing-board with a lamp fixed above it.

Hari stared down at a letter from the bank, turning it over in her hands, almost afraid to take up the paper-knife and tear open the envelope. Her heart raced and her mouth was dry, she feared there were new problems to contend with before the old ones had begun to sort themselves out.

The letter was quite pleasant in tone, informing Hari

that a new sum of money had been placed at her disposal. She scanned the page quickly and then put down the letter with a trembling hand. Bethan Hopkins had known the difficulties Hari would face and had injected a further £2,000 into the project. She sighed in relief, at least for now there would be no problems. Yet in a way she was becoming deeper in debt and the thought was frightening.

Hari rose and made her way across the rubble of the hall towards the back of the house. She moved past the kitchens and out into the grounds. There, an outbuilding was slowly taking shape as a large workshop. New machines were in place, a cutting machine and a machine for stitching the leather. All that was left for the workmen to do was to put the finishing touches to the window-frames.

She would make a start in the morning, let the men work around her. Some shoes would simply be finished by hand, others, costing a great deal more, would be entirely handmade.

Hari would need to find a young apprentice as well as an experienced shoemaker. She would work on the designs herself and take on some of the manual work, at least until the business began to make a profit, if it ever did. Profit, what a wonderful word.

She felt a hand on her shoulder and turned to see Craig looking down at her with such tenderness in his eyes that she immediately turned and buried her face against the crispness of his shirt-front.

'We will make a go of it, won't we, Craig?' she asked almost fearfully.

'Of course we will. I can't offer many skills, except that of choosing good leather but my back is strong, I can fetch the stocks from the tannery for you.'

The thought of her husband acting as a labourer cut deep into Hari's heart. At his age, Craig should be able to relax, to take life easy and here he was, offering to take an active part in the business.

'If we pull together, we'll make it.' He spoke with a confidence Hari knew was forced.

'We'll have to,' she said, 'otherwise we'll end up even deeper in debt than before. We can't have that, can we?'

He laughed out loud, throwing back his head, the strong column of his neck was tempting and Hari reached up and kissed him, just below where his beard was beginning to turn grey.

'Why are you laughing at me?' she asked in mock indignation.

'Because you suddenly reminded me of the little monster girl I first saw in a tiny kitchen that smelt of cooking and leather.' He drew her closer in his arms. 'My little Welsh *cariad*, my own Hari.'

She nestled against him, they had so much to be thankful for, they had each other.

She then pushed him away. 'Now then, let's see if this fine talk of yours has any substance to it, shall we?'

He looked at her, his eyebrows raised, waiting for her next words with a hint of a smile on his face.

'If I'm to make a start on my first pair of shoes tomorrow morning as planned, I'm going to need some fine calf for the uppers.'

'Yes, boss,' Craig bowed his head. 'Anything you say, boss.'

Hari slapped out at him playfully. 'You think you are being funny, don't you, but you're going to find out exactly just how bossy a woman can be, my lad.'

He took her hand. 'Before I become totally subservient, please may I have the honour of taking my boss to bed? I suddenly feel very much in need of love and comfort.'

'Craig!' Hari looked round, wondering if any of the men working inside the building had heard. Craig laughed and pulled at her, drawing her towards the house.

'It's quite legal to want to make love to you, you are my wife, after all.'

Hari looked at him sternly. 'That's as maybe, but now you have to conserve your energy, I need that calf here by tonight so that I can make...' She stopped speaking as he put his hand gently across her mouth.

'I know, so that you can start first thing in the morning. You'll have your leather but only if I have what I want first.'

Giggling like a young girl, Hari allowed Craig to lead her towards the house and suddenly her heart was light, her new venture was going to be all right or she would break her back in the attempt.

CHAPTER ELEVEN

The unseasonal weather swept in on Honey's Farm with torrential rain fading the landscape to grey and beating the crops into submission. The fields of once proud, golden corn were flattened and rotting, turning the meadows to swamps and bringing the danger of disease to the beasts.

Catherine looked out at the dismal weather and with her finger traced the tracks of a raindrop slipping like a tear along the window-pane. The silence in the kitchen was oppressive, if only she had someone to talk to. She sighed, she would have to brave the storm and do some work, there was no-one else to do it for her, not now.

She faced the fact, standing there in the dismal darkness of the unlit kitchen, that she was not managing the farm very well, not managing at all, if the truth be told. Contrary to her mother's prophesy that she would bring the lands back to their former glory, she had done nothing but make one mistake after another and now, with even the weather against her, it was almost certain that the farm would face ruin. The precious crop of corn would rot in the ground and there would be no seed to sow in spring.

Catherine sighed heavily, reluctant to step outside and face the beating rain. What did it matter, anyway, what was the point in struggling? There would be no profit this autumn, no money at all, not unless she sold some of the stock.

She had been giving it some thought; the most valuable asset she had at her disposal was the prize bull that her father had been so proud of. He was a huge creature kept solely for breeding, docile enough while there were enough cows to service but moody and even bad-

128

tempered when he was left idle for too long. Catherine was a little afraid of the animal and it would be no hardship to get rid of him.

She glanced round uneasily, it was so quiet that the silence was almost tangible. Occasionally a coal shifted in the grate but otherwise the only sound was the ticking of the clock on the mantelpiece.

A coal fell through the bars in a shower of sparks and Catherine turned briefly to look at the fireplace. The flames were dying, it was about time she fetched in some logs from the shed across the yard. And yet the rain was sweeping now, rushing against the window in gusts, rattling the glass in the small frames.

But she must stir herself; whatever happened, the cows needed to be milked before nightfall, the hens shut in the coops for safety, for there were always foxes about the farm. She did not relish doing the chores in such weather but she had no choice, the entire work of the farm now rested on her shoulders. Only that morning she had paid off the two remaining labourers, there was no more money in the wages box. Both the men had promised to hold on till the end of the harvest, managing without pay, but Catherine had taken a lingering look at the beaten corn and had shaken her head, there would be no harvest.

So now she was entirely alone, alone on the farmlands that spread across the hill like a patchwork quilt washed by rain and greyness. She was facing a crisis and she knew it.

She took her coat from the back of the door and wrapped herself in it, buttoning it up to her neck. She tied a scarf around her long hair and then pulled on her boots.

It was a battle to open the door, the wind tugged and twisted her clothes and swept the fallen leaves into the kitchen. The rain fell in spiteful darts against her face and briefly she wondered why she was still struggling to survive. And yet she knew why, farming was in her blood as it had been in her father's before her. She only needed one good crop to recoup all her losses, one good harvest of corn would see her right. In the meantime she would just have to do the best she could.

In the milking sheds the animals moved softly, udders uncomfortably full. Catherine drew the old worn stool towards one of the animals and, with practised fingers, began to work, bringing the milk down into the pail with a cheerful drumming sound. Things had come to a pretty pass when even the company of the animals was enough to cheer her.

It was some time later that she carried the heavy pails of milk across the yard and into the stone-flagged coldness of the creamery. There, she filled the churns, splashing some of the pearly liquid onto the floor, watching as a strand of grass floated on the surface.

The milk would be picked up in the morning by Jones-the-milk, who would drive the horse and cart into Swansea and sell the milk by the gill to the townspeople. At least there would be some income from the dairy products, small enough by all accounts but enough to keep her in food and clothing for a time.

She worried about the new seed she would have to buy to replace the beaten corn, she doubted she would save anything from the battered ears that lay flattened against the sodden land. She smiled wryly, staring at the spreading stain on the flags, it was no use crying over spilt milk, wasn't that how the old saying went?

Once more she ventured outside and made for the hen-house, she would bring in the eggs and see the birds safe for the night and then, only then, would she be able to rest.

CHAPTER TWELVE

Bethan turned the pages of accounts and frowned, shaking her head; she had her sources and they had informed her that Honey's Farm was running into debt, soon the girl would be in over her head and then Catherine O'Conner would be taught the lesson she deserved. She would realize that to steal another woman's husband was a sin and should be punished.

Catherine O'Conner was to blame for everything. Not content with crawling into Boyo's bed and turning him against his own wife, she had upset Bethan so badly that she had lost the precious baby she had been carrying.

Everyone knew that babies born perfect and beautiful did not die without reason. No, the tragedy had been brought about by the distress Catherine had caused Bethan at a time when she should have been happy.

Oh, it was all right for her, Miss O'Conner, she was young and strong. The hard-hearted girl was able to go blithely on her way, enjoying her life, taking her pleasures where she may.

She was probably, even now, plotting new schemes; the bitch was bent on wrecking Bethan's life by getting Boyo into her web once again. Well, she wouldn't get away with it, she would learn a hard lesson: that blessings in this life need to be earned.

Boyo entered the room and Bethan drew a blotter over the pages before her.

'What are you doing?' He helped himself to a brandy and lifted the decanter enquiringly. She shook her head.

'Just a bit of accounting.' She put the papers in the drawer and locked it. 'I've decided to sell the Gomerian Inn.'

She moved to the warmth of the fire, the wind was

rising and darts of rain fell against the curtained windows.

Boyo looked at her in surprise. 'Is that wise?'

'I think I should know what is best for my own property,' Bethan said quietly. 'I feel the time is right to go into some other kind of business and if I sell now, the inn will bring me a handsome profit.'

Boyo shrugged. 'Well, it's up to you, of course. What does your father say about it?'

'I do not need to consult my father or anyone else, I know what I am about.' Her words were a rebuke and she knew by Boyo's expression that he had taken it as such.

'You are quite right, what you do with your own assets is your business.' He sank into a chair and Bethan took the seat on the opposite side of the cheerful fire. She looked into the flames, the yellow and red glow misted before her eyes. What had happened to the harmony that once existed between herself and her husband? They had been friends at least, now, thanks to that hussy, they had lost even the closeness of friendship.

After the fiasco that had occurred last time she had shared a bed with her husband, he had moved back into his own room. Since then, neither of them had broached the subject of her wish to try for another baby.

She saw Boyo stare into his drink, his expression morose, and she knew with a feeling of pain that he was thinking of Catherine O'Conner.

Suddenly she rose to her feet in a fury. 'For God's sake go to her if that's what you want!' She was surprised to hear the hysteria in her voice. Her control had snapped, she could no longer pretend that everything was all right. Even if she lost Boyo for ever, she needed to have her say.

'I am sick and tired of seeing you mooning about the place like a lovesick child.' She paced across the carpet, rubbing her hands together. 'If you want this . . . this hussy so much, then have her, I'm not stopping you.'

Boyo had risen to his feet at her outburst, his face was suddenly pale. 'I only wish to God I could "have her" as you put it, but I can't.'

She stared at him. 'Why can't you? What's stopping

you? Not a sudden sense of morality I'm sure, so what is the truth?'

'She does not want to see me any more.'

A feeling of relief poured through Bethan, shedding a little sense on her chaotic thoughts; so the girl had finished with him, probably found a more eligible man to latch on to. Boyo's next words were like an icy blast.

'Catherine will have nothing to do with me. It would be different if I were not married to you.'

Rage ran afresh through Bethan's veins. Was he asking for a divorce? Was that what his no-good piece of garbage wanted now?

'She should have thought of that before, shouldn't she?'

'Well, she didn't.' Boyo's voice was heavy with sarcasm. 'It was only after interference by someone or other that she came to such a conclusion at all. Was it your fault, Bethan? Did you go to Catherine, beg her to keep away from me? Is that what happened?'

'If your intention is to hurt and insult me then you are succeeding.' She drew herself up to her full height and looked at him disdainfully. 'I do not need to beg for anything, you should know me better than that.'

'Do I know you at all?' He turned away from her. 'Do I want to go on sharing the same house with you? I really don't know if I can stand it any longer. You wanted the truth and there you have it.'

He moved to the door and with his hand on the handle, paused. 'I have decided, I shall take up residence at the house in Caswell, I'll leave first thing in the morning.'

'Go on to your shabby love-nest then, go tonight if you like, you're no use to me. Half a man, a man who cannot make love to his own wife, but I tell you this, I shan't divorce you, divorce has no place in my scheme of things, you know my feelings on the matter.'

He didn't answer; Bethan stared at him and in that moment, hated him. 'What sort of man are you, Boyo?' The words were torn from her. He turned and looked her full in the face.

'I'm a man who does not wish to play the part of a hypocrite; that's the sort I am. I cannot make love to you because I am not sure I even like you any more.'

He opened the door just as Bethan took up the full decanter of brandy and flung it towards him.

'Go back to the gutter where you belong!' The glass shattered against the closed door and the brandy ran along the wood panelling, trickling onto the rich carpet like so many tears. But Bethan was past tears, she felt empty and lost. She stormed to the window, pushing the curtains aside with such force she almost tore them from their hangings. Suddenly, replacing the pain, came a white-hot anger. Catherine O'Conner was a she-devil, a wrecker of homes. The woman must be made to pay, and pay dearly, for all the trials and humiliations she had heaped on Bethan's head.

Bethan sank into a chair. First she would sell the inn, accumulate as much capital as she could, then she would enjoy the task of destroying the O'Conner woman's character; make sure no self-respecting banker would lend her any funds. And, when the time was right, Bethan would move in and take the farm, sell off the land in small parcels so that there would be nothing left. She would be even richer than she had been before and Honey's Farm would be nothing but a memory.

Boyo could hear Bethan's bitter words beat in his brain. She had accused him of being impotent and had told him to return to the gutter from whence he had come. Her words were spoken in anger but they made him doubt she had ever loved him.

Women, did any of them mean what they said? Catherine, so soft in love, had become hard and unyielding, refusing even to see him. And what of her cousin, was he still hanging about the place, mooning about Catherine's skirts, probably promising to make an honest woman of her?

He had arrived at Caswell wet through; his mount had needed prompt attention, for the creature was shivering

134

with cold and the effort of being ridden mercilessly across the fields. There was no sign of the man who was supposed to be taking care of the house and the place had a chill air about it.

The fire in the drawing-room had been stubborn, refusing to light, but now at last, bathed and dressed in a warm smoking jacket and casual trousers, Boyo sat before the roaring flames, a glass of fine brandy in his hand. He put it down abruptly, spilling a little of the liquid onto the polished surface of the small table.

The house was well-appointed and there was still a plentiful supply of drinks but Boyo was tired of drinking, tired of using liquor as a means of dulling his senses. He was a young man but he would soon become haggard and dissolute if he didn't curb his excesses.

He smiled wryly, perhaps he should have availed himself of the comforts of his wife's inn for a night or two, found himself a happy whore who would share his bed and make no demands on him. But then would he be any more successful with a loose woman than he had been with his wife? It was Catherine his body cried out for, Catherine with her pure skin and glossy hair. No other woman would ever be enough for him, not now.

He must have dozed in front of the fire because he woke to the sound of the wind rattling the windows. He rose and moved aside one of the heavy curtains and looked out on a blustery autumn morning. Leaves were driven across the drive, the trees, quickly losing the colourful foliage that marked the season, were bending with the force of the wind. The sea below the house was phosphorescent in the dimness, white-capped waves rushing shorewards.

He must alter his life, leave the area, begin afresh somewhere else, America perhaps. One thing was clear, if he didn't drag himself out of the mood he was in, he would be sucked into a vortex of helplessness from which he might never escape.

He thought briefly of Bethan but dismissed her at once from his mind, she would be all right, she had more than

135

enough money, she had her hard-nosed father on her side and he would doubtless tell her she had had a lucky escape.

Later, he would go to Honey's Farm, make one more attempt to see Catherine, talk to her, beg her to reconsider her attitude towards him. Perhaps by now she was seeing things more clearly. If not, he would clear out, leave the area, put as much distance between himself and his past as he possibly could.

There was no food, so he made himself hot, strong tea and carried it to the fire in the drawing-room. The house which he had bought in happiness now seemed empty and cold. A house, any house, needed people in it, people who loved and laughed. How long was it since he had laughed?

Perhaps he would sell the house, get rid of it, but first he would have to freshen it up a little. He spent an hour lighting fires in all the rooms and opening windows to the fresh air. He felt no better, the house held memories of Catherine everywhere he went.

In the morning, dressed in fresh clothes from the wardrobe, he made his way to Swansea and to Honey's Farm.

As soon as he approached the borders of the land he knew things had not gone well for Catherine. The corn lay flat against the land, rotting now in the slant of sun. It appeared that the entire crop was ruined, it would never now be harvested.

The farmhouse was empty, there was no-one about. A cheerful fire burnt in the grate and the sight of the bright, leaping flames gave him heart, Catherine must be somewhere around. He sat down at the scrubbed table prepared to wait for her, however long it took.

He listened to the ticking of the clock, built up the fire when it sank low in the grate and then pushed the kettle onto the rekindled flames. He moved to the doorway and stood staring down the path to the roadway as if he could draw her to him with the force of his will.

Then he saw her, hair bright and uncovered, as red as

136

the leaves of autumn drifting from the trees. His heart seemed to leap within him, he longed to run to her, to clasp her in his arms and yet caution restrained him. Catherine was a strong-minded woman, she would not welcome him with open arms; she would need persuading and persuade her he would, even if it took all day.

Her greeting was not encouraging. 'What are you doing here?' She brushed past him and he breathed in the scent of her, the freshness, the beauty and pain swamped him.

'How did I lose you, Catherine, what did I do wrong?' His voice shook and he imagined her stony look softened a little.

She took off her coat and laid it over the back of a chair. She seemed to need time to compose herself and he hoped that she was feeling as moved as he was by their meeting.

'It wasn't meant to be.' Her tone was flat, final and she turned to face him, her hands crossed around her body as though she was cold.

'How can you say that! We love each other.' He made a move towards her but she held up her hand.

'No, don't come near me. I don't want you, Boyo, you must see that.'

'I've left my wife,' he said quickly. 'We parted in bitterness. I've taken up residence in our house, yours and mine, the house in Caswell.'

'I can't help any of that,' she said. She avoided his eyes and sank into a chair. 'Please go, this can do no good. I don't want to see you again, I can't make myself any clearer than that, can I?'

'I want you to come to live with me, Catherine. I need you so badly, I can't sleep for thinking about you.'

He was suddenly facing the full glare of the anger in her eyes. 'Where were you when I needed you? My father was sick, dying and you were too busy with your own affairs to care.'

'But Catherine, I had to be with Bethan. The baby, she lost it, you must know that.'

'I didn't know anything except what titbits of

137

information came to me through casual gossip in the market-place.' She shook her head and the red hair flew across her pale face. 'Please, this is pointless, can't you just go, leave me alone, I've been hurt enough.'

He was suddenly angry, angry with the pain of rejection. He stared down at her. 'And I suppose Liam was here, holding your hand, comforting you; got his feet well and truly under the table, hasn't he?'

Catherine was raking him with her eyes again. 'Yes, he was wonderful, he helped me in every way he could, he even shaved and washed my father when he was too weak to do anything for himself. Liam is a good man, a caring man, the sort a woman needs in a crisis.'

'And I am not?' Pain made Boyo's voice harsh. She met his gaze and held it.

'Tomorrow I sail for Ireland, the arrangements have been made. I shall be seeing Liam again and I shall be visiting my mother but then you wouldn't know that my mother has left here, would you? You come along now and expect me to be sweet and kind to you and yet you have shown me nothing but indifference these past months.'

'I called and was turned away,' Boyo protested. 'You are not being fair, Catherine.'

'You were not very persistent in your efforts to see me, were you?' Her voice was small, distant. She rose to her feet. 'Perhaps you will oblige me by leaving my house, I have work to do.'

He moved towards her with a sudden surge of anger and clasped her in his arms, kissing her mouth, her throat, touching the swell of her sweet breasts, straining the soft cotton of her blouse. Desire flared in him, replacing his anger, his fingers sought her buttons and, though he half-recognized her puny efforts at resistance, he could not stop himself. He had her against the rag mat on the floor, blood pounded inside his head, he tasted her nipples and failed to feel the blows she aimed at his face with her small fists. He was caught up in his passion, taking her roughly, pounding at her, grasping her slim hips in his hands, holding her closer. How he loved her, how he wanted her to be his for ever. Why did she fail to understand that?

She would respond to him, once she felt the need that both shared, her passion would grow and she would want him as he wanted her. She was quiescent and he was jubilant, she no longer resisted him. He kissed her throat, her breasts, tasting her sweetness with such hunger that he felt he would never find release. And then, at last, the hot surging flames of his release swept sweetly through his blood. He felt as though he had touched the golden gates of heaven and then he was lying beside her still body, gasping for breath.

He became aware then that she was crying, soft, bitter tears that racked her. He sat up and looked at her, she had covered her face with her hands, her skirts were above her waist, the pale skin of her thighs and belly were exposed and the dark colour of bruising was becoming evident. Shame engulfed him, he had raped her, raped the only woman he could ever love. Had he gone mad?

He covered her with her skirts and made a move to cradle her in his arms. She looked up at him, her eyes dark, unfathomable.

'Get out of my house, Boyo Hopkins.' She spoke quietly, so quietly he hardly heard her. 'Get out now.' She pushed him away and rose to her feet; she was tiny and defenceless and he was appalled by his own behaviour.

'Catherine, my love . . .'

'Stop!' Her face was a mask of anger. 'Love? You don't know the meaning of the word. If ever you wanted to prove that you felt only lust for me then you have done just that today. I hate you, Boyo Hopkins, I hate you and worse, I despise you. A man who needs to force a woman is no sort of man at all, you are pathetic.'

Ashamed, he straightened his clothing. 'Catherine, I don't know what happened to me, I never meant to hurt you, God knows I . . .'

'You dare mention God after what you have done? May God forgive you because I never will.' She turned her back on him and her shoulders shook. He felt sick as he realized how deeply she was distressed.

'I thought you would want me as I wanted you.' It sounded lame and he knew it. He had taken her, uncaring of her feelings, at least he could be honest with himself if not with her.

'Get out!'

He shook his head and moved towards her. As he touched her shoulders she shrugged him away. 'What? Do you want to rape me again, Boyo? Have your pound of flesh? Is this the repayment you require for the gifts you have given me?'

She turned to face him. 'I will be away from here tomorrow and when I do return there will be a gun kept loaded by my side and I will use it, believe me.'

'I'm sorry, Catherine, more sorry than I can ever tell you, I behaved like an animal, I don't blame you for hating me.'

'I don't care about your feelings, can't you get that through your thick skull? Go to hell!' She pushed at him suddenly and unresisting, he left the cottage. The door closed heavily and there was the sound of locks being put in place.

He walked towards the fields and sat for a long time on the stile staring out across the land and down to the sea. What had he come to? Were there any further depths to which he might sink? He was a young, strong man and he had taken, no, he had raped, a helpless girl who had no strength to fight him.

He covered his face with his hands, seeing again in his mind's eye her slim nakedness and the blue of the bruises he had inflicted with his rough passion. He had wanted her so much, wanted all of her, not just her body and now he had alienated her for ever.

He glanced back at the farmhouse, it stood silent, the windows blank like accusing eyes. He shook his head, there was no point in going back, she had finished with him for good and he really couldn't expect anything else; he had hurt her too badly for forgiveness.

Wearily, he made his way back to the house in Caswell; tormented by shame and guilt, he rode hard as if he could outrun his feelings.

Once back at Caswell, he sat staring out at the sea rushing into the shore below. The waves were white-capped, soon autumn would fade and the cold of winter would take hold of the land.

He suddenly remembered, the rotting harvest at Honey's Farm and sat up straight. Catherine must be in trouble, with no money coming in for the corn, she would need help and all that had concerned him was his own needs. What a selfish bastard he was.

There was no way she would accept help from him, not now. He crashed his fist against the window-sill, what a fool he had been, what a crazy maddened fool.

It was a few days later when he was summoned by messenger to Bethan's presence. He was angered by her arrogant attitude but he went to see her nevertheless.

She faced him coolly across the expanse of carpet in the blue drawing-room and when her glasses slipped along her nose he felt a sudden dart of nostalgia for what had been. He who had everything had lost it all. In the space of a few weeks he had alienated his wife and damaged his lover, what was happening to him?

'It appears that there is something you must sign before I can close the deal on the inn.' She spoke as though he was an employee not a husband. 'Because I had included you in the profits from the business, you have, apparently, a legal right to read and agree the sale documents.'

'I don't wish to read anything and of course I'll sign, the business is yours, I've never claimed anything else.'

'No,' she conceded. She handed him the document and he signed it. She placed it on the table beside her and turned to look at him. 'One more thing, I feel as this is your house I should return it to you.' She handed him an envelope. 'Here are the deeds. I shall be moving back with my father at Ty Craig and you can live here or dispose of the house as you see fit.'

'There is really no need for this.' He felt almost intimi-
dated by his wife's cool attitude, but then Bethan had
always been an imposing woman, strong and self-
sufficient, that was what had attracted him to her. 'Keep
the house if you wish.'

'No,' she shook her head, 'it was useful when I needed
to keep an eye on the inn but now that I am disposing of
that, I don't need to live this far out of town.' She eyed
him almost smiling. 'How is your little mistress?'

He looked at her sharply. 'She is not my mistress, not
any longer.'

'Tut, tut, losing your charms so soon? Has she made so
much money herself that she doesn't need yours?'

'She did not take the money I settled on her when her
father was sick. She will not take it now when she must be
facing ruin with the failure of the harvest.'

'So, the harvest of corn is lost, is that critical then?' She
half smiled.

'Of course, a farmer needs new seed for the crops that
must be planted soon; without income there is not much
hope of that.'

'Assets? Surely the girl has something she can sell,
cattle or land or something?'

He wondered why Bethan was concerned, women were
strange creatures, he would never understand them. He
shrugged. 'The only thing she could dispose of that has
any real value would be the bull. She needs the other
beasts to make any sort of living, the milk yield is a good
source of revenue.'

'But not good enough without the harvest of corn, is
that it?'

Boyo rose to his feet. 'I don't know why you are asking
me all these questions about Catherine,' he said uneasily.
'I don't really see what it has to do with you one way or
another.'

Bethan rose and faced him. 'Well, you never did see
further than the end of your nose, did you? You need to
grow up a great deal yet before you can call yourself a
man of the world.'

'I was a man of the world before most men are aware that women exist,' he retorted angrily.

'Oh, yes, in matters physical I don't doubt it. What you have not yet realized is that a woman has a brain too, it would pay you to remember that.'

He stared at her, wondering for a moment if she knew about the way he had violated Catherine, grasping at her like a greedy child. But no, that was ridiculous, that was something she could not possibly know.

'That's all, I think.' Bethan moved towards the door. 'I shall be moving out some time next week, I hope that suits you.' She might have been a stranger conducting a business arrangement for all the warmth she showed.

'It does not affect me one way or another,' he said. 'I don't really know why you wanted me here, unless it was to torment me.'

'Don't be melodramatic, I got you here to conclude a business deal, that is all. You may go now.'

He left the house feeling somehow that he had been manipulated into answering questions that were important to Bethan. But why would she care about Catherine? He was becoming over-sensitive, a feeling brought about by shame and guilt, perhaps. He turned away from the house and made for home.

CHAPTER THIRTEEN

Ireland was as beautiful as her father had told her it would be. Catherine clung onto the sides of the cart that bumped and lurched over the uneven ground and looked around her at the fields, lush and green in the autumn rain.

Liam had been delighted that she was coming to Ireland and had arranged to meet her at the port of Cork. He sat beside her now, his red hair blowing in the breeze as he drove her towards Kinsale, the small seaside village where he lived.

'You are looking a little pale, Catherine.' Liam broke the silence, the lilting of his voice was somehow comforting, reminding her of her father.

'I am worried about the farm, Liam, that's the reason I've come to you. And I want to see my mother, of course.' She looked up at him, his eyes met hers and she read love in them and was briefly cheered.

'I wasn't going to throw my woes at you suddenly like this but I might as well get it over with and tell you the worst. The harvest has failed, I've laid off the labourers, I'm losing money at an alarming rate and I don't know what to do.'

'You did right to come to me, colleen.' He spoke softly. 'My own farm is doing so well, I can afford to put some capital into yours, help it along until times are better.'

'No, that's not what I want at all,' Catherine said quickly. 'I want advice. I thought I might sell the bull, that seems the best way of raising capital quickly, but on the other hand, he fetches a lot of money at stud.'

Liam glanced down at her again, as though to reassure himself she was actually sitting there, at his side. 'I don't see why you can't accept some financial help from me, we could make it a business venture, I would willingly act as your partner.'

'No,' Catherine shook her head. 'I would feel beholden to you, but I appreciate your offer.' She drew a ragged breath, Liam was offering an easy way out of her dilemma but what would the implications be?

'Well, if you won't let me help, then I suppose you must sell the bull. The big creature is your most disposable asset, sure enough.'

He swung closer to her as the cart swayed and, for a moment, Catherine was tempted to rest her head on his shoulder. He was so big, so reassuring, such a handsome man.

'Who's caring for the beasts while you are over here in Ireland, Catherine?'

'Cliff, my neighbour, and his sons. They will see to the hens and the cows but I can't be away long.' She looked down at her hands, thinking of the beaten land, the ruined crop, the empty barns and she felt a sense of despair.

'Your mother's looking forward to your visit.' Liam's voice was light, he was changing the subject deliberately. 'She's happy at the convent, she seems to have found peace there with the sisters.' He looked out into the distance. 'Folks don't believe in dying of a broken heart but I think your mam was until she came here.'

'Dying?' Catherine was alarmed, all the problems of the farm faded into insignificance at the prospect of losing her mother.

Liam put his hand over hers for a moment. 'Don't take on, she's looking fine. I would not lie to you, now would I?'

Catherine's mouth was dry, she had been so wrapped up in her own problems that she had not thought about her mother very much in the past weeks. She looked up at Liam and, sensing her look, he smiled.

'Sure, there's no need to worry, your mam knew you'd come over when you could spare the time. I can take you to her first thing in the morning if you like.' He smiled

145

reassuringly. 'Don't fret so, Catherine, everything is going to be all right, your mam has family here, we'll make sure she's happy, so we will.'

'You are wonderful, Liam.' Catherine slipped her arm through his, leaning against his shoulder for comfort, feeling warmth and gratitude flood through her.

'Aye, so I've been told,' he laughed easily. 'Maeve has killed the fatted calf, well, a few chickens anyway, I hope you have a fine good appetite, my grandmother gets offended if her food isn't appreciated.'

'I couldn't eat a thing,' Catherine protested and she felt Liam's breath against her hair as he turned to look down at her.

'You'll eat once you get a smell of Maeve's cooking.'

The small village of Kinsale came into sight, the sea curling against the shore, the sky clear of clouds. The sun was shining and, in spite of the cold breeze blowing in from the sea, it was a fine day.

The farm was situated on the outskirts of the village, the lands spread as far as the eye could see. The fields nearest the lane were cut, the stooks of corn plump and rich and Catherine wondered at the vagaries of the weather that destroyed one crop, yet brought another to ripe fruition.

'Do you get much rain here, Liam?' she asked, forcing her mind back to her problems.

'Aye, rain enough but this has been a good month for farmers, plenty of time to take up the corn and dry it out.' He looked up at the sky. 'It will not last, though, soon my men will bring the corn indoors to finish off the drying.'

She looked at him with fresh interest. Back in Wales, Liam had seemed a little lost, out of place somehow; here in his own country, on his own land, he had somehow grown in stature. She thought, not for the first time, what a pity it was she had not met him sooner, before she had fallen so hopelessly in love with Boyo Hopkins.

Inside the parlour of the farmhouse, the family were waiting to greet her. A cheerful fire burned in the grate and the table was spread with a spotless cloth ready for tea.

146

Maeve Cullen regarded Catherine with a gaze that was more than a little curious, she was a shrewd woman with bright, intelligent eyes and a crinkle of humour about her mouth.

Brad Cullen came forward warmly and hugged her close. Catherine could smell the heather and grass scent on him, the tang of the open air. She was reminded of her father and she felt tears spring to her eyes. They were so warm, so generous, these Irish kinsmen of hers, they were treating her like a member of their family and yet she was little more than a stranger to them.

'Sit down, Catherine, warm yourself by the fire and have a bit of supper with us. Sure an' you are so pinched and pale I'm of a mind to think you need feeding up.' Brad led her to a chair and Catherine sat down, still dressed in her outdoor clothes.

Maeve Cullen tutted. 'Sure an' can't you let the girl get her coat off before you start running her life?' She spoke briskly and Brad, grown man as he was, looked suitably chastened.

Laughing, Liam moved forward and took the coat which Catherine had slipped hastily from her shoulders. 'Don't take too much notice of Gran, she's an old witch but with a heart of gold beneath all that sternness.'

Catherine wasn't so sure about the heart of gold, the rest was an apt description of the old lady.

A girl entered the room, her hair pinned up in a severe style which did nothing to enhance her rather plain looks. She nodded distantly to Catherine and then took up the pot, warmed it and made the tea.

'This is my sister,' Liam explained. 'Patricia keeps all our noses to the grindstone, don't you, love?' He planted a kiss on her cheek and the girl flipped him away impatiently.

'Behave yourself, Liam, you're like a naughty child sometimes.'

He made a wry face and sat in one of the high-backed upholstered chairs pretending to be subdued. 'I don't know what the world is coming to,' he complained, 'once a woman had respect for her menfolk.'

'When was that?' Patricia said without looking at him. 'It surely wasn't in my lifetime or I'd have noticed.'

'Sourpuss,' Liam said without rancour.

Catherine felt an outsider, as though she was looking in on a charmed circle. It was one she could belong to if she were to accept Liam as her husband. That he would still want her, there was no doubt in her mind, his every look, his every gesture, told her more than words could how much he cared for her. She found the thought comforting.

She found to her surprise that she was hungry. The chicken in a rich gravy was tender, the vegetables cooked to perfection. She even managed to eat some of the fine fruit cake and thinly sliced bread and butter that was set out before her. She saw Maeve nod in approval.

'Got the appetite of a good farm girl anyways,' she said and Catherine felt the words were some sort of compliment. No wonder her mother had felt at home in Ireland among these people who were kin only by marriage.

'I was up at the convent visiting your mam yesterday,' Maeve said in her dry voice and Catherine glanced at her in surprise, wondering how she had picked up on her train of thought.

'How was she?' Her mouth was dry as she waited for an answer.

'I don't think she could be called a well woman but then she is a widow grieving for her husband, what can you expect? At least she looks at peace with herself and no-one can ask more of the good Lord.'

'We'll go up there at first light, don't you fret.' Liam touched Catherine's hand as he looked towards his grandmother.

'Will you excuse us if we leave the table, Gran, Catherine and me; we have some talking to do?'

The old woman inclined her head, it was for all the world as if she were royalty.

Liam led the way into the small, snug parlour. Here everything was lovingly polished so that the firelight threw

148

a glow that was reflected on the surface of the small table and the wood of the tall dresser that stood against the wall.

'Did you bring any figures with you, Catherine?' Liam asked. 'I could see just how much money you need to make to put the farm on its feet again.'

Catherine shook her head feeling foolish and inadequate. Suddenly she was weeping and Liam took her in his arms, holding her close, letting her cry.

'There, there, colleen, sure you are not alone, I'll come over to Wales with you, help you out for a few weeks at least. Now don't say no, I won't have it.'

Catherine drew away from him and rubbed at her face with her handkerchief. Liam made her feel protected and it was a good feeling.

They talked then, about the farm, about Fon's life at the convent and soon Catherine found she was feeling better, more confident and relaxed than she had been for some time. A knock on the door disturbed them.

'I'm off to my bed, son.' It was Brad's voice. 'Don't stay up too late now, that little girl needs her rest.'

Catherine rose to her feet hurriedly. What must the family think of her, shutting herself away with Liam for so long?

'I'd better go to bed, too,' she said softly, 'and you will need some sleep if you are taking me to the convent first thing in the morning.'

He took her arm and led her upstairs to her room. 'I hope you'll be comfortable, colleen.'

She saw a cosy room with the curtains drawn against the night and a cheerful fire burning in the small hearth. The bed was turned down and looked so inviting that Catherine wanted to crawl in between the blankets and sleep for ever. 'Good night, Liam, and thank you, I can't tell you how grateful I am.'

He kissed the tip of her nose lightly. 'No need for thanks, you are part of the family and don't you forget it.'

When she was alone, Catherine closed her eyes, leaning against the warmth of the door. She had forgotten

149

what it was like to be with people, she had become used to the solitude of the farm and yet now, she realized just how much she had missed the sound of a human voice, a touch, a warm look. Well, for a couple of days at least, she could relax, be taken care of, it was a wonderful feeling.

The morning was bright and sunny but with a chill of autumn in the air. Catherine, wrapped in a thick shawl, was seated in the trap beside Liam, heading away from the farm and out into the open country.

'Is it far, the convent I mean?' She was aware of the anxiety in her voice and Liam must have noticed it too because he held her hand and squeezed it before taking the reins again.

'Only a few miles, we will be at the convent in a little over an hour.'

She sat beside him in silence, half-eager, half-fearful of the coming meeting. What did she expect to see? Her mother in tears, perhaps pale and thin, but then Fon had looked that way when she had left Honey's Farm.

It was going to be difficult not to beg Fon to come home, to help her through this difficult time, just to be there in the silent, empty farmhouse. She knew, even as the thoughts formed in her mind, that she could never show her mother how lonely and afraid she was, could never disturb the feelings of peace that Fon was experiencing at the convent. She squared her shoulders, she would pretend that everything was going well, that she was managing the farm without difficulty and that the harvest had been good. But it would take all her courage to put a brave face on things and she knew it.

'Well, I don't think she's good enough for our Liam.' Patricia Cullen was standing with her hands on her slim hips, her face was flushed and her eyes gleamed in the light from the lamps.

''Tis not for you to say, girl.' Brad shifted uneasily in his seat. 'Liam is a man, he has his own opinions, neither you nor I can shape him into what we think he should be.'

'But she has been living with a married man!' Patricia

said indignantly. 'How do we know she has not conceived a child by him and looks on our Liam as a substitute father, a man who can make her appear respectable?'

'Keep calm, don't let your imagination run away with you. All we know at the moment is that she wishes to visit her mother,' Brad said flatly.

'That is not all we know,' Patricia said hotly. 'We know she has come to Ireland with some kind of problem which she wants my brother to sort out for her. It sounds suspicious to me and I think she should be sent packing as soon as possible.'

Brad frowned. 'It is none of your business, Pat,' he said sharply. 'Now can't a man have a bit of peace at his own fireside?'

Maeve Cullen spoke for the first time. 'It is our business, Brad, Liam is a very rich man and handsome with it. Still, I like the girl, she's got spirit, but then again . . .'

'Enough!' Brad rose to his feet. 'I will have quiet in my own house.' He looked at his daughter. 'You look to your own future, my girl, you will end up an old maid if you don't find yourself a husband soon.'

'Dad!' Patricia looked at him in astonishment. 'Does that mean I am not welcome here in the house where I was born?'

'You will not be welcome for long if you don't keep that tongue still in your head.' Brad moved to the door. 'I'm going down to the village, I can't stand you nagging women a moment longer.'

The door slammed and Patricia eyed her grandmother. 'Well, Gran, it looks as if this Catherine O'Conner is causing trouble in our family after only one night under our roof. I think it's up to you and me to do something about it.'

The grey walls of the convent came into view, the ancient stone rising high against the darkening sky. The only sign of habitation was a single light shining from one of the windows. It appeared a forbidding place and Catherine shivered.

151

The nun who opened the gate to admit them was small, covered entirely in black from her head to her black-booted feet. She looked into Catherine's face smiling a welcome. 'I'm Sister Teresa and sure I can see you are a fine Irish girl by the red in your hair.'

'We've come to see Mrs O'Conner,' Liam explained; 'this is her daughter, Catherine.'

Was it Catherine's imagination or did the smile fade a little?

'Well, come inside, the good lady will be happy to see you, I'm sure.'

She seemed to wobble her way along the drive with a rolling gait that indicated a problem with her legs or feet. She was very old, were all the nuns so old? If so, life must be very dull for her mother, Catherine thought unhappily.

Inside the convent were the familiar artefacts of the Catholic faith. A giant effigy of Christ on the cross dominated the hallway and along the walls were pictures depicting the stations of the cross.

'Wait here awhile.' Sister Teresa made her way, unsteadily, across the hall and disappeared through a doorway. Catherine looked up at Liam.

'I'm worried about Mam,' she said, 'it's so bleak here, so cold.'

He put his arm around her shoulders and hugged her to him, dropping a kiss on the top of her head.

'I know, colleen, but it's what your mammy wants, remember that. And another thing, you must remember, your problems are my problems, you are not alone.'

But she was alone. When she returned home she must sort out the finances of the farm, do her best to make a go of the business her father had built up over the years. She could not let Honey's Farm die.

A woman with a serene face and a bearing that spoke of authority entered the hallway and Catherine guessed she was the Mother Superior.

'Miss O'Conner, would you like to come with me?' Her glance swept over Liam. 'I am afraid I will have to ask you to wait here.' She smiled briefly. 'We do not often allow any man within the cloisters you understand?'

Catherine found herself being led along a dark corridor, she shivered, the building was unheated, it felt damp and chill and she wondered how her mother could bear to live in such an environment.

'In here, child.' The woman made a gesture towards a cell-like room with a bed standing in the corner and with only a small shaft of light from a narrow window piercing the gloom.

Fon O'Conner was seated on the edge of the neatly made bed, she was dressed in a long skirt and a crisp white blouse over which she wore a thick woollen shawl. She looked up and her eyes were bright with unshed tears as they rested on her daughter.

'Mam?' Catherine moved uncertainly forward, then they were in each other's arms and Catherine was hugging her mother as if she would never let her go.

'Are you keeping well, Mam?' She held her mother at arm's length and studied her carefully. Fon was still pale and wan, a little too thin but Maeve was right, it was as though her mother had found an inner peace.

The Mother Superior touched Catherine's arm. 'Stay for a little while, child, but remember your mother is used to peace and the silence of the convent, don't tire her.'

When they were alone, Catherine hugged her mother once more and, kissing her cheek, wanting to rekindle the closeness they had always shared, but now something was missing.

'I'll never get over losing your dad, love,' Fon said softly, 'but I am content here. I know things must be difficult for you at home, the farm is a lot of responsibility for you but you have to make your own way now, I can't help you any more, you are a woman now.'

'I know, Mam, and everything is fine, I can take care of myself, you know I can. The work on the farm is second nature to me, I could do it with my eyes shut.'

'Are the labourers good men?' Fon asked. 'You need

good men about you when it's harvest time.'

Catherine swallowed hard. 'Yes, Mam, don't worry, everything is fine.'

They talked quietly for some time and, though the love was still there between them, it was as if they had grown apart from each other. The thought saddened Catherine.

The door opened and a young nun stood casting a shadow into the cell-like room. She made a gesture towards the door, 'Time for prayer, Sister Fon.'

Reluctantly, Catherine rose and moved away from her mother. 'I should have come sooner, Mam, I've been selfish.' Swallowing hard she said, 'I have been so wrapped up in my own problems that I didn't stop to think how you were getting on.'

'What problems?' Fon asked anxiously. Catherine thought quickly.

'Oh you know, Boyo, all that.'

'It will sort itself out for the best,' Fon said. 'I must go, I don't want to keep the sisters waiting.' She kissed Catherine warmly. 'And you are not to worry about me, I'm doing just fine.'

Near the main entrance, the nun who had met Catherine at the gate led her out of the convent. The old woman paused for a fraction of a second and then seemed to make her mind up to speak.

'We are a poor order and while we do not turn away the needy, a donation would be very gratefully received, anything you can spare, you understand? Your mother is not yet strong enough to take on the tasks which the other sisters do so ably and yet she still needs to be fed and clothed.'

'I can't give you anything at all,' Catherine said in a low voice. 'I am in difficulties, you see, I am struggling to keep the farm going as it is.' She glanced to where Liam was waiting for her, hoping he could not hear the conversation, he would only take on the responsibility himself and she did not want that. 'I might be better placed soon,' she added, 'if so, of course I'll send what I can.'

'There's nothing more to be said on the matter.' The

nun smiled. 'Go in peace, child.'

'I'm so sorry, I didn't realize that the order needed money, I didn't stop to think. I'm so selfish.'

'My dear child, forget I mentioned it, this is a place of God, a place where there is peace and tranquillity. We will take care of your mother, she is one of us, you need have no worries on that score.'

Catherine bent forward and took the nun's hand in her own and kissed the wrinkled flesh. 'Thank you, Sister.'

'Go on with you now, your kinsman is waiting. Go home, Catherine O'Conner, try to make something good and worthwhile from the life your parents gave you and go to confession as a good Catholic girl should.'

Liam smiled in relief when he saw Catherine coming towards him; as she approached, he took her arm. 'Let's get out of here, this place is enough to give me goose bumps, it reminds me too much of all my sins.'

'Thank you for bringing me,' Catherine said softly and slipped her arm through his.

Once they were outside the gates, Catherine took deep gulps of air. She closed her eyes, turned her face up to the skies and felt the gentle autumn rain fall against her closed lids. She might have sent up a small prayer for her mother and for herself but then Liam was drawing her towards the horse and cart, anxious to be away.

'Do you think Mam is happy there, really happy?'

Liam cleared his throat. 'I only know what my grandmother tells me, that your mammy came here sick with grief. Now she has a bit of peace and quiet and it seems to be doing her good.'

He helped Catherine into the seat of the cart and climbed up beside her. 'Maeve is a good soul, she visits here every week in spite of her bone ache. Calls it doing her penance, hoping God will forgive her life of sin.' He laughed. 'What sins I daren't begin to imagine; with Maeve anything is possible.'

'Why are your family so kind?' Catherine asked. 'And to someone who is no relation except by marriage?'

'It's what any Irish family would do,' Liam said softly.

'Uncle Jamie was always a good man, always one of us. Not that we saw a great deal of him, at least, not until the last few years.'

'But my father wasn't really your uncle, was he?' Catherine looked up into Liam's face.

'Well, he was a distant cousin to my father, something like that. It makes no odds, he was still kin.'

'I don't know how I can ever thank you enough,' Catherine said.

His hands rested briefly on her knee and he laughed, 'Don't tempt me into making an indecent suggestion, colleen.'

She was laughing with him, her head tossed back, her arm clinging to his for support.

'Sure that's the first time I've seen you laugh in a long time,' Liam said. 'A right sourpuss, that's what you've become young lady.'

'I know and I'm sorry.' Catherine looked up at him feeling grateful and troubled at the same time. He wanted her as his wife, though heaven only knew why; wouldn't it be easier to give everything into his hands, allow him to take charge of her life?

She leaned against his shoulder and he looked down at her, his lips brushing her hair. 'Feel better now you've seen your mam for yourself?' he asked quietly.

She sighed heavily. 'I suppose so, though it's not the sort of life I'd want for myself.'

'No, I don't think you'd be a very good nun.' He was laughing again. 'You are such a sinful wretch, you drink and gamble and chase the fellers. Oh, no, you could not be a nun, never, ever.'

She slapped his hand and chuckling, he clucked at the horse and flicked the reins, urging the animal to go faster over the uneven ground.

'Sure it's going to pour down any minute now, I can feel the rain getting heavier.'

Catherine closed her eyes and saw the sodden fields of Honey's Farm. The corn was ruined, a little more rain could not do any further damage. She opened her eyes

156

suddenly. 'What about your corn?' She was anxious for him, picturing the golden stooks drenched and mouldering.

'That's all right,' he said, 'the men will have brought it all in by now. I took on extra workers to make sure; knew the weather would turn some time today.'

As if to underline his words, the rain began in earnest, beating down with tremendous force, bouncing off the boards of the trap.

Liam changed direction and drew off the road and into a gateway leading along a rutted track. 'We'll take shelter in that barn over there until the worst is over.'

The barn smelled of rotting hay and animals but at least here the cruel spikes of rain could not reach them.

Catherine climbed down from the cart, aware that her skirts were clinging wetly to her legs. She shivered and Liam took her in his arms.

'Cold?' he asked and she nodded. She could feel the beating of his heart and his strong arms around her. She felt the young hardness of him and suddenly, she knew she wanted to feel alive once more. She had become so miserable, so lacking in humour lately, she wanted to taste life to the full, to remember she was a young woman with her life before her. She wound her arms around Liam's neck and clung to him, lifting her face to his.

He hesitated for only a moment and then he was crushing his mouth against hers. She knew that he desired her and the knowledge was like a balm on an open wound. She felt comforted, reassured that she was a woman and not just a cast-off mistress facing financial ruin. She became aware that Liam was touching her breasts, his hands sure and skilful.

Gently, she drew him to the softness of the hay on the floor of the barn. They were close to the pony and trap. She smelled the wood, damp and reeking of resin. The horse stirred in the shafts and Catherine heard the creature breathe softly. Everything had taken on a sharpness, her senses were alert, it was as though she was coming awake after a long sleep.

Liam was undressing her with deft hands, she could hardly see his face in the gloom but she could hear his ragged breath and it gave her a sense of triumph, almost of power.

He was beside her then, his hands on the soft skin of her thighs. He began to caress her gently, with skill, and she moaned softly. She felt a million miles removed from Honey's Farm, from the troubled person who had stepped onto Irish soil yesterday. She felt the sensations of passion rush through her as Liam entered her.

She clung to him, her hands pressing the firm flesh of his buttocks. He gasped; then he was kissing her neck and her breasts. She smelt the rain in his hair and in that moment she felt an overwhelming feeling of joy. He was here, making love to her, he cared, he wanted her, he really loved her.

Liam was a good lover, in some part of her mind she acknowledged the fact that she was not the first. Liam Cullen was a man of experience, he combined skilfulness with vigour and strength.

She heard herself cry out as she arched backwards and knew the sweetness of release thundering through her loins and her breasts, sending her brain reeling.

Afterwards, she lay quietly in Liam's arms. She could not speak, she was ashamed, knowing herself for a woman of weakness, a woman of little virtue. What sort of person was she? A woman who could give herself to a married man, swear love for him and then turn so easily to another lover was beneath contempt.

And then her thoughts dissolved into sensations. Liam was with her again, touching her, caressing her so skilfully that she wanted him more than she had the first time. She writhed beneath him, moving with his rhythms as though she had always known them. She heard her own moans and then the fire began low in her belly, spreading outwards and upwards. She cried out and clung to Liam's broad shoulders, holding him close to her, tears running into her mouth.

Later, he dressed her as though she was a child. 'I love

you, Catherine, my darling,' he said, his voice vibrant, 'I know now I can make you happy.' He kissed her mouth briefly. 'Come on, the rain has stopped, we can go home.'

He lifted her into the seat of the trap and guided the horse out on to the road again. The world seemed a misty place, raindrops hung in the hedgerows like diamonds. Catherine closed her eyes and soon, she drifted into a haze that was half exhaustion, half sleep.

She opened her eyes some time later to find that they were home. It had grown dark, the nights were drawing in. The lights blazed from the front windows of Liam's house and from somewhere within was the cheerful sound of a piano being played.

Liam lifted her to the ground and pressed her close and she allowed him to kiss her lips. She was stirred by him, was the feeling love? She was so confused, she did not know what she felt any more.

He took her hand and led her into the hall and along the passage to the parlour. Outside the door, he paused and smoothed back her damp hair. 'My beautiful Catherine, my love, you've made me so happy,' he said gently. Then he was leading her into the parlour where the family were sitting. A blazing fire warmed the room, the curtains were drawn against the night.

Maeve was seated at the piano and Brad was before the fire, feet stretched out to the blaze. Patricia was sewing and she did not look up as they entered.

'Dad, Gran, I have something I wish to say to you, something very important, something I know will make you happy.' He put his arm around Catherine's shoulders and drew her against him.

'Catherine and I are going to be wed, just as soon as we can.' He smiled down at her proudly and even as the shock waves fired through Catherine's veins, she was aware that she had made a strange sort of commitment to Liam. He believed she loved him as he loved her and at this moment, in the glow of lovemaking and with the warmth of his family around her, she believed he might be right.

CHAPTER FOURTEEN

Catherine stood on the hillside overlooking the sea and breathed in the damp air, worried by the strangeness of the events that had taken place over the last few days. Liam's sudden announcement to the family that he and Catherine were going to be married had completely taken her by surprise and, though she had wanted to protest that it was not true, the words had died on her lips.

Liam had been so happy since the moment they had made love in the shelter of the barn. His arms had been comforting, she had sought solace in the heat of his body and the urgency of his ardour, and yet, she felt she had betrayed Boyo, that she had been unfaithful to him. What a fool she was even thinking of him now, he had taken her with the roughness of a man taking a whore. Was he thinking of her at this moment? She doubted it.

She would be returning home to Honey's Farm soon and then she would be able to evaluate her feelings, make decisions about her future: either she married Liam and became a respectable married woman, living comfortably on her husband's money or she struggled on alone at Honey's Farm.

She warmed whenever she thought of being with Liam, lying in his arms, having him adore her so openly. But was that enough? What about love?

She was weak, a fool, she should have spoken up immediately, not allowed Liam or his family to believe that she was going to be married to him. To make matters worse, his family, with the exception of his sister, had taken her to their hearts.

Brad had been warm and welcoming from the first, Maeve, harder to win round, was a staunchly independent old lady with strong views on life but she had softened as the days went on and had even offered Catherine advice: 'Love is sometimes a mirage, here today and gone tomorrow. You know what they say, a bird in the hand is worth two in a bush.'

Catherine had not credited Maeve with such perception, that she was a woman of sound common sense was obvious, but Catherine felt that in Liam's grandmother, she had found a friend.

She looked up at the clouds scudding across the sky. Soon it would be winter, the lands of Honey's Farm would be lying asleep, waiting only for the spring sunshine to bring forth a new harvest.

She shook her head, without seed there would be nothing to grow, no harvest to gather. The farm would be plunged into desolation, the fields would grow wild with untamed grasses that would be hard to shift. Brambles, prickly, strong and remorseless, would reclaim the lower slopes of the farm.

She could picture it now: Honey's Farm, little more than a wild hill on which children would play. Would it be such a bad thing? But she could not give up her birthright so easily; for the sake of her father's memory, if nothing else, she must try to build the farm into a thriving business once more.

She felt strength surge through her. No! She would not give in without a struggle, she would just have to sell the bull. With the money she could make a fresh start, try to pull the lands back into shape, see the fields rich with golden corn once more.

She must go home, stand again on Welsh soil, breathe in the fresh sea breeze, stare at her beloved coastline; there, perhaps, she would find the courage to decide on her future. She might even entice her mother home to Honey's Farm, one day.

Catherine felt fired with enthusiasm, she would show them all, especially Boyo Hopkins, just what she was made of. She would have to tell Liam of her decision as soon as possible. He had wanted to marry her right away, here in Ireland and, for a while, she wondered if that was what she wanted too. She rubbed her eyes, she did not know what she felt, for Liam or for Boyo. Damn them! Damn the men in her life, they tossed her emotions about as if they were playing God with her life. Well, she would find her own way, without either of them. Then, when she was financially secure, perhaps she could think about love and marriage and relationships with a clearer mind.

If she could put the farm back on its feet, she could consider selling it for a reasonable price, she would be free to make a fresh start in whatever direction she chose.

She rose to her feet and stared out at the coastline of Ireland; the green of the trees had turned to the brown of autumn, the sea washed the shore with clean white-edged waves. Ireland was a beautiful land but it was not her land; she must go home.

'I don't know why you are even thinking of taking this girl as your wife.' Patricia was peeling potatoes, the bowl in her lap, the peelings dropping onto newspaper on the floor. 'She's nothing better than a street girl. She could be with child, have you thought of that, Liam?'

Oh, she was not with child, had she been pregnant Catherine would have hastily accepted his offer of an early marriage. In any case, she was not like that, she was the sort who would tell the truth and shame the devil. Catherine knew he would take her as his bride whatever the circumstances. He loved her, that much would be obvious to a blind man.

He was about to speak when his grandmother leaned forward and tapped her stick on the flagged floor. 'Don't be hasty, Patricia.' She looked dryly at her grand-daughter, 'Just because your blood has never flowed hot enough for you to lie with a man, don't blame those women who have been more fortunate.'

'Gran!' Patricia was outraged, 'Anyone would think you admired the girl for her sordid past.'

Maeve smiled a dry little smile. 'There are those of us who would not wish to see our past brought up before us, we are the women who are fortunate, who have enjoyed the favours of more than one man, who have lived, child, lived.'

'So you think it fine to be loose then, do you, Grandmother?' Patricia stopped peeling potatoes and stared across the room, her eyes hot and angry. Maeve shrugged.

'I think 'tis sad to be a virgin when you are past five and twenty years.'

Patricia rose and banged the bowl against the table with a resounding thump. 'So, if I go and lie in the barn with one of the field hands I will be considered fortunate, is that it?'

'At least you would be considered human.' Maeve sat back in her chair and closed her eyes indicating that the conversation was at an end. Patricia stared at her with two spots of colour in her cheeks, it was clear she was about to launch into an argument and Liam held up his hand.

'No need for everyone to get so angry,' he said evenly. 'I am going to marry Catherine and that's an end to it.' He moved to the door and looked back into the kitchen. 'Pat, try to like her, it would be so much easier if you did, we will be living together after all.'

Patricia turned her face away and, after a moment, Liam shook his head and closed the door behind him. He strode out across the fields, forging uphill to where he knew Catherine would be sitting.

The top of May's field had become a favourite spot, perhaps one day he would build her a house up there so that she could watch the moods of the tide from the windows. There was enough land and enough money for him to do just as he liked. The farm had passed to Liam from his mother, his father had a stake in it, but only a small one, for it was Liam who had turned the land into the profitable arable and dairy farm it now was.

It had been troubling at first, the way he had spent money on newfangled ideas – the steam-ploughing machine had been a great bone of contention but it had paid off very quickly. The crops in the outer fields grew without the problems of root rot or worm; it seemed he

163

had the touch, the golden touch which made everything turn into profit.

He had been a happy and contented man, enjoying the occasional favours of the country girls, making no commitments, wanting nothing more from life, until Catherine. Now he wanted her with a fire that burnt in his heart and in his guts. He would have her, however long he had to wait and instinct told him that he would need to be patient.

In the first flush of having consummated their union, he had believed she would marry him; later, he had not been so sure. Catherine, he learnt, was not the usual sort of woman, she did not take one night of lovemaking for a declaration of undying love. Once, Liam had welcomed such liberal thinking, enjoying the freedom of indulging in passion without the necessity of offering more. With Catherine it was different, so different.

She was there up on the hill, standing with the wind moulding her clothes to the lithe lines of her beautiful body. Her hair, free of ribbons, streamed like red-gold silk behind her, she was a goddess and he worshipped at her feet.

As he drew near, she turned to him with a smile and he took her in his arms, burying his face against the warmth of her neck. He breathed her sweetness and the urge to possess her rose irresistibly within him.

He drew her down into a hollow and touched the swell of her breasts. She clung to him, her eyes closed, not resisting him but not welcoming him either. He drew away from her. 'Catherine, I would not take you against your will,' he said softly, looking down into her face.

'I'm glad,' she said simply, 'not all men are as considerate.'

Anger flared in him, so Hopkins had taken her by force, that was why Catherine had become his mistress. He felt the urge to kill and sat up, running his hand through the dark redness of his hair.

'Liam, I've come to a decision: it's time I went home,' Catherine said and he turned to her, striving to keep control of his feelings.

164

'When shall we leave?' He was surprised to hear that his voice was calm.

'Not us, me, I must do this alone. I will sell the bull and with the money buy seed, employ labourers again, try to pull the farm back to its feet. Then and only then can I think about marriage.'

'I do have a chance then, do I?' His attempt at lightness failed.

She reached towards him and touched his hand. 'Of course you have a chance, Liam. You are a wonderful man, you do not sit in judgement on me, you do not try to force your will on me and I love you for it.'

So that was the secret of her, she needed to be gentled, like a nervous beast; led, not pushed. He rose to his feet. 'Come on, then, let's get back in time for supper or Gran will take her stick to my back.'

Catherine laughed, 'Not much danger of that, my boy!'

'You don't know Grandma, a real dragon she is when she is angry.'

Together, they ran, hand in hand, like children, down the slope of the hillside and towards the welcoming smoke rising from the chimney of the farmhouse.

Resting in the large room that looked on to the grey rock-face, Bethan stared unseeingly into the darkness. She had successfully completed her sale of the inn and all its contents and her bank balance was even healthier than it had been before. But that brought her small consolation.

She had left the home she had shared with Boyo since her marriage and moved to Ty Craig to be with her father. He had told her not to harbour any regrets, that Boyo was not worthy of her, but none of it made her feel any better.

As for regrets, she had a great many of them but she also had an iron core of determination. She could not and would not endure being scorned by her husband, have him sleeping under the same roof but knowing it was another woman he wanted.

She had believed, at first, that she could deal with it,

weather the storm, so to speak; after all, many husbands strayed. But in the end, his love for Catherine had become like a wound festering inside her.

A knock on the door startled her, she knew who it would be. She had arranged for him to call during the time her father took his afternoon rest. She moved slowly from her chair and crossed the room, opening the door just enough to admit the man standing outside in the corridor. Behind him, a maid fluttered anxiously and Bethan waved her away impatiently.

'It's done.' The man was well-dressed as he should be; he was one of her father's oldest acquaintances.

'Well done, Uncle Tom.' She led the way towards the ornate fireplace and gestured towards one of the upholstered chairs. 'Tell me all about it.'

Tom took a seat and stared at her, a small smile curving his mouth beneath the greying moustache. 'The beast has been gelded, there will be no more prize heifers from that source.'

'The creature has not been harmed?'

Tom smiled more broadly. 'Well, the taking away of a creature's fertility is no laughing matter, especially when it is such a fine specimen as the bull on Honey's Farm turned out to be, but no, the animal will live a healthy life, but its only use will be as beef to put on the table.'

For a moment, Bethan felt a pang of horror at what she had done. It had been quite calculating, she had wiped out the one disposable asset that might save Honey's Farm. Well, it was no more than that bitch deserved! If you took another woman's husband, you asked for all you got.

'You will be able to buy the land at a rock-bottom price in a matter of only a few weeks, though why you should want it beats me.'

'Don't worry about it, Uncle Tom,' Bethan said quietly. 'I have been feeling restless lately, not knowing what it is I want out of life, perhaps the farm will prove a new challenge for me.'

'Look, *cariad*,' Tom said quietly, 'the girl is ruined, the farm is in a terrible state, forget it, the land will be a

166

liability to you.' He paused, waiting for Bethan to speak but she remained silent.

'In any case,' he said hastily, 'you and that fine husband of yours can patch things up, can't you? After all, a great many men have a little fancy piece on the side, it means nothing and I should know, I wasn't always faithful and yet I loved my wife dearly.'

Bethan sighed. 'This girl, the one who owns the farm, I just can't forgive her, she's beautiful, she could have any man but she took mine.' She felt the heat of anger rise to her cheeks as she waited for Tom to tell her she was a wicked woman. Instead, she heard him chuckle.

'Well, well, it's true then, hell hath no fury!'

She sat up straighter. 'That's right, Uncle Tom, I'm a scorned woman, my husband would prefer a little tramp to me. Well, he can have her and she can have him but she must feel hurt as I feel hurt, she must learn that one cannot have everything in life.'

Tom sighed, his laughter vanished. 'Just so long as you don't hurt yourself, my lovely girl; revenge is not very sweet, take it from me.'

When he had gone, Bethan sat in the chair near the window and stared out into the darkness for a long time, lost in unhappy thoughts. At last she closed the curtains and lit the lamp, her eyes blinded for a moment by the sudden light.

Over the fireplace, the portrait of Elizabeth Llewellyn looked down at her and it seemed there was a hint of sympathy in those dark eyes, but that was just a trick of the lamplight.

Bethan prepared herself to join her father for dinner but her thoughts kept returning to Boyo and to that woman who had ruined everything for them.

What would Catherine O'Conner feel when she came home and learned that her prize bull had been castrated? Would she know, with some deep, womanly instinct, who was behind the evil deed? Bethan clasped her hands together, a thin smile on her lips, she hoped so, she sincerely hoped so. It was time Catherine learned that she had made a very powerful enemy.

It was strange to be back in Swansea. Liam had wanted to come with her but Catherine had persuaded him she would be better off going alone. She needed to be her own woman, to give herself time to think clearly about her life.

She walked from town up the hill towards the farm, pausing once or twice to regain her breath. Turning, she looked back to where, in the valley, the untidy buildings of Swansea huddled together, lit here and there with lamps as the darkness moved in. It was a long walk and a tiring one but soon she would be in her own house, asleep in her own bed, the thought warmed her.

As she neared the house, she saw that lights gleamed from the farmhouse window. Her neighbours had been told of her return and it seemed that Cliff Jones had been kind enough to make her homecoming a pleasant one.

The door stood open and Catherine stepped inside the kitchen, seeing the soaring flames of the fire and hearing the singing of the kettle with a feeling of joy. Here she would be able to think, here she must learn to deal with the loneliness of her life on the farm.

A figure stepped out of the shadows and Catherine put her hand to her mouth, to prevent herself from crying out in fear.

'I'm sorry, I didn't mean to startle you. I had to see you, Catherine, I've missed you so much.'

Boyo stood before her, tall and handsome, his young face held a pleading expression and his eyes were shadowed. 'I want to apologize for the way I behaved last time we met, I was like an animal and I couldn't blame you if you never wanted to see me again.'

She pushed away the memory of him above her, forcing himself on her, it was too painful to bear. It was a betrayal of all she had believed him to be.

'Why are you here? I told you never to come near me again.' She walked towards the fire, the silence seemed loud, she was mesmerized by it. A coal shifting in the grate made her look up. 'Did you do all this?' She waved her hand around the kitchen, encompassing the cheerful fire, a fresh cloth on the table, cups and saucers neatly set out. She did not wait for a reply. 'How did you know I was coming home today?'

'I have been up here several times this week,' he said. 'Your neighbour was glad of my help. Cliff has been having a few difficulties on his own farm lately so for a few days, I have taken over the running of Honey's Farm completely.'

Catherine dumped her bag on the stone flags. 'Well, thank you.' Her voice was cold, flat.

'Cat,' his voice was soft, he came closer and tried to catch her hands but she stared up at him angrily.

'I'm very tired, Boyo. Please, just go, leave me alone will you?'

'Let me at least make you a cup of tea.' He moved to the fire and she sank into a chair, watching dully as Boyo moved to the fire and made the tea. 'Here, drink this,' he said, 'it's hot and sweet, it will make you feel better. I've put a hot-water bottle in your bed, I don't want you catching cold.'

Suddenly Catherine was furious, how dare he come into her house as though he owned it? How dare he assume that his interference would be welcome?

'You take too much on yourself, Boyo.' She looked up at him, the steam from the tea in the cup gripped tightly between her fingers making her blink. 'You are not welcome here, don't you understand that? You treat me like a whore and then you think a few little niceties will make me forget the humiliation. Well I won't forget, not ever. You and I are finished, I'm going to be married to Liam Cullen.'

Suddenly she felt tears restrict her throat but she forced herself to go on speaking. 'I will be respectable, a word you have never associated with me. Please, just go, leave me alone, you have brought me nothing but pain and I just want an end to it.'

Boyo stood looking down at her for a long time, he

169

seemed carved out of stone. 'Very well, Catherine, if that's what you really want then I have no right to stand in your way.'

He moved to the door and paused for a moment. 'I want you to know that I love you, I will always love you and I will come if you call, wherever you are.'

He went out and closed the door behind him and in the silence Catherine heard her own heart beating so hard she felt it would choke her.

She drank her tea and then crouched on the mat before the fire trying to sort out the chaos of her thoughts. It was in anger she had spoken of marrying Liam but perhaps that was the path she would eventually tread. First she had to put the farm back on its feet, make it viable again, the thriving, rich farmlands it had once been. Surely that would not prove too difficult for the daughter of Fon and Jamie O'Conner?

In the cosy room, she felt warmed by the house, by the familiarity. Here alone, she could almost believe her mother was still in the kitchen preparing for the morning. Her father would be taking a last look at the hens before turning in for the night.

She climbed into bed and found she was grateful for the stone bottle which had warmed the sheets, they closed comfortingly around her, she felt almost as though she was being held in an embrace. Outside, the night was cold, winter would soon hold the land in an icy grip. She had borrowed heavily from the bank already, how could she survive till spring? Wearily, she closed her eyes, nothing could be solved tonight; she would rest and in the morning, she would be able to think more clearly.

She was woken by the sun streaming through the window, it seemed the cold weather had relented and the blessing of an Indian summer was upon Honey's Farm. She stood in the coldness of her bedroom looking out at the sloping fields. Here she had spent her childhood, here she had been happy, cared for by her parents, they had seemed so strong, so indestructible to her then.

Even after April had died so unexpectedly, Catherine

had been secure in the belief that her mother and father would live for ever. How foolish she had been. She had believed then in dreams, she had watched Boyo Hopkins grow tall and handsome and even as a child she must have loved him.

A sad smile twisted her mouth, she had been a little brat, taunting and teasing April, intruding on the couple whenever she found the opportunity, chasing them across the lands of Honey's Farm, spying on them as they kissed under the cover of the barn. Perhaps she had not even recognized that her feelings of anger against April had stemmed from jealousy; it was clear that Boyo loved her to distraction.

Then April had died one awful day, swept away by the sickness that had gripped the town, taking old and young like a scythe cutting through the grass, how Boyo had mourned.

Catherine moved impatiently from the window. Well, he was gone now, gone from her life for ever. Boyo was not for her, he was a married man, a wealthy man, he had lived a different life these past years and he had left her behind. How could she go with him into the houses of the rich? Even if he had not been married, Boyo was now accepted by the higher echelons of Swansea society. A girl from the farmlands would be unwelcome in such company.

When she was dressed for outdoors with her boots firmly laced and a scarf around her head, she went into the yard and felt the sunshine on her face. She could hear the sounds of activity from the cowshed across the stretch of brown earth and knew with a feeling of relief that her neighbour had come in to help.

It was dim in the sheds, with the familiar mingling of smells of animal and milk that she would always associate with her childhood.

She stopped short as she saw the strong shoulders beneath the flannel shirt, the strong forearms and hands which were bringing the milk into the pail with deft, expert movements.

'What are you doing here?' She stood, arms across her

body, and looked down at Boyo's bent head.

'I wanted to help, just for today, until you settle in.' He glanced over his shoulder at her. 'There is surely no need for us to squabble like children, can't we at least act like civilized adults?'

She longed to go to him, to kiss his mouth, to feel his arms around her, holding her close. She closed her eyes suddenly seeing an image of herself and Liam lying in each other's arms and a wash of pain and guilt ran through her.

'Catherine . . .' his voice was soft, tender and her eyes opened quickly. She kicked out at the bucket, startling the cow and sending a stream of milk mingling with the dirt on the floor.

'Get out!' she said between gritted teeth. 'Get out of my life and leave me alone, I won't tell you again but if I see you on my land I'll take a shotgun to you.' She turned and fled back to the house, tears burning her eyes. What a mess she had made of her life, what an inept, pathetic creature she had become.

She did not see him leave, she did not want to watch as he strode away out of her life for ever. When he was gone, she felt lonelier than ever, how was she going to survive the winter with not a soul to talk to in the dark winter evenings? She sighed and made her way back to the shed, there was work to be done and no-one was going to do it for her.

It was almost a week later when she advertised the bull for sale. The creature was running wild in the fields, she simply could not manage him. From the numerous enquiries that came in, Catherine chose the one which seemed the most sincere.

Farmer Whitestone was a small, leathery man with warm blue eyes and a thatch of white hair jutting from under a much-worn cap. With him was the local vet.

'Good day to you, Miss O'Conner, come to see the beast, hope you don't mind old Willie Fern taking a look at him.'

Catherine smiled, it was the usual practice and she nodded in the direction of the field where the cows were

172

grazing. 'Go ahead, take your time, the bull is in a good mood today, though I must warn you that he's been off his food.'

Farmer Whitestone smiled showing uneven teeth. 'Had himself a good time, I expect? Found himself more than one willing lass among your herd no doubt.' He touched his cap and ambled away across the yard, the vet with his black bag following him more slowly. Bulls could be of uncertain temper and Willie Fern had experienced more than one brush with danger on his farm visits.

Catherine was carrying milk across the yard when she saw the two men walking across the fields, heads close together. She knew at once there was something wrong by the worried look on Farmer Whitestone's face.

'Put the creature out to breed, lately?' It was the vet who asked the question. Catherine shook her head.

'No, not since last spring. My neighbour Cliff Jones brought two of his heifers up here, very pleased with the results, he was, you can ask him if you have any doubts.'

'I see.' Willie Fern rubbed at his cheek.

'What is it, what's wrong, is the bull sick?'

'Oh, no, the creature's in good health, never been better I'd say.' He looked uneasily at the farmer and then shrugged.

'No other way but to tell you the plain truth, the bull's been gelded. You didn't know nothing about it then?'

Catherine felt a shock of fear run through her. 'That's not possible,' she said faintly, 'the bull is a prize animal kept only for breeding, there is no way I would have him gelded.'

'Thought it odd myself. Looks as if someone got it in for you, girl, the creature has been got at, he is only good for a bit of beef now, anyways up.'

Catherine felt embarrassed, a foolish inept girl trying to do a man's job. She scarcely heard the sympathetic words of the farmer. How could she not have noticed the change in the bull? But then, she had been so engrossed in her own worries, even when she was tending the animals she had been rehearsing in her mind a plea to the bank manager to lend her more money.

She watched with a feeling of unreality as the two men left the yard. Catherine bit her lip, searching for some explanation for the disaster, there was none, the bull was ruined for breeding for ever. Who could have done something so wicked?

She returned to the farmhouse and sank heavily onto one of the kitchen chairs. She felt faint and sick and saw her future as a farmer disappearing. She put her head down on the scrubbed table and closed her eyes, too weary even for tears.

CHAPTER FIFTEEN

It was dim in the kitchen but Catherine was not aware of it, she stared into the fire, not caring that it was burning low. Outside, winter was gripping the land, the frost had come suddenly and the winds blowing in from the sea were cold and punishing. She felt lonely, hopeless, as though every ounce of courage she possessed had been snatched from her.

She had pondered long and hard about what had happened while she was away. She had asked herself what she had done to deserve such spite? She simply could not believe that anyone would cruelly ruin such a fine creature as the prize bull.

The answer came at last, reluctantly. Bethan Hopkins was capable of anything and who could blame her for wanting revenge? Catherine had stolen the woman's husband and this was her punishment.

The knocking on the door roused her, she rose to open it and knew it would be the constable from town, no-one else ever called at Honey's Farm, not these days. Old Farmer Whitestone had spoken to the police but an investigation was pointless, the bull was worthless.

'Evening, miss, I'm Constable Danby.' The policeman was young, handsome and his eyes lit up as they rested on her. 'I came about your prize bull.'

Catherine stood back to allow the constable inside and then, carelessly, she threw some logs in the grate and watched them flare brightly. She moved to the dresser and lit the lamp and the light flickered and gleamed on the plates resting on the shelves. She made an effort to listen to what the policeman was saying.

'Been gelded, is that the right term for it, miss?'

'That's right, the animal has been ruined, he's

worthless, I can no longer use the bull for stud. Whoever has done this terrible thing knew exactly how valuable the animal was.' She sank down into a chair. 'I just can't understand anyone being so wicked.'

'Is it all right if I take a seat, miss?' The policeman removed his helmet and placed it on the table and when Catherine nodded, he drew out a kitchen chair and seated himself opposite her.

'This is an act of mischief, miss, done by someone who bears a grudge against you. Can you think of anyone like that?'

Catherine shook her head. 'It wouldn't be a farmer, I can assure you of that.'

'Why, miss? I'm a townie, see, don't know anything much about country life.'

'A farmer might be tempted to steal such a valuable animal', Catherine said, 'to serve his herd but no respecting farmer could bring himself to destroy such a beautiful creature.'

The policeman looked doubtful. 'But the . . . the job, it was done right, proper-like, the animal wasn't harmed.'

'The operation was done by a vet, yes, it was an expert job, as you say, calculated to make the bull worthless without killing him.'

'Can't you come up with the name of anyone, anyone at all, however unlikely, who might have wanted to spite you?'

Catherine looked at him bleakly. 'Only the wife of the married man I was having an . . . an affair with. Does that shock you, Constable Danby?'

The policeman frowned and shook his head. 'No, miss, nothing much shocks you after a few years in this job. I've seen murder most horrible, I've seen arson, beautiful places burned to the ground, I've seen a great many crimes committed and all in the names of greed or spite. You have to keep an open mind doing this sort of job.' He paused for a moment and studied her. 'Would you like to give me the name of this . . . this wife, local is she?'

Catherine shook her head. 'No, it's too silly, the

woman is rich, influential, she is not a farmer, she would not know how valuable the animal was. Forget I mentioned it.'

He closed his notebook. 'Right then, miss, I'll get onto it. Can't promise much, mind, but I'll do my best.'

'How will you even begin?' Catherine said despairingly.

'Oh, we have our ways. In spite of what everyone thinks of us, we often get it right.' He looked down at her and she read interest in his eyes, an interest that she did not welcome. She rose to her feet and moved to the door.

'Thank you, Constable Danby, you've been very kind.' She stood looking at him as he pencilled a few words into a notebook. He tucked the book into a pocket and then smiled down at her.

'If I find anything out, anything at all, I'll come and report to you at once, how does that sound?' He was trying to jolly her, to lift her spirits and she relaxed a little.

'I know you will do all you can, thank you.'

She watched as the young policeman strode away from the house and disappeared over the brow of the hill. He had been kind, very kind, but there was little hope of discovering the culprit and they both knew it. In any case, what good would it do her now? The bull was worthless.

Catherine took her coat from the back of the door and buttoned it around her throat. It was cold outside, a bleak December night with the stars brilliant in a clear sky. She shivered, glancing back regretfully at the glowing fire she was leaving behind but there was work to be done, cows to be milked, animals to feed, the chickens to be shut in for the night, she had neglected her chores for long enough.

As she sat in the shed with her head against the warm flank of one of the animals, she felt calmer. The everyday job of drawing down the milk, hearing it drum against the bottom of the pail, had a soporific effect on her. Suddenly she realized she was very tired.

She could not go on trying to cope with the work alone, she realized, even if she worked from morning until night, she would never manage. In the spring, when the lambs were born, she would need extra hands and where would she find the money for wages? She might just as well give up and sell the farm now, as it was, at least there was a good dairy herd and fine rich soil in the fields, these were enough surely to attract a buyer?

By the time she left the shed, the skies had become overcast. Clouds raced across the moon obscuring it and then the rain began, a heavy chilling rain that quickly soaked through her wool coat.

Doggedly, Catherine carried the milk, pail by pail, across the yard to the dairy. By the time she had finished she could have taken the hem of her coat and wrung the water from it and there were still the hens to be fed.

Standing miserably in the dairy, pouring the milk into churns, Catherine became aware of noises in the yard. She tensed, straining her eyes to see through the dark window on to the ground beyond. The hens began to shriek and Catherine hurried from the dairy to the kitchen to pick up her gun. A fox must have got into the hen-house; it was her fault, she should have seen to the poor creatures before this.

She paused to light a storm-lantern, for now it was completely dark without even the moonlight to cast a glow over the yard. Catherine went outside and the wind buffeted her, blowing darts of cold hard rain into her face, taking her breath away.

The hens were still screeching and as Catherine approached the shed, a flurry of feathers caught up by the wind scattered over her. She paused, this was no ordinary fox, the noise was too great. The sound of splintering wood confirmed her suspicion that the intruder was human. She put down the lantern and cocked the gun, moving slowly forward.

'Come out of there!' Her voice sounded frail and light and was carried away by the wind. She stood still for a moment, uncertain what she should do. If she went inside the run, she might be trapped with the maniac who was plundering the hen-house. She moved nearer to the wire-covered door, lifted the gun and fired some shot into the air.

178

The effect was startling: a huge frame hurtled towards her, crashing into her and knocking her to the ground. The gun spun away from her hands and she scrabbled in the mud for it but the barrel was just out of reach.

The figure loomed over her and then the world exploded as a fist connected with her temple. A booted foot crushed against her side and she gasped with shock. She felt another blow catch her mouth and then there was nothing but blackness.

Catherine regained consciousness slowly and became aware of the chill and dampness that settled over her like a blanket. She realized with a shock of fear that she was still lying in the mud near the hen-house. A few yards away, the storm-lantern flickered and died. She lay still for a moment, straining her ears for the slightest sound. There was nothing except the wind in the trees and the soft clucking of the hens who were free of the run and scratching, bedraggled and wet, in the mud of the yard.

She tried to rise and fell back to the ground. She realized she could scarcely move and then the feeling in her face began with a slow throbbing that rose to a crescendo of pain.

She dragged herself onto her knees, her hair hung around her eyes in soaked, muddy strands and, for a moment, the world seemed to swing away from her as the darkness threatened to draw her downwards once more.

She began to make her way towards the farmhouse, she could see the lamplight glimmering through the open doorway.

She lost count of the times she fell, face down in the mud, but, time after time, she struggled to her knees and crawled towards the light that seemed to offer comfort and solace.

At last, she fell inside the door and lay for a moment, trying to ward off the circles of darkness that pressed against her eyes. With her feet, she pushed the door shut and gasping with pain at every movement, dragged herself across the floor towards the fire. It was almost dead in the grate, only the flickering embers remained. Catherine forced herself to her knees and pushed a log onto the fire. She fell back onto the mat, watching the log spark and splutter and then, thankfully, spring into bright flame. She knew instinctively she needed warmth to survive the night.

She seemed to lapse into bouts of unconsciousness, rousing only to throw another log into the grate. Each time she moved, she felt the waves of faintness wash over her.

Towards morning, she became aware that her clothes were chilling her, clinging damply to her skin. She braced herself for the effort of undressing and with each garment she removed, she felt sick and ill; the pain in her face and body almost defeated her.

When she was naked, she dragged a shawl from the back of the rocking-chair and wrapped it around her, trembling violently. The shawl had the scent of her mother about it and suddenly, Catherine was crying hot bitter tears.

When she woke, it was daylight. The fire was still flickering in the grate and Catherine realized that she must have kept it alight even after she had undressed though she had no recollection of it.

She could not open one of her eyes. Gingerly, she touched the swollen lid and winced as she felt the swelling with her fingertips. She tried to rise to her feet but a sharp stab in her side brought her to her knees.

More cautiously, she tried again and then, holding onto the table leg, she pushed herself upright. She cried out loud as the pain began in her ankle, rising up through her knee to her thigh. She looked down and saw that her foot was blue and swollen and she bit her lip wondering if she had broken a bone.

She sank into the rocking-chair and closed her eyes, fighting the waves of pain and blackness. She felt the salt of tears on her cheeks, perhaps she would die here alone and the animals, they would die too, all of them would starve slowly, painfully, lingeringly. She tried to tell herself to stop being melodramatic, someone would come but lying to herself did not work. She lay quietly, sometimes she drifted into unconsciousness, but towards midday, she came fully awake and she knew that she must do something positive or she would die.

She threw some blocks from the bottom of the basket onto the fire, aware that the stock was getting alarmingly low. She looked around for something to strap to her ankle to try to ease the pain. From the dresser, she pulled out some linen and when the pile of cloths fell to the floor, she smelled the scent of the dried lavender her mother had put in the drawer last summer.

The pain in her side caught her breath and she guessed that at least one of her ribs was cracked. She became aware of the smell of oil from the lamp and realized that it had burnt away hours ago.

Among the linen she found a runner, edged with lace, which her mother had made herself to protect the top of the dresser. Carefully, she bound it round her ankle and beneath her foot and the pain eased a little.

She found an old bolster cover and wound it around her aching body. Now would come the difficult part, she would have to get upstairs to find herself some clean warm clothes.

Several times she tried to get up from the floor and the pain made her gag. She did not know where she hurt the most, her ankle, her ribs or her face. Very slowly she forced herself upright, clinging onto the edge of the dresser and then, on one foot, she moved towards the stairs.

She was sweating as she sank onto the first stair, she wanted to remain there, still and quiet with the warmth of the fire drifting towards her but she had to get upstairs; somehow she would do it. She needed a wash badly, there would be water in the jug in her room, it would be cold but it would have to do. She could sit on the bed and try to get the worst of the mud off her skin.

Fresh waves of pain and despair washed over her as she tried another few steps but she forced her mind to work on the problems ahead of her and forget the pain.

'One step at a time, Catherine.' It was as if she could hear her mother's voice encouraging her. But that was foolishness, her mother wasn't dead, she wasn't a voice from beyond the grave offering solace; her mother was in a convent in Ireland, happy to think her daughter was restoring the farm to its former glory.

Inch by painful inch, Catherine made her way up the stairs. They reared before her like a mountain that needed to be conquered.

In the bedroom, a pale sun slanted through the window and fell on the bright patchwork quilt that had always reminded Catherine of the pattern of the fields of Honey's Farm.

Slowly, Catherine washed as best she could, though it was agony to reach her legs and feet. At last, dressed in warm thick clothes, she began to feel more hopeful. She had come this far with sheer determination and as for the next step, the task of finding help, well, she would just have to sort something out.

The journey back to the kitchen was accomplished by the simple procedure of sitting on the stairs and negotiating each one with her foot stuck out before her. Near the door to the kitchen stood the stick that her father had used in the last days of his illness and, gingerly, she took the smooth wood in her hands and experimented with it, leaning on it heavily and hopping forward.

She reached the back door of the kitchen and looked outside with a feeling of dismay, the rain was still teeming down and the yard was a quagmire presenting difficulties which she knew would be almost insurmountable.

Cliff Jones's farmhouse was the closest building to Honey's Farm but how would she get there? She would never be able to hitch the cart up to the horse, she would have to ride the animal bareback. That was going to be easier said than done, she thought ruefully.

She drew on a heavy topcoat and wound a thick woollen scarf around her head and leaning heavily on the stick, began to make her way towards the stables.

Liam stepped off the boat at Swansea docks and turned up his collar at the flurry of cold rain which greeted him. His overfilled bag bumped against his side as he turned to look back at the Celtic Star, the cargo ship on which he had bought passage and he shuddered. It had been a most uncomfortable journey across from Cork, he was glad to reach dry land, though dry was hardly the word for it, he thought ruefully.

He had worried for days, seeing in his mind's eye the pale face and haunted eyes of the woman he loved. She had lain in his arms, given herself sweetly to him and then, with the stubborn streak of the Irish, she had told him she was going home to run the farm.

Liam sighed, the problems of the farm were too much for her, the land needed strong men who worked hard to tame it. She needed men to plough the land and fresh seed to plant in the furrows.

Liam loved her for wanting to be independent but, though he respected her efforts to clear up the debts and make the farm a viable proposition again, he doubted that she had the strength to achieve it.

She had not written to him, not after the first week when she had sent a pitifully small offering for the convent where her mother was lodged. He had added substantially to the sum before having it sent up to the Reverend Mother.

He looked around for some means of transport but there seemed to be no cabs about. A few wagons stood near the dockside and a horse-drawn cart loaded with coal was making its way unsteadily over the cobbles. With a sigh of resignation, he set out to walk the few miles to Honey's Farm. Normally the walk would have been pleasant. The streets around the docklands teemed with life. Cockle women, baskets over arms, the contents covered with pristine white cloths, called their wares in raucous voices. Vans trundled by and a big wagon drawn by four fine dray-horses pulled into the curbside near him to unload huge barrels of ale.

After a time, Liam left the busy streets behind and began the walk uphill away from the town. The rain had abated a little but by now he was soaked, his hat dripping water down his face. He hoped Catherine had a warm fire waiting but somehow there was an edge of doubt in his mind that all was not well.

As he negotiated the muddy lane leading to the farm-house, he saw that the kitchen door was open. Some chickens were scratching in the yard and he breathed a sigh of relief, his fears had been unfounded. What he had imagined, he did not know. That Catherine had sold the farm perhaps, that she had fallen sick and was lying in her bed alone. But no, she would be near the fire, boiling up mutton for dinner, perhaps, or out milking her large herd of cows.

He called her name as he pushed the door open and then stood just within the kitchen staring around him in dismay. The fire was dead in the grate, the coals dusty. He moved forward and touched the hob, it was cold, there had been no fire lit there for some time.

He moved quickly around the rest of the house and his search of the rooms proved only that Catherine was not here. In one of the bedrooms, the bedclothes were dis-arrayed, a bolster lay on the floor and a jug of water had been overturned.

He returned quickly to the kitchen, the stock of logs was almost gone, usually in this sort of weather any country girl would be sure to have a large stock at hand. His instincts had been right, something had happened.

He stood on the doorstep and looked around him, straining his eyes to see through the mist and rain. He caught the hint of smoke rising from a chimney-stack and realized it must belong to Catherine's nearest neighbour.

He crossed the yard and looked into the barn. Some of the animals were crouched on the ground and it took him a few minutes to see that the creatures were in dis-tress, their udders heavy with milk. He touched one swollen belly and felt by the heat there that the cow was sick and engorged. Something needed to be done, and quickly, but his first priority was to find out where Catherine was.

He made his way towards the distant farmhouse, slipping on the wet hillside. He tried to keep his feelings of panic at bay, praying he would find her safe with her neighbours. 'Mother of God keep Catherine from harm,' he said softly.

Cliff Jones was a young, sandy-haired man with a plump wife and a brood of children in various stages of growth. He drew Liam into his house with a smile of welcome. 'What can I do for you, sir?' He had noted the good cut of Liam's clothes and clearly felt it was wise to be a little deferential.

'I'm looking for Catherine O'Conner, have you seen her in the last few days?'

'No, sir. Sorry but the weather's been so bad-like, got enough to do on my own farm, much as I'd like to help. Done all I can for the lady, mind, helped when she was away but it's all too much for one man. "Get out of there," I told her, "sell up, make life easy for yourself." Perhaps that's what she's done.'

'Has there been anyone else here asking about her?' Liam tried again but the man shook his head.

'Sorry, sir. Could we offer you a cup of something to warm you up, it's an awful day for a man to be about.'

''Tis kind of you,' Liam said quickly, 'but I shall have to go into town, see the police, perhaps they know something.'

'Oh!' The farmer looked at Liam with raised eyebrows, 'I just remembered something.'

'Go on then.' A small hope flickered within Liam but the man's next words extinguished it at once.

'Jeremiah Danby been up here, asking questions he was, about the bull.'

Liam looked at him blankly. 'Jeremiah Danby?'

'Police constable hereabouts, he is. Seems the bull was got at.' He lowered his voice. 'Some bastard cut the beast's balls off, useless the creature was then, good only for the cooking pot.'

185

Liam digested this information in silence, aware that the rain was now stealing down the collar of his coat in chill streams. 'Where will I find the policeman?'

'Got a house down in town, Moriah Street, that's where he lives. Be there this time of day I 'spects, havin' his dinner.'

Liam refused a cup of tea but took out some money and placed it on the table. 'I'd be obliged if you would see to the animals up at Honey's Farm, just until I can sort something out.'

'Oh, right sir, I'll do that, don't you fret. Should sell up, I told her, told her more than once; it's more than any young girl can handle, is farming.'

Once outside the farm door, Liam began to run towards the town. It took him almost an hour to locate Moriah Street which was tucked away on the fringes of the town. He knocked on the door and stood on the step, impatiently waiting for someone to answer.

The door was opened by a huge-breasted woman in a spotless white apron. She clucked when she saw him and drew him into the warmth of the kitchen.

'*Duw*, look at the state of you, catch your death, you will, your poor old coat is soaked through. She was drawing it away from his shoulders before he had time to protest and then she drew out a chair and set it before the fire. 'A nice mug of stew is what you need, get some colour back into your cheeks.'

'Are you Mrs Danby then?' he asked. 'The policeman's wife, is it?' He was touched at the woman's hospitality and he sat back, allowing her to take charge. In any case, to stop her would be like trying to halt a herd of wild horses at full gallop.

'Love you for a good man, I'm Jeremiah's mother, not his wife, though thank you for the compliment anyway.'

'I'm after a talk with your son, then.' He rubbed his hands together, trying to infuse some warmth into his chilled fingers. 'I don't suppose he's at home is he?'

'Love you, no, down at the station he is, working hard. Well, that's what my Jeremiah tells 'is mam, anyway.'

186

She brought him the stew and his mouth watered at the pea-and-ham flavour that rose from the brimming mug. She drew a chair closer to the fire and sat opposite him lifting her skirts and exposing plump knees to the blaze. Liam averted his eyes.

'Don't mind me!' she giggled like a girl. 'Now come on, tell me what's wrong, Lovie. I know as much about the goings on in Swansea as my son does.'

He hesitated and then decided it could do no harm to confide in her. 'I'm looking for Catherine O'Conner,' he said slowly. 'She's close kin and I'm worried about her, she's not at the farm, you see, and the beasts are falling sick and the chicks running loose . . .' The words trailed away and he shook his head helplessly.

'Well now, there's been a bit of nastiness up at Honey's Farm lately, the old bull got dealt with good and proper, won't have any more fun, not him.'

'I know, I heard about that from the neighbouring farmer,' Liam said, his despondency growing.

'Someone got it in for the young lady, someone with a grudge,' Mrs Danby said. Her nod was knowing. 'My son is working on that now, thinks he knows who the culprit is.'

'Sure then he's a clever man.' Liam leaned forward in his chair. 'Has he told you who this person is?'

To his disappointment, Mrs Danby shook her head. 'No, it's confidential like, couldn't tell me nothing about his job, not him.'

'When do you expect him home?' Liam asked wearily and watched as the woman's brows drew together.

'No tellin', can't say when he'll get off work, treat him like a slave at that station they do.'

Liam rose and placed the mug on the table. 'Thank you for the hospitality, sure an' I'll call back this evening, will that be all right?'

'You're welcome any time to sit at my hearth. Now don't forget your bag, there's a good man. Who shall I tell my boy was looking for him then?'

'Liam Cullen, Catherine's kinsman.' Liam stepped out

into the rainy street and placed his damp hat on his head. He strode out along the street and realized, too late, he should have asked Mrs Danby for the name of a good hotel, somewhere cheap and warm where they served good plain food. He had no time for the fiddling dishes they set before a man in some of the more elegant establishments.

Once in the heart of the town, he picked up a cab easily enough and told the driver exactly what he was looking for. Then, he sank back in the seat, feelings of anxiety crowding in on him. Catherine had disappeared but he would find her, if he had to stay the rest of his life in Swansea.

CHAPTER SIXTEEN

It was cold in the drawing-room of the grey-stone house known as Ty Craig, even though a fire burned brightly in the grate. Bethan stared around her as though she had suddenly found herself in a lost world. However many times she had the fire stoked up in the rooms, the place still retained a damp, somewhat sickly atmosphere that reminded Bethan of a churchyard. Why had she returned to the place? Because of her father whose health was failing or because the valley in which the house stood was tucked well away in the folds of the surrounding hills?

Ty Craig was a gloomy house and sometimes she felt she sensed a presence, more than one presence, a host of ghostly images which faded on closer inspection with a well-lit lamp. She dismissed the idea as the fancies of a lonely woman and tried to put it out of her mind.

The door opened and the elderly butler, who had served at Ty Craig for as long as Bethan could remember, came into the room inclining his head in deference. 'A gentleman to see you, madam, a Mr Thomas Butler.'

Bethan rose at once, a smile on her face as she went forward to greet her visitor. 'Uncle Tom, I wasn't expecting to see you today, so this is indeed a pleasure for me.'

She took her uncle's hands and over her shoulder gave an order that some refreshments be brought at once.

'Sit here beside the fire, Uncle Tom, it's not a very nice day, is it?'

Tom looked at her ruefully. 'Outside it is beautiful but here in this mausoleum it is as cold as the grave. How is your father, my dear, is he up to a visit from me?'

'I should think so but first, is there something you want to tell me?' Bethan smiled to herself.

'You always were too wise for your own good, couldn't this just be a social call?'

'It's lovely to see you, Tom, but I can see this is not just a social call, you have something on your mind so come on, out with it, am I to have a lecture on the perils of living the life of a scorned wife again?'

Tom frowned. 'I'd better come straight to the point.' He paused as the maid Bethan had brought with her to Ty Craig bobbed a curtsey and placed a tray on the table. Bethan waved Cara away impatiently. She poured the tea and handed Tom a cup and then waited for him to speak.

'My man, the one I sent up to keep watch at Honey's Farm, he's come to me with a problem.'

'What sort of problem?' Bethan asked warily. She put her cup of tea untasted on the tray. 'What has happened?'

'It seems the O'Conner girl surprised young Jacob, he was forced to hide and the fool chose the hen-house. The young woman had a gun, I'm afraid he acted somewhat hastily.'

'And?' Bethan probed, wishing he would get on with it.

'Well, he injured the girl rather badly I'm afraid.'

Bethan resisted the urge to smile, she put her hand to her mouth and feigned disapproval. 'This was not what I intended, how badly was she hurt?'

'Bruises, perhaps broken bones, I'm not sure. Jacob hung around for a while as he was instructed to do and later, he found her in the yard, lying in the mud, her face almost unrecognizable. He took her to his hovel and she's there now, sick with a fever. What am I to do with her, Bethan?'

Bethan thought of the girl, sick and injured, in a hovel with a halfwit and felt a glow of almost self-righteous joy; it was where a girl of that sort belonged.

'What can I do?' Bethan asked holding her hands palms up as though dismissing any responsibility. 'I can hardly bring her here, can I, that would make people suspicious to say the least. I can't see that it matters much where she is, can you?'

'Well, no, except that some Irish cousin, a man by the

name of Liam Cullen, is going about Swansea, talking to people, trying to learn the whereabouts of the girl.'

'I doubt he will be able to trace her,' Bethan said. 'How could he?'

'I don't know but I am uneasy about it. She needs care, it's quite possible she could die, then all sorts of hell will break loose. You must think of something Bethan.'

'And what am I to do, then? Murder her, hide her body beneath the stones in the courtyard?' She was angry with him, this was his problem, he had made the mess, he could clean it up. 'If you recall, I did not agree to any violence, Uncle Tom, so I can't be held responsible for what your man has done.'

'But what if she dies?' Tom asked, he was almost pleading with her now, anxious in the face of Bethan's displeasure.

'Get her medical attention if you are so concerned, make up a story, any story. Use your intelligence, Uncle Tom, you have plenty of it.'

'Aye, I may be a learned man but it seems I have a great deal yet to know about the devious workings of a woman's mind.' It dawned on him that she was not going to help in any way and as he subsided in his chair, he suddenly looked old.

'Don't let's quarrel,' Bethan rose and in an uncharacteristic gesture, kissed Tom's brow. 'Drink your tea, let us calm down and discuss this sensibly, there is bound to be a solution.'

Her mind was racing; what would happen to the farm with the O'Conner girl out of the way? Would it be put up for sale by this kinsman of hers? Alternatively, the place could be left to moulder away in neglect. Perhaps she should take a trip into Swansea and find out for herself just what was going on. In the meantime, she must placate Tom, persuade him to leave the girl where she was, at least for the moment.

Catherine opened her eyes slowly, a pale wintry light was filtering through the grimy window to the left of her. She realized that she was in bed in a strange room. The room was small and bare, the only furniture was a small table and the bed on which she was lying. Fearfully, she sat upright and immediately a pain tore her side, running down to her ankle. She gasped and paused for a moment before pushing herself upright.

She saw herself then in the speckled mirror on the shabby table facing her and she hardly recognized herself. Her face was dappled with bruises, her eyes blackened and swollen, her lip cut. Memory came flooding back, she felt again the blows rained on her by the intruder, the horror and fear of the attack made her tremble even now.

She tried to clear her mind, she remembered crouching for what seemed like hours on the floor, half unconscious. Finally, she had made her way into the mud-soaked yard attempting to reach her neighbour's farm and then all was blackness.

She pushed back the bedclothes and shivered in the cold. She glanced down the length of her body, she had been undressed and garbed in a decent, cotton nightgown but who had brought her here? And why had she not been taken back to the farmhouse?

She tried to get out of bed and the pain made her cry out. She hung onto the worn brass head-rail, forcing back the waves of nausea, she must get out of the room, find someone who could tell her what was happening.

She managed to inch her way to the door but every movement made her wince in agony. She turned the handle but it resisted and after a moment, she realized that she was locked in. Slowly, she edged towards the window but it was far too high for her to see out of the small panes.

She was shivering violently with cold and fatigue and, defeated, she made her way back to the bed; at least there she could be warm.

She must have dozed because, when she opened her eyes once more, the room was dark. The door was opening and a woman carrying a lamp entered. She was tall, austere and she wore a big flapping cloth around her hair.

For a confused moment, Catherine wondered if she was in a convent but then she saw that this woman was dressed in poor garments, a heavy sack hung around her thick waist and her arms beneath the rolled-up sleeves were those of a working woman.

'There's a doctor here to see you.' The woman said sullenly and Catherine stared past her at the man who bustled towards the bed, a black bag in his hand. He offered neither his name nor his hand but he gave her a tablet which she obediently swallowed and then examined her bruises in silence. After a while he pulled back the bedclothes and clucked in disapproval at the state of the self-made bandage on her leg.

'Fetch me some clean water, I must bathe this ankle and bandage it properly. Find some strips of clean cloth if you please.'

'Who are you and why am I here?' Catherine asked, her voice thin with fear. He looked at her in surprise, as if she had risen up and bitten him.

'I'm just a visiting doctor, girl,' he peered into her eyes. 'You might well have sustained some injury to the head when you fell.' He glanced at the woman who was still hovering in the doorway. 'Well, go on then, hurry up, I haven't all day.'

'All right then, Doctor, but I warn you, this girl is a terrible liar, you must not believe a word she says, she can make up stories like no-one I ever saw before.'

Catherine was bewildered, 'I have never seen that woman before and yet she talks as if she knows me, am I going mad?' she asked, fear gripping her.

'You have had a fall and that led to a fever, you might even have some injury to the brain, nothing I can do about that! You are bound to be a little confused but time will heal all, so don't worry.'

'I am more than a little confused, Doctor. The last thing I remember was being attacked, trying to go for help and then I woke up in this house.'

'As I said, you are confused.' The doctor began running his hand expertly up her leg, testing for injuries.

'You must realize, young woman, you can expect the occasional "incident" of this kind to happen, it's the lot of common man; woman too, of course.' He gave a glimmer of a smile.

She looked at him. 'I'm a farmer and of course accidents happen on a farm but not the sort of beating I got, that was no accident.'

He stared at her trying to assess the truth of her words. 'Do you not have a husband with a hasty temper?'

'No, I haven't,' Catherine said shortly.

He became businesslike. 'That's what I was told. Well it's none of my business, I'm just a doctor, not a priest, I'm not interested in your private life, my dear.'

She looked at him in despair. 'Please, Doctor, I don't know what you have been told, or what you believe of me but can't you help me to get back to my home?'

Before he could reply the woman had returned to the room, her gimlet eyes fixed on Catherine.

'I hope you ain't takin' no mind of this trollop's hardluck stories, Doctor,' she said, handing him a few strips of rag.

'This may hurt a little.' He ignored the woman and spoke gently to Catherine; as he bound the clean strips of rag around her ankle his hands were deft.

'I think you have been very lucky,' he said. 'The injury to your ankle could have been worse, you could easily have sustained a broken bone.' He looked at the bandage in satisfaction.

'Now let us look at these ribs, shall we?' He lifted her gown and though she shrunk from him, she allowed him to take off the bolster and to press her ribs experimentally. 'Hmm, should be all right in a week or two, then you'll be ready to go . . . well, wherever you wish. For the moment I think it would be foolish to move you.'

Before Catherine could speak he was being ushered out of the room by the tall, austere woman whose headscarf flapped about her ears like a gaggle of agitated sea birds.

Catherine heard the lock turn and knew she was a prisoner again, though she did not understand why.

194

Tired, she fell back against the pillows. She could not make any sense of what the doctor had said, it was almost as though he believed she belonged in the mean house where she lay. But she was too tired to think it all out just now. She closed her eyes and as the tablet the doctor had given her began to take effect, she slept.

The farm looked desolate as Bethan, in riding habit, strode about the place, her eyes taking in every detail of the obvious neglect and decay that made the farm appear long abandoned. There was no sign of any animals except for the sheep which roamed in the fields sweeping down from Honey's Farm and a few thin hens scratching in the stunted grass at the verge of the yard.

'I should get this place for next to nothing.' She glanced at Tom who was stepping gingerly through the mud, careful of his highly polished shoes. 'I told you to put on a pair of old boots but would you listen to me, would you hell!'

'Bethan, it is not seemly for a woman to swear. What would your dear father say?'

'Oh, Uncle Tom, you are stupid, disapproving of my manners when we both know that we are accomplices in an abduction.'

Tom looked alarmed. 'No-one could trace what's happened back to us, could they?'

Bethan shook her head. 'You are such an innocent, Uncle Tom, the girl has been kept locked in a hovel against her will. If pressed, this man Jacob would talk his head off. Had any of us really meant to help her we would have taken her to the nearest hospital.'

'I suppose you are right,' he sighed. 'I don't know how we are going to get out of this mess.'

'We'll think about that once I have bought the farm,' Bethan said, reassuringly. 'Just don't you worry about it now.'

She lifted her head, her shoulders tense. 'I can hear the beat of hooves, perhaps this is the Irishman nosing around again.'

Tom was suddenly pale and Bethan touched his arm. 'Keep calm, let me do the talking, no need for any of us to panic, is there?'

The rider came into view and, as the flying hooves lifted the turf and the large stallion covered the ground, Bethan drew a ragged breath, waves of pain and shock washing through her.

'Boyo!' She trembled as he came towards her, pulling at the animal's reins and her heart turned over as he smiled down at her.

He slid from the saddle and stood close to her, his eyes looking down at her held an expression of concern. He was as handsome as ever, his face rosy with the coldness of the breeze, his hair ruffled over his forehead. She still loved him, there was no denying it.

'Bethan, what are you doing here?'

She longed to reach out to him, to touch his cheek and kiss his dear mouth.

'I had to come, I needed to know where you were, I wondered if you were living up here with *her*,' she lied smoothly. 'But it looks as if the place is deserted.'

'That's very strange, I can't believe Catherine would neglect the farm. What about the animals?'

She realized then that the concern in her husband's face had not been for her but for the O'Conner slut. 'The stock have all gone,' Bethan said tightly. 'There is no sign of the milking cows or anything other than the sheep roaming the hills.'

'But where can Catherine be? I'm worried about her.' Boyo said and Bethan was suddenly coldly angry with him. Had he no sensitivity? Here he was, calmly discussing the disappearance of his paramour with his wife, as though she had no feelings at all.

'Oh, I think I know where she's gone,' Bethan said quickly. 'It appears some sort of kinsman came over from Ireland looking for her, he has probably taken her away with him. I understand he is a very handsome young man.'

'I don't think Catherine or Liam Cullen would

abandon Honey's Farm,' Boyo said firmly. 'It has been in the family for such a long time that Catherine would not leave here unless she was forced into it. Perhaps I should go over to Ireland myself, see what I can find out.'

Stung, Bethan resisted the urge to goad Boyo further. 'That might be a very good idea.' She forced herself to speak evenly. 'It would certainly do no harm.' It would also give her the chance to study the affairs of the farm and to sort out what she should do with Catherine O'Conner; the girl was becoming more of a liability with every passing day.

She became aware that Boyo was looking at her strangely. 'You wouldn't know anything about her disappearance, would you?' he asked, his eyes narrowed with suspicion.

'Why should I know anything about the silly girl?' Bethan said, her head raised in challenge.

'I wonder what really brought you here, perhaps this place is up for sale, I wouldn't be surprised, the state it's in. Not interested in the farm yourself are you by any chance?'

'Are you mad? This run-down place, I wouldn't be so foolish. You forget, I was a businesswoman when you were still in baby clothes. No Boyo, it was to see if you were here. I have not heard from you for some time and believe it or not, *I* was worried about *you*.'

'I see.' Boyo looked out across the fields. 'I'm sorry, I should have let you know I was all right.'

With a feeling of relief, Bethan saw that he had accepted her story. As his eyes swept over Honey's Farm, Bethan felt she could read him well; he was considering putting in a bid for the place himself. Well, the bank was holding the deeds against the huge debts the O'Conner girl owed them. The weasel of a manager was in her power, a little matter of some misplaced funds at one time, over which she had not made too much of a fuss. She had reckoned, rightly, that the man's gratitude might prove useful at some later date.

'Come along, Uncle Tom,' she said taking the old

man's arm, 'I think we have stayed here too long, I see my husband is fine and does not need my concern. Let's go home, you are looking tired.'

She paused to glance at this man, this handsome stranger who was so much out of her reach, her husband. Her face softened. 'Perhaps you will come home with us, Boyo? My father is not at all well, I'm sure he would be happy to see you. After all, he still thinks of you as his son-in-law.' This was far from the case but it suited Bethan to pretend otherwise.

Boyo seemed to struggle with his reply and when he spoke, his voice was guarded. 'I don't really think it would be a good idea, Bethan.'

'Please. Uncle Tom and I could do with company on the way home, the nights are drawing in so early now aren't they? Makes me quite nervous to be on the road.'

He considered her words and then nodded. 'I'll follow your carriage.'

When she was seated in the creaking leather seat, she saw her uncle glance at her in exasperation. 'Why do you encourage that man?' he asked flatly.

'You forget, Uncle, that man, as you call him, is my husband.'

'Your estranged husband who seems to care more about the whereabouts of his strumpet than he does about you. Don't you see what he is up to?'

'I don't believe he can be up to anything, after all, *I* asked him to accompany us back to the house.'

'Well, I think he wants to look round the place, to find out if you have the girl hidden there. He is suspicious of you, my dear. Be careful your emotions do not override your good sense.'

She regarded her uncle carefully, could he be right? Was Boyo so cunning, so devious? Well, she would watch him, she would soon learn his real reason for going with her to Ty Craig.

'Perhaps you had better get back to your own house, you appear tired,' she said abruptly. 'I'll have the carriage take you there as soon as we reach Ty Craig. In the meantime you'd better think of a way of getting that girl off your hands.'

'Off my hands? But you said . . .' Tom's voice faltered for a moment as he looked at her in dismay. He was obviously choosing his words carefully. 'I had hoped you would come up with a solution to the problem, my dear.'

'Just keep her hidden for a while, leave her in that hovel until I get my hands on the farm and then you can have your men take her miles from here and dump her. By the time she makes her way back to Swansea she won't know what has happened to her.'

'Very well, perhaps that is the best way out of this mess. She could hardly find Jacob's place again, not unless she knew where to look.'

He paused, 'How long will it take you to complete the purchase of the farm do you think?'

'I'll buy as soon as I can possibly arrange it, I'll let you know. It can't be soon enough for me.'

Bethan was relieved when the carriage drew to a halt at the arched door of the house. She kissed her uncle and waved as the carriage rolled away along the drive. Taking a deep breath, she turned and smiled up at Boyo who had reined his horse alongside the doorway.

'I'll get a groom to see to the animal,' she said as the butler opened the door. 'Come along in, I'm sure you could do with something to eat and perhaps a nice strong glass of porter.'

She gestured to one of the maids to help Boyo off with his riding boots. 'See that they are polished at once.' Then, taking his arm, she led him through to the sitting-room where a cheerful fire burned in the large, ornate grate.

She felt his arm against her breast and hugged it closer. How she longed to throw herself into Boyo's embrace, to cling to him, beg him to come back to her. She almost spoke her thoughts out loud but then he extricated himself and took a seat near the fire.

'It's very cold in here, Bethan, perhaps the servants allowed the fire to go out and then rebuilt it before you returned.'

'Perhaps.' She did not tell him that Ty Craig was always cold; even when the sun shone into the garden the house remained in shadow. 'We will have some refreshment and then you can see father.' She smiled but she was watching his face carefully.

'Will you really go to Ireland to look for this girl?' She could not help but question him even though she knew his reply would probably hurt her.

'If she's not here in Swansea, then yes, I will go to Ireland.'

They talked about other matters over a tea of light sandwiches and small cakes and Bethan saw that he drank little of the fine wine she had served him. He was looking about him as though his eyes could see through the ceilings into the floors above.

'Would you like to see the improvements I've made to the house while I've been staying with Daddy?' she asked innocently. Boyo's gaze rested on her and there was a question in his eyes.

'Very much.' His reply was wary but she sensed the curiosity in his response.

'Then please, help yourself. Perhaps you would care to explore alone, I have some instructions to give to the servants. I have a guest for dinner this evening, a very important guest.'

He rose at once and she was disappointed that her hint concerning her guest fell on stony ground. She frowned, her thoughts bitter, he did not care if she entertained a regiment of men and took each and every one of them to her bed.

She watched him look into the ground-floor rooms and then make his way upstairs. Well, he would find nothing, his harlot was safely locked in a room far away from here. A glow of warmth filled her at the thought. What a pity the girl had not lost her memory, traumas sometimes had that effect. If that had happened, the girl could have remained where she was indefinitely and would probably have been used by the beast, Jacob. Such a fate would serve her right. The bitch had slept with Boyo without a qualm of conscience and doubtless she'd been intimate with this Irishman too. Living with a boor and a bully would be what her kind deserved.

Bethan found herself smiling at the thought of what Catherine's fate might be. Suddenly, for just a moment, she was appalled, wondering what was happening to her. Had she always been so vindictive and cruel? But no, none of this was her fault, it was the betrayal of her love that had made Bethan so bitter. After all she had been to Boyo he had turned to that strumpet with no breeding and no brains and had put her before his own wife.

Bethan went upstairs and looked into her father's room, he was asleep, his face turned into the pillow. Bethan was relieved, she did not feel up to coping with his ill humour should he learn that her husband was in the house.

Boyo returned after a time and stood before the fire, shivering a little. 'This is an odd house,' he said, 'it gives you the feeling of being watched.'

Bethan looked up at him, so he felt it too. 'Nonsense!' she said briskly. 'It's a very ordinary house.'

Boyo appeared not to have heard her. 'I suppose it's because there's no view, no outlook, nothing but the towering hills rising above the house.'

'Well, *you* do not have to live here, do you, so please do not criticize my family home.'

'I'm sorry, it was rude of me.' He frowned. 'How many cellars are there here?'

'Three; they are filled with discarded furniture and stores of wine. You can examine them, if you like, but if you have satisfied yourself that I am not hiding your little paramour in chains somewhere under my roof perhaps you'd better leave.'

She could see by the expression on his face that her barb had found its mark. He did not protest his innocence and somehow that only angered her more.

'Well, that's what you thought, isn't it?' she demanded. 'You imagined I had a hand in this girl's departure from

Honey's Farm, you might as well admit it.'

He looked down at her as though she was a stranger. 'You are remarkably interested in the farm,' he said, 'that in itself is suspicious.'

'Oh, Boyo,' deftly Bethan changed tack, 'if only you could see how empty my life is without you.' The words were spoken before she could think clearly but for once she knew she spoke the truth.

She began to cry, much to her own astonishment. After a moment's hesitation, Boyo took her in his arms and held her, smoothing her hair.

'I never meant to hurt you so badly, Bethan,' he said softly. 'I believed ours was a marriage of mutual respect and liking and perhaps of a little love. I never thought you would be so hurt when I . . .' his voice trailed away.

She looked up at him, her defences down. 'I know, Boyo, I thought our marriage was mainly one of convenience at first. But I grew to love you and to need you and now my life is empty without you.'

'I'm so sorry.' He kissed the top of her head and in that moment Bethan was tempted to tell him everything: how she'd had Catherine watched, how everything had gone wrong and how, in the end, Tom had called in a doctor to care for the girl. Surely Boyo would understand that none of this was Bethan's fault. She even opened her mouth to speak but then he released her, moving away from her, his shoulders bent, his eyes unwilling to meet hers.

'I love Catherine, God help me, I love her more than life itself. I can't help it, Bethan, I just can't help it.'

She drew herself up to her full height and forced back the tears. 'Go your own way to hell then and that slut with you.' She turned her back on him and did not look round even when she heard the door close quietly behind him.

She remained frozen for some minutes, hearing his voice in the hall as he asked the maid for his boots and she flinched as the outer door slammed.

The beat of horse's hooves on the gravel outside

seemed to echo within her and she sank down onto the carpet before the fire, trying to warm herself at the flames. But she was alone now, alone in a house with a sick old man, alone in a house that did not welcome her, where the ghosts of the past inhabited the rooms. She crashed her fist against the marble hearth.

'Catherine O'Conner, I could kill you!' Her words rang out harshly and Bethan almost believed she heard the sound of ghostly laughter echoing around her in the gloomy emptiness of the room.

CHAPTER SEVENTEEN

'Why are you keeping me locked up when all I want is to go home?' Catherine was sitting in a chair beneath the high window, her foot resting on a stool. The raw-boned woman who brought her food looked at her without expression.

'How can you go home when we don't know where you live?' She placed the bowl of thin stew on the rickety table.

'Can't I talk to whoever brought me here?' Catherine asked tightly, her hands gripped in her lap until her knuckles gleamed white. She longed to strike out at someone. 'Speak to me, damn it!'

The woman straightened and stared down at her with unwavering eyes. '*Duw*, cursing now, is it? Grateful to be waited on hand and foot like this, you should be, madam. Why, you even had a doctor in to look at you which is more than I've ever had.'

'But why am I being kept prisoner?'

'I told you, don't grumble, just think if you hadn't been found you might have died all alone in the wet and cold. A word of advice: just don't go asking questions. I can't answer nothing so you are wasting your time.'

'You can tell me your name, can't you?' Catherine said more quietly. 'You are the only person I see, it can't do any harm if I know what to call you, can it?'

'Winnie, that's my name, now are you satisfied?' The woman went to the door and looked back over her shoulder. She stared at Catherine, a long hard look and then her face softened.

'Look, love, your foot is getting better and your bruises are all but gone. Now just think, how would you have managed on your own? No doctor, no-one to bring you food and keep you warm, how long do you think you'd have lived if you hadn't been cared for by me? She nodded as though to reinforce what she was saying. 'Now just be grateful and show a bit of patience. You are a pretty girl, no real harm has been done to you and look, I'm sure you'll be able to go home soon, so be good and don't give me any trouble, right?'

When she was alone, Catherine looked around her helplessly. If only she could get out of this room she might find out where she was, she imagined she must be quite a few miles from Swansea, Winnie spoke with a different accent to that of the townsfolk.

She closed her eyes, the woman was right, of course, she would have died out there in the mud of the farm if someone had not taken her in. But unanswered questions still raced through her head.

With a sigh she fell back against the pillows. There was a gleam of hope now, Winnie had said that Catherine might be sent home soon; she hoped so, she could not stand this room for much longer.

And when she got home, what then? The farm would be in a dreadful state and the animals, what had happened to the milk cows? Had they all died of milk fever by now?

She was a failure, she had to face it, she had no money, no ability to run a farm properly and her love life was a mess. She was what her mother would call a loose woman.

Outside the window, darkness was closing in on the unremarkable landscape. Catherine was tired, so very tired. She climbed painfully onto the bed. It was cold in the room, she pulled the worn blankets over her and closing her eyes, she drifted into an exhausted sleep.

It was still dark when she woke to find Winnie beside the bed holding a lighted candle. Outside the birds were beginning to sing, it must be early morning.

'Get up, love, I thought you might like a bath.' Winnie's attitude seemed to have softened and Catherine felt a lift of hope, perhaps this was it, perhaps, at last, she was going home.

'I would love a bath, Winnie.' And she would welcome the chance to be out of the room where she'd been kept for what seemed an eternity.

Winnie helped her to her feet, 'There, see, you are nearly able to walk on your own now.' She helped Catherine through the open door into a spotless but spartan kitchen. There were bare flags on the floor and in the centre of the room stood a huge scrubbed table. To the side was a battered dresser full of oddments of crockery, but a cheerful fire burned in the grate and before it stood a tin bath filled with steaming water.

'If I can get you into the bath do you think you could stick your bad leg out of the water?' Winnie asked and Catherine resisted the desire to burst into hysterical laughter.

'I think I can manage,' she said shakily. It took a great deal of manoeuvring but at last. Catherine sank into the hot water with such a sigh of pleasure that Winnie's stern features relaxed into something of a smile. She leant over Catherine like a mother and began to wash her hands and arms.

'What's going to happen to me now, Winnie, am I to go home?' Catherine asked, taking advantage of the change in the woman's attitude.

'I don't know, love, all I have been told is that you are to be washed and dressed.'

'Am I to meet whoever brought me here, then?' Catherine asked eagerly and Winnie shook back a curl of grey hair that had fallen across her forehead.

'What a girl for asking questions; questions I don't know the answers to. Now shut up and let me wash your hair.'

Afterwards, Winnie brought her clothes, washed and pressed and mended, and helped Catherine to dress in them. A pair of boots, much mended, stood ready for her. Catherine's feet slipped into them easily, they were several sizes too big. She wondered what had happened to her own boots but that was not really of any importance now, she was going home.

As Winnie dragged the bath easily through the door, Catherine felt the rush of cold air and shivered. She huddled near the fire and then, lifting her head, became aware that someone was talking to Winnie outside.

Winnie returned and fetched one of her own shawls from the back of the door. 'Wear this, you're off out of here. Take care, love, just take care.'

Catherine stood quite still for a moment, unable to believe the suddenness with which she was being released.

'Go on then you daft girl, don't look a gift horse in the mouth.'

Galvanized into movement, Catherine hurried out of the kitchen into the dark of the early dawn. A man was standing in the shadows, holding the reins of a horse which was harnessed to a small cart.

'Get in, miss.' The voice was gruff, that of a working man. Catherine shivered in the misty dampness that hung over the land, obscuring the view.

'Where are we going?' she asked meekly. The man was silent for a moment.

'Swansea, miss. Get in the cart.' Catherine climbed awkwardly onto the cold, damp boards and as she sank back into the wooden seat, she felt relief pour through her; she was going home.

But home to what? On the heels of relief, she felt frightened for her future. The farm would be neglected, the house unused and damp, the fields would be overgrown with weeds. There would be a lot of work needed to get the land under control again and no money with which to accomplish it. And worse, out there, in the darkness, was someone who had attacked her and might attack her again.

As the cart jerked into motion, Catherine looked back at the building she was leaving. It was difficult to distinguish anything through the mist but she could see that the house was small, little more than a hut, and it was set against the folds of an unfamiliar hill. Where was this place where she had been kept? Still, it did not matter now, nothing mattered so long as she was free.

She was jolted against the hardness of the seat and she winced at the pain in her bruised bones, closing her eyes, telling herself that everything was going to be all right. She would soon be home.

She still could not quite believe it, after fearing the worst she had been released. Sometimes, in the dark of the night, she had believed that she would eventually be killed off in this remote place, Winnie had grumbled enough about what a trial she was.

The journey seemed endless, though she had no way of knowing exactly how many miles she had covered. Suddenly, the cart rocked as the driver climbed down from his seat. He took her arm and drew her unceremoniously onto the rough track. She grew tense, imagining that he would take an axe and put an end to her out here miles away from anywhere.

'Sorry, love, wheel is broken, can't take you any further.'

Catherine looked at him in alarm. 'But there's nothing wrong with the wheels, even I can see that.' As soon as she spoke, she regretted her words, why antagonize the man? She backed away from him, looking round her, trying to find some place she could run to.

The driver ignored her and swung himself into the driving seat, pulling at the reins so that the horse jerked forward in the shafts. Dust spurted up from the ground as the wheels turned and the cart began to move away from her at speed. She watched, long after horse and cart were out of sight, sighing with relief. She looked round at the hazy greyness of the land and it dawned on her that she had been abandoned miles from anywhere. But at least she was alive.

She stared around her at the empty hillside and the seriousness of her situation swept over her. Here she was, standing in the wet grass, in boots that were too big for her and a shawl that hung around her like a shroud, not knowing where she was.

'You are still alive.' She said the words aloud but

208

instead of giving her courage, her voice echoed away from her emphasizing her loneliness. She began to hobble forward, making her way with painful slowness over the uneven land. The drizzle had turned to heavy rain and the path leading uphill had become slippery with mud. If only she had some way of knowing which direction she should go in but the mist, if anything, was becoming more dense.

She struggled up the rise in the land. Once, slipping to her knees, her hands in the mud, she nearly cried out at the pain in her ribs but she bit her lip and got to her feet again.

At the brow of the hill, she looked around her, here the mist was even thicker. Nearby, Catherine could hear the sound of a brook. Was she near home? Was it the Burlais brook she could hear?

Some of the mist cleared for a moment and Catherine saw only unfamiliar land, spreading away as far as the eye could see. Her heart sank but she forced herself to go on towards the next hill. Would she see yet another unfamiliar hill and another and another? she wondered desperately.

At one point, she felt as if she would have to give up the attempt to reach home, her foot was aching so badly now that every step was painful. The too-large boots did not make things any easier. She took deep breaths considering her position, she could remain here, try to find a hollow tree or an outcrop of rocks where she could shelter. She looked round, peering through the rain that was falling now in heavy darts against her face. There was no friendly tree, no outcrop of rocks, there was nothing but the unrelenting countryside rolling away out of her sight.

She tried to buoy herself up with hope, Honey's Farm was her home, her refuge, once there she would be all right. She listed the homely chores she could do; light the fire, put on the kettle, make herself some tea. Most wonderful of all, she could climb into her own bed, in the room she had known since childhood, and sleep away her aches and pains. Then, when she was rested, she could try to work out how to bring the farm back to the thriving business it had once been.

She seemed to walk for hours, once she thought of changing direction but some instinct drove her on the same pathway. Exhausted now, barely able to stand, Catherine struggled on. She paused, tears running down her cheeks and she could not find the strength to brush them away.

She closed her eyes for a long moment, trying to picture her home, the farm, the hills sloping to the sea. The sea. She lifted her head, she smelt salt, she was close to the sea. Excitement filled her, she could not be far from Honey's Farm. With renewed hope, she walked on, numb now, ignoring the pain that every step brought her. She would be home, soon, she would be home and then everything would be all right. As she topped the rise, she saw the sea. It was there, spread out before her as she had known it would be but it was not the gentle tide that ran into Swansea harbour. The craggy rocks echoed to the buffeting of the waves and Catherine sank down on the ground, knowing that she was as far away from home as ever.

'Why have you done it?' Boyo said angrily. 'You told me you had no interest in the farm, you lied.' He strode to and fro in the gloomy sitting-room at Ty Craig, his hands thrust into his pockets. 'You have taken Catherine's home from her, deprived her of her livelihood; is your blood-lust satisfied now or do you have other schemes in mind?

'Don't be absurd, I didn't lie. It was you who put the idea of buying the farm into my mind. The place was up for sale and for a very good price. I might develop the land, save it from becoming nothing more than a wilderness.'

Bethan stared at Boyo coldly. 'Be reasonable. If this woman could not pay her debts that was her own fault, no-one could expect the bank to support her failures forever more.'

'So you moved in like a bird of prey and took away the only home she has ever had. I wondered why you were taking an interest in the place but I never suspected you of such a low, vicious desire for revenge.'

'Calm down, you are being melodramatic,' Bethan said. 'I saw a good prospect and I bought it, I am a businesswoman or have you forgotten?'

Boyo did not answer her question, he stared at her for a long time and shook his head. 'Did I ever know you? To think I even liked you – once.'

Bethan rose to her feet, the colour flaring into her face. 'Liked me? How kind of you, how very kind.' Her eyes glittered with tears.

'I *loved* you, Boyo, loved you, do you understand? I would have done anything for you but you had to sleep with a whore, shatter the marriage vows we made together. Can you blame me if I take back a little of what is owed to me?'

Boyo was silent. He stared at the woman who was his wife, would always be his wife if she had her way and anger swept over him in a powerful wave.

'I have never hit a woman but I feel I could make an exception in your case.' He turned on his heel and moved towards the door; there, he paused. 'So where is she now? Tell me that. No-one can find her, not even that cousin of hers. Cullen has searched Swansea from one end to the other, by all accounts, and drawn a blank. What have you done, how did you get her to leave the farm, for she would never leave willingly?'

'How do I know where the slut is?' Bethan turned away from him. Then, slyly, she looked up at him from under her lashes, 'Though I did hear a rumour . . .' She broke off apparently considering her words and Boyo waited in a fever of impatience. 'I did hear she had gone off with some ruffian, a common man of her own sort and is living with him somewhere far away from here. You see, she did not want you, after all, she's just a little whore who will go to any man's bed.'

'Liar!'

'Go and look for her then, if you are so sure.' Bethan shook him away. 'But I tell you this, you do not know the half of that woman. She sleeps with whomsoever she likes, she's been intimate with that Irishman as well as with you and why should she stop there? She's nothing but a slut, Boyo, will you never learn sense?'

Boyo left the coldness of the house but he did not feel the chill of the air. He was feverish with anger and with the need to find Catherine. He did not believe a word Bethan had said to him, she was out of her mind, a cruel vindictive woman and he was afraid she might have harmed Catherine in some way.

He mounted his horse and rode away down the track between the folding hills. He looked around him at the dripping trees and the boulder-strewn lane and shuddered, feeling as though he had just left a graveyard.

He rode his horse mercilessly over farmlands towards Rhosilli Downs. Even though Bethan no longer owned the inn, she knew the present owner well enough to beg a favour. Boyo felt sure she would have taken Catherine there, it would be the best place to keep her hidden until the sale of the farm was complete.

His horse was quivering with sweat by the time Boyo reined the animal in at the yard of the hotel. Here, the mists had cleared and the sea ran in to the long shoreline, white-capped and swift.

Inside the hallway, he paused as a discreet footman appeared at his side. 'I'm Todd, can I help you, sir?' The man wrinkled his nose and Boyo smiled at him disarmingly.

'I have been riding hard,' he explained, 'I could do with a hot drink and my animal needs attention.' He slipped some money into the man's willing hand. 'Is the owner here? It is important that I see him.'

'I am expecting him back at any time, sir, perhaps you would like to pay me in advance, sir?'

Boyo followed the man upstairs to the first floor and was shown into a room with a cheerful fire burning in the ornate fireplace.

'If sir would care to go into the dressing-room and

change into the robe that is provided then I could have your clothes laundered by morning, sir.'

Boyo shook his head. 'I will attend to that later. When the owner of the inn returns let me know at once.'

The man nodded and moved backwards through the door. 'How many rooms are there in the hotel?' Boyo asked suddenly. The man looked surprised.

'I don't rightly know, sir, about thirty, in all, I'd say.' He looked curiously at Boyo and there was a trace of disapproval in the way his mouth turned down at the corners. 'Is there any particular reason for the question, sir?' Todd's eyes were guarded.

'No, just idle curiosity.' Boyo palmed some coins into the man's hand which quickly disappeared into his pocket.

'The hotel has just changed hands, as it happens, the new owner is a man by the name of Mr Cousins, a gentleman from Devon, a good Quaker gentleman. Changing the place, he is, making it respectable, if you get my meaning. Now, if there's nothing else I can do for you?'

Todd withdrew and closed the door and Boyo waited a moment before crossing the room and pouring himself a drink from the decanter.

A quietness descended over the corridor outside and Boyo moved to the door, it might be as well to begin searching the place. If Catherine was here, which he was beginning to doubt in the light of what Todd had told him, she would be in an attic room away from prying eyes.

He opened the door carefully and looked out into the corridor, it stretched long and silent towards the curving staircase leading to the hall below. To his left and facing him was a door marked 'Private' and he made towards it as quietly as he could. As he thought, behind the door was a staircase, plain and carpeted in cheap jute; here, he felt sure, he would find the servants' quarters.

It did not take him long to search the upper floor, the rooms were empty, the servants would be working until the early hours. His spirits dropped as he saw there was no sign of Catherine's presence, no locked rooms, no evidence at all that anything untoward had happened here.

'Have you lost your way, sir?' He turned to see Todd looking at him with a careful expression on his face. Boyo decided to take a chance, it was clear he was getting nowhere alone.

'I'm looking for a young girl, a girl with red hair; Catherine her name is, have you seen her?'

Todd shook his head. 'No-one of that description in the hotel, sir and I know.' He smiled, 'The place is practically empty, the new owner's spoiled a good thing, the old customers liked the inn as it was. No, there is no young girl here, sir.'

'But has she been here; please, this is very important, I must find her.'

The man looked around quickly as though fearing being overheard. 'What's it worth to you, sir?' Todd said.

'It could be worth quite a lot of money, if you give me the right information,' Boyo said.

'Well, I heard of a young girl, such as you describe, being found sick, near to death like. Jacob, who is a bit . . .' Todd tapped his forehead meaningfully, 'he took her to the hovel he calls his house, had old Winnie take care of her.'

Boyo moved closer to him, his shoulders hunched threateningly. 'How do you know this? Why should she be brought all this way from her home?'

'The tale is common gossip, this is a small village, see. As for why and wherefore, I can't answer that, sir, but I tried to tell you that Jacob, he's a halfwit, see?'

Boyo stared hard at the man. 'Where does this "halfwit" live?'

'Dunno that, sir, I told you the gossip; that's all I know, honest, sir.' He held out his hand and Boyo thrust some money at him and pushed the man aside.

'My horse been stabled?'

'Aye, sir, nice and warm the creature is, rubbed down and fed, like a pig in clover he is.'

Boyo made his way down to the bar. Here, near the

fire, a few old men were sitting, obviously locals. One had a sheepdog at his side. Boyo sat down with them and ordered a round, getting information from them might take some time.

CHAPTER EIGHTEEN

The rain was beating down outside the window of his hotel room but Liam did not notice. Anger raged within him: Honey's Farm had been sold. First repossessed by the bank, it had later gone to the highest bidder, at least that was what he had been told. The fact that Catherine was missing did not seem to bother anyone, least of all that bastard Hopkins. Something crooked was going on, Liam was becoming more and more convinced that Catherine was being kept out of the way for some reason. He thumped the window-sill in frustration, he had been unable to find the remotest trace of Catherine's whereabouts, every lead became a dead end. Where in the name of all the saints was she?

The records of the sale named Mrs Bethan Hopkins as the new owner but clearly it was her husband who was behind the deal. Someone had been well-paid to put off all opposition. Liam leaned against the coolness of the glass; now he would have expert help, he had written to a big firm of lawyers in Cork, a firm with which his family had done business for years.

Seamus O'Sullivan had been trained in London, a clever man, a man who, some said, sailed pretty close to the wind to get what he wanted. Seamus had arrived that morning and was installed in the room next door, sifting through the evidence, as he put it.

Liam rubbed his eyes tiredly. Evidence? There was none. Had he not gone over and over every detail of Catherine's disappearance, asked questions until folks became impatient with him? Still Liam had every confidence that Seamus would ferret around, ask the right questions; at least now he had someone on his side. He returned to his chair and closed his eyes and the image of

Catherine rose to the surface of his mind. Where was she, was she lying hurt somewhere, injured, in pain? His imaginings tortured him. He sat up straight and stared down at his hands, at least he was confident that Seamus would sort out the petty crooks who seemed to be running things to suit themselves. Seamus could and would question the Hopkins pair directly, they would not fool him.

Liam had done his best, he had travelled the streets of Swansea, searched from the finest hotels to the seediest lodging-houses and there was no sign of her.

He looked down at the newspaper delivered to the hotel room every morning and the black print seemed to mock him. Why were there no headlines, no questions about the disappearance of an innocent young woman? He pushed the paper away from him. It fell to the floor and the pages fanned out across the carpet. He cursed angrily, bending to screw up the pages, then he hesitated as a name caught his eye.

His mouth dry, he lifted the paper and read the item in the business news; here it was, confirmation of his suspicions. A picture of Boyo Hopkins smiling into the camera stared up at him and he longed to punch the man's smug face.

The report said that Mr Hopkins was about to extend his business interests throughout Swansea and Liam knew exactly what that meant.

Hopkins wanted power over Catherine, he was offering a bribe in the shape of Honey's Farm. Perhaps that was exactly what she wanted; perhaps she was, even now, living with the man. Is that where she had been hidden away all this time? It seemed a likely enough explanation.

Liam closed his fists around the picture feeling a cold anger within him, an urge to choke the breath out of Hopkins, to force him to tell the truth for once in his shabby life.

He heard the clock in the foyer of the hotel strike the hour and rose to his feet. It was time he was on his way to meet Seamus in the foyer. He smoothed out the

217

newspaper report, it might prove useful to the lawyer.

'One day, Hopkins, I will make you pay for what you have done!' He spoke aloud but his words sounded hollow even to his own ears. He knew, if only he could have Catherine safe in his arms, he would be happy to forget that Boyo Hopkins had ever existed.

Catherine did not remember how long she had lain on the rough ground crying like a lost child but, at last, the sound of the birds in the trees and the twittering of small creatures in the grass penetrated her misery and she knew that it was morning. She pulled herself to her feet, she had to go on, try to find her way to the farm, there she could rest, get back her strength. Once she was fit she could begin the battle to put the farm on its feet again.

As she raised her head, she saw that a stout branch, fallen from one of the trees, lay in the grass beside her; the hand of providence was on her side. She took up the stick and leant on it gratefully.

'I'll make it home, somehow,' she said fervently. Slowly, she began the long walk, trying to ignore the pain in her foot, buoying herself up with images of her kitchen, the fire blazing in the grate, the table laid for tea, cups set on a pristine cloth and the familiar all-pervading scent of the farm around her.

She frowned, what if Cliff Jones hadn't been able to spare any time to work at Honey's Farm? The house would be unused and damp, the fields overgrown with weeds, the animals straying, uncared for. It would be an almighty task to begin again but she would do it somehow, she promised herself.

She looked up at the sky and tried to get her bearings. The town was at the edge of the sea, above it sprawled the farmlands, if she headed uphill, away from the coast, surely she would be going in the right direction.

She walked for what seemed hours, her pain numbed now, her movements slow; she tried to lift her mind above it all, to let some deep instinct lead her, there was nothing else she could do.

At last, she came to a familiar landmark, over to the other side of the valley rose the slopes of Kilvey. With renewed vigour, she moved on, forgetting the ache in her bones. She breasted the crest of a hill and tears of weakness came to her eyes, she was on the perimeter of Honey's Farm.

She was weak with joy as the whitewashed buildings came into sight. She paused for a moment, savouring the sight and then she headed towards the gate leading to the house. She pushed it open and took a few unsteady steps forward. The door stood open, the fire was lit and hope blossomed in Catherine's heart.

'Boyo?' her voice sounded strange in the silence. She looked around, the room was a shambles, stale crusts of bread littered the table, cups stood unwashed and she knew that whoever had been in her house, it was not Boyo Hopkins.

She sat down in the old rocking-chair, her head resting against the warm wooden back and, exhausted, she slept.

She was woken by the feeling that she was not alone. She turned, looking fearfully over her shoulder, remembering the way she had been so viciously attacked. She forced herself to move towards the door, her ankle was throbbing, like toothache. Her mouth was suddenly dry. She gave a small scream as the door sprung open and a man with a gun over his arm stood staring at her.

'What are you doing here, this is private property, can't you read?' He gestured towards a sign swinging outside on the fence and Catherine stared at it in disbelief.

'I can read.' She held herself upright with difficulty and faced the man. 'It says that this is private property and it is, it's my property.'

'And who do you think you are then?' The man was the bullying sort, thick of jaw and with a forehead that jutted aggressively over his narrow eyes.

'I'm Catherine O'Conner, I own Honey's Farm.'

He gave a slow, unpleasant smile. 'Not any more you don't, love.' He swung his arm in a wide arc. 'This dump

219

belongs to the Hopkins family, though why they should want it I don't know.'

'No! Catherine protested, 'Honey's Farm is mine, I haven't sold it to anyone.'

He shrugged. 'That's not what I've been told. Now clear off before I set my dogs on you.'

'But I've nowhere to go.' Catherine fought the despair that threatened to engulf her, she was tired, so very tired.

'You could always stay here, I suppose.' The man was looking at her carefully. 'If you was putting yourself out to be nice to me like.'

Wearily, Catherine shook her head, she hobbled past the man, wanting only to get away from him. Her eyes were stinging, her head ached, she shivered as though she had a fever. Outside the house, she looked out over the hills she loved, the farm which had been hers, the one place she felt she belonged and she flung back her head and screamed out her fear and pain.

'Clear off you mad bugger!' She heard the panic in the man's voice, he thought she was deranged, perhaps she was.

She stumbled away from the farmhouse, downhill towards the town, her throat ached and she felt she could not go on. Almost blindly, in a daze of pain and despair, Catherine found herself back in the streets of Swansea.

Beaten, she leaned against the window of the Grenfell Emporium, wondering if she could pluck up enough courage to go inside and ask for help. She rested her head against the cool glass, her eyes staring into the dim interior and, slowly, she realized that the windows of the emporium were grimy, streaked with dust; the place was empty, closed up, fallen into disuse.

It had begun to rain; heavy, spiteful drops of rain that stung her face and ran down her neck with the chill of icy fingers. Catherine closed her eyes, feeling the sounds of the street receding into the distance; she was weak and ill and she had nowhere to go.

The door of the emporium opened, Catherine heard the jangle of keys. 'Are you all right?' The voice was familiar, Catherine forced herself to concentrate.

'You'd better come with me.' Hari Grenfell's face swam into focus. She took Catherine's arm and led her towards a cab that stood at the curb. Listlessly, she sank back into the cold leather of the seat. 'Good thing I came to check if there was any mail here for me.' Mrs Grenfell's voice echoed faintly in Catherine's ears.

The cab journey was short but Catherine would not have minded how long it was, she was warm and dry and someone else was taking charge of her life.

The cab jolted to a halt outside the imposing exterior of Summer Lodge, a very different Summer Lodge to the one Catherine had admired from afar. It had been altered, the façade had been changed so that the once grand house now appeared to be an emporium.

'As you can see, Catherine,' Hari said, 'my home is now my place of work; you might have heard gossip about my misfortunes. Anyway, it's a long story, I'll tell you about it some time. For now, what you need is care and attention.'

She helped Catherine along a passageway towards the back of the building and into a small suite of rooms. 'This is where my ladies have their rest times. The stove is kept alight day and night, otherwise the rooms become very cold.' Hari sounded cheerful, her voice was normal, as though bringing a desperate woman into her home was an everyday occurrence.

She handed Catherine a cup of tea and then set about stoking up the fire. It was only when she had washed her hands that she sat with Catherine, looking at her with obvious sympathy. 'It's clear you are very distressed, Catherine, do you want to talk about it?'

Catherine shook her head. Hari leaned forward and put her hand on her arm. 'Your mother and father were well respected in the area, surely you can trust me to offer a helping hand?'

'No-one can help,' Catherine said. 'I have lost the farm and I don't know how it happened.' She shrugged, 'I know well enough what it means though: that I no longer have a home.'

221

'Tell me about it, perhaps things are not so bad as you seem to think. Possibly I might be able to help.'

Catherine shook her head. 'It's too late, the farm has been taken from me, I can only think it's because of my debt to the bank.' She paused and looked at Hari Grenfell. 'I have nothing, no home, no money and no friends.'

'Look, there's nothing so bad that we can't make it better.' Hari smiled reassuringly. 'For now you can stay here in the house, that's if you don't mind the girls coming to and fro to make tea during the shop hours. At least you can spend the night in warmth and safety and try to work out exactly what you are facing.'

Catherine looked around her at what seemed to be a haven of peace. 'Thank you, Mrs Grenfell.' There was a constriction in Catherine's throat.

'There's food in the kitchen, bread and a little cheese,' Mrs Grenfell said. 'In the morning, I'll bring supplies from my own kitchen upstairs. In the meantime, I'll find out all I can about the farm, I have my own sources of information and they are usually reliable.'

She patted Catherine's arm. 'It seems that things have changed a great deal for both of us. Don't look so lost, I'm sure if there is any misunderstanding, it can soon be cleared up.'

She rose and moved towards the door. 'And by the way, there are some of my things in the wardrobe in the bedroom, a few skirts and coats that I wear when I help out on the shop-floor. Take what you need, I think we are about the same size.'

Catherine looked down at her clothes ruefully, they were wet and mud-stained; she tried to stand and then the room seemed to swim around her. She suppressed a small cry and falling back into her chair, clutched her ankle.

Hari shook her head. 'You are hurt, why didn't you tell me?' she knelt and unlaced the over-large boots. 'My Lord, will you look at that.' Hari stared in consternation at Catherine's bruised and swollen ankle.

'My dear child, you shouldn't be walking about on this.' She leaned back on her heels. 'That was a stupid thing to say, you obviously had no choice in the matter.'

Deftly, Hari washed and then bound the swollen ankle. 'I'm not the best nurse in the world but at least that will make you feel a little easier.'

'You are so kind but I'll repay you, I promise you,' Catherine said in a thick voice.

'Look, my dear, I needed help myself these past weeks. When you reach rock-bottom, there is usually someone to help you up again. Now, I think it might be as well if you were to get into bed and try to rest. Is there anything else you want before I go?'

Catherine shook her head, her throat was full of tears though her eyes were hot and dry.

'Try not to worry too much,' Hari seemed reluctant to leave her alone, 'I'm going to lock up, now.' She smiled, 'Things will seem a lot brighter in the morning, I promise you.'

When Hari had gone, Catherine made her way, with painful slowness, towards the bedroom. The bed was covered in a bright quilt and the pillows were fresh and clean and smelt of lavender. Gratefully, Catherine took off her clothes and slid between the sheets. She turned on her side, buried her face in the pillow and slept.

'I wanted to bring her up here with me.' Hari sat at the long dining table, cramped in the small rooms of the upper-floor apartment, barely touching the food on her plate. 'Poor child, she looks so lost and alone.'

Craig looked at her with wise eyes. 'Nothing changes, does it, my love?'

'I don't know what you mean,' Hari said, pretending to be offended.

'I mean that you were always on the side of the under-dog and you still have enough humanity to show the rest of the world how shabby it can be.'

'Nonsense,' Hari said briskly. 'How could anyone turn away the poor child? You should see her, Craig, bedraggled and woebegone, her foot badly swollen and signs of bruising around her face. Something has happened to that girl, something she doesn't wish to talk about.'

'Well, you have done all you can, you have provided her with food and shelter and tomorrow, I've no doubt, you'll set about interfering in her affairs. That's the sort of woman you are.'

Hari laughed suddenly. 'I don't know why I put up with you, you insult me, you make fun of me and somehow, in spite of it all, I still love you very much indeed.'

'Quite rightly.' Craig took up his glass and watching him, Hari thought what a handsome man he still was. There was a touch of grey at his temples, there were creases around his mouth but his lips were still as tantalizing as ever; his body strong, his shoulders broad.

'Remember how we first met?' She leant her chin on her hands and stared across the table at him.

'How could I ever forget? There you were, a scared little rabbit, standing in the kitchen of the house at World's End. You were staring at me with those huge eyes and yet defying me at every turn in spite of your fear.'

'And you looked like a wild man,' Hari retorted. 'Hair hanging over your shoulders, your clothes in tatters, I thought a mad man had come into my kitchen.'

'I think I fell in love with you then.' Craig spoke soberly. 'I had never met a girl like you, a girl of spirit, of fire as well as beauty.'

'Go on, I was far beneath you,' Hari said softly. 'I was Angharad Morgan, shoemaker's daughter and you were the great Craig Grenfell, owner of a thriving leather business.'

'Ah! But I was also a convicted criminal, accused of betraying the trust of my shareholders. But you believed in my innocence, I'll never forget that, not if I live to be a hundred.'

He rose from the table and took her hand, drawing her from her chair. 'Come here, I want to make love to you.'

He kissed her neck, his mouth warm and Hari responded, as she always did, to his touch.

'Have I ever told you how much I love you?' he whispered against her hair. He placed his hands on her cheeks and looked down at her. 'Don't ever leave me, will you, Hari? And don't ever change from the lovely, loving woman you are.'

She closed her eyes and leaned against him. 'I want to go to bed with you.' She whispered the words though no-one else was there to hear her.

In the bedroom, she fell across the silk quilt. 'What would our strait-laced neighbours think of us?' she giggled. 'Behaving like children at our time of life.'

'I think the neighbours must be used to our funny ways by now, Hari, don't you? In any case, we have much more interesting things to do than talk about them.'

His mouth was hot on hers and her laughter vanished as she clung to him, loving him, wanting him as much as she had when she was seventeen years old.

'You'd better start talking before I beat the living daylights out of you!' Boyo shook the man, his hands around his skinny throat. 'Talk to me, where is she? Where is Catherine O'Conner?'

'Leave him alone.' The voice rang out behind him and Boyo, turning, saw a tall woman bearing down on him, her sacking apron flapping in the wind. 'Jacob don't know nothing, I'll tell you what I know but leave the boy alone.'

Boyo released the man so suddenly that he fell on his back into the mud of the yard.

'The girl was brought here by Jacob and it's grateful to him you should be, not shaking the living daylights out of him. Bad she was, hurt, like; I cared for her as if she was my own.'

'Where is she now?' He strode towards the small hut and held his breath at the meanness of the place. Through an open door, he saw a narrow bed and his heart contracted in fear as he thought of Catherine lying there sick and in pain.

'Where is she now?' He repeated the words in a hard voice and the woman looked away.

'Gorn 'ome I suppose, left here some days ago.'

'How? Did she walk? Was she driven? Speak, woman.'

The woman swallowed hard. 'Jacob took her in the cart, wheel broke though and he had to let her off, somewhere between here and Swansea. She'd be 'ome by now I 'spects.'

'You said she was sick, hurt. What happened to her and was she taken proper care of?'

'Don' know what happened but we had the doctor to her. Not too bad, she wasn't, just bruises like.'

'And who paid for the doctor?' Boyo said quickly, too quickly. The woman looked away.

'Came for nothing, friend of mine, see. She's not here now though and I can't tell you no more.'

It was clear that there was more behind the story than the woman was prepared to tell, someone had paid her very well to keep her mouth shut.

He caught the skinny young man by his collar. 'You are coming with me, you are going to show me exactly where you took Catherine.' He turned for a moment to glance back at the hut and he shuddered. 'Come on,' he said harshly to the cowering man, 'the sooner we get on our way the better.'

Catherine woke to the sound of birdsong and, at first, when she opened her eyes, she thought she was home in Honey's Farm, safe in her own bed. Then the unfamiliar room came into focus, the light of the morning spreading patterns across the bed. Catherine blinked and sat up straight and memories came flooding back. She was destitute, she had lost everything.

She rose and washed quickly, shivering in the cold bedroom. Tentatively, feeling as though she was prying, she opened the wardrobe and took out a few of Hari Grenfell's clothes. After a moment, she selected a clean blouse and a dark, sensible skirt and a neat jacket which buttoned all the way down the front from throat to hip.

226

It was warmer in the small living-room, the stove was still alight but it was clear it would need stoking. Careful not to damage the borrowed clothes, Catherine built up the coals and soon the stove began to roar like a beast, the flames bursting into comforting life.

With tea on the way, Catherine began to feel her spirits rise. She moved to the small window and looked out at the green of the grounds around the big house. She felt hope rise within her, perhaps today Hari Grenfell would learn something more about the farm. She was a powerful lady, there was no doubt about that, but even Hari Grenfell could not claim back the farm for Catherine if it really had been sold.

Soon Catherine began to hear sounds of movement on the shop-floor, the girls were arriving for work, chattering voices drew nearer to the door and then the room seemed full of people.

'*Duw*, what are you doing here. New girl, are you?' A tall thin young woman was looking down at Catherine with some surprise, her rather elegant hat slipping from her head, her coat buttoned unevenly so that the hem dipped lopsidedly over her thin legs.

'I'm just staying here for a few days,' Catherine explained, liking the girl's open expression and strangely odd appearance.

'I'm Doreen Meadows, chief hatter here, though you wouldn't think of it to look at me would you?' she said ruefully. 'Cup of tea on the go, is there, love?'

Catherine refilled the kettle. 'Sorry, I seem to have drunk the potful.'

'Don't be sorry, that's my salvation first thing in the morning, a nice cuppa, couldn't come to without it. Aye, as I was saying, I'm chief hatter, make the designs and supervise the cutting and shaping, been doing it all my life. These young things here work in the glove department, noisy lot they are too.'

A few of the girls stared at Catherine in curiosity but Doreen flapped them away with her hands. 'Go on then, the work won't do itself, mind. There's shelves to be filled, chairs to be dusted, plenty of things to do before the customers start arriving.'

When they were alone, Doreen turned her cheerful smile on Catherine. 'How come you're staying here, then?' Doreen looked neat now in a black skirt and matching jacket which, with care, she had buttoned correctly.

'I had nowhere else to go.'

'Right, that sounds like the boss.' Doreen was making a futile effort to tidy her bird's nest of hair. 'Bugger it, it will have to do, the customers won't be looking at my kisser anyway. Too busy looking down their noses at the likes of me to actually notice me.'

'Don't you live in, any of you?' Catherine asked and Doreen shook her head.

'No spare rooms here except these few. In any case, Mrs Grenfell takes on married women, mostly, like me, with sick husbands or no husbands at all. Lets us all live out 'cos it's handy-like for the kids. Don't moan if we have to take a day off now and then, don't dock our pay, either. Marvellous woman Mrs Grenfell, not many bosses like her about. Well, I suppose I'd better be getting my girls organized or there will be no orders filled this side of Christmas!'

When Doreen had departed, the room seemed strangely empty and Catherine refilled the kettle. She needed hot water to wash up the accumulation of cups and saucers. Apart from the ache in her ankle, Catherine felt almost normal, as if she was beginning to rejoin the human race.

It was late afternoon when Hari Grenfell let herself quietly into the rooms at the back of the emporium. She seated herself in a chair and folded her gloves in her lap. It was clear she had just returned home from town and had news for Catherine.

'Have you found out anything?' Catherine could hardly breathe for the suspense she felt as she waited for a reply to her question. Hari looked at her for a long moment.

'It seems that there were two bidders for the farm.' Her words fell into the silence and Catherine felt her heart sink; so it was true her home was gone for ever.

'Who were they?' tears threatened to run, humiliatingly, down Catherine's cheeks.

'One, the successful bidder, was Mrs Hopkins, wife of Boyo Hopkins who owns the local tannery.'

Catherine bit her lip. So Boyo's wife had bought the farm, though what interest she had in farming was a mystery.

'The other interested party was someone I don't know,' Hari said, 'a Mr Liam Cullen from Ireland.'

'I see.' Catherine was silent. Liam and Boyo, both of them wanting to take her home from her, to make her beholden to them. Well, they could both go to hell, they would find she could not be bought, not at any price.

'Mrs Grenfell, do you think you could find me a job here?' she asked. 'I know I'm ignorant of shop work, I don't know if I would fit in but I promise I would do my best to be a good worker.'

'Of course I can find you a job and I'm sorry about the farm, I know it's been in the family for a long time.'

'Well, that's in the past, I have to make my own way in the world now. I've been frightened, I've felt beaten and ill-used, now I am just angry and I am determined to make my life a success without depending on any man.'

Hari smiled. 'You remind me of myself when I was your age,' she said softly.

'Well, I don't think I have a chance of being as successful as you, Mrs Grenfell.' Catherine's tone was rueful. 'You are talented, poised and beautiful, I'm just a simple farm girl, a foolish girl, putting my trust in faithless men. From now on I'm going to put all my energies into working and making something of myself.'

'Don't be too hard on men,' Hari said, 'they are not all rogues and despots.'

'I know,' Catherine said, 'I can't blame anyone but myself for what's happened. But I was a fool, I gave too freely of myself and I realize it doesn't pay.'

Hari Grenfell sighed and shook her head. 'You will get over your bitterness in time. You are a lovely young

229

woman, with the most glorious hair and such looks that would turn any man's head. One day, you will find true love. In the meantime, like me, you need to be your own woman.'

Mrs Grenfell rose to her feet. 'Take this week to recuperate from your accident and then you can start work in the store. You will start at the bottom as all my ladies did, you will be making the tea and cleaning the floors at night. Show aptitude and you will earn promotion. For the time being, until you are better suited, please treat these rooms as your home.'

Catherine watched as Hari took up her gloves and moved to the door. 'Mrs Grenfell, thank you for giving me this chance, you won't regret it, I promise you.'

When she was alone, Catherine stared around her, she had a home and she had a job, at least that was a start. She was well aware that Mrs Grenfell took in women who were lame ducks but, she thought, she would rise above it, she would drag herself up out of the mire and, one day, she would show the world what she was really made of.

CHAPTER NINETEEN

'What do you mean, someone is out to make trouble for me, who is it?' Bethan stared at her solicitor, her brow furrowed, anger surging through her.

'This man, this kin of Catherine O'Conner's, he wishes to have an inquiry into the way the farm was sold.'

'I see, you mean that Irishman, Cullen. Well, Riddler, if you can't deal with this person yourself, then perhaps I can.'

'Take care, Mrs Hopkins, you must handle this with caution. Please do not do anything hasty.'

'Caution? Don't be so weak-kneed, man, this Irish fellow needs to be drummed out of town. Who does he think he is, coming here and dictating to his betters?' Bethan glared at the man and he looked away, unable to meet the scorn in her eyes.

'Liam Cullen,' the solicitor said uneasily, 'is no fool and you and I know that the sale was rather . . . rather . . .' his words trailed away and Riddler rubbed his nose anxiously.

'Rather hasty? So what? There's nothing to worry about, not if you keep your nerve. Where will I find this Cullen fellow?'

'He's staying at a hotel in town, he is a very rich and influential young man. He has brought a clever Irish lawyer over here with him; he means to make trouble, I think it would be just as well to placate him.'

'You could be right.' Bethan rose to her feet. 'The name and address of this hotel, if you please.'

Riddler sighed and tore a leaf from his notepad, writing hurriedly. 'Again, I urge you to be cautious.' He looked at her but avoided her eyes. 'You must be seen to be an honourable businesswoman, there can be no hint of

231

anything untoward.'

'I am well aware of that, I am not an idiot.' Bethan gave him a withering glance. 'I had expected more guts from you but there, you are a mere man, easily outwitted. Good day to you.'

Outside, Bethan waved away the coach driver and began to walk towards the Castle Hotel. A pale sun was shimmering through the trees but Bethan did not notice, she had more important matters to think about.

She found Liam Cullen in residence. A servant showed her into the plush sitting-room where a few middle-aged men and an elderly lady working at her needle-point were sitting.

'That's Mr Cullen there, madam.' The servant pointed to a young man with reddish hair relaxing near the sunny window.

Bethan saw that he was immersed in a newspaper and she studied him for a moment noting his youth and his clear pale complexion. He would be very easy to manipulate, she had no doubt.

'Mr Cullen?' She spoke gently, almost hesitantly and he was on his feet immediately offering her his chair. She sat on the edge of the chair as if she was nervous and when she spoke again, it was with a tremor in her voice.

'I'm sorry to intrude like this but I had no choice.' She glanced up at him from under her lashes and saw a look of concern on his face that gladdened her heart; this was going to be easier than she had anticipated.

'I'm Mrs Hopkins, Boyo is my husband.' She swallowed hard, congratulating herself on the effect she was having on the young man. She drew a shuddering breath before speaking again.

'He urged me to buy Honey's Farm in my name but he put up the money. He has a moral right to the place. What I fear is that it will become a love-nest for him and for his . . . his . . .' she broke off and fumbled in her bag for a handkerchief.

'Please, can I get you something, a glass of water, tea? To be sure, you look very pale.' Liam Cullen was bending over her and Bethan sat up straighter.

'I'll be all right, all I need is your co-operation.'

'In what way?' Liam asked taking a chair and drawing it closer to her.

'Bide your time, call off your ideas of an inquiry.' She dabbed at her eyes. 'I know that Miss O'Conner wishes to live at the farm with my husband and that is what I do not want. I want him back, Mr Cullen.'

She saw the rush of mixed emotions on the young man's face and she felt a sense of triumph. She remained silent, waiting for him to speak.

'But how will biding my time help? Sure I can't see the sense in that, begging your pardon, Mrs Hopkins.' Liam Cullen spoke doubtfully.

'I fancy that if they live together they will soon learn how mismatched they are. If I have time on my side perhaps I can win him from her. He thinks they'll be happy together but it will not work, not in the long run.' She paused, 'One thing is certain, if obstacles are put in their path they will fight all the harder to be together.'

'And you feel that by demanding an inquiry, I will drive them into each other's arms,' Liam said in his soft Irish brogue.

Her lips trembled, a masterly touch, she felt. 'Yes, don't you agree?' She paused and looked up at him waiting for a reply. When there was none forthcoming, she continued speaking.

'Catherine O'Conner wants Honey's Farm, she also wants my husband, this way she can enjoy them both.'

Liam rose and paced across the room, his hands thrust into his pockets, his brow furrowed. At last he came to stand before her, looking down at her in a way that made Bethan feel uncomfortable.

'You know what I think, Mrs Hopkins?' Liam spoke softly, leaning towards her and, instinctively, she pressed herself back into her chair. 'I think you wanted this farm very badly and you used every trick in the book to get it.'

Bethan rose and looked down at her feet. 'I am sorry but you have misread my intentions.' It was imperative that she kept up the façade of a woman in trouble, pleading for help. 'You must do whatever you think fit, of course. I am just sorry I have taken up your time.'

She left the hotel and made her way back into the street clenching her hands into fists. She stood for a moment looking across the busy road, hearing the roar of the traffic, without really noticing the noise. So Liam Cullen was not as gullible as she had imagined. Well, now she would have to adopt stronger measures to persuade him of the folly of his ways.

She smiled to herself, there was more than one way to skin a rabbit. She realized she was enjoying the sensation of doing battle, she felt charged with life as she had not been in a long time. She was changing, she was aware of that. She had never been a prissy miss, she had always had the courage of her convictions but marriage had softened the edges of her character, happiness had made her a nicer woman, or should she say a more malleable woman? Well, she would not be manipulated any longer, she had bought Honey's Farm and, shortly, she would offload it. Liam Cullen did not yet realize it but he had arrived on the scene just a little too late.

Liam sat for a long time, staring into the empty sitting-room, unaware of the furniture or of the sunshine slanting in the window, unaware of the sound of the birds in the garden or the tinkle of teacups from the dining-room. He was pondering over his conversation with Mrs Hopkins, she had been out to fool him into delaying his hand, keeping quiet until whatever plan she was hatching was complete.

Yet on reflection, it did make sense that Catherine would want to keep Honey's Farm and if that entailed selling herself to a married man, then perhaps that was a sacrifice she was willing to make.

He frowned, would it be a sacrifice or did she want to be with this man, whatever it cost her? He was restless, his efforts to find her had come to nought, it might well be that she did not wish to be found. But if only he could talk to her again, try to persuade her that he could offer her not only a successful farm in Ireland but the respectability of marriage too.

The most likely way to find Catherine was to seek out Hopkins. If Boyo's wife had told even a fraction of the truth, then her husband would know exactly where Catherine was.

Liam could not find Seamus anywhere in the hotel, the lawyer must be out working on his case, perhaps he would have more information by the time they met up again in the evening.

Outside, the pavement was damp with rain but the shower had been brief and now vapour was rising into the air as the sun warmed the streets.

Liam raised his hand to summon one of the cabs that stood waiting outside the hotel. As he climbed aboard, he gave the driver the address of Hopkins's offices in town and then sank back in his seat. Something was very wrong, his uneasiness was growing, he had a gut feeling that Catherine was not with Hopkins but soon he would prove it one way or another.

Hopkins agreed to see him immediately which came as a surprise to Liam. He had expected to be kept waiting in the elegant hallway of the ornate old building. As he rose and made his way towards the inner office, Liam could not help noticing the rich panelling and the patina on the old wood that covered the walls of the corridors. It was clear that Boyo Hopkins was a very rich man indeed.

Boyo did not rise to greet him, he simply gestured for Liam to take a seat on the opposite side of his enormous desk. He appeared relaxed, in complete control of the situation and why shouldn't he, the man was holding all the cards?

'How can I help you?' He spoke strongly in a fine English accent that denoted a man of letters and yet had he not once been just a simple tannery worker? In spite of himself, Liam found he had a grudging admiration for Hopkins.

'I want to know where Catherine is,' Liam said, his voice giving nothing away. If Hopkins could play his cards close to his chest then so could he, Liam thought.

'You have echoed my own thoughts exactly.' The answer was quietly spoken but rang with truth. Liam frowned.

'Then she is not with you?'

'I only wish she was.' Hopkins was still relaxed but his eyes were alive, taking everything in. 'What made you think I would know where Catherine was hiding herself?'

'Is that what she's doing then, hiding herself?' It was like a game of cat and mouse, neither man willing to give too much away.

'You tell me. Look, Mr Cullen, I don't know why you are here. If I knew where Catherine was I would be with her, it's as simple as that.'

'Are you not concerned with finding her, then?' Liam asked, his composure slipping a little.

'Of course I am concerned. I have tried to trace Catherine without success. I had almost come round to believing she was with you.'

'It seems we were both barking up the wrong tree.' Liam leaned forward.

'Your wife came to me, begging me to call off my inquiry into the sale of Honey's Farm. Why did she do that, have you any idea?'

Boyo's eyes narrowed. 'I have no idea and I am not in the mood to speculate on what my wife does. I would appreciate it if you would keep my wife out of this.'

'How can I? She told me that you and Catherine wished to set up home on the farm, is that true?'

'I would like nothing better than to set up home with Catherine but it would not be on a farm, I assure you.' He rose, he was a big man, well-built, handsome, no wonder Catherine was in love with him.

'I suggest we conclude this meeting, neither of us appears to be gaining anything from it.'

Liam rose and walked to the door. There, he turned and looked back at Hopkins. 'Sure 'tis an awful thing to ache to hold a woman in your arms again, to make love to her – again.'

He saw Hopkins wince at his words and Liam knew that his barb had struck home. 'Why don't you keep out of her life?' Liam's tone was harsh. 'I offered Catherine the one thing you could not, a respectable marriage.' Liam wanted to turn the knife, 'She was sweet and loving and I want to taste that again. I want her to bear my children. I want to put a ring on her finger.'

Boyo was staring at him with anger. 'Are you sure you do not mean through her nose?' he said. 'Now good day to you, Mr Cullen, you have taken up enough of my time.'

Liam left the office feeling his satisfaction fade, what had he gained? Nothing except to score a cheap point over a man who quite obviously loved Catherine as much as he did, judging by the expression in his eyes.

Liam looked around wishing he had the power of second sight, the power to search out Catherine with his mind and bring her to him from wherever she was. A dray rumbled past him, too close for comfort and turning, Liam began to walk back to his hotel.

As he entered the faded portals of the Castle Hotel he was confronted by two burly constables. They flanked him in a way that could only mean trouble and Liam felt his hackles rise.

'Yes?' He tensed as one of the men moved a little closer to him.

'Mr Cullen, Mr Liam Cullen?' The man seemed to tower above Liam, his moustache quivered, as though with anticipation, and Liam's gut reaction was to flee.

'I'm Sergeant Meadows, this is Constable Danby, we want to ask you a few questions, sir, that's all.' The constable smiled almost apologetically.

'Right then, ask,' Liam said, standing his ground, blocking the exit to the street.

'Wouldn't you be more comfortable in your room, less public-like, sir?'

'Just state your business,' Liam said. 'What do you want with me?'

237

'It is a matter of a gold-and-diamond pin, a pin belonging to a Mrs Hopkins. Do you deny she came to see you this morning?'

Liam began to see what was happening, Mrs Bethan Hopkins wanted him out of the way, she wanted to stop him making an issue of the way the sale of the farm had been handled.

Before he could stop to reason, he had spun on his heel and was out of the door, racing along the street, dodging between the traffic, putting as much distance between himself and the two policemen as he could.

He ran down narrow courts and through buildings long unused and at last found himself in the Strand, a long road that led towards the docks, a road that teemed with seedy lodging-houses. He paused for breath, leaned against a crumbling wall and tried to think clearly. The woman had set him up, that meant she was afraid, really afraid of being found out.

Sweat ran into his eyes as, more slowly now, he made his way into a public bar that was empty, except for the surly landlord. He took a drink, then sank into a corner seat and waited for his heartbeat to return to normal.

Liam sipped the warm ale and leaned back closing his eyes and he knew, in that moment, that in running away from the police he had made the biggest mistake of his life.

Catherine began to settle into the life of the emporium with an ease which surprised her. She rose early and cleaned the fixtures and fittings on the various floors of the lovely old house. She made tea and sandwiches, chatting familiarly with the other girls and as the days passed, she came to feel that she was part of a family once more.

'Hey there, Cath,' Doreen came into the back room and flopped into a chair, 'give us a cuppa, there's a love.'

Catherine smiled, Doreen and she had become friends, drawn together by loneliness. Doreen had been a much-loved child before her disastrous marriage to a policeman. She had served only half her apprenticeship as a milliner when her parents both died in the flu epidemic that had swept through Swansea, the same epidemic that had taken Catherine's sister's life.

Doreen never stopped singing the praises of Mrs Grenfell who had taken her on in faith, given her a new aim in life and money of her own in her pocket.

'What's happening then, love, not getting into a rut are you?'

Catherine looked at her friend sharply. 'What do you mean?'

'I mean where is the fire in your belly? Why aren't you out there fighting tooth and nail to get your place back?'

Catherine sighed. 'Doreen, you only know a little bit of the story.' She pushed the teapot across the table. 'I have no money, what can I do about the farm?'

'You can go to the bank, that's what;' Doreen spoke calmly, 'get them to make you a loan. It can be done, you know.'

Catherine shook her head doubtfully. 'It was because of the loan from the bank that I lost the farm.' She shook her head. 'It's all signed and sealed, I've lost my home for ever.'

'Well, there's still no need to lie down like a sick cat and take a beating. Fight for what you want, girl!'

Catherine leaned on her elbows, perhaps Doreen was right, perhaps she should be doing something about her future. But then what did she want? She no longer knew. It was comfortable to work in the store, surrounded by girls who accepted her as one of them.

'You are not the sort to spend the rest of your life indoors, mind.' It was as if Doreen had read her mind. 'You are cut out for the open land and the sun and the good earth beneath your feet. Don't settle for second best.'

'I may not be cut out for shop work but at least I won't starve,' Catherine said wryly.

'No, but you might fade away with boredom. Sort out your future while you are young, love, you don't want to be working for someone else for the rest of your life, do you?'

Catherine rose to her feet. 'Doreen, the farm failed because I was not good enough at working it, I might as well face the fact that even if I did get it back the same problems would be there waiting for me.'

'Well, if you are sure in your mind that this is what you want, then you will do your best at it but think on what I've said and think hard.'

The door opened and the two unmarried shop girls came into the room. They were sisters, alike and well-groomed, their clothes ironed to perfection probably by their doting widowed mother. For a moment, Catherine felt very alone.

'I'm starving, any biscuits in the tin?'

'Give over, Jess,' Doreen said, 'you eat like a cart-horse and stay as thin as a reed, there's no justice in this world.'

'Go on, look at the pot calling the kettle black.' Jess Painter pushed Doreen's arm playfully, spilling a little of her tea. 'Oops! Sorry!'

'Always was awkward, her,' Doreen spoke as if Jess was not there. 'Must have been born awkward, silly cow.'

Catherine knew the banter was good-natured, she felt part of it and it was a good feeling. She took the tin from the cupboard and placed it on the table.

'Where's the china plate and the doily then?' Jess asked in mock indignation.

'Fish and find out.' Doreen pushed a biscuit into her tea and sucked on it in delight.

'Pig!' Jess said good-naturedly.

'Oh, look at this picture in the paper,' – Pippa nudged her sister – 'I could swoon over him, such lovely eyes. Wonder what he's done to have the police after him.'

Jess took the paper and shook the pages flat. '*Duw*, he's a right good-looker.' She was quiet for a moment and then she looked up. 'Poor man's been accused of stealing from some rich piece by the name of Hopkins, an old biddy by what it says here. Don't believe such a hand-some man would need to steal anything, I'd give him any-thing he wanted for nothing, me.'

The name registered on Catherine and instinctively she

moved forward to look over Jess's shoulder. She stared at the picture in silence, shock washing over her as the face of Liam Cullen looked out at her from the pages of *The Swansea Times*.

'Let me read that.' She took the paper from Jess's hands and sank into a chair, her hands trembling.

'What's the matter, Cath? You look like you seen a ghost.' Doreen, more perceptive than the others, leaned anxiously towards her. 'Do you know this geezer or what?'

'I know him, he's my cousin, well sort of.'

Pippa smiled knowingly. 'Oh, aye, kissing cousins like, is that it?'

Catherine shook her head ignoring the good-natured banter. 'Liam wouldn't need to steal anything, he has lots of money of his own. He's got a farm in Ireland, a very good farm. Why should he want to take a brooch of all things and why should he have run away? It doesn't make sense.'

'Men do that all the time, love,' Doreen said dryly. 'Steal things and then run away. Still, you better get round to the police and tell them what you know; might just let this Liam chap off the hook.'

Catherine bit her lip, she had been happy to remain as she was, out of the reach of both Liam and Boyo, left in peace to try to sort out her life but now fate had stepped in to shake her out of her rut. She sighed heavily, Doreen was right, she must go to the police station, she could hardly allow Liam to be accused of such a silly crime without at least trying to help.

'I'll ask for time off this afternoon.' She turned away from the table and busied herself building up the fire. Her back and shoulders were tense, a warning to the others not to pursue the matter. Her mind was racing, her tranquillity was smashed to pieces, she had been enjoying a quiet life but now it appeared all that was about to end.

It was late afternoon by the time she was able to make her way to the small station just off one of the side-streets

241

of the town. She moved in through the doors, glancing round nervously.

'Yes, miss, can I help? I'm Police Sergeant Meadows.' A police officer was staring down at her and, with a shock, Catherine realized this huge, hard-faced man was Doreen's husband. His brow was furrowed as he stared at her and Catherine swallowed hard.

'Can I speak to someone in charge of the Liam Cullen case, please?'

'Well, now, if you have any information about this man's whereabouts you can tell me.' He had suddenly become alert, she had all his attention. He took out a pencil and sucked on the end before drawing a sheet of paper towards him. 'What's your name and where have you seen this man?'

'I'm Catherine O'Conner.' She could see the name meant nothing to him. If he had ever known about her disappearance from Swansea, the matter had been of little or no importance to him.

'I haven't seen him, I mean, I know him. He's a very rich man, he wouldn't want to steal anything.'

The sergeant was looking suspiciously at Catherine, his eyes running over her, noting her good clothes and her well-polished shoes. 'Where is he now?'

'I don't know,' Catherine said, shaking her head.

'Well, there seems little point in you coming here wasting my time then.'

Sergeant Meadows looked down at her. 'The charge against this itinerant was brought by Mrs Bethan Hopkins. It is a matter of great importance; Mrs Hopkins is a very respectable lady.'

'Rich and influential too.' Catherine was angry, she spoke with a sarcasm that was lost on the man.

'Precisely. Now, miss, if you have nothing else to say I would ask you to go about your business and stop wasting my time.'

He was so pompous Catherine could have slapped him. She turned on her heel and left the station and headed along the road, not seeing the traffic, not aware of a tall figure stopping before her until a hand grasped her arm.

'Catherine!'

She looked up into the face of Boyo Hopkins and the shock of seeing him brought tears to her eyes. She brushed them away angrily and shook off his hand.

'If only you knew how hard I've searched for you,' he said, drawing her into a doorway. 'I've been out of my mind with worry.'

'Worried that you might not get my farm away from me, that's about the size of it.' She stared up at him, her eyes hard now, her heart slowing to a quieter pace.

'I never wanted your farm.' He shook his head, 'Catherine, I never asked you for anything, did I?'

'Let's get this clear, you bought the farm, which you didn't want. You searched so hard for me that you didn't find me.' She stared up at him, her cheeks flushed.

He was silent and Catherine felt her anger build like a sheet of flame. 'I have had nothing but trouble since I became your . . . your mistress. My prize bull was ruined, I was attacked in my own home, then I was kept prisoner in some hovel miles from anywhere. If that wasn't part of the plot to get my farm away from me then what was it; answer me that?'

'I can only say it was none of my doing. Catherine, I love you.'

'Then you have a very funny way of showing it,' Catherine said abruptly. The last thing she needed now was for Boyo to talk to her of love. She was so confused, so angry, she could hardly think straight. She turned away and he caught her arm.

'Listen, I know my wife has been acting strangely, she's not herself lately. I know she has made a foolish accusation against your cousin but I'm trying to put things right. I was on my way to the police station to say that the damn pin has been found, the police will drop the charges against your cousin.'

She looked back at him. 'You found the pin?'

'No, I didn't find the pin, I don't believe it was lost in the first place. Catherine—' He made a move to take her in his arms but she waved him away impatiently.

'Get one thing into your head, it's over between us; all that you can do for me now is to go on your way to the police station and clear Liam's name,' she moved away from him, 'and leave me in peace.'

She was hurrying along the road then, her skirts flying, her eyes filled with tears. She still loved him, she knew she was a fool to even think of him that way and yet the blood had sung in her veins as she had stood close enough to touch him.

Suddenly, the comfort of her life at the store, the pleasant acceptance of the changes that had taken place in her life vanished and she saw herself as she really was, penniless, unloved and alone.

'I'm afraid my husband was mistaken, Sergeant Meadows, I am sorry you have found it necessary to make a trip all the way out here.' Bethan smiled and the policeman took her hand and deftly palmed the money she held out to him.

'No trouble at all, Mrs Hopkins. In any event, I thought it wise to wait for your word on the matter before I called off the search for the rogue.'

'Very wise, I appreciate that.' Bethan smiled. 'I will make sure I mention your vigilance to your superiors.'

She nodded to the young maid who bobbed a curtsey and opened the double doors of the sitting-room before leading the policeman into the hall.

Bethan rose to her feet, her face twisting into a sneer; so Boyo had thought to spoil her plans, had he? Well, he would have to be much cleverer than that if he wanted to outwit her.

She moved to the window and looked out at the grim rocks, hovering like a threat above the house. Why had she come here to this strangely haunted place? Why did she stay? She longed to pack up her bags and leave; she almost did leave but her father had fallen sick. Quite suddenly, he had turned from an intelligent, able man into an invalid, confined to his bed. Bethan found herself more and more irritated by his querulous demands but he was her father and he would be leaving her a considerable fortune. When he died she would be among the richest women in the country. The thought gave her a tremendous sense of power. Money bought you anything you wanted. Anything. Her heart dipped in pain, it would not buy her husband back. She pushed the thought away. How long would her father linger? Would he become more and more of a burden to her as each day passed?

She pushed the uneasy thoughts away and turned to matters of more immediate importance. Her plans for revenge on Mr Liam Cullen were well underway, she had men out in Ireland at this moment, making for the farm near Cork. There they would begin work, poisoning the crops on the Cullen lands. Slowly she would destroy Liam Cullen, take from him all that he owned. He had dared to threaten her, so now he must suffer the same fate as his precious cousin.

Bethan's fist clenched, she could picture Catherine's face, pale, delicate, surrounded with a cloud of lovely hair. The girl was everything Bethan was not, seductive, small of stature, the sort of woman who could stir the blood of any man.

She forced herself to relax and stretched her fingers wide to relieve the ache that had begun in them. She was getting pain in her bones lately, it was this house, damp and unwelcoming and yet, she was beginning to feel she could not leave here. It was hers, it was part of her; perhaps she had always been meant to live here, alone, a dried-up spinster.

'Damn!' She thumped her fist on one of the occasional tables, spilling a vase of flowers. She watched the blooms fall to the carpet and rivulets of water pour along the polished surface and down the ornate legs of the furniture, and suddenly she smiled.

She rose from her chair and called cheerfully for Cara to clear up the mess. 'I've had a little accident,' she said easily, 'but no real harm done, I think.'

She swept from the room and up the stairs to the

bedrooms. Here she could talk to herself in peace and here, sometimes, she felt sure voices answered her.

In the master bedroom, the one she should be sharing with her husband, she settled herself on the bed and crossed her arms over her body, as though such an act could prevent her from feeling alone.

'I'm content,' she said softly; 'my revenge has begun, I've torn that woman away from my husband's arms, caused a breach that they will never mend. And what's more, Honey's Farm is mine, all mine, to dispose of as I wish. Catherine O'Conner, you will rue the day you crossed Bethan Hopkins. Gloat while you may, your troubles are just beginning.'

CHAPTER TWENTY

'I'll do what I can, sir,' Constable Danby frowned over his notes while behind him, his mother, her great shelf of a bosom shaking with laughter, poured hot, fragrant tea into dainty china cups.

'I'm grateful to you.' Liam leaned back in his chair, relaxing a little now that the purpose of his visit had been achieved. His case had been considered calmly and coldly. He had brought his solicitor with him and Seamus was imposing in his dark suit and crisp high collar.

'*Duw*, anyone with half an eye can see the young gent wouldn't need to steal anything.' Mrs Danby lowered her great bulk into a chair. 'Good clothes, shoes polished to an inch of their life. Oh, no, Mr Cullen is no thief, you can take that from me, Jerry Danby, I've got a nose for these things.' To emphasize the point, she tapped her nose, a small button of a nose for such a large face and winked meaningfully at Liam.

'Aye, feelings are all right, Ma, it's proof that is needed in cases like this.' Jerry Danby spoke dryly and his mother shrugged and shook her head.

'Well, didn't her old man come in the station and say there had been a mistake and he should know.'

'Yes, Ma but then Mrs Hopkins came back to tell us the pin was still missing.' He looked at Liam, 'I think it might be better if you came with me to the station. I'm not arresting you, see, just giving good advice.'

'What then?' Liam knew the constable was right, running away had been a mistake, one he must do his best to correct.

'Then you may have to be detained, perhaps until a judge can try to sort it all out.'

'I don't think so,' Seamus said slowly. 'With lack of

even one shred of evidence there would be no reason to hold my client. Indeed, I'm surprised he was accused in the first place on so flimsy a story. Still,' he turned to Liam, 'it would be better if you went into the station voluntarily.'

Liam nodded. 'Sure an' I know you are right.'

'Mr Cullen was going to be questioned on the word of a very influential lady. When Mr Cullen ran away, it looked very bad for him.'

Constable Danby rose to his feet and shrugged his broad shoulders into his coat, sometime in the not too distant future the policeman would be as large as his mother, Liam thought.

'The matter can easily be cleared up, I'm sure,' Jerry Danby said easily. 'The important question is, were you ever alone with the lady?'

Liam shook his head. 'No, I was in the sitting-room when Mrs Hopkins called to see me and there were several other guests there at the time.'

'So, if the lady did lose her pin, and I must say there seems to be some doubt about that, then anyone could have picked it up.'

'I suppose so.'

'Right then, I can't see there's any problem, shall we go Mr Cullen?'

The trip to the police station was a short one and as Liam entered the ornate portico, he took a deep breath.

'Don't worry, sir,' Constable Danby said, 'everything is going to be all right.'

Sergeant Meadows was at the desk, his hair was grizzled grey and his colour high, he drank too much gin and longed for retirement. He looked up at Liam and then turned with raised eyebrows to Jerry Danby.

'Mr Cullen has come in voluntarily,' Danby said easily. 'Gave himself into my charge, he did, and, as far as I can see, there's no reason to detain him.'

'Oh, so you are an authority on the law now, are you, son?' The older police officer rose to his feet and stared at Constable Danby with narrowed eyes.

Seamus stepped forward. 'I think I can claim *I* know something about it, I'm a lawyer,' he said easily. 'It seems that there were other people seated in the lounge of the Castle Hotel when the pin went missing. I fail to see why my client should be held responsible any more than the other guests present at the time.'

'But Mr Cullen was the one talking to Mrs Hopkins, he was the one who was close enough to take the item.'

'So you think he might have unpinned it from the lady's bodice then?'

Sergeant Meadows looked confused. 'Well, no.'

'No,' Seamus said equitably, 'I am sure Mrs Hopkins would have noticed such an obvious move.'

'Well, she dropped it, that's clear as daylight.'

'And where exactly did the lady drop the pin; in the street, in the lobby of the hotel, in the sitting-room, where?'

'Well, I don't know.' Sergeant Meadows shook his head as though to clear it.

'I would advise you that with such a flimsy case you would put your own career in jeopardy if you were to detain my client.'

'Better take his details and let him go, sir,' Constable Danby advised in a low voice.

Meadows shot him a venomous look and sat down at his desk, taking up a pen and dipping it into the ink with fierce jabs of his hand.

Liam sighed with relief. He was careful not to look at the young policeman, he could see that Danby would come in for a certain amount of ire from his older colleague.

It was less than half an hour later when Liam walked from the station a free man, his name cleared. He turned to Seamus and shook his hand. 'Thank the good Lord you were here.'

'Ah well, save your thanks,' Seamus looked grave. 'I've had disturbing news from home, your farm is in some sort of trouble.' He paused, 'Look, I think I've got a lead on the whereabouts of Catherine O'Conner, something

249

Danby said. I'll continue the search here. You'd best get back to Ireland on the next boat.'

Catherine moved along the floor of the shop, her head high, her hands smoothing down her skirt nervously. She was very aware of her new clothes. Even more aware of the fine, comfortable boots made for her by Hari Grenfell. She felt she was taking some sort of test, she was about to serve her first customer.

'Good morning, madam, can I help you?' Catherine hoped that her tone was the right mixture of deference and confidence.

'Catherine! How are you? I must say this is a surprise.' Ellie Bennett held out her hand, it was warm and, with a feeling of self-consciousness, Catherine shook it briefly.

'I'm working for Mrs Grenfell now,' Catherine said. 'Hoping I have the makings of a good saleslady.'

'But Catherine, what on earth made you leave Honey's Farm? It was where you were born.'

'I had no choice,' Catherine said, 'I couldn't afford to keep up my payments to the bank and the farm was sold.'

'Well, I hope it went to someone who loved the land as you did,' Ellie said gently.

'Mrs Hopkins bought it, Boyo . . . Boyo Hopkins's wife.'

'Perhaps it's for the best,' Ellie was sympathetic. 'It must have been lonely and very hard work for you and at least you know that Boyo will care for the farm, make it thrive again. Honey's Farm is part of his life as well as yours, he will do his very best to make it work. I'm sure you two are still very good friends aren't you?'

'What can I show you, Mrs Bennett?' Catherine turned to hide the hot colour that came to her face. She led Ellie towards one of the ornate chairs that graced the shop floor.

Catherine was aware of Doreen placing a finished hat on a stand and watching her, urging her on to success. When Catherine glanced towards her, Doreen winked and mouthed the words 'Give 'em hell!'

Catherine resisted the urge to laugh. 'Is it boots you want, Mrs Bennett, or slippers? We have a fine new stock of both.'

Ellie relaxed and placed her bag on the carpet, drawing off her gloves with quick movements. 'Oh, I can't afford to buy boots and slippers, Catherine, I'm just the wife of a poor cleric, remember?'

Catherine did remember, she remembered the shock waves that shook the town when Ellie Bennett handed over *Glyn Hir* tannery and the fortune that went with it to Boyo. It was only much later that Ellie's reasons had become clear. Boyo, so the gossips said, was old Jubilee Hopkins's grandson.

Now Ellie was Mrs Daniel Bennett and she seemed completely happy with her role as the wife of a struggling cleric, as she put it.

'No, it's just a pair of house slippers, that's all I want for now. Can you show me something not too expensive?'

Catherine's feelings of nervousness vanished, she felt exhilarated as she brought a selection of slippers for Ellie's inspection. She even found she was enjoying herself. She eventually sold Ellie a pair of slippers in black brocade, decorated with tiny jet beads. And, in spite of Ellie's protestations of poverty, persuaded her to buy a fine pair of walking boots that were marked down in price because of a scuff on one of the heels.

'Thank you, Catherine,' Ellie smiled ruefully as she pulled on her gloves and rose to her feet. 'I think you are going to make an excellent saleslady.'

When Ellie had left, Doreen came forward, smiling her approval.

'Well done, little Cath, like the lady said, we'll make a saleslady of you yet.' She touched Catherine's shoulder, 'And the more sales you make, the more commission you get, so it's all up to you.'

'That's news to me,' Catherine said, her eyebrows raised. 'I didn't think I would get anything except my wages for selling shoes.'

'Well, you learn something every day, don't you? Mrs

Grenfell believes in encouraging us to do well, not in pushing us like slaves the way some bosses do.'

'If I work hard, sell plenty of shoes, perhaps soon I'll be able to get my own place,' Catherine said wistfully. 'It's good of Mrs Grenfell to let me stay here in the house but I feel I'm intruding, taking advantage of her good nature.'

'Look,' Doreen rubbed her cheek with her forefinger, 'why don't you have a room at my place?'

'Sounds lovely,' Catherine said, 'but what about your husband, won't he have something to say about that?'

'*Duw*, I haven't got no husband! Pete Meadows ran out on me years ago and good riddance to him I say. Policeman he is, so-called respectable, well I could tell you a thing or two about him that would make your hair curl.'

She paused to take a breath. 'Anyway, I could let you have the big bedroom, we could turn it into a sitting-room so that you could be private like.'

'But wouldn't I be in the way?' Catherine wanted badly to accept Doreen's offer, the loneliness in the evenings was becoming unbearable and yet she was reluctant to impose on the other woman's friendship.

'The extra rent would help me, mind.' Doreen urged as if sensing something of Catherine's thoughts.

'In that case, I'd love to come and live with you.' Catherine felt like hugging Doreen but at that moment, the door opened and a group of women swept into the shop.

'Give me the weekend to get the place right and then I'll take you over there Monday, right?'

Doreen swept away and lowered her head to the ladies as though they were royalty. The women preened and Catherine smiled to herself, she could learn a thing or two from Doreen Meadows.

It was late in the evening when she heard a knocking on the back door of the flat. Cautiously, Catherine moved to the small window and peered outside. It was growing dark and all she could see was a shadowy figure outlined against the glow of the lamplight. The figure moved and she saw a glint of red hair.

'Who's there?' she called. With mixed feelings she hesitated, knowing full well who was standing outside. But she didn't want to see Liam, he was part of her past; a lover for one night but she had never loved him, had she?

'It's me, Catherine, open the door, please.' He sounded anxious, unlike his usual calm self and Catherine drew back the bolts.

'Come in, Liam,' Catherine spoke grudgingly. 'How did you find out where I was staying?'

'I had a great deal of help. Thank God you are safe and well.' Liam flopped into a chair and she saw that his clothes were mud-stained, his hair awry. There were shadows beneath his eyes.

'What is it, Liam, what's wrong?' She sat down quickly beside him and took one of his hands in hers. He was cold, his fingers, gripping hers, felt icy to the touch.

'I've been to Ireland, I've just got back.' He looked directly at her, 'It's bad news; the crops are poisoned, the new machinery broken and useless. My investment is gone, the profit I made last year has vanished into the blue.'

'But Liam, how could this happen, you were doing so well?'

'Someone has it in for me that's sure enough, Catherine, and I think I know just who the bastard that wants me ruined is.'

Catherine put her hand to her mouth trying to sort out her tangled thoughts. 'Liam, now be calm, don't jump to conclusions.'

'I'm not jumping to conclusions, colleen, the only man who hates my guts enough to sicken my animals, sour the milk and try to destroy my livelihood is Boyo Hopkins. I've come back to have it out with him, make him wish he had never been born, I'll burn his house around his ears.'

'No! He wouldn't do a thing like that.' Catherine spoke without thinking. She felt a cold hand of fear trickle through her, Boyo's wife could be capable of such an act but even she would not go to such lengths, surely?

'The man is offloading Honey's Farm in small parcels like so much ballast,' Liam said.

'I don't believe it.' Catherine's voice sounded hoarse even to her own ears.

'Don't you know what's going on under your nose, Cath? The man is wreaking revenge on me and on you.'

'But why, what have we done?'

Liam held her hands even tighter. 'He knows we are lovers. Hopkins is far from stupid and I reckon that if the man can't have you himself then he'll ruin both our lives rather than let us be happy.'

'Liam, we slept together once, that doesn't make us lovers.' She faced him squarely. 'I'm sorry, Liam, I should have been honest with you; I am not in love with you.'

'I could make you love me,' Liam said softly, 'and for now, liking will do, sure it will.'

Catherine shook her head. 'No, it wouldn't work, I can't marry you, Liam, I just can't.'

'Is it because I'm ruined that you don't want me, is money so important to you then, Catherine?'

'No!' She put her arm around him and tried to lead him to a chair near the fire. 'It's not that at all. Sit down Liam, I'll get us something to drink.'

He ignored her words and pulled her closer and then his mouth was on hers. She felt him tremble and held him closer, pity turning her stomach to ice.

'Don't turn away from me now, Catherine, not now when I need you so badly.' He sounded near to tears.

'Liam, you'll always be my friend.' She tried to draw away from him but he held her fast.

'Catherine, please think about it. I'll work hard, I'll sell up what is left of my place in Ireland. I'll take a job here, bring in good money for us, we could have such a wonderful life if we work together.'

'Take it slowly, now,' Catherine urged. 'Before you make any hasty decisions, think of what it will mean to your family. Where would Maeve live and your father and your sister? Where would they go? How would they manage without you?'

He released her and sank into the chair, his head in his hands. 'You're right sure enough, I have responsibilities, I can't desert my family, not now.'

Catherine felt a sense of relief, she had her life mapped out, her job, her new home with Doreen. The only one she would be responsible for was herself.

'At least think about us, Catherine, I don't think I can live without you.'

'All right, Liam,' Catherine said softly. 'I'll think about what you have said, I promise.'

Liam seemed beaten, his hair was tangled, his eyes shadowed with weariness. New lines of worry were forming about his eyes and mouth. On an impulse, Catherine knelt before him and put her hands on his cheeks.

'Liam, nothing is as bad as it first seems, I've learned that much. Perhaps, even now, you can rescue the farm; the land is lush and good, the house you live in is large and roomy, surely there is a way around your difficulties.'

'Things are bad in Ireland just now,' Liam replied. 'Prices are falling, there is no money about for investments. Whoever has done this thing to me chose the right moment to bring about my downfall.'

'It wouldn't be Boyo, I know that much,' Catherine said quickly. 'It's more likely to be that wife of his.'

Liam rested his head on her shoulder. 'You could well be right but what's done is done; my reputation, my fine way of life, my farm, all that is ruined.'

She patted him gently, as though he was a child. He looked up into her eyes. 'Cath, let me stay here tonight, just for tonight.'

Catherine took a deep breath. 'If I let you stay, will you promise that you will go back to Ireland, try to sort things out?'

'Aye, I'll promise you that.'

'And you won't try to avenge yourself on Boyo because none of this is his fault, take my word for it.'

'I will not do anything foolish, that's all I can promise

Cath. Before I go back home, I must try to find out who has done this to me. If I don't do that, then I won't be able to look at myself in the mirror in the mornings.'

'Come on, there's hot water to bathe. You look so tired, Liam, a good night's sleep will make you feel . . .'

He caught her hand in his, ''Tis not a good night's sleep I'll be wanting, Catherine.'

His meaning was clear and she was suddenly angry with him. She turned away to hide the flush that rose to her cheeks and made an effort to compose herself.

'Liam, I . . .'

His hand was on her shoulder. 'Hush, now, no more talking, lead me to this hot bath you spoke of, it sounds like a fine idea to me.'

Catherine sat alone near the fire, her head was aching, she was suddenly weary of the complications in her life. And yet, she had brought it on herself. She had encouraged Liam to make love to her. As for Boyo, she had become his mistress within a matter of days and it was her own fault she had fallen in love with him.

Now she was sick of it all: sick of Boyo, sick of the unhappiness knowing him had caused her. Liam had suffered too, he had lost everything because of her involvement with Boyo Hopkins. He was right, who else would want to harm him or his lands? Only a woman who cared nothing for farmland or the creatures on it.

She sighed heavily and closed her eyes, she was quite sure that Bethan Hopkins was behind the attack on Liam's farm. Who else would be so cruel, so vengeful? Tomorrow, she would persuade Liam to leave well alone, to go home, try his best to salvage something from the ruins of his livelihood. As for tonight, what was the point in rebuffing him? Surely she owed him the comfort of her arms? That much at least, she could give him.

And yet, later, as she lay beside him in the narrow bed, she was dry-eyed and restless. He was sleeping now like a baby, his arm flung across Catherine's breast, his curly head against her shoulder. A great tenderness filled her,

256

he was good and kind and he did not deserve the wrongs that had been done to him.

It was a long time before Catherine slept and when she did, she dreamed of Boyo, of his smile, his eyes adoring her. She felt, in sleep, the ecstasy of his lovemaking and she woke to find that she was moaning softly.

She turned quickly, light was filtering in through the window; it was morning. Liam was still asleep and, quietly, Catherine crept out of the bed. She would make breakfast for Liam and send him on his way. Then, perhaps, she would be able to turn her thoughts to the way she was going to run the rest of her life.

CHAPTER TWENTY-ONE

Bethan was in her bedroom at the back of the house, staring out at the towering hill that forever cast a shadow over the building. It was a room she had come, if not to like, at least to be comfortable in. She was becoming reclusive and she was aware of it but she lived her life in her own way. Trying to please other people did not always pay dividends.

Bethan lifted her head, listening, she thought she heard a voice, low, sibilant. She turned, there was no-one, only the painting of her ancestor, Elizabeth Llewellyn, the eyes seeming to look through her, into her soul. Bethan was not quite sure what had made her put the portrait in her bedroom, perhaps it was some foolish idea of having a companion, someone who was blood of her blood beside her in the dark, lonely nights.

A knocking on the door jolted her out of her reverie; the young maid stood there, agitated, her thin face white, her eyes round with fear.

'Come quick, Mrs Hopkins!'

Bethan rose slowly to her feet. 'What's wrong?'

'It's Mr Llewellyn, I think he's sick.'

Bethan pushed the trembling girl aside and hurried along the landing towards her father's room. The door stood open, the tray brought by the maid leaning drunkenly on the bed.

'Father,' Bethan moved to his side and looked down at the old man in the bed. He seemed diminished since her return to Ty Craig and now his frame made scarcely any impression beneath the bedclothes.

Bethan removed the tray and, with her hand, touched her father's cheek. It was cold.

'Daddy! Open your eyes, speak to me!' She shook him

and his head lolled to one side, his mouth gaping tooth-lessly. Death, Bethan realized, was not the heroic exit from life portrayed by the novelists, death had an ugly face.

She stepped back, away from the still form. 'Daddy!' Her voice was thin, far away and then Bethan felt the room spin into a vortex of darkness.

The funeral took place a week later. It was a dark day with clouds scudding over the graveyard but it had remained dry. Bethan listened to the words of the vicar with a feeling of numbness. That body in the coffin was not her father, her father had gone from her without warning, had left her alone in the world.

'Bethan, I'm sorry to hear of your father's sudden death, I had no idea he was ill.'

She looked up into Boyo's face and, in spite of every-thing, she felt warmed by his presence. 'I am alone in the world now, what am I going to do?' She knew it was weak of her to appeal to his sense of guilt but she could not help herself.

He held her arm and stood beside her just as a proper husband would. She leaned against him gratefully. 'Will you come back to the house with me afterwards?'

'I can't, Bethan, I'm sorry, it wouldn't work, believe me.'

So, even now, in her moment of loss, he would not bend, would not make an effort to comfort her, he was not worthy of her love. She stood upright and took a deep breath.

'Very well, I will not ask you again.' She watched the coffin being lowered into the grave, heard the thud of earth on wood and felt suddenly bereft. She had never been close to her father, he had never held her or teased her or played games with her but he had been a good father, a man of great intellect and now he was gone.

Bethan realized how much she had taken him for granted these past months. How little she had considered his needs or his health. She should have noticed he was growing feeble but then she had been worried and upset about her own problems. No-one could blame her for anything; she had done her best by her father she had kept him company in his old age.

In a daze, she walked back to the carriage and climbed into the seat alone. She glanced over the heads of the few people who had come to pay their last respects and saw Boyo mount his horse and without a backward glance, ride away.

For a moment, hate superseded her love for him, how dare he be so insensitive to her needs, he was her husband after all. And what would people think, she, travelling alone back to her home and her husband going off in another direction? And then she was crying. She held her head erect beneath the black hat and veil, her shoulders were square and tense, no-one would see her grief, no-one. Bethan Hopkins had her pride.

For several days after the funeral, Bethan kept to her bed with a chill, brought on by standing in the cold wind at the cemetery. The days had passed in a haze of coughing and sleeping and generally feeling sick.

At last, she opened her eyes and knew she was over the worst. She sat up and drew the bedclothes around her, it was cold in the room and dimly lit. It was night-time.

She looked up at the portrait of Elizabeth. 'Well, here I am, sick and alone and my husband having a wonderful time with his fancy piece no doubt. Damnation take Catherine O'Conner.'

She heard the bitterness in her voice and then, it was as if Elizabeth was talking to her. There came a soft insistent whispering, it was in Bethan's head, echoing there, telling her what she must do. Her mission had only just begun, the voice said, retribution was her right, she must claim it.

The presence was near, so close that Bethan knew if she reached out her hand she could touch it. She leaned back against the pillows and closed her eyes, the spirit would be her solace, her comfort, for there was no-one on earth who cared about her. Her life had become empty, barren. She laughed bitterly, barren, the word was painfully apt.

She brooded on the wrongs that had been done to her. She was alone and unhappy and it was Boyo's fault. If he had not deserted her, spending every minute he could with that arrogant hussy, everything would have been all right. But show him a pretty face, a young face and he was away like a dog on heat.

'I hate him,' she said, to the spirit who leaned above her with the breath of cold winter. 'That woman has intoxicated my husband, offered him her very obvious charms and he went to her, with no thought for me.'

The spirit sighed and shifted a little and Bethan sank back against the pillows. It was the pain and the despair of Boyo's betrayal that had robbed Bethan of her child, had brought her to live in a house that was empty now, inhabited only by ghosts of the past.

Oh, she had a great deal to answer for, the red-haired bitch, the sorceress. She had turned everyone against Bethan Hopkins, the citizens of Swansea did not wish to know her, she had no friends. They all saw her as a woman abandoned, ugly, old and alone.

'They must pay, all of them, for what they have done to me, they must pay, mustn't they?' Bethan said softly.

The voice was there again, closer, next to Bethan's ear and suddenly she knew what it was she must do, she must plot to pay them all back.

Hari Grenfell had taken the O'Conner slut into her so-called business, well she would be the first to feel Bethan's displeasure. Anyone who crossed her would pay, they would all learn that she was not a woman to trifle with. She allowed the thought to seep into her being. Once she had exacted her revenge, put the record books straight, the world would begin to right itself; Boyo would come to his senses, he would know where it was he belonged. The chain of wicked fascination would be broken. He would have to be punished, of course, he could not be allowed to get away scot-free with the hurt he had inflicted upon his wife. But in the end she would forgive him.

Bethan raised herself onto her elbows and stared out of

the window. A grey dawn light was penetrating the gloom now, throwing the rocks outside into relief. The gaunt cliff face was running with rain, dark grey like gravestones. The grave, it was a place of peace, where she would one day rest with her spirit friends but, in the meantime, she had work to do. She must get up and dress herself.

She ate a good breakfast, feeling the strength flow into her body. The tea was hot and sweet; warmed and heartened, she began to make her plans. Bethan knew exactly where she would find Catherine O'Conner; she thought she could hide away, work with Hari Grenfell without anyone knowing, but she did not allow for Bethan's spies. Uncle Tom had continued to do Bethan's bidding, taking her advice to employ no more halfwits who would make the same mistakes as Jacob had done.

When the time was right, when her plans were fully formed, Bethan would strike. She did not know exactly how but her voices would tell her. In the meantime, it would be satisfying to destroy all that was close to Catherine O'Conner, all that she had come to hold dear, including her job at the Grenfell Emporium.

A smile curved Bethan's mouth as she considered the havoc her men had wreaked on that fool, Liam Cullen, the Irishman who had dared to oppose her. His farm was ruined, poisoned, it would take years to restore the fields to healthy land again.

She did not feel one ounce of pity for Cullen. He deserved everything he got, he had enjoyed the charms of Catherine and then, on the order from the slut, he had sought to cross Bethan in her bid to buy Honey's Farm. Poor foolish man, he did not realize he was no match for the powers that Bethan had at her disposal.

He had been discredited in Swansea, accused of stealing from one of the upright citizens of the town and, though he had been bailed out by his clever lawyer, who had insisted there was no proof that Liam Cullen had taken the brooch, the mud would still stick, Bethan would see to that. The man must suffer, he must pay, as all who crossed Bethan Hopkins must pay.

Hari looked at Doreen's narrow, sharp face, the bright, intelligent eyes, full of enthusiasm and eased herself back in her chair, pushing aside the accounts she'd been studying; they could wait.

'So you think Catherine is going to make a first-class saleslady, do you?'

'I'm sure of it, Mrs Grenfell. I hope you don't mind me butting in like this but I wanted to tell you how well she's working out.'

'That's very commendable of you, Doreen, but then you always did give praise where it was due.'

Doreen ignored the compliment, though Hari could tell by the blush on the girl's cheeks that she was pleased.

'Catherine is willing to be told and she learns fast. I'm even teaching her a bit about the hatting, she's very bright at picking things up, believe me.'

'I do believe you. Is it working out at home? It was good of you to rent a room to Catherine, she must have been very lonely living here.'

'Aye, it's going well, she's a nice soul. Daft in the way she thinks of men, mind, she hasn't yet learned that they are rotters, each and every one.'

Hari knew about the way Doreen's husband had bullied and abused her. Meadows had chosen to leave his wife only after beating her half to death, and consequently, Doreen had been happier than she had been in years.

Doreen glanced at Hari from under her sparse eyelashes. 'Got a gentleman caller, she has, mind; that nice Police Constable Danby. She's not interested though, she still thinks she's in love with that Mr Hopkins. Wasting her chances she is.'

'She's very young,' Hari said softly. 'Plenty of time for her to settle down. In any case, these days women have more opportunities to make a success of life alone, you've proved that.'

'You have too, Mrs Grenfell,' Doreen said quietly. 'Heard the stories, I have, of how you made yourself rich and famous. I wish I was more like you.'

Hari laughed, 'I had a lot of luck.'

'Luck indeed! You was gifted, you worked hard and when the going got tough you rolled up your sleeves and got going again.' Doreen looked down at her roughened hands in sudden embarrassment and Hari hid a smile.

'Any new hats on the stocks then, Doreen?' She came to the girl's rescue and Doreen's face lit up with enthusiasm.

'Yes, Mrs Grenfell, I got a lovely hat on the block just right for that rich biddy that came in yesterday. Mother of the bride she is, and proud as a pouter pigeon.'

'I expect you mean Mrs Charles, do you?'

'That's right, a funny woman, don't know what she wants except that it has to be bigger and better than anything the other folks got.'

Hari smiled. 'Well, you keep her happy, Doreen, she'll come back to us again if she gets what she wants.'

'Oh, she'll get what she wants, Mrs Grenfell, but it will be a much nicer hat than she ever expected. Come to think of it, I'd better get on, the hats won't make themselves; if you'll pardon me, Mrs Grenfell.' Doreen hurried from the room and closed the door quietly after her.

When she was alone in her small office at the top of the stairs, Hari gave her attention to the accounts once more. Matters were going better than she expected. News of the strange shop, situated in what had once been a fine old home had brought in the curious who fortunately had remained to spend their money. It would be some time before the debts would be paid but the business was beginning to make a profit, slowly but surely she was making progress.

The door opened and Craig looked into the room, his sleeves rolled up above the elbow, his face grimy with sweat. 'I've brought the last of the leather over from the tannery.' He sank into the chair opposite the desk and rubbed at his face. 'None left after this, my love. Can we afford to buy more stock?'

She pushed the accounts over to him. 'Have a look for

yourself, I think I can safely say we are beginning to turn back the tide.'

Craig perused the figures in silence for a time and then nodded. 'I see, yes, we are beginning to see daylight.' He looked up at her, 'It's all due to you and your enormous strength and courage, I couldn't have faced it alone.'

Hari left her chair and put her arms around Craig's shoulders, hugging his head to her breast. 'We are a team, what we have achieved we have done together. I know there's a long way to go yet but we'll make it, you'll see.'

'You'll get filthy if you hug me like that.' Craig's hand was on her waist, holding her close to him and Hari laughed.

'I can see you don't like it! I have a suggestion to make, what if I take you to the bathroom and give you a lovely hot bath?'

'You are a wicked woman! But I can see the benefits of combining business and pleasure.' Craig rose to his feet and towered over her. 'Don't tempt me too much, my girl, or there won't be any more work done today.'

'I see,' Hari pretended to sulk. 'So I am going to have to wait until my lord and master is ready for me, am I?'

Craig bent and kissed her mouth, his lips lingering on hers. Then he straightened. 'I am always ready for you, Hari, but one of us has to go out and do some work, we can't all sit around at a desk doing nothing all day.'

He dodged through the door, laughing, as Hari lifted a paperweight from the desk and made as if to throw it after him. She stood and watched as he descended the stairs almost at a run. He was enjoying the challenge of their temporary lack of funds. At first he had been despondent but once Hari began to urge him to try again, he had shown an enthusiasm that would not have shamed a man half his age.

Sighing, she returned to her desk, there was a great deal to do, the business was not out of the woods yet, not by a long chalk.

Doreen's house was situated at the end of Watkin Street,

a tall building with steps leading up to the door. Doreen rented only the lower floor of the property but the rooms were spacious and light and Catherine had begun to feel at home there.

'*Duw*, my feet are aching like billy-oh.' Doreen kicked off her shoes and stretched her toes into a bowl of hot water, her face reflecting her satisfaction.

'Better than having a roll in the hay, is this, any day.' She grinned up at Catherine who was cutting bread into neat thin slices to go with the cold pie she had bought on her way home.

'Course, you wouldn't know about that, would you, being a single girl, like?'

'Don't be nosy.' Catherine laughed out loud. 'Never did know anyone like you for prying.'

'Only interested, mind, don't mean no harm.' Doreen ruffled the water with her feet. 'Got the look of a girl who's had a man, you have, and such beauty that most would kill for. Have you then; had a man I mean?'

Catherine glanced at her. 'I've had two lovers; now then, are you satisfied?'

Doreen sat up straighter. 'Do you mean it or are you having me on?'

'Figure it out for yourself. Come on, tea's ready, I don't know about you but I'm starving.'

'Oh, pass a plate of pie over by here, love, can't waste this lovely hot water now, can I?'

Catherine sighed in mock exasperation. 'Didn't know I was going to end up being head cook and bottle washer when I came to live here.'

'Go on, used to it, you are, being a farm girl.' Doreen looked at her. 'Don't you miss it, going to bed with a man, I mean?'

Catherine bit into her pie and shrugged her shoulders, how could she tell Doreen she longed to be in Boyo's arms every night when she went to her bed? That sometimes she would wake up with tears on her pillow aching to be held, to be loved.

'No need to answer, I can see it in your face that you

266

do. In love, poor sod, that's what you are, hopelessly in love.'

'Right, well, shall we change the subject?'

'Aye, suppose so. What do you think of that confection I made for Mrs whatsername?'

'The mother of the bride, you mean?' Catherine smiled wickedly. 'She seems pleased enough but it's a bit . . . well, a bit fussy for my tastes.'

'Ah, but these rich people like to know they're having their money's worth, proper mean they are and the tips they give are not worth holding your hand out for. Still, it's a good job and Mrs Grenfell pays our wages on time, not like most toffs.'

A sudden loud knocking on the door wiped the smile from Doreen's face. 'Oh, my lord, that sounds like 'im!' She looked up at Catherine with fear reflected in her face. 'Go and answer, love, try to put 'im off, I can't stand a row, not now.'

Catherine moved to the door, her heart had begun to beat rapidly but she held her head high. Why should she be afraid of Doreen's husband? Surely the man could not be such a monster as Doreen made out.

'Yes?' She opened the door and started back as the huge figure of the policeman swayed in the doorway. 'Sergeant Meadows, your wife is not at home. Please go away, you're drunk.'

He pushed her aside as though she were a rag doll, ignoring her cries as she fell heavily. He stepped over her and made his way unsteadily through to the living-room.

She heard a crack of a hand against flesh and shakily, Catherine scrambled to her feet and followed Meadows, so frightened, she felt she could not breathe. He was standing over his wife and she was pressed back in her chair, a livid mark across her cheek.

'What do you want?' Her voice was thin, it was clear she was close to tears.

'What do you think?' He tore at Doreen's clothing revealing her thin body.

'No, please, Peter, I can't stand it.'

He smacked her hard and Catherine rushed forward, grasping at his arm, trying to pull him away. He shook her off with ease and turned on her, his mouth drawn back over his teeth.

'Keep out of this if you know what's good for you. This woman is my wife and I have rights over her, do you understand?'

'Get out, Cath,' Doreen said breathlessly. 'Just get out while you're all right.'

Sergeant Meadows grasped his wife's arm and forced her towards the door. 'First I'm going to give you a good hiding and then I'm going to claim what's mine. Why should I pay whores for a service my wife is bound to give me for free?'

He thrust Doreen from the room and Catherine, her hands to her face, heard the sound of blows from the bedroom at the back of the house. Then there was an awful silence and Catherine closed her eyes, imagining the big beast of a man forcing himself on the defenceless Doreen.

She turned suddenly and ran up the stairs and hammered on the door of the first-floor apartment. It was opened a crack by a small elderly woman who stared at her suspiciously.

'Can you help?' Catherine gasped. 'I think that man is going to kill Doreen.'

The woman shrugged. 'People quarrel, love, that's life. Any road, what can I do against him?'

'Haven't you got a husband or a son who can help, please?' Catherine said desperately.

'Bless you, love, don't you know better than not to interfere between a man and his wife? In any case, he's a copper, don't do to cross that kind.' She closed the door and Catherine heard the sounds of bolts being shot home.

She turned, ran back down the stairs and stood wondering what she should do, should she run into the street or should she try once more to tackle Meadows herself? She moved into the kitchen looking for some sort of weapon. From the fireside, she picked up a heavy poker.

The door to the kitchen crashed back on its hinges and

Meadows came into the room, his shirt was unbuttoned and his trousers hung loosely round his hips. He ignored Catherine and opened the lid of the biscuit tin, taking out the money and stuffing it into his pocket.

'Silly cow knows I'll find it wherever she hides it.' He spoke more to himself than to Catherine. Incensed, she moved forward and barred his path.

'Some of that is my money. Give it back at once.' She brandished the poker, she was so angry that she forgot her fear. He leaned forward and leered down at her.

'Not any more it isn't, it's mine, right; got it?' He poked his finger in her chest and angrily, Catherine smacked it away. He lifted his hand as if to strike her and she faced up to him, her chin high.

'Go on, hit me and then I can make a complaint against you; I am not your wife, do you understand?' she said furiously.

He looked at her for a long moment and then spat on the ground at her feet. 'Bitch!'

He pushed past her and lurched through the door and out along the passage into the roadway. Catherine slammed the front door after him, locking it with savage movements of her fingers.

Slowly, she made her way to the back bedroom, almost afraid to look in case the monster had murdered Doreen. The room was in darkness and she drew back the curtain allowing the light from the lamp outside to filter into the room.

Doreen was hugging her knees, blood trickling from a cut on her brow and her mouth was swollen.

'Oh Doreen.' Catherine sat on the bed and hugged her, feeling the thinness of the girl with a dart of pity. 'How could he do this to you?'

'He thinks it's his right, what he deserves because he hasn't disgraced me by getting a divorce.' She tried to smile. 'One good thing, it never lasts long; not very good at it is Meadows, for all he thinks he's a great stud.'

'I'll boil water for a bath,' Catherine said, 'the warm water might ease the pain.'

'Aye and it will wash away the stink of that bastard as well,' Doreen said bitterly.

Catherine bathed Doreen's thin body as though she was a sickly child. She felt her throat constrict as she saw the bruising on Doreen's thighs and breasts and around her throat.

'That's lovely, Cath. Fetch me a gin, will you?' She sloughed the water over her shoulders and arms before taking the glass which Catherine held out to her.

'I do this each time in case the bastard's put me in the way. Never has mind, hasn't got the necessary if you asks me. But gin's supposed to be good for shifting what might be put there and in any case, it makes me feel a bit better.' She tried to smile, though her lips were swollen now to twice their ordinary size.

'You can't go to work looking like that, Dor,' Catherine said. 'I'll tell Mrs Grenfell that you're sick.'

'Aye, she won't believe it but she's a good sort. Ask her if I can have my stuff at home so that I can finish that blessed hat for Mrs Charles.'

'Don't worry about that now,' Catherine said, 'you just think of yourself for a change.'

She helped Doreen out of the water, handed her a towel and then dragged the zinc bath out through the back door into the yard.

The moon was high in the heavens, a bright shining orb. The clouds hung motionless, as though painted against the sky and Catherine took deep breaths trying to calm herself. Never had she witnessed such savagery; how one human being could be so brutal to another she could not understand. But one thing she knew: Peter Meadows must be prevented from molesting his wife again, or next time he might finish her for good.

She spent the night in bed with Doreen, soothing her when she cried out in her sleep, watching over her like a mother. Doreen was older than Catherine but, tonight, it was almost as though the roles were reversed.

It was the same feeling she had had when her mother had been so low after her dad's death; the urge to comfort, to take away some of the pain. Catherine's eyes misted with tears, she remembered the happy childhood she had spent on Honey's Farm, loved and cherished by both her parents and she wanted to weep for what she could never have again.

In the morning, Doreen looked even worse than she had the previous night. Both her eyes were closed to mere slits and her mouth was swollen to twice its size.

'*Duw*! Would you look at that kisser, not even my own mam would recognize me.' Doreen spoke with difficulty.

'He's a beast!' Catherine said angrily. 'That man should be locked up and the key thrown away. You should make a complaint against him.'

'No love, it's not done, not for a woman to complain about her old man, especially not when he's a copper.'

'I know,' Catherine sighed, 'but there must be something we can do. Anyway, I'll make us some porridge and then I'd better get off to work. I'll try to come home at dinner time and make something nice to eat.'

'Now don't you go worrying about me,' Doreen said quickly. 'I can get us a bite to eat, you stay in the shop and I'll see to the food. So long as I don't have to go out and face people I'll be all right.'

As she walked to work, Catherine felt anger boiling up within her. She wished she'd been stronger, had used the poker on Meadows, he deserved to be hurt as he hurt others.

'Catherine!' She heard the familiar voice and stopped in her tracks, the colour leaving her face. 'Catherine, wait, just talk to me, won't you?'

Boyo was looking down at her, his eyes pleading but Catherine was in no mood to listen.

'Can't you take to be told?' she said hotly. 'I don't want to speak to you, not now, not ever.'

'Catherine, if only you knew how much I have longed for you. I must have been mad to think I could make a life with Bethan once I had you.'

'Oh yes, you can say that now but when I needed you most you put your precious Bethan first, didn't you? You hurt me, betrayed me and what I hate most of all, you turned your back on me. All for the sake of a bitter, vindictive woman who'd stop at nothing to destroy anyone who stood in her way.'

'We have to talk. Will you just let me walk with you, Catherine, I'm trying my best to apologize. What I did was unforgivable, I know that, I've been a bastard. I apologize for it all but I can't apologize for staying with my wife when she was so sick.'

'My father was sick, too. I needed you so much then Boyo, I really needed you and you weren't there for me.'

'Try to understand that it has been bad for me, too,' Boyo said urgently. 'I had lost my child, I was not thinking straight.'

Catherine faced him angrily. 'Don't expect me to be sorry for you. Look, I have made my own way in life. It's too late for us. I don't need you, I don't need anybody.'

'Not even your dear cousin, Liam Cullen?' Boyo was angry now, his hands clenched into fists as though he would strike somebody. 'Your cousin can offer you a way out, a comfortable life and you'd settle for second-best just for a little bit of security.'

'You are obviously as ill-informed about my cousin as you were about me and what my family were going through.'

'I don't know what you mean.'

'No, you don't. Liam's farm is ruined, his crops spoiled, his livestock poisoned. It appears that your precious Bethan is behind the destruction. Go on, say you didn't know that.'

He stared at her in silence and Catherine turned abruptly and walked away from him. She was trembling, though whether it was with anger or the longing to be in Boyo's arms she didn't know. She closed her eyes and took a deep breath. She must forget Boyo Hopkins, forget he ever held her in his arms and made her sing with happiness.

The emporium was bustling with early-morning activity. Within the mellow walls, fires were springing to life in the ornate grates, floors were being swept and Catherine realized that she was late.

Hari Grenfell was in her office, she looked up when Catherine knocked on the open door and beckoned her inside.

'It's Doreen, Mrs Grenfell, she . . . she isn't well this morning.'

Hari rose abruptly and strode across the room, closing the door firmly. 'Her husband is up to his old tricks again is he?'

Catherine looked down at her shoes, dusty now from the long walk. 'He's a monster!' The words were torn from her. 'He beat Doreen and raped her and before he left, he took all our money.' She looked up at Hari, 'We were saving for some new curtains and covers. Doreen wanted the place to look nice, it's not much to ask of life is it?'

'Sit down, Catherine, you look washed out.' Hari's voice was full of concern. 'The man didn't touch you, did he?'

Catherine sank into a chair. 'He pushed me a little, nothing terrible, it's what he did to Doreen that upset me.' She swallowed hard. 'You should see her face, Mrs Grenfell, her lip is cut, her eyes almost closed and bruises everywhere. How could the man be so cruel to a defenceless woman?'

Hari Grenfell drew open the desk. 'Here's some money,' she said quietly, 'I want you to go out now and buy some material, Doreen can at least occupy herself making those curtains she wanted so badly.'

Catherine looked at Hari doubtfully. 'I don't think Doreen would like to take charity, Mrs Grenfell, I know you mean it kindly but . . .'

'It's not charity, I assure you.' Hari smiled. 'Mrs Charles is being charged above the odds for the very special hat Doreen's making for the wedding. This is only what Doreen has earned, a bonus for the work she put in, the long hours she spent here after time.'

Catherine smiled and took the money. 'If you put it

that way, how can Doreen refuse?'

'Right, now off you go to the shops and take the rest of the day off. Help Doreen, she could do with it.'

Hari rose to her feet and Catherine knew that the interview was over. 'I'll send some work home for Doreen to do over the next week or two until she's recovered.' Hari opened the door and Catherine paused on the threshold.

'I wish I could be more like you, Mrs Grenfell,' she said earnestly.

Hari smiled and rested a hand on Catherine's shoulder. 'I think you are already, very much like me. Go on, now, I'll see you tomorrow.'

The walk back into town was accomplished with comparative ease, it was mostly downhill with the sea spread as a backdrop to the untidy town. Houses, pale in the morning light, spread over the floor of the valley, rising to encroach on the hills above the town.

Catherine felt suddenly elated, warmed by Mrs Grenfell's act of kindness and by her faith in Catherine's ability to make good. She would rise above the setbacks, Catherine decided, she would fight to make herself independent, needing no-one but herself to survive. She lifted her head high as a shaft of weak sunlight gleamed brightly on the rain-soaked pavement. Everything was going to be all right.

Amongst the dark hills, in a dark house overshadowed by huge grey rocks, Bethan Hopkins was beginning to put her plans into action.

CHAPTER TWENTY-TWO

The land beneath his feet was hard and dead, with little sign of recovery, and Liam felt tears burn in his eyes. He had returned across the Irish Sea with a mingling of happiness and anger burning inside him: happiness that he had once more taken Catherine into his arms and made her his and bitterness at what Hopkins had done to him and to his lands.

He sank down on his haunches and dug his fingers deep into the hardness of the soil, scraping skin from bone in his pain and anger. He ought to thrash Hopkins to within an inch of his life. Some part of Liam's mind accepted that he was jealous of Boyo Hopkins, the man was young, strong and rich; why did he have to inflict devastation on good arable land? In a way it made little sense. And yet who else *could* be responsible?

'Sure, it does no good to cry over spilt milk, my boy.' The voice behind him startled him out of his reverie, he rose and faced his grandmother.

'What are you doing out here in the fields, Gran?' He thrust his bleeding hand into his pockets but Maeve's eagle eye missed nothing.

'Same as you. I'm wondering if the soil will come good again.' She dug at the ground with the heel of her shoe.

'It'll come, given a few years.'

'That's what I thought.' Maeve folded her arms across her high-necked bodice and stared out across the acres, her eyes shrewd.

'By then we'll be ruined.' Liam's voice was heavy.

'I don't think so.' Maeve dipped into the pocket of her voluminous apron and took out a thick document. 'This is for you, Liam.'

It was the last will and testament of Maeve Cullen and

Liam, frowning, read through it quickly.

'Gran, you are going to live for a long time yet.'

'You bet I am!' Maeve smiled. 'Still, there's nothing stopping me tearing that up and giving you what is yours a little before time, is there?'

'But Gran, I never realized . . .'

'Never realized I had other lands? A wise head keeps a still tongue, my boy. Anyway, those lands are for you.'

'But what about Dad, and what about my sister? Sure she'll go mad when she hears of this.'

'I want the Cullen line to go on and it doesn't look like your sister will ever get herself a man, let alone a child. In any case, any children she might have will not be Cullens. Patricia will be as mad as hell, as you say, but she'll just have to put up with it.' There was a gleam of laughter in her eyes.

'As to your dad, he knows what I intend to do with my land and he approves.'

Liam smiled, it would be just the same if his father did not approve, Maeve was the sort of woman who had her own way. Unbidden came the thought that Catherine was cut from the same cloth as his grandmother.

'Get yourself a good wife.' Maeve might have been reading his thoughts. 'Catherine O'Conner is a fine, spirited woman, be determined enough and you will win her.'

Liam smiled. 'Are you a witch, Gran?'

She tapped her nose with her forefinger. 'That's for me to know and you to find out.'

Maeve talked in clichés, it was a habit of hers but she was as sharp, quick-witted and more perceptive than most.

'What are you waiting for? Go and claim your new farmlands, see for yourself what fine land I've given you. Oh, and Liam, put this place up for sale.'

'But who would buy ruined land, Gran?' Liam said in exasperation.

'Men who want to build houses, churches, or factories, there are still some of those about the place. Advertise the land, use your brain box, boy.'

Liam leaned forward and kissed his grandmother, his lips brushing the lined face with fondness.

'You know something, you are not so bad.'

'Get away with you, Liam Cullen, if that's your idea of a compliment then 'tis clear you haven't kissed the Blarney Stone.'

They returned to the house together, Liam matching his steps to Maeve's slower ones, her arm through his. They walked in silence but there was a bond between them that needed no words.

Patricia was standing in the kitchen, her bags packed on the floor beside her.

'What's going on here?' Maeve spoke more out of curiosity than concern.

'Well, since there's nothing here for me I've decided to move in with Terrence Duffy.' She lifted her chin, 'Any objections?'

'Rat leaving a sinking ship, sort of thing,' Maeve said. 'You are a fool, you know the man can't put a ring on your finger, he's already got a wife.'

'I'm not stupid, I know that.' Patricia put her hands on her hips and Liam noticed with a dart of surprise that, though his sister was plain, she had a well-rounded figure.

'So, you are going to become part of the human race after all,' Maeve sank into her rocking chair; 'going to give up your virginity at last.'

'Gran, do you have to be so crude?' Patricia's colour rose alarmingly. 'I haven't said I'd go to his bed, only keep house for him while his wife is sick.'

'Sick in the mind, pour soul,' Maeve spoke contemplatively; 'thin as a rake and long as a piece of streaky bacon. She's been no wife at all to poor Terry these past years.' Her glance ran over her granddaughter's tightly buttoned bodice and neat skirt. 'Take my word for it, Patricia, he'll be wanting more than a housekeeper.'

Liam stepped forward. 'Look, Pat, no need for this.' He glanced towards Maeve. 'Can I tell her, Gran?' Maeve shrugged.

'Gran has given me some land, I can begin again, we

can make a go of it. Come with me, be my housekeeper if that's the sort of job you're after.'

'I see, so once again the blue-eyed boy has fallen on his feet. Well, I don't want to come with you and take the crumbs from your table and I don't want to stay here with Dad and Gran either. If I'm to be a housekeeper, then I'll earn my living honestly.'

Maeve concealed a smile. Patricia glared at her angrily. 'Don't you laugh at me, Gran. As I remember it was you who urged me to get out into the world and find myself a man.'

'Well, I'm glad to see that my advice didn't fall on deaf ears.' Maeve closed her eyes and leaned back in her chair, determined not to be drawn into any further discussion.

'Right then, I'll be going.' Patricia picked up her bags and moved towards the door.

'Hadn't you better wait till Dad gets in?' Liam asked her anxiously.

'My father knows exactly what I intend to do, it was he who told me it was for the best.' She glanced around the farmhouse. 'The place is ruined, a wasteland, what good is it to anyone now?'

The rumble of wheels sounded on the gravel outside. Maeve opened her eyes and there was an impish gleam in their dark depths.

'Looks like your knight in shining armour has arrived.'

'Oh very funny, Gran.' Patricia paused for a moment, her shoulders sagging as she stared through the door at the portly man seated on the cart. He lifted his hat and his bald pate shone in the pale sunlight.

'You can always change your mind,' Liam said. Patricia smiled with rare humour.

'Half a loaf is better than none.' She glanced at her gran, Maeve's smile was suddenly warm.

'I think there's a bit of me in you yet, Patricia. Treasure it, it'll be the saving of you, believe me.'

Liam watched as Terrence Duffy helped Patricia into the cart, his weathered face was alight and Liam wondered if perhaps Patricia had not made such a bad bargain after all. When the cart had rolled out of sight, Liam turned from the window.

'Want some supper, Gran?' His voice fell into the silent room, Maeve was asleep.

'I think I'm having the bastard's baby.' Doreen looked up at Catherine, her eyes shadowed and heavy. The bruises inflicted by her husband had long since faded from her face and body but as the weeks had passed, her dread had increased and now she was sure, sure that her husband's last, brutal attack on her had filled her with his child.

Catherine pushed the kettle onto the flames and Doreen could see that she was searching for something to say.

'I don't want it,' Doreen said harshly. 'I never wanted anything of his.'

Catherine came and sat beside her. 'Perhaps you'll change your mind when it's born.'

'And how will I keep it?' Doreen felt anger burn within her. 'How can I earn my living and carry a baby at the same time? It just can't be done.'

'I'll help,' Catherine said, 'and I'm sure Mrs Grenfell will let you work at home. When your time comes, I'll support us until you are strong again.'

'Love you, child, you can't take on such a burden, don't talk so soft.' Doreen rose to her feet. 'I've tried hot baths and gin, tried jumping off a chair, nothing will shift it.'

She could see that Catherine was shocked by the seemingly callous words.

'Look Cath, I hate that man, I don't want his seed growing inside me. What if I had a boy? Would he be a bully like Meadows?'

'It might be a lovely little girl,' Catherine said gently and Doreen shook her head.

'I just don't want it, can't you understand that?'

'Well, there's not a lot you can do about it now, is there?' Catherine said.

'Oh, isn't there. Well, just you wait and see, I won't

have Meadows's child; I don't want it and I won't keep it.'

'You can't mean to go to old Ma Piper!' Catherine's tone was filled with horror. Mrs Piper lived in a run-down house in the poorest part of town, she was old and dirty but adept with a hot crochet hook. Most of the women who went to her for help survived with little harm done; the unlucky few did not.

Doreen knew all of that but she was prepared to face the dangers rather than carry her loathsome husband's child.

'Don't look so worried, love, I know what I'm doing. Now, let's drop the subject, tell me what's been going on at the shop, is Mrs Grenfell making a profit do you think?'

Catherine shook her head. 'I don't know anything about that but she doesn't seem so worried these days.'

'Well, let's hope she's pulling herself out of the slump otherwise it's down the privie for all of us.'

Catherine was still a little naïve, still a bit of a child in spite of her chequered love life. Doreen allowed herself a glimmer of humour, at least Catherine had not been fool enough to get herself married to the first man who bedded her.

It was early next morning when Doreen found herself seated in the front parlour of Mrs Piper's house.

'Well, Doreen Meadows, got yourself with child from a seed that's not your husband's, is it?'

Doreen smiled thinly. 'It's my husband that's put me like this and I don't want anything of his, ever.'

'Can't say I blame you, knocked you about a bit in his time, hasn't he? But then, they're all the same, give 'em plenty of beer and a willing woman and they're happy.'

Doreen wished the old woman would stop blathering, her hands were sweating, her mouth was dry and suddenly she was afraid. 'Meadows is not fussy about "willing", so long as he has his way. Are you going to get on with the job, Mrs Piper, or not?'

'Get in the kitchen, if you're in such a hurry, and get your drawers off. Don't worry, it'll be over before you know it.'

It was cold in the kitchen, a thin strip of light pierced the gloom between the shabby curtains and the room smelt of stale food. Doreen swallowed hard.

'Get up on the table then.' Mrs Piper quickly spread newspaper over the grimy table top. 'Don't look so worried, I don't lose my girls; well, not many of them.'

Doreen hesitated, she felt the urge to run, to get right away from the old woman.

'Do you want this brat or not?' The words fell into the silence and Doreen was galvanized into life. She clambered awkwardly onto the table and looked up at the cracked ceiling festooned with cobwebs.

'Let me get at it then, girl. Come on, you're no trembling virgin, let's see what I'm about.'

Doreen closed her eyes, she was cold, she had never been so terrified in all her life, not even when Meadows had beaten her almost senseless. Violence of that kind, she knew; this ordeal before her was very different.

She felt Mrs Piper probe into the deep recesses of her being and reacted abruptly.

'There, there, don't clamp your knees together or I can't do nothing to help. Be easy now, this won't hurt, I promise you.'

Mrs Piper had, quite clearly, never undergone an operation of this kind, for the pain, when it came, was sharp, searing, threatening to tear Doreen in two.

'That's it.' Mrs Piper sounded pleased with herself. 'That's shaken the little birdie off its perch. Want a cup of tea? Don't charge for that.'

Doreen sat up shakily, reading the kindly phrased offer correctly. She dug in her pocket and brought out the purse of money, money that represented the month's wages Hari Grenfell had advanced her.

'Now, get off home with you, do a bit of housework, get the blood flowing, that's what's needed now to clear you out good an' proper.'

Doreen found herself out in the cold air, she felt disorientated, her eyes did not appear to focus clearly on the roadway stretching out before her. It seemed a long way back to her house, though in reality it was a mere two streets away.

Indoors, she sank into a chair, her eyes closing. She smiled weakly remembering Mrs Piper's exhortations to do a bit of housework and knew she had no strength to lift her arms, let alone wield a broom.

Perhaps she was going to die and perhaps it served her right. What she had done was a mortal sin, at least in the eyes of the Catholic Church to which Doreen had once belonged. But that was when life was clean and simple, that was before she had married Meadows.

The blood came suddenly. Doreen watched abstractedly as the stain spread across her skirt. The room was growing dim, perhaps she should light the lamp. It was too much trouble, the darkness was closing in and it was warm and welcoming.

Catherine walked briskly along the high street turning uphill towards Baptist Well. She was tired, it had been a long day at work but she knew Doreen would have a hot meal waiting and a good fire to welcome her home.

'Catherine.' The voice stopped her abruptly. She closed her eyes against the rush of anger, her hands clenching into fists before she composed herself and faced him.

'What do you want now, Boyo?' Her tone was as cold as the air around her. 'Hasn't it sunk in yet that I've got nothing to say to you?'

'I have to talk to you.' Boyo reached out towards her but she side-stepped his hand.

'Go away.' She pushed past him and stepped into the dim porch of Doreen's house. She moved along the passage towards the kitchen and, suddenly, the smell of blood, like old iron, was almost tangible. Through the gloom she saw the still figure of Doreen lying on the floor and she cried out in terror.

Footsteps pounded along the passageway behind her. 'What is it?' Boyo was beside her, gripping her arms. She shook her head, unable to speak and pointed to where

Doreen was slumped against the cold flags.

'Light the lamp,' Boyo instructed and she obeyed him with fumbling fingers. 'Bring it over here.' Boyo was kneeling down beside the inert figure and as she approached, Catherine could see the dark stain that covered Doreen's skirt from waist to hem.

'Is she dead?' Her voice sounded insubstantial, as though she was whispering in a high-ceilinged church. She held the lamp higher and in the flickering flame she saw that Doreen was waxen, unmoving.

'Not far from it.' Boyo rose to his feet. 'Stay here, I'll fetch a cab, we'll take her to the hospital.' He turned briefly, 'Get something to wrap her in, she's like ice, she's lost a lot of blood.'

Catherine put the lamp carefully on the table and hurried upstairs. She took a thick woollen shawl from one of the beds and paused for a moment, trying to push away the knowledge of what her friend had done, what she must have faced alone. She forced herself to hurry as she retraced her steps back to the kitchen.

She entered the room at the same moment as Boyo did, he took the shawl from her and carefully wrapped it around Doreen before lifting her gently in his arms. The cab driver looked down at them doubtfully but at Boyo's sharp command, he took up the reins and urged the horse forward.

The hospital corridors were quiet, the brown and green painted walls sombre in the dim lighting. Doreen was taken from Boyo's arms and swept away behind closed doors.

Boyo took Catherine's arm and led her to a bench near the entrance of the hospital. Outside, a pale moon glinted through the branches of the young trees planted near the gates.

'How did this happen?' Boyo said, leaning towards Catherine.

Catherine shook her head. 'Doreen was having a child.' Her voice was strained. 'Her husband raped her and she didn't want it. She must have gone to old Ma Piper. Poor Doreen, will she be all right?'

283

'I don't know but it's something she has brought on herself isn't it?' Boyo said quietly. Catherine looked up at him, straining to see him clearly in the gloom.

'Don't you dare to judge.' Her tone was hard. 'What gives you the right to be so holy and good?'

'I lost my son, though perhaps you have forgotten that. It didn't touch you, after all.'

She leaned closer to him. 'I know the memory must be painful for you but that was a different situation entirely. Doreen's husband is an animal, he beats her whenever he feels like it. She couldn't go on carrying his child, it would have given Meadows even more of a hold on her than ever.'

She touched Boyo's hand and his fingers grasped hers, strong and warm.

'I wonder what's happening in there, I don't think I could bear it if Doreen dies.' Catherine's voice trembled and Boyo's hand held hers firmly.

'We can only wait and see, Cat.' The old endearment slipped out unnoticed by Boyo but Catherine winced. How easy it would be to slip back into the old ways, to become Boyo's woman again. He would take her back to their house in Caswell, he would take her away from the hardness of the life she was now leading. The thought was very tempting and Catherine closed her eyes, resting her head against his shoulder, glad that she was not alone.

It was going to be more difficult than Liam had imagined to farm the new lands to the north of Cork. The ground had been allowed to grow wild for years, it would need many seasons before good crops could be grown there.

The farmhouse was spacious, sprawling over almost half an acre of land, there were more rooms than Liam could ever inhabit alone. He smiled as he set the kindling in the huge fireplace. Once he brought Catherine here, gave her babies to care for, the house would be filled with love and laughter.

Maeve's advice about the spoiled farmland had proved sound. Cork was expanding, building land was needed and prices were set to rise. Good had been wrought from evil; what had seemed an insurmountable problem had been resolved in a most satisfactory way. Soon, he would have a great deal to offer Catherine: a fine house, for he intended to renovate the old farmhouse, and prime farm-land supporting rich crops and fine milk herds and further up into the hills, pasture lands for sheep.

Once Liam had the money from the sale of the old land, he could begin his work, start afresh. He sank down onto a log and looked up towards the sky. He would have the last laugh over Boyo Hopkins, after all.

His gaze sharpened as he saw a figure toiling up the hill towards him. He rose to his feet, his hand shading his eyes from the dying light and for a moment, he wondered if Catherine was coming to him. Then he recognized the figure, it was Patricia.

He ran down the hill towards her and took the bag from her hand. He could see she was tired, her eyes were shadowed, her footsteps slow. He did not have to ask her what was wrong for when her shawl slipped apart, the curve of her belly was plain to see.

In the farmhouse, she sank into a chair near the fire and held out her hands to the glow. Liam made her some hot tea and sat with her, looking at her in compassion.

'He kicked me out,' she said at last. 'Once the baby began to show Terrence wanted nothing more to do with me.'

'I thought he was in love with you,' Liam said, 'the way he looked at you, as though you were the best prize this side of the Irish Sea.'

'Sure, so did I,' Patricia said dryly. 'What he was in love with was the thought of breaking in a virgin, he kept on about it enough to whoever would listen to him.' She smiled mirthlessly. 'It wasn't even worth it, all that gasp-ing and pushing and shoving. If that's what love is about then sure I can do without it.'

She began to cry, silent tears ran along her cheeks and she dashed them away with shaking fingers. Liam, moved, took her in his arms. 'Why didn't you go to live with Dad?' he asked, rocking her as though she was a child. 'The cottage I found for them is big enough for three, heaven knows.'

'And have Gran laugh at me?' Patricia's voice rose. 'Have her saying "I told you so".' She leaned back in his arms. 'Say I can stay here, Liam. I'll work, I'll keep house for you, I won't be any trouble, I promise.'

'Of course you can stay here.' Liam rubbed gently at her eyes with the heel of his hand. 'Though how I'm going to put up with that acid tongue of yours, sure only the good Lord knows!'

Patricia was laughing then, laughing and crying at the same time.

'At least Gran was right about something,' Liam said, smiling to soften his words; 'sleeping with a man has certainly made you one of the human race at last.'

She reached out and slapped his face lightly with her fingertips. 'Monster!' It was the first time he had seen her laugh so easily. It seemed his sister, during her time away, had found a new sense of humour.

CHAPTER TWENTY-THREE

Bethan looked at her husband with narrowed eyes. 'It's good of you to worry about me but really there's no need. I like being here alone.' Her voice was soft, for the spirit of Elizabeth was with her, urging her to make the most of this unexpected opportunity to regain Boyo's sympathy if not his love.

When he had called, she had been sitting alone in the upstairs room but no, not quite alone. Elizabeth had been close, comforting her. When Boyo had arrived Elizabeth had withdrawn to the corner of the room, watching, waiting.

'I'm concerned, that's all.' Boyo moved towards the window and Bethan saw him frown at the overhang of dark rocks, knowing he hated the enclosed feeling the greyness gave him. She smiled to herself, Boyo Hopkins would be hers again, one day, when the time was right.

He was looking very handsome, her husband, but there was a light in his eyes that she didn't like the look of. Suspicion rose within her like a monster and became a certainty.

'You've been with *her*, haven't you?' It sounded like an accusation and Boyo looked at her in surprise.

'Sometimes I wonder where you get your powers of perception from, Bethan.'

She knew, oh, yes, she knew all right, the spirits were around her now, friends brought by Elizabeth gathered close, supporting her, leading her. Elizabeth spoke from within her, Bethan's mouth opened and the words came out. 'She's evil, she will do you harm. You must keep away from Catherine O'Conner or she will bring about your downfall.'

Boyo's shoulders stiffened but he didn't look at her.

When he spoke, he sounded defensive. 'She's an ordinary girl, she has had everything she knew and loved snatched away from her. The harm you speak of has been done to her, not to me.'

It was a rebuke, Bethan knew that and she longed to cry out to her husband, tell him that what had happened to Catherine O'Conner was simple justice. The girl would be the death of Boyo, he was a fool not to realize it. She held her tongue as the door opened and a maid bobbed a curtsey, her eyes downcast.

Cara was afraid of Bethan, her manner made that obvious. She thought her fey, mysterious and had talked below stairs of hushed voices in the bedroom. Bethan was aware of the maid's feelings but did not feel it necessary to do anything to dispel the girl's fears.

'There's a . . . gentleman to see you, Mrs Hopkins.' Bethan stared at her, aware of the hesitation before the word 'gentleman'. She knew at once who the caller was.

'Take him to the drawing-room, give him tea, tell him I shall be with him presently.'

'A gentleman caller, is it?' Boyo's attempt to lighten the atmosphere fell on stony ground. Bethan rose from her chair and faced her husband.

'If you will excuse me, I have some business I must attend to. Perhaps you will call to see me again, Boyo; I'd like that.' She rested her hand for a moment on his cheek and with an involuntary movement, he drew away.

Behind her, the spirits whispered their disapproval and in her mind she comforted them, telling them it was the evil influence of Catherine O'Conner that made Boyo act in such a way. Boyo must be worked on, persuaded to see where his best interests lay. Bethan was confident that he would be a loving husband once more, given time.

Boyo paused at the front door, peering across the dark hall towards the sitting-room, trying to see who her visitor might be. Bethan hid a smile, so he was not so insensitive to her as he liked to pretend, perhaps he was even a little jealous of her mysterious caller.

She watched as the groom helped Boyo to mount his

horse. As he rode away, he looked tall and handsome, it was only when he was hidden from sight by the sheltering trees that Bethan turned towards the drawing-room.

As she entered the room, Meadows rose to his feet, bowing slightly as though she were royalty.

'Please sit, Sergeant Meadows. Tell me, have you found out anything I should know?'

He half smiled. 'I certainly have. I put one of my trusted men to watch on the household where this woman lives.' He paused and Bethan waved her hand impatiently.

'Go on.'

'Catherine O'Conner paid a visit to a certain type of woman, a medical woman, if you get my meaning.'

'Speak plainly, man.' Bethan felt a prickling of excitement as she recognized what the policeman was trying to say but she wanted him to spell it out, so that she could be sure.

'This woman was a backstreet midwife, of sorts, the type more inclined to get rid of a nipper rather than bring one into the world.'

'An abortionist, a backstreet abortionist, that's what you mean isn't it?'

'Yes Mrs Hopkins, that's just what I mean.'

'Any idea who the man is?'

'Well, Jerry Danby, one of my constables, has been hanging round the house quite a lot lately. Fancies the girl, he does, been sniffing round the place like a dog after a bitch on heat.'

Bethan, who had urged the man to speak plainly, now deplored his crude remarks. Nevertheless, the gist of what he was saying pleased her. It was clear that Catherine O'Conner, not content with bedding a married man, was now sleeping with this Constable Danby and had found herself in trouble.

Bethan took a deep breath of triumph, the O'Conner slut had conceived a child and it had been aborted. That choice piece of information would be useful. She could picture the disbelief on Boyo's face but that disbelief

289

would be wiped away by the testimony of Sergeant Meadows.

She moved to the ornate sideboard, seeing her own reflection in the oval mirror above it with a sigh of displeasure. She was old, an old woman and Catherine was young, zestful, eager for the joys of the flesh. Bethan sighed; but those joys would turn to sorrow, when the time was right.

She took out an envelope containing some money and handed it to Meadows. 'You have done very well, keep up the good work.' She forced a smile even though she despised the man for his gauche, common manner. She despised his false air of servility, his coarse speech, his dirty nails. Yet he was useful to her, at least for the moment. He was the perfect spy: he had access to the house because of his estranged wife, so he could watch on Catherine O'Conner at close quarters.

When Meadows left, Bethan sank down in a chair and closed her eyes. The room was quiet, dreamy in the soft sunlight. Outside the windows the birds sang, bees droned in the honeysuckle but Bethan heard none of it, she had retreated into the private, comforting place where the spirits communed with her. They were her comfort and support, the spirits were her friends, they would take care of her, lead her to her destiny. She sighed softly as she felt herself drop into the other world, the world where she could forget she was old, where she could be beautiful and loved, where she could be happy.

Catherine opened the door and froze as she saw Meadows standing on the doorstep. His mouth twisted into a sneer as he pushed past her into the heat of the sunlit kitchen.

'What do you want?' Catherine demanded, hiding her hands as she tried to stop them trembling. The man moved closer and Catherine could smell the stale odour of him.

'Shut your gob, slut.' He spoke the words so casually that Catherine did not at first believe she had heard right.

290

Anger burned through her, replacing her fear.

'How dare you speak to me like that?' she said hotly. He caught her arm and twisted it behind her back.

'I'll speak to you any way I want to, whore!' He slipped his hand into her bodice, grasping her breast with cruel fingers.

Catherine moved swiftly, she kicked Meadows as hard as she could and put the breadth of the kitchen table between them. She dragged open a drawer and took out a knife. 'Touch me again and I'll kill you.' She said in a cold flat voice. Meadows drew back a little, seeing that she meant every word.

'Like you killed that baby you were carrying?' His words were like stones and for a moment, he wondered if he was wrong when he saw the naked surprise on her face. 'It was you saw that old woman, wasn't it?' His voice had hardened.

Catherine swallowed hard, her thoughts were whirling, she could not give Doreen away, could not tell this man that Doreen's hatred of him was so great she could not stand the thought of his child growing within her. 'And if it was me, is that any business of yours?' she hedged.

'So you can let Jerry Danby up your skirts but not old Meadows.' He had recovered his composure and sat astride one of the kitchen chairs leering at her. 'Like to ride the young bucks, is that it? Well, don't forget there's many a fine tune played on an old fiddle, I could show you some things that Danby hasn't even learned yet.'

Catherine swallowed hard, she had driven herself into a corner and it was going to be difficult to escape from it. She forced herself to speak firmly. 'Mind your own business, I don't have to answer to anyone, least of all you, do you understand me?'

He rose threateningly and Catherine stood her ground staring up at him, the knife held before her, challenging him to come any nearer.

'I could break you in two with my bare hands, you silly bitch,' he said in a growl. 'I could have my way with you and you couldn't stop me.'

'You would have to kill me then,' Catherine said, her voice deadly calm. 'Because after you'd done with me, I would be straight round to your superiors to make a complaint about you. You'd be discredited, out of a job, all your petty power gone and I don't think you'd like that one bit.'

Her words had the desired effect, Meadows was silent for a moment and then he shrugged. 'I wouldn't want you anyway, soiled goods are not to my liking, fussy I am about where I gives my favours.' He looked round. 'Where's my wife?'

'Gone to the market. Search the place if you don't believe me.' Catherine stared at him unwaveringly. He turned without another word and left the house and she sank down into a chair, feeling suddenly weak. She dropped the knife, she had been clutching it so hard that there were grooves along the palm of her hand.

She was still sitting there when Doreen came into the house, her steps slow, she was still weak after losing the baby. She was carrying a bag, from which jutted a stiff piece of board and she smiled cheerfully. 'I've been buying materials for making some new hats.' She was still pale and thin, her eyes shadowed, but she was as perceptive as ever.

'Hell fire, what's got into you?' She dumped her bag on the table and leaned forward, her bony shoulders protruding through the thin material of her coat. 'You are as white as a sheet, love you, what's happened?'

Catherine swallowed hard. 'It's nothing, Meadows...'

'So that bastard has been here, has he?'

Catherine made an effort to gather her wits and sat back in her chair, easing the tension from her arms and hands. 'Aye, he's been here, he knows about the . . . the visit you paid to that woman.'

Doreen sank down into a chair opposite her and shook her head, her mouth compressed into a straight line. Appearing suddenly, as though painted on with a brush, harrowed lines settled across her forehead. 'Oh, my Gawd!'

Catherine forced herself to speak reassuringly. 'Don't worry, I let him think it was me who was seeing Ma Piper.'

Doreen banged the table with her fist. 'The bastard had no right to come here in the first place, we pay the rent, not 'im.' She looked down at the knife, pushing it away gingerly with her foot. 'He threatened you, didn't he?'

'He tried to, I said I'd report him to his superiors if he touched me, that stopped him in his tracks.'

Doreen sighed heavily. 'Your good name will be dragged through the mud, that's what my precious husband will do. He can't stand anyone facing up to him. He'll have it in for you now, girl.'

Catherine rubbed her eyes, 'Why can't he leave you alone? What makes him come back here time after time, can't he see you don't care about him any more?'

'He likes to have me in his power, he can't dampen my spirit, not for long, but he tries his best. He thinks he'll win with his beatings and by using force to get "his rights" as he calls them but he won't grind me down, the bastard.' She looked at Catherine with worried eyes. 'Don't walk anywhere dark, Cath, 'cos he'll get even one way or another. He'll pounce where no-one can see him, so that you can't prove nothing against him, clever he is, evil and clever.'

Catherine tried not to show how frightened she was by Doreen's words. She had seen the hate in Meadows's eyes, seen the lecherous way he'd looked at her. It was clear he would like to hurt and humiliate her in any way he could.

'Let's forget him,' she said, suddenly brisk. 'Tell me what you've brought home with you, show me again how to make a fine hat for a toff, you never know when it will come in useful.'

Doreen smiled wanly. 'You got guts, I'll give you that. Right, we'll do some work but not before we have a hot, sweet cup of tea. Your turn, love, I made the last one.'

Catherine returned her smile. 'A likely story but all right then, I'll make the tea you old dragon.'

★

Bethan was lying in bed, the clothes drawn up to her chin. She was waiting for Boyo, she had sent a servant to fetch him with a message that she was not well. He had replied saying he would be there within the hour.

Bethan looked across the room towards the cliffs and saw the ghostly figure sitting there, on a ledge outside the window. Once Bethan had walked to the top of the cliffs and looked down into her bedroom and was not surprised to see that the entire room was visible from outside. Below her was a sheer rock-face, falling away below the fence that supported the perimeter of her garden.

Her house was built on what must have once been a plateau in the rocks, a flat piece of ground broken away over the years from the face that towered behind and above it. From the front of the house, the land sloped downwards, guarded by random outcrops of grey rock, making the traffic of carriages difficult. But Ty Craig was her house, part of her; it had always been waiting for her to come home, she realized that now.

The oil painting she had taken to her room took pride of place above the mantel. The face of the young Elizabeth Llewellyn was strong, lovely, the eyes large, the mouth firm. The same face now looked into her bedroom from the rock-face outside, smiling at her, encouraging her.

Elizabeth had owned the house once. She had died young, at least that was what Bethan's father had told her. Elizabeth had never married, never had children. They shared the same family name and Bethan was becoming more fond of her, more dependent on her, with every day that passed.

Usually she would invite Elizabeth inside her bedroom and they would talk at great length about the problems that beset Bethan's marriage. Now, Elizabeth would wait in patience, knowing that Bethan must be alone with her husband, she had something of importance to tell him.

Bethan sat up and looked into the mirror on the far side of the room. Her face looked thin, her cheek-bones high, she appeared wan and helpless, a woman in need of care.

She smiled, oh, yes, that's what Boyo would believe, she knew him inside out, knew the guilt that drove him, the conscience that smote him whenever he was with his wife.

She heard footsteps outside the door and fell back against the pillows, closing her eyes. The door opened and she sensed Boyo crossing the room, his feet making no sound on the deep carpet. She felt his weight as he sank onto the bed beside her. 'Bethan, how are you, love?'

Slowly she opened her eyes and allowed a smile to turn up the corners of her mouth. She held out her hand and he took it, thrilling her with his strong grip. 'I'm so happy to see you, thank you for coming, Boyo. I'm sorry to be a trouble but I feel so sick and I had no-one else to turn to.'

'It's no trouble, don't be silly.' He smoothed the skin on the back of her hand with gentle, soothing movements and Bethan felt love for him well up in her. She had no need to force her tears, her emotion was real.

'Oh, Boyo, take me in your arms, hold me, I've been so alone.'

After a momentary hesitation, he drew her to him and as her head fell against his shoulder, he patted her back awkwardly. 'It's all right, I'm here. Now, you are not alone any more.'

'I've felt so lost, so ill, I don't know what's wrong with me.' Her lips rested against the warmth of his neck. She breathed in the scent of him, loving him, feeling the pain of losing him all over again. Mingling with the pain came a surge of bitterness against the one who had caused the rift – Catherine O'Conner.

'Have you had the doctor?' Boyo held her away and looked anxiously into her face. 'You're so thin and pale, Bethan, you are not taking care of yourself, are you?'

'I don't want the doctor,' she said slowly, 'I know what he'll tell me, the same thing he did last time he came.'

'And what was that?' Boyo asked, frowning.

'He told me to get out more, to breathe in the fresh air and to stop grieving over you.'

She felt Boyo stiffen and she knew that her words sounded like a rebuke.

'I told him that was all stuff and nonsense!' she added hastily. 'I told him that we were nothing more than friends, now, that you and I had respect for each other and that you were always kind to me. You are kind, Boyo, you came when I needed you. Say you'll stay a few days, please, will you, just until I feel stronger?'

She sensed the conflict going on behind the deliberately bland expression on his face. 'Please, Boyo, only for a few days, I won't be any trouble, I promise.'

'All right. Yes, of course I'll stay.'

Bethan sighed with relief. 'Go and get some supper, now, Cook has a hot meal ready for you.'

'Were you so sure I'd stay?'

Bethan shook her head. 'It never occurred to me to ask you until this moment, Boyo, but I couldn't let you ride home without giving you a good meal, could I?' She allowed herself a smile. 'I can see you are not getting enough to eat.'

He rose from the bed. 'I will have to go home, get some clothes. I can be back before nightfall, though.'

'No need, love,' Bethan said. 'I found when I moved here that I'd brought some of your things with me.'

She saw the trapped look on his face and felt a momentary dart of pity for him. But it was for his own good, she would have time over the next few days to work on his good nature, to make him feel even more responsible for her than he did now. And in the meantime, she could count on the little maid Cara to acquaint Boyo with the latest gossip concerning Catherine O'Conner, that way the revelation of the girl's wanton ways would not look like spite on Bethan's part.

'Go and have something to eat. Don't worry so much, if you really must go home, then I can't keep you here by force, can I?' She allowed herself to speak lightly, making him feel foolish and unreasonable. Oh, she knew him all right.

When he left the room, Bethan looked towards the

figure on the rocks. Elizabeth was coming nearer, she was in the room, standing beside the bed, smiling approvingly. Her lips were the same scarlet as they were in the painting. She was so vivid this time, she mouthed the words 'well done'. Bethan closed her eyes and slept.

'This pie is delicious, Mrs Frayne, Bethan was lucky to find a cook like you.' Boyo had elected to sit in the warmth of the kitchen instead of having his dinner served in the long cold dining-room. The fire glowed in the hearth and, at the large sink, the young maid was washing dishes.

'Go on with you, flatterer.' Mrs Frayne deftly lifted his plate and replenished it with another helping of beef pie. 'Wasted I am here, mind, poor Mrs Hopkins hardly eats enough to keep a bird alive.'

Boyo nodded. 'I know, she's very thin and frail, I wish she would have proper advice, her doctor doesn't seem a very sympathetic sort of man.'

'Bless you, she won't have no doctor in the house, don't hold with them, she says.'

'He has never been here?' Boyo asked carefully and watched as Mrs Frayne shook her head. 'Not to my knowledge. But she's a strong lady, right enough, strong-willed that is. A bit strange at times but with a good head on her shoulders for all that.'

The young maid came and sat at the end of the table and the cook served her meal. 'Are you sure you want to eat with us, Mr Hopkins?' Mrs Frayne asked, frowning a little at the girl.

'Of course, I'm not one for standing on ceremony. In any case, the kitchen seems to me to be the most cheerful room in the house.'

'You're right there.' Mrs Frayne seated herself and picked up her knife and fork. 'Ghostly, that's what this house is; there's a feeling about it, some say it's haunted but that's a lot of bunkum.'

'I don't know,' Cara said softly, 'sometimes even I think I can see things, just out of sight, around a corner or in the shadows.' She shivered.

For a moment there was silence in the kitchen and then Mrs Frayne spoke, giving Cara just the opening she had been waiting for. Mrs Hopkins had been very insistent that she pass on one particular piece of gossip, heaven knows why, perhaps as a diversion for this young handsome husband of hers.

'Hear anything interesting in the market today, Cara?' She looked towards Boyo. 'This girl is a one for picking up gossip, like a sponge she is, folks will tell her anything.' She smiled. 'Must be that long nose you got, Cara.'

Cara touched the tip of her perfect nose indignantly. 'I'm not nosy, Mrs Frayne, just interested in what folks have to say.'

'Well, what are folks saying today? Get on with it, we haven't got all night, mind.'

Cara spun out some stories about people Boyo didn't know and he allowed himself to fall into a reverie, wondering how soon he could leave Bethan's house. When he heard Catherine's name being mentioned, he was suddenly alert. He forced himself to remain still, though every sense was now tinglingly alive.

'Went to that old woman down by Wassail Square there, that midwife, you know the one . . .'

'Aye, I know the one,' Mrs Frayne said darkly. 'Butcher, that's what she is and none too clean into the bargain. It's a wonder the poor girl is still alive.'

'Well, the babe she was carrying is gone, that's for sure.' Cara glanced towards Boyo. 'Poor little mite, not wanted by anyone, not even its mammy.'

He relaxed; it wasn't Catherine they were talking about, he had been there when her friend miscarried the baby, had gone to the hospital with them, sat for long hours with Catherine at his side, waiting for news of Doreen Meadows.

'Who's the father, then?' Mrs Frayne was leaning forward eagerly now, her cap falling unnoticed to one side of her grey hair.

'Well, they're saying that nice Jerry Danby been a regular caller, courting the girl strong, so they say. Catherine

O'Conner and Jerry Danby go everywhere together, least-ways that's what I heard.'

Boyo forced himself to be calm, that titbit of gossip had been altered in the telling just as the rest of the story had been. And yet jealousy twisted within him like a knife.

Cara was looking at him as though she could see the turmoil within him but her expression remained bland. 'Catherine O'Conner is working for Mrs Grenfell in her new shop. Pretty girl with lovely red hair, a real beauty, she is. Jerry walks her home every night, lovey-dovey they are, the pair of them, lucky things.'

Boyo rose from the table and left the kitchen without another word leaving the two women to stare at each other with raised eyebrows.

As he mounted the stairs, he fought with his jealousy but suspicion and anger were mounting within him. Outside his wife's door, he rehearsed the words he would say to Bethan, words that would tell her he could not stay with her, that he had urgent business in town. And he had.

He must speak to Catherine at once, ask her to tell him the truth about Jerry Danby; could she be walking out with the constable? It seemed unlikely, it was only a few weeks ago that he had been with her at the hospital, so close that hope for their future together had risen within him like the blossoming of a flower.

Since then, he had been away on business, he'd had no opportunity to see her or speak with her. As soon as he had returned to Caswell, there had been a message waiting for him from Bethan.

In her room, Bethan was lying against the pillows, her greying hair spread out around her shoulders, her face as white as the sheets around her.

'Bethan,' he spoke her name softly but there was no response. 'Bethan, are you all right?'

She opened her eyes slowly. 'I don't feel well at all, Boyo, I seem to get so confused these days. Please sit beside me, hold my hand.'

He was impatient to be gone but he sat on the side of

the bed and took her hand in his. Her flesh was cold to the touch and he bent closer to her.

'Bethan, we had better get the doctor out to see you, I know you say you've seen him before but he must pay you another visit, I'm worried about you.'

'All right, Boyo, get him if you like but wait until the morning.'

'I can't wait, Bethan, I have decided not to stay after all. I'm sorry.'

'I understand you have been listening to Cara's gossip. Go, if you must, see the girl but can you be sure you are not doing more harm than good?'

'What do you mean?' Boyo was on edge, suspicious of anything Bethan might say.

'Look, I don't want to hurt you but what Cara has told you is the truth, at least some of her gossip is accurate. The girl has been seen with Constable Danby on several occasions. Have you thought that perhaps you should leave her alone, allow her to make her own way in the world?'

He rose to his feet and moved away from her, knowing that there was a thread of common sense in what she was saying.

'Sergeant Meadows told me about a visit the girl made to a backstreet abortionist. In some ways, I feel almost sorry for the girl.'

Boyo smiled thinly. 'No need to feel sorry for Catherine, she is perfectly all right, I assure you. As for Meadows, he is about as reliable as a leaking boat, I wouldn't believe a word he says.' He paused, realizing there would be repercussions for Doreen if he told Bethan the truth of the matter. Bethan seemed to gather strength from his silence.

'Go to her then, she'll tell you the truth herself, if she has any decency in her. Look, Boyo, she's young, she needs to spread her wings and who could blame her for that?'

Boyo turned to look at his wife. Though she had always hated Catherine, she was right about one thing, he should leave Catherine alone, let her find a man who could care for her, a man who could marry her. Looking at his wife, sick and weak in the bed, he knew he could not bring himself to urge her to divorce him as he had intended to do.

'Sergeant Meadows's estranged wife lives in the same house as Catherine O'Conner,' Bethan said. 'He calls there sometimes with gifts for his wife. On more than one occasion, your lady friend was sitting in the kitchen in the company of this young policeman.' She sighed heavily. 'I'm only thinking of you, Boyo, I don't want to see you hurt and upset any more than you have been.'

She fell back against the pillows, coughing so violently that her colour rose alarmingly. He knew he could not go to Catherine, not tonight at least. He must call out the doctor, for if he left Bethan now, he felt she might not live to see the morning light.

CHAPTER TWENTY-FOUR

'It's just like Cath to stick up for me.' Doreen poured home-made wine into a glass and handed it to Boyo. 'If Meadows knew it was me who saw the old woman, he'd kill me, that's why Cath lied to him. Thank you for being such a rock, Mr Hopkins, I was sick as Mother Murphy's pig when you took me to the 'ospital.'

'I was glad to help.' Boyo sipped the wine, wincing at the sharp taste of it. 'When will Catherine be home?'

'You're married, aren't you?' Doreen folded her arms across her thin chest. 'Can't make an honest woman of Cath, can you?'

'That's my business, Doreen. Look, I've heard she's going out with Constable Danby. If that's the case, I'll get out of her life, for good.'

'Best thing to do, an' all. Most men are selfish bastards, I get the idea that you are different, so why don't you do Cath a favour and go back to your wife?'

'Just tell me something, is she happy with this policeman?'

'She could be, given time.'

'So she is seeing him?'

Doreen shrugged. 'She sees Jerry Danby, course she do. He walks her home from work most nights but, if you ask me, she'd be better off with that cousin of hers.'

Boyo felt himself tense, Liam Cullen was a threat, a real threat. He had made love to Catherine, he had stood by her when she needed a friend.

'So he's back in Swansea?'

'Aye, for a day or two, comes over here regular, like. A long story he had to tell us this time.'

Boyo looked at her sharply. 'What story was that?' His voice cracked and Doreen poured him more wine.

'First off, his farm was poisoned, the lands ruined, the cattle dying in the fields.'

'These things happen in farming.' Boyo was aware he sounded unsympathetic but set-backs were not unusual when it came to country matters.

'Not natural this, the work of a man's hand not that of God; it was done deliberate, like.'

Boyo suppressed the surge of uncharitable triumph that raced through him. 'So he's ruined then, is he?'

Doreen shook her head. 'That's exactly what some-body planned would happen but his old grannie had other ideas. No, he's not ruined, Liam Cullen is a good fighting man, won't give in under the first blow.'

It was clear to Boyo that Doreen had come to know and like Liam Cullen and why not? He was personable, honest, he wanted to marry Catherine. It was as though Doreen read the pattern of his thoughts.

'Not cut out to be a fancy piece, not Catherine.' She looked at him levelly. 'She's young, beautiful, she needs to make her own choices in life. You are a good sort for a toff but Catherine deserves more than the dregs of a mar-ried man's life.'

He rose abruptly and moved to the door, the woman's words stung but he could not deny the truth of them.

'Sorry to be hard on you, I am, mind, but it needed to be said. Leave her alone, Mr Hopkins, let her be happy.'

He heard the door closing but did not turn around. He seethed inwardly, his guts in turmoil as he thought of Catherine with Liam Cullen. Perhaps, even now, they were alone somewhere, making love. Cullen would be stroking Catherine's alabaster skin, the round high breasts, the slender thighs. Her hair would be against his skin, cool, silky. He groaned, at that moment he could have cheerfully killed Liam Cullen. How foolish he had been to worry about Jerry Danby, the policeman would not stand a chance against the Irishman's blarney.

He turned to step into the nearest public bar and peered through the gloom of smoke and beer fumes as though searching for a friend. He had no friend. It was a sudden realization. He was a loner, a man with a wife he did not love, a man without offspring. In spite of all his wealth, no-one would miss him if he vanished from the face of the earth this minute.

He knew he was indulging himself in self-pity and that was weak, despicable even, but as he took his glass of ale from the landlord, he had the feeling that he needed to drown his sorrows, to forget his barren existence, if only for a while.

It came to him then how badly Bethan must feel, she was childless, unloved, turning inward on herself. She was growing strange, almost detached from reality. She seemed to hear voices that no-one else could hear, see beings that were invisible to the eyes of others.

He shuddered, he had heard rumours that Ty Craig was haunted and it certainly seemed to have a presence that was not altogether wholesome. Even the servants felt it.

He drunk deeply of the ale and told himself not to be foolish; his wife was not herself, the loss of her child and then the break up of their marriage had taken its toll, she would get over it, she would have to, she was getting stranger every day. It was high time he got away from Bethan and from the cold atmosphere of Ty Craig.

He sank back in his chair and closed his eyes; perhaps he should turn his mind to good works, expiate his guilt and his longing to be with a woman, not his wife, by helping those less fortunate than he was. Less fortunate, that was rich, even when he had been dirt poor, he had lived his life in hope and anticipation, he had been alive, now he felt half-dead.

He lifted his hand and called through the babble of voices, 'Landlord, another drink.' He saw men turn and stare in curiosity, and he closed his eyes in self-disgust. He threw a few coins on the beer-soaked table and ignoring the open-mouthed surprise of the landlord, walked out into the cooling evening air.

'Good of the Danby's to put me up,' Liam Cullen was

holding her arm, guiding her over the railway tracks towards the moonlit beach.

He smiled at Catherine. 'Well, colleen, I've come over from Ireland especially to tell you that I'm well set-up now. The old farm lands sold at a fine profit and my new land's being cleared. By this time next year I should have a rich harvest in and the land lying asleep resting for the following spring.'

By this time next year where would she be? Catherine looked towards the sea, watching as the small waves lapped the shore and then fell away, pebbles and shells tumbling back on the tide with a sound almost like music. It was a fine night with the stars clear in the heavens.

She glanced at Liam, he was handsome in the pale moonlight, his jaw strong, his reddish hair falling across his brow. Catherine felt a dart of affection for him but could affection take the place of love?

He turned, catching her glance and he took her hands into his own. 'Catherine, I want to marry you, I'm asking you for the last time. Cath, please, give me the answer I want to hear.'

She took a deep breath, her mind was a haze of memories, of the beginning of their love affair when Boyo was so ardent, so attentive. But since that night at the hospital when Boyo had been so strong, so tender, she had not seen him, not once. Perhaps loving alone was not enough, look where falling in love had got Doreen Meadows. Love could turn sour, surely friendship was the best beginning to any marriage?

'I will marry you.' She held her finger to his lips, 'But not yet, Liam, be patient, please try to understand I have to prove to myself that I can be independent, make my own way in the world. Let's wait until next year when your farm is running smoothly, until then you will need to give it all your attention.'

He looked at her for a long moment and sighed. 'All right, Catherine, but we are promised to each other. You won't change your mind, will you? For sure I couldn't bear it.' Liam's voice was persuasive and Catherine touched his cheek gently.

'Yes, we are betrothed and no, I won't change my mind. Are *you* sure this is what you want?'

'I am,' Liam said. 'So that's settled, isn't it, Catherine?' Catherine felt a moment of terrifying doubt and then she forced a smile. 'It's settled, I've made you a promise, I won't break it.' It was what Jamie had wished and her father had been a wise and a good man.

Liam dipped into his pocket and took out a small leather purse. 'Inside here is my mammy's ring,' he said. 'If she could have known you, she would have loved you as I do. Please wear it for me, Catherine.'

She looked down at the dark red garnets glowing softly in a setting of gold and allowed Liam to slip the ring on her finger. Had he been sure she would agree to marry him, then?

'There, it fits; I knew it would.' Liam sounded triumphant as though something important had been confirmed. 'My mother had small fingers just like you, Catherine.'

He bent towards her and as his lips touched hers, Catherine felt a shiver of fear, she had burned her boats, she had destroyed any last hope of being with Boyo.

Liam was caressing her and she felt herself warm to him. His scent was not the same as Boyo's, Liam did not use expensive soaps but he had about him the clean smell of the grass in the meadows.

She wound her arms around his neck. His touch felt familiar, as though they had been together for years, almost as if they were meant for each other. He kissed her gently at first and she responded, her head spinning, her senses alive. She was stirred by his masculinity, she stopped thinking rationally and breathed in the moment of intimacy between them.

She heard a sound, not even a sound, a breath beside her and looking up she saw Boyo standing a few feet away from the bench where she sat wrapped in Liam's arms.

'Hopkins, what do you want?' Liam's voice had a hard

306

edge to it. He rose to his feet. 'Leave Catherine alone, just keep away from her or I'll kill you.' He spoke without heat but with a cold conviction in his voice that sent a shiver of fear through Catherine, fear for Boyo, who seemed at a loss, a man adrift without direction.

'We will be married next year, is that plain enough for you?' Liam held up Catherine's hand and the ring sparkled in the moonlight. 'She is to be my wife, do you understand? Now, just go away and leave us in peace, I'm asking you for your own good.'

Boyo shook his head, under the light from the moon, his face was drawn. 'I'll leave you alone.' He was speaking to Catherine, 'I am no good for you, no good for anyone or anything.' He turned and stumbled away across the sands, his shoulders bowed, his head on his chest and suddenly, Catherine was crying.

'There, there, colleen, don't cry, it's over now, he's gone, he won't trouble you again.'

Even as Liam held her close, Catherine knew that she would always be troubled by Boyo, he had come back into her life and turned it upside down. He had aroused feeling in her that she'd never had before. However hard she might try to be faithful to Liam, she would never forget Boyo Hopkins.

'Hold me, Liam, I want you to make love to me.' She must seal her fate, cut herself off from Boyo once and for all.

Liam kissed her mouth with growing passion, his hands touching her breasts, his body hard against hers. For a moment she thought he would take her there on the bench but then he was leading her into the deepness of the dunes. He was gentle, easing into her with a tenderness that brought tears to her eyes. He was young and strong, his body finely muscled, the column of his neck curved gracefully as he bent to take her nipple in his mouth, his red hair dark in the moonlight curling against her face. It felt so right.

She arched backwards as he became more eager, more vigorous. She felt the explosion of sensation rip through her and knew that this giving of herself utterly was cutting the final cord that bound her to Boyo Hopkins.

Doreen was sitting before the fire when Catherine and Liam entered the house; opposite her sat Jerry Danby, his feet stretched out towards the fire. He looked so much at home that Catherine realized, with a shock, that he did not come calling out of duty. All those times he had walked Catherine home from work had been merely an excuse to see Doreen. From the look on his face, it was quite clear he was falling in love with her.

'Hello you two,' Doreen shifted her chair back a little. 'Come and sit by the fire with us, Liam.' Doreen was flushed and not with the heat of the fire alone. Catherine kissed her cheek and whispered in her ear.

'Who's a dark horse then?'

Doreen flipped her away. 'Behave yourself, Catherine O'Conner. You can make a fresh pot of tea for your cheek, or is it so long since you brewed up that you've forgotten how?'

Catherine felt her spirits lighten as she busied herself at the table, she had put Boyo out of her life for ever and it was the right decision. She knew it in her head, pity her heart did not believe her.

Catherine lifted the kettle onto the fire and then turned and held out her hand. The ring sparkled in the glow of the flames and Doreen took her hand, looking from Catherine to Liam, a smile lighting up her face.

'You've come to your senses at last then. Got a good man there, lucky you got him hooked or I might have set my cap at him. I'm glad for you both.' She kissed Liam and then hugged Catherine tightly. 'Well done, Cath.'

Catherine knew Doreen had been worried about her future. She had pointed out often enough that love was an illusion, marriage should be entered into with a clear head.

Doreen rose to her feet. 'Right, in honour of the occasion, we'll forget the cup of tea and have a drink of that blackberry wine I made last year.'

She lifted the kettle back off the hob and moved

towards the pantry. 'Jerry, you'll join in the celebrations with us won't you?'

He had risen to his feet uncertainly but he sat down again with alacrity. Catherine smiled, why had she failed to see it before? It was so obvious that Jerry Danby was madly in love with Doreen. If Meadows ever found out about it, there would be murder committed.

He must not find out. Soon Liam would return home to his farm; when he was gone, Catherine would pretend that she was walking out with Jerry, no-one could invent evil gossip about that. She would protect Doreen from her monster of a husband if it was the last thing she did.

The wine poured, the women sat close together raising eyebrows in mock exasperation as the men began to discuss the rights and wrongs of the law. They laughed together as Jerry Danby asserted that the methods of the police were not methods at all but a hit-and-miss affair which sometimes worked to their advantage.

Doreen leaned close to Catherine's ear, 'I see by your face that you've been well and truly bedded, there's a sort of glow about you.'

Catherine, lulled by the wine, responded in kind. 'That's the pot calling the kettle black, is it?'

Doreen's eyebrows shot up almost into her hairline. 'How the hell do you know?'

'Same way you know about me, it's the look in the eyes, the cat-got-the-cream look, know what I mean?'

'If Meadows ever found out.' Doreen drew her finger across her throat in a cutting gesture and Catherine caught her hand, holding firmly.

'I've thought about that, we'll say Jerry is calling on me, that's what everyone thinks anyway, isn't it?'

Doreen nodded, 'Aye, I suppose so.' She glanced at Liam and Catherine read her mind. 'He's my cousin, it's natural he'll visit me when he's in the country, isn't it?'

Doreen nodded. 'Aye, suppose so. Thanks, Cath, I got to make the most of it, it might not last, see.' She glanced at Jerry Danby, younger than herself by several years and he looked up and met her gaze and his smile was unmistakably that of a man in love.

'Got all the elements of a lasting romance from where I sit,' Catherine said dryly.

'Oh, you, miss country girl, what do you know?' Doreen was pink with pleasure. She rose to her feet. 'Right, then, it's home for you two boys. We got our reputation to think of, mind.'

Catherine looked up and met Liam's eyes. He smiled. 'When we are married and living in Ireland there will be no need for all this palaver, you will be Mrs Liam Cullen and sure won't you be the envy of all the girls in County Cork?'

'Go on, out, you conceited Irishman.' Catherine pushed him playfully.

The two women stood in the doorway, watching as, together, the men walked along the street in the direction of Jerry Danby's house.

'Are we lucky girls, Cath?' Doreen said dreamily. 'Good, strong men to love us, isn't that what every woman dreams of?'

'Yes, I suppose it is,' Catherine said softly. Doreen looked at her shrewdly.

'Know something, Cath? I don't think you know your own mind. I think you are half in love with Liam only you won't admit it.'

'You could be right,' Catherine said but suddenly she was troubled, the laughter and fun of the last few hours vanished as if caught up in the breeze coming in from the sea.

'Forget Boyo Hopkins,' Doreen said firmly. She drew Catherine inside and closed the front door firmly. 'He's married, will always be married, face it, you'll always be the other woman where Boyo Hopkins is concerned.'

The other woman; Catherine winced, it was true, she had allowed herself to become a fancy piece, a woman taking the leavings of another woman's marriage. She could never walk out with Boyo in the sunlight, never be at his side when he attended formal occasions, never sit with him of an evening in the company of others. She would always be a secret, hidden away in dark corners, well she wanted more than that from life.

In the kitchen, she sank down onto the rag mat before the fire, pulling absently at one of the coloured strands of old cloth.

'You're doing the right thing, you know.' Doreen poured them each a small amount of wine, it sparkled red like the garnets on Catherine's finger. The ring seemed to tighten, holding her in a vice-like grip, imprisoning her.

'Am I?' she said softly.

It was clear to Bethan now what she must do, she had talked with the spirits of her dead ancestors and they had told her to go to Hari Grenfell, talk to her as one businesswoman to another, warn her against the whore of Babylon Catherine O'Conner.

Bethan rarely left her home these days but today she had a purpose. She felt stimulated, her eyes gleamed back at her from the mirror in her bedroom and, over her shoulder, she saw Elizabeth nodding her approval.

Elizabeth had become a friend, a ghost of the past perhaps but not to Bethan. To her, Elizabeth was solid, real, closer than any flesh-and-blood being could ever be, except perhaps Boyo but then he was her husband.

'I'm ready.' She held her head high and watched Elizabeth retreat as a knock resounded through the room and the door was opened a fraction.

'Your carriage is here, Mrs Hopkins.' Cara scarcely looked in, she hated this room more than any other in the house. It was cold, always cold and it smelled of evil.

'Don't stand in the doorway dithering, come in, speak to me properly, how do you expect me to hear when you will mumble?'

Reluctantly, the girl came over the threshold, she shivered and looked around her and Bethan found it difficult not to laugh out loud.

'The carriage is there at the door waiting, Mrs Hopkins.'

'Well, why didn't you say so in the first place?'

Bethan closed her bedroom door carefully, encouraged

by a nod from Elizabeth who was looking more vivid each day, it was almost as though she was drawing life from Bethan's knowledge of her existence. Bethan smiled, Elizabeth was a friend, a real friend, she approved of what Bethan was doing. More, she encouraged her with ideas of her own, words of ancient wisdom, knowledge of a woman who has existed through the ages.

Bethan blinked a little at the sudden lightness of the day outside the walls of her house. A pale sunshine was washing the drive with colour, the stones gleamed like diamonds, and at the borders small white flowers were beginning to bloom.

The drive into town was uncomfortable, the hard seat of the carriage unyielding against the rough roads. Bethan cursed the driver under her breath, he should be horse-whipped for his carelessness.

In days gone by, when her father ruled his staff with a rod of iron, the punishment meted out to the man would have been harsh indeed.

She felt as though every bone in her body was aching by the time the carriage drew to a halt outside the once imposing entrance of Summer Lodge. Now the house had been extended and altered. Large, commercial-looking windows faced the driveway, a gaudy sign informed any callers that this was a place of business and no longer a gracious home. Mrs Hari Grenfell had indeed come down in the world.

Still, she would honour Bethan's wishes to be rid of Catherine O'Conner. Oh, yes, once Mrs Grenfell knew the truth about the Jezebel she had taken on to her staff, the girl would be given short shrift. If she proved difficult, there was always the matter of the investment Bethan had made in the woman's business.

Mrs Grenfell took an inordinately long time in coming to see Bethan who sat on a tiny upright chair and fumed with impatience. But at last, Hari Grenfell, elegant enough by any standards, came towards her, smiling a welcome, no doubt expecting to do business with one of the richest women in Swansea.

'Mrs Hopkins, I am honoured to have you patronize my emporium.'

Bethan barely concealed her disdain, the woman had a marked Welsh accent, she was uneducated, clearly not such a lady as her appearance suggested. 'I have come to warn you about a member of your staff; I think you should know what sort of person you are trusting to work with you.'

Hari Grenfell's smile faded. She straightened her back and her mouth drew into a firm line. She remained silent. Bethan, at a disadvantage, was forced to go on. 'Catherine O'Conner is a cheap whore, she takes her wanton pleasure with whatever man crosses her path.'

Hari Grenfell was silent for so long that Bethan thought she would never speak. When she did, her voice was controlled but with a hint of hardness that Bethan had not suspected her capable of.

'What my employees do in their private lives is none of my business.' Mrs Grenfell spoke evenly but with authority and Bethan was momentarily thrown off balance. She quickly rallied.

'The woman has been seen on the premises of a back-street abortionist. Miss O'Conner is an infamous woman, not fussy which man she takes to her bed, be he married or single.'

Hari Grenfell squared her shoulders. 'Mrs Hopkins,' she said slowly, 'if I can help you with a purchase of shoes or boots, that I will gladly do. What I will not do is listen to gossip concerning one of my girls.'

Bethan rose to her feet, her cheeks suddenly hot. 'It is not gossip!' She fanned her face with her gloved hand. 'The harlot took my husband from me, twisted his mind against me. If you are not careful she might do the same to you one day.'

'I see.' Hari Grenfell studied Bethan's face as though memorizing each feature and Bethan turned away from her clear gaze, suddenly self-conscious.

'Someone like that cannot be trusted with any man. If you can't see that, then perhaps I should withdraw the investment I made in your business.'

'Perhaps, Mrs Hopkins, it would be wise of you to leave my shop now.'

Bethan stared at the woman unable to believe her ears, the commonly spoken Mrs Grenfell was throwing her out. She calmed herself, knowing that she must return home and speak of her anger to Elizabeth. She would understand, she always understood and she would know what the suitable punishment for such an outrage should be.

'I cannot be involved any longer in this foolish scheme of yours,' Bethan said scornfully. 'I see you are obdurate, unable to listen to good advice, so on your own head be it.'

Bethan was aware that the woman was accompanying her to the entrance of the emporium; around her were the signs of trade and Bethan sniffed. She saw fine hats, delicate gloves, elegant shoes and, for a moment, she was sorry that she had not bided her time, given herself a chance to really look at the assets this woman possessed. One never knew when such information might be useful.

'I won't forget this slight, Mrs Grenfell.' Bethan stood for a moment looking past the woman's shoulder, so angry that she longed to strike out physically. But that would not do, a lady never lost her dignity, whatever the provocation.

'I'm sure you won't, Mrs Hopkins, and neither will I,' Hari Grenfell said quietly.

Bethan climbed into the carriage and sank back in the seat feeling suddenly weak, all this effort for nothing, her advice had fallen on deaf ears. She drew off her gloves with short stabbing movements of her fingers, anger flaring through her. How dare such a woman turn her, Bethan Hopkins, away from the door? Well, she would be dealt with, of that there was no doubt. Mrs Hari Grenfell would pay for the insult, just as all who crossed Bethan Hopkins must pay.

Back home, she hurried into her room, flinging off her hat and coat, stamping her feet for the maid to build up the fire, taking her ire out on anyone who ventured into her path. At last she was alone, lying in the darkened room, a cloth watered with cologne across her brow.

'Elizabeth, what shall I do?' she said softly. Elizabeth came into the room silently as she always did but Bethan knew she was there by the sudden lowering of the temperature. It was as though a window had been opened and a gust of icy air had fallen over the bed.

'She was hateful to me, Elizabeth.' Elizabeth soothed her, telling her the woman was of common stock, nothing better could be expected of her. She was probably possessed of easy morals herself.

'What shall we do to punish her, Elizabeth?' Bethan asked in a whisper and she was answered, as always, with sound advice. She must study the woman and her means of financing her business, learn the weaknesses and strengths of her affairs, look into her marriage, see what damage could be done there. And then, when she was fully armed, strike Hari Grenfell in the heart.

'Yes, I see,' Bethan said, nodding her head. She knew how to hurt the woman, it was easy, really, trust Elizabeth to put her finger on the correct solution. Bethan must take away all the things Hari Grenfell held most precious in her life, it was as simple as that.

CHAPTER TWENTY-FIVE

Catherine felt chilled in spite of the warmth of the deeply carpeted showrooms. Near the door sat a group of customers trying on boots. To her right, Doreen was carefully arranging feathers on a velvet hat. It all seemed so normal that, for a moment, she could not comprehend what Mrs Grenfell had told her.

'Bethan Hopkins came here and threatened you?' she asked incredulously. She looked at Mrs Grenfell's calm face and wondered at her composure. 'Why now? Whatever there was between Boyo and me has been over for some time. And why threaten you?'

'Mrs Hopkins is a little . . . unbalanced, I think,' Hari said carefully. 'You know what they say about hell having no fury and all that, well, it's true in Bethan Hopkins's case.'

'I'm sorry for her, in a way,' Catherine said quietly. 'I don't expect her to forget what's happened or to forgive, she's been hurt and she's striking out at anyone in her path, but I think she is taking her revenge too far. It seems she wants to hurt not only me but anyone who is kind to me.'

She saw Hari Grenfell frown. 'Don't waste your time being sorry for her, she wanted me to fire you from your job. She is a bitter woman, a dangerous woman. I think you should be on your guard against her.'

Catherine looked up at Mrs Grenfell anxiously. 'You don't think she would harm any of us, do you?'

'I think she might try. As I say, she is unbalanced.' Hari Grenfell moved towards the stairs. 'Anyway, try to forget about her for now, just be careful.'

Doreen watched as Mrs Grenfell disappeared up the stairs and crossed to where Catherine was standing.

'What's the matter? What's happened?' Doreen caught her arm. 'Catherine, why are you looking so dazed? Not bad news is it?'

Catherine shook her head. 'No, it's just that Mrs Hopkins has tried to get me the sack.'

'The old witch!' Doreen caught Catherine's arm. 'Come on, it's time for a tea break. Let the other girls carry on for a while, I need a sit-down, my feet are killing me.'

She drew Catherine into the small quarters at the back of the building and pushed the kettle onto the stove. 'It's too bad of that cow to try to get you the boot like that, I hope Mrs Grenfell told her where to go.'

Catherine sank into a chair. 'Bethan Hopkins had the nerve to threaten Mrs Grenfell with goodness knows what if she didn't sack me. What I don't understand is, why now when it's all over between me and him?'

'The nerve of the woman.' Doreen quickly made the tea and poured out the fragrant liquid, spooning a liberal helping of sugar into Catherine's cup. 'Come on, drink up, you look as white as a ghost.' Doreen sat down. 'The old cow, she's done her worst and it didn't work, you still got your place here, snug as a bug, you are.'

Catherine was thoughtful. 'I don't think Bethan Hopkins has done her worst, not by a long chalk. I wouldn't put anything past that woman, she's taken my farm from me, hasn't she? She's poisoned Liam's land. What might she do to Mrs Grenfell?'

'Well, don't let her bother you,' Doreen said. 'The old cow will get her comeuppance, one day. God do not sleep, mind.'

Catherine smiled suddenly. 'Aye, you're right, it's daft to worry about what might happen, there's enough to be going on with, what with us two sharing a lover.'

Doreen picked up a small silk cushion and aimed it at Catherine's head. 'Shut your mouth, you, I don't have no lover. Well, perhaps just one and he's mine, all mine, so don't go getting any ideas on that score, madam.'

She sank into a chair, blushing like a girl. 'Don't it sound grand: a lover, so romantic.' She stared at Catherine ruefully. 'That's not what other folks would call it though, is it? I'd be a whore, a slice out of a half-eaten meat pie. Still, so long as Meadows don't get to hear of it, I'll be all right.'

'He won't hear of it, don't worry, how could he? Everyone thinks Jerry Danby is my gentleman caller.'

'I hope so, Cath, I really do hope so but you don't know Meadows as I do, he 'as a knack of knowing everything that goes on round Swansea. Anyway, drink up, girl, we'd better be getting back to work or we'll both be getting the order of the boot.'

Later that evening, Catherine was sitting quietly in the kitchen of number four Watkins Street when the door was pushed open with such force that it screeched against the hinges and banged against the wall.

Meadows came into the house, stinking of ale, his eyes narrowed as he looked around the kitchen. 'Where's that bitch got to now? I'll strangle her if she's out gallivanting.'

'If you mean Doreen, she's working late, she has a special hat to finish by tomorrow.' Catherine was tense, watching the man's every move, she did not trust Pete Meadows one inch.

'Damn and blast, I felt like a bit of fun, an' all.' He came closer. 'I suppose you would do, any port in a storm as they say.'

'Get out of here,' Catherine said in a low voice. 'If you come any nearer, I'll scream blue murder, get the neighbours in, they'll all see you for what you are: a man who can only get a woman by force.'

'You scrawny bitch! I've taken enough cheek from you!' He lashed out with his bunched fist and Catherine ducked instinctively so that the blow passed harmlessly over her shoulder. Off balance, Meadows fell, cracking his head against the fender. For a moment he lay unmoving and Catherine stood hand to her mouth, wondering if he was dead.

He began to groan and turned over onto his side, a trickle of blood running from his temple. He lurched to his feet and stared around him, his eyes feverish. 'I'll pay you back, bitch, I'll get even with you if it's the last thing I do.'

He leaned against the small dresser, heaving against it until the china plates fell to the floor with a crash. Meadows smiled as if the act had given him pleasure and then, systematically, he began to destroy everything in the once-neat kitchen.

Catherine edged away from him, he was drunk beyond reason, there was no knowing what he would do next. She tried to make for the door but he was blundering about like a charging bull. He took up the teapot, hurling it against the wall. Catherine watched in terror as a stain spread outwards on the patterned wallpaper. He turned towards her, his face a mask of hate. 'Now to deal with you, you dirty whore!'

Catherine screamed, backing against the wall. Suddenly the room seemed full of people. Doreen, white-faced, was pushing through the debris towards Catherine, with her was Liam, with Jerry Danby close behind him.

'All right, sir, calm down now, this can do no good. Let me take you back to your lodgings so you can sleep it off.' Jerry Danby moved confidently forward expecting his superior officer to go with him quietly. He was mistaken.

'Bugger off. Do you think I'd take orders from a green bastard like you?' Meadows's voice was slurred but his meaning was clear as he picked up the poker from the hearth and lifted it above his head.

Liam moved sharply, catching Meadows's hand, twisting it hard. Meadows struggled grimly, clinging to the poker, he was a strong man and maddened by drink, he was dangerous.

A silent battle of will and muscle was taking place and Catherine stood frozen to the spot, too frightened to make a sound. She knew if Liam lost the struggle he would be battered mercilessly with the heavy iron poker.

Meadows's face was red, streaked with sweat, his eyes bulging as he exerted all his strength. Liam had his back to Catherine, she could see the veins in his hands stand proud as he struggled to take the weapon away from Meadows.

'For God's sake, Pete, give up before someone gets killed.' Doreen's voice carried to where Meadows was grappling with Liam and momentarily, he was distracted. Liam twisted the man's arm with such force that a sickening crack reverberated through the kitchen.

Meadows fell to the floor screaming in pain, the poker rattling into the fireplace beside him.

'You've broken my arm, you Irish bastard!' He stared up at Liam, his mouth contorted, his eyes filled with venom. 'I'll get you for this, you see if I don't.'

He struggled to sit up against the wall, clutching his arm. 'What are you waiting for, Danby, arrest this man; he's attacked me, injured a police officer, why don't you do something?'

Jerry Danby was barely able to conceal his disgust, his face grim, he helped Meadows to his feet. 'I'd better get you to the hospital, sir,' he said through his teeth. 'It seems to me that you had a slight accident here in your wife's home. Bit of damage done to the place, sir, don't know who will be liable to pay for that. Perhaps this incident is a case of "least said, soonest mended", think so, sir?'

Meadows seemed to have sobered up a little with the pain, he glanced around him, seeing the havoc he had wreaked and his lips twisted into a sneer. 'All right, you load of twicers, you might think you've got me beat but Pete Meadows never forgets. You lot better watch your backs when you walk in a dark alley, because I might just be there behind you.'

He followed Jerry to the door and, as a final gesture, kicked it shut behind him.

'Thank God he's gone.' Doreen picked up a chair and sat down on it suddenly as though her legs would not support her.

'Liam,' Catherine moved towards him, her eyes anxious, 'are you hurt?'

He had a bruise above one eye but he was smiling cheerfully. 'I'm fine, sure enough, takes more than a drunken bully to put one over an Irishman.'

Catherine put her arms around his waist hugging him, filled suddenly with relief. 'Thank God for that.' She leaned against his shoulder and he smoothed her hair from her hot face.

'You all right, colleen, he did not get too near you did he?'

Catherine shook her head. 'You came just in time,' she smiled wanly. 'My knight in shining armour, well, almost.'

'What do you mean, "almost"?' He tilted her face up to his and she struggled to smile through the tears that welled, burning behind her eyes. Now that the danger was over, she realized just how frightened she had been.

'Well, look at you, torn shirt, tangled hair, not exactly Sir Lancelot, are you? Still, you'll do until something better comes along.'

Doreen spoke suddenly. 'I don't think I can stand living here, not after this.' She was close to tears and Catherine went to her side, hugging her warmly.

'Don't worry, love, we'll get this place tidied up in no time.'

'It's not just that,' Doreen looked around her with dull eyes, 'it's him, Meadows, coming here, taking "his rights" as he calls them. I don't think I can put up with it any more.'

Liam busied himself picking up the dresser and stood it against the wall. He stared around him at the smashed plates and broken furniture. 'Look, why don't I take you two back with me to Ireland for a few days? A bit of Irish luck might be just the thing you need.'

'It's a fine idea but will Mrs Grenfell give us time off?' Doreen said doubtfully.

Catherine began picking up pieces of china, stacking them into the coal bucket. 'It might be the solution to all our problems,' she said thoughtfully. 'Meadows will have time to calm down and if I'm out of the way perhaps Bethan Hopkins will leave Mrs Grenfell alone.'

'All right, you've convinced me.' Doreen rose tiredly to her feet. 'We'll get this place tidy in the morning, for now,

I think I need to get myself a good night's sleep.'

Liam smiled down at Catherine and winked like a conspirator and Catherine returned his smile, feeling closer to him than she had ever done before.

He reached out and rested his hand on her hair as she crouched over the coal bucket, full now of shards of china. Suddenly, Catherine felt lost, it was all too much for her, all this emotional turmoil, this questioning of herself and her own feelings. She had fought against the memories of Boyo holding her in his arms, making love to her and yet, sometimes, in the stillness of the night, she could not help remembering the happiness she had shared with him.

The fields of Ireland were growing lush with the onset of spring. Flag irises stood queen-like at the edge of the marshlands. The air was clean and fresh.

'*Duw*, nearly as lovely as Wales, is this country of yours Liam.' Doreen took in a deep breath and stared around her in wonder. Towards the west, she saw the blue of the sea merging on the horizon with the sky. 'No wonder they say this is a land of little people and magic and all that sort of thing.'

'Glad you appreciate it, madam,' Liam said gravely. 'We do our best to please our visitors. You know who I mean, those barbarians from across the water.'

'Oh, *you*!' Doreen flipped at him with her hand. 'You can't believe that Ireland, lovely as it is, is half as good as Wales, you can't be that dull.'

'Well, I suppose you do miss the stink from the works, the coal dust, the . . .'

'Shut up!' Doreen sank down onto the grass and glanced back over her shoulder at the tall presence of the convent behind them.

'Wonder how Cath is getting on in there.'

'You could have gone in with her,' Liam said. 'Not like me, the nuns won't let a man anywhere near the inner sanctum.'

'I should think not.' Doreen looked up as Liam sat

beside her. 'Not many good men about the place, are there? Rotters the lot of you, that's what I thinks anyway.'

'Well, isn't there at least one exception?' Liam's voice held a teasing note. 'Jerry Danby seems a decent enough sort.'

'Oh him?' Doreen's assumed indifference covered the sudden jolting of her heart. What was wrong with her? She was like a young, green girl, in love for the first time. Did she really think she stood a chance of a lasting love affair with such a handsome man? Perhaps, even now, with the width of the Irish Sea between them, Jerry was walking out with some other girl. She bit her lip and Liam touched her arm.

'What's wrong, colleen? Why so worried, think he'll find another woman?'

'You a mind-reader or what?' Doreen looked up at him and suddenly she knew this was a good man, a man she could talk to, a man who would not put his tongue to gossip. 'I love him, Liam, that's the long and the short of it, damn and blast it, I love the man.'

'From what I've seen, the feeling is mutual.' Liam spoke softly.

'If you mean he feels the same, I suppose you are right but will it last? What's in it for Jerry? I'm married to an evil monster. Meadows would never let me go and if he got wind of anything going on, he'd break Jerry's neck and mine too.'

'Take it a bit at a time, move house if you like, don't tell Meadows where you are going. Enjoy what's there while you've got it. When you are with Jerry, you are happy, make that enough for now.'

'Aye, that's good advice, I suppose.' Suddenly Doreen felt easier in her mind, Liam had the knack of making everything seem so simple.

'Now you've put my life in order, what about yours? Yours and Cath's?' Doreen looked up at Liam with a bland expression and he laughed out loud.

'You are right, who am I to solve other people's problems when I can't solve my own?'

'Won't she name a day, then?'

Liam shook his head. 'Can't pin her down, she's like a gorgeous butterfly, beautiful and elusive.'

'She's a warm, loving girl is Cath but it don't do to try to force her into anything. Got a mind of her own, has that one. Mind, I wish I was single like her, you wouldn't see me waiting round, I'd be with Jerry all the hours God made.'

It was the truth. Lying alone in her bed, Doreen had longed to have Jerry sleep beside her for the whole of the night. Just once, she wanted to wake to the dawn with him beside her, his head on the pillow next to hers.

'Take your own medicine, Irish boy,' she said with mock severity. 'The advice you gave me was good enough, enjoy what you have while you have it.'

'Clever clogs.'

'She'll come round, give her time.' Doreen was serious now, her eyes searching Liam's face. 'Cath is a lovely girl, she's good and honest and she deserves someone like you.'

'Why does she still hanker for that bastard Hopkins then?' Liam's head was on his knees now, so that Doreen could no longer see his expression, but he could not conceal the pain in his voice.

'Women are daft creatures.' Doreen felt she must explain, make him feel easier in his mind, the way he had done for her. 'They sometimes fall in love with the wrong man, look at me with Meadows, what a fool I was for years, hoping he would change. Anyway, it takes a long time to break the mould and make a new pattern, do you know what I mean?'

'I know exactly what you mean.' Liam's voice was muffled.

Doreen put her hand on his arm. 'Think of this, who is the one she's with now? Who is the one loving her, holding her in the dark of the night? It's not Boyo Hopkins, it's you and I bet the man would give all the money he's got to change places with you.'

Liam looked up and smiled. 'You're good for me, Doreen Meadows, do you know that?'

'We're good for each other,' she said, touched. 'We're pals, real pals, aren't we?'

He took her hand and squeezed it, 'Sure enough, we'll pledge a bond of friendship right here before the little people.' He lifted his head. 'Now witness all you gnomes and goblins and fairy folk, that Doreen Meadows and Liam Cullen are friends for life.'

He bent forward and kissed her cheek and Doreen smiled, though there was a suspicious moistness gathering in her eyes.

'She's been working constantly in the garden, she's the one with green fingers all right.' The young Sister Monica led the way along the path towards the allotments, her gown sweeping the dry earth. 'Our Fon O'Conner is an asset to this order, a wonderful woman with any growing thing, a born woman of the land, she is sure enough.'

Catherine suppressed a smile, if she explained to the young nun that her mother had been born Irfonwy Parks, living on the edge of the oyster-beds, moving only to farming on her marriage, it would break the illusion.

'I'm so glad that Mam is happier now.' Catherine ached for the sight of her mother. She had been so wrapped up in her own problems, selfishly putting Fon out of her mind. Now, she wanted to see this new, strong Fon for herself.

She saw her then, bent over the ground, her once-abundant tawny locks greying now, tied up beneath a square of linen.

'Mammy!' As Fon looked up from her task, Catherine began to run towards her, stumbling a little over the uneven ground, then they were in each other's arms.

'Mam, I love you.' Fon smelled of the earth, of flowers and new-mown grass. Catherine held her at arms length seeing the brown of her mother's skin and the light in her eyes with a feeling of joy.

'My lovely little girl,' Fon touched her cheek, her hair; 'so like your father, so like him.'

Sister Monica spoke in soft tones. 'Sure there's good to

325

see a girl and her mammy together again. I'll put some refreshments in the quad, you can sit there together for a while and talk to your hearts' content.'

Arm in arm, Catherine and Fon followed the sister back towards the great gaunt building. The sound of a bell echoed across the grounds and Fon crossed herself. 'The sisters are at prayer,' she whispered.

As they drew nearer to the buildings, Catherine heard the sound of voices rising in song, a sweet haunting melody hung in the still air and Catherine felt moved to tears by the beauty of it.

As she sat with her mother in the open square of green between the high walls of the convent, Catherine felt at peace. It was almost as though the sound of prayerful singing and the tranquillity of the ancient walls and the hollow ringing of a bell on the still air had the power to ease the troubled state of her mind.

'It's so wonderful here, I only wish your dad could see me now.' Fon's voice was wistful. 'I still miss him, Cath, I suppose I always will but at least here I've found peace and a funny sort of contentment. Can you understand that?'

Catherine rubbed at her eyes. 'Yes, I can understand it, Mam, this is just the sort of place to heal wounds.'

She knew, with a feeling of sadness, there would be no possibility of her mother coming home to Wales; not now, perhaps not ever.

They were silent for a long moment and then Fon leaned forward eagerly, her eyes alight. 'Come on, tell me, when are you and Liam getting married?' She touched the garnet ring and smiled, 'I see you have made the first move, that's something.'

Catherine forced a smile. 'Liam is outside the grounds, waiting for me.' She spoke brightly. 'We brought a friend to Ireland with us, Doreen, her name is. She's had a bit of a tough time of it and we thought she needed a rest.'

'You didn't answer my question,' Fon said gently. 'You are going to marry Liam, aren't you, Cath?'

'Oh, yes, of course I am but, Mam, I've got the most

wonderful job, I don't want to give it up, not yet.'

'Job? What do you mean, job? Why aren't you working on Honey's Farm? Catherine, you can't have sold it, the place where you were born, where Jamie and I lived so happily together for so many years?'

'Mam, I can't hide the truth from you any longer, at first you were in too much pain and grief to take it all in but, now you are strong again, I have to tell you what happened.'

Fon slumped back in her chair, her face suddenly drained of colour. 'Go on then, tell me everything.'

'I couldn't make the farm pay, Mam,' Cath said awkwardly. 'The harvest failed, the bull got sick . . . everything went wrong. I was in so much debt that the bank moved in.' She hesitated, 'Anyway, the outcome of it was the farm was sold.'

'Sold, to who?'

Catherine swallowed hard. 'Bethan Hopkins, Boyo's wife, bought it.'

Fon was silent for a long time. 'I can't believe it of Boyo, I always thought he was such a fine boy. But then he came into a lot of money and money can corrupt the nicest of people. He's been bad news for you from the moment you met him.'

'Mam, it wasn't like that at all, it wasn't his fault, his wife, Bethan, she wanted to punish me for . . .'

'I know,' Fon said softly, 'I know why she wanted to punish you. You can't really blame her for that, I suppose I would have felt the same if some young girl had tried to take your father away from me.'

Catherine felt like a snail withdrawing into a shell. She was hurt by her mother's rebuke but she realized that, to Fon, in her new life, everything was black and white, the choices were simple, you did what was right. Her mother had become removed from her.

'So what's this wonderful new job then?' Fon asked tartly.

Catherine took a deep breath. 'It's at Mrs Grenfell's emporium, Mam. Mrs Grenfell is kind and considerate and she says I have every chance of bettering myself if I stick it out.'

'So what will you be when you "better yourself?" '

'I'll be head shop girl, maybe even manageress, I don't know.'

'And you really think all this is better than being wife to a good man like Liam Cullen?' Fon did not look at her. 'You intend to break the promise you made your father on his deathbed, then?'

'No, Mam.' Catherine tried not to show her sudden anger. 'I just want a little independence. I was brought up to have Dad care for me, I never did have to stand on my own two feet. If I marry now I'll never know what I might achieve. I must try being my own woman, Mam, at least for a year or two.'

'Catherine, by then your chance might be gone, Liam could easily grow tired of waiting, find another girl more grateful than you are. Why not get married now, stay in Ireland? It would be wonderful if I could see you more often.'

'Look, Mam, I'd better go.' Catherine rose to her feet. 'I'll come again before I go home.'

'Oh, don't put yourself out, you go and live your life of independence, I don't want you to feel obligated to me in any way.'

'Please, Mam, don't be like that. I just can't make you understand, can I?'

'I understand that you have let your father down, it was his dearest wish that you marry Liam. You are throwing that away for some headstrong foolish idea about being your own woman.' Fon's voice had risen a little and Catherine bit her lip, trying to keep at bay the waves of pain flowing over her.

'Give me a kiss, Mam, I'll see you in a few days' time and we can talk again.'

Fon allowed Catherine to kiss her cheek but there was no warmth in the tautness of her face or in the stiffness of her shoulders.

With a sigh of resignation, Catherine turned and

walked across the quadrangle and into the shade of the old building. She glanced behind her but the square of grass was empty, Fon had disappeared.

Outside, in the wide open spaces of the Irish hills, she took a deep breath, tears stung her eyes but she brushed them away impatiently. Why couldn't her mother try to understand how she felt? She would marry Liam, one day, but not yet.

For just a little while she wanted her freedom, wanted to explore the world she lived in. She had not even explored the town of Swansea yet. She was drawn to the oyster-beds at Mumbles, the place where her mother was born. She knew nothing of Swansea except for the occasional visit on market-day. What she really meant was that she wanted to explore life as an independent woman, just for a while.

Once she was married, she would have to leave it all behind her, leave Mrs Grenfell and worst of all leave Doreen, the only friend she had in the world.

She saw Liam sitting on the edge of the hill, his arm outstretched as he pointed something out to Doreen. She swallowed hard, could she fall in love with Liam if she tried really hard?

'Hello there, Cath, you're looking down in the mouth, what's the matter?' Doreen had seen her coming and was hurrying towards her. She slipped her arm through Catherine's and hugged it. 'Your mammy, bad is she?'

'No, she's very well, she looks better than I've seen her in a long time, brown as a berry . . .' her voice trailed away.

'So what's wrong then?' Doreen leaned closer. 'Is your mam nagging you to get wed?'

'Worse than that, she is angry with me, angry about the farm, angry about Boyo and disappointed that I won't marry Liam now, while I'm here in Ireland.' Catherine sighed heavily. 'I'll tell you all about it later.'

'What are you two girls whispering about then?' Liam was standing looking at them, his hands in his pockets, the breeze ruffling his reddish hair. He was very handsome, a rugged man, part of the countryside just as her father had been and Catherine's heart missed a beat. Why was she so reluctant to tie herself to him in marriage? What was wrong with her?

She knew why of course, she knew exactly why she wanted to be free: just in case, by some miracle, Boyo might come for her and carry her off to a love-nest where they would live happily ever after. It was a dream, a child's dream, it would never happen.

'Girl talk, so mind your own business, right?' Doreen smiled impishly and Catherine's throat constricted with tears. She was surrounded by fine people, good people; why couldn't she just be happy with her lot?

'Come on, then, let's go home.' Liam walked easily, as if sure of his ground. He put his hand on her shoulder and kissed her on the mouth.

'Patricia is in fine form, her condition seems to suit her.' His hand remained on her shoulder, as though he was asserting his right to be close to her. 'Pat will have made us a fine broth and some crispy bread and sure I can tell you now, I'm fair famished.'

He took her hand as they walked away down the hill and Catherine turned briefly to look at the tall buildings of the convent rising against the sky. She thought of her mother within the walls and for a moment, longed to run back, retrace her steps, tell her mother how much she loved her, would always love her. Liam tightened his grip on her fingers, she looked up at him and caught his eye.

'Don't worry, love,' he said softly, 'we'll come back again tomorrow and you can talk to your mammy some more.'

Comforted, she rested her head on his shoulder. 'You're such a kind man, Liam Cullen, I don't deserve you.'

He was silent and she saw the frown on his brow and knew that she had hurt him with her lukewarm praise.

'We'll be married soon, I promise.' The words tumbled out before she could stop them and echoed inside her head, mocking her weakness.

Liam made no reply and Catherine knew that she could not hold him at arm's length any longer, decisions would have to be made. No, not decisions, the deciding had already been done. She must name the day, that's all there was to it. She took a deep breath, feeling the unhappiness well up inside her and she wondered if she could ever again be the carefree girl who had climbed into bed with Boyo Hopkins.

CHAPTER TWENTY-SIX

Bethan was still angry with Hari Grenfell, she had tried to talk reasonably to the woman and she would not listen. She would be punished, along with all those others who tried to thwart Bethan Hopkins in her bid for justice.

Bethan had spent many days in her room with Elizabeth, who was becoming more solid and real as each day passed. Elizabeth, her confidante and friend, the only person she could trust with her true thoughts.

Hari Grenfell's business was rocky, made even more so by Bethan recalling her loan, but it was clear that the main thrust of Bethan's attack on the woman would be through the husband she adored, Craig Grenfell.

A smile curved Bethan's mouth, her plans had been put into action, soon Hari Grenfell would be sorry she had not listened to reason, had not dismissed the whore, Catherine O'Conner, on the spot.

The alacrity with which Hari Grenfell had repaid her debt had disconcerted Bethan at first but she had the consolation that it was money the woman could ill afford to do without. And then Bethan, with Elizabeth's help, had hatched the most brilliant idea, one that would ruin the common little shop owner and make her sorry that she had ever crossed Bethan Hopkins.

That slut O'Conner would be out of work then, all right; she would be on the streets, if Bethan had her way, shunned by everyone for the cheap trollop she was.

Bethan looked up at the overhanging trees, the garden was small but secluded, a place for secret meetings. Bethan had found that wherever she was, Elizabeth would find her, come to her. This afternoon, full of pale sunshine, was no exception. Elizabeth sat down, her full crinoline touching the grass, a contrast to Bethan's modern skirt and high-necked blouse with the cameo at the throat.

Elizabeth had exciting news: she leaned closer and whispered to Bethan that, while she could not have Boyo with her in the flesh, she could enjoy his company by calling his spirit to her whenever she chose.

Bethan nodded and smiled, Boyo could come to her bedroom, lie with her as he used to when they were first married. He could be her husband in spirit until the moment came when she possessed him once more in the flesh.

Bethan was elated, this was a gift indeed, the finest gift anyone could wish for. She asked Elizabeth what she required in return, some favour, something tangible that Bethan could do for her. The answer was quite simple, the grave at Dan-y-Craig was overgrown, the headstone fallen to the ground. A new marble monument to Elizabeth would please her, as would fresh flowers every day. Bethan nodded, that was a small price to pay for having Boyo back with her once more.

If anyone at the graveyard thought it odd that after many years the resting place of the Llewellyns was being beautified, no-one spoke of it. The fine marble angel with wings spread wide as if rising up to heaven graced the head of Elizabeth Llewellyn's tomb, glinting like white icing in the sun. Men worked for a week to cut the grass and place marble stones around the perimeter of the grave and it was Bethan Hopkins, née Llewellyn, who herself came every day to lay fresh flowers.

Bethan knew that Elizabeth was pleased, for once the work was done, as promised, the spirit of Boyo came to her in the night.

Bethan thrashed about the bed in a frenzy of passion such as she had never experienced before. Boyo was full of vigour as if his long absence from her had made him more eager. He was there in her arms, his mouth was on hers, his body possessing hers. She felt herself grow hot and in her joy she cried out his name.

At the door, the maid stood shivering, staring into the

moonlit bedroom where her mistress was apparently having some sort of fit. Mrs Hopkins's pale arms protruded from her nightgown, she heaved beneath the bedclothes, grunts escaping from her open lips. They were, Cara recognized with a shock, the sounds of a woman in the arms of her lover.

Cara crossed herself hurriedly, her mistress must surely be possessed by the devil. She wondered if she should call someone but by now the fit seemed to be over, Bethan Hopkins was quiet. A cold wind seemed to blow through the corridor and the maid turned and hurried back to her bedroom, scurrying up the narrow staircase and sliding into her still warm bed with a sigh of relief. She pulled the bedclothes over her head and squeezed her eyes tightly shut, promising herself that, whatever she heard, she would never venture to her mistress's bedroom in the still of the night again.

Boyo was tired of the unsatisfactory relationship he shared with Catherine. One minute he thought she was softening towards him and the next the barriers would go up again. Now that she was back from Ireland, he must see her, talk some sense into her. They would go away, leave Swansea and start a new life somewhere where they would not be recognized. He could not offer her marriage but he could make provision for her for the rest of her life.

It was evening, cool and growing dark, rain-clouds raced across the sky and, as he walked along the street, he wondered at the feeling of lethargy that had overtaken him lately. It was almost as though some invisible force was sapping away his energy, except that it was a fanciful idea, more suited to his superstitious wife than to a man like him with his feet planted firmly on the ground.

The front door stood ajar and from the house came the sound of laughter, feminine laughter. He knocked hard and absorbed the sudden, startled silence with a touch of dismay.

It was Catherine who came along the passage, a candle in her hand, her eyes enormous as they stared at him. 'Boyo, it's you.' Her voice was breathless, as though she had been running, her eyes were large as though she was frightened of something.

'Who were you expecting, Catherine?' he asked gently, knowing that if anyone was threatening to hurt her he would kill them with his bare hands. Had that bastard Meadows been back here?

Catherine mistook his concern for reproach. 'Is it any of your business who I am expecting?' Now her voice was cool, in control, and as he lifted his hand in protest, she spoke again. 'Boyo, will you never learn that I am my own woman, I make my own decisions and what they are has nothing to do with you.'

'Let's put the past behind us, go away somewhere. You are still in this awful house, you have not yet found other accommodation. I hate to see you living like this. We could be together as man and wife, no-one would know the truth.'

'*I* would know the truth,' Catherine said. 'Look, Boyo, it's too late, far too late for this. I should never have taken what you offered in the first place, it simply wasn't enough.'

'I gave you my love.' He felt a constriction in his throat. He swallowed hard and tried to speak again but she forestalled him.

'You gave me what you had left over from your marriage, you gave me passion but you gave me pain too, and I don't want to go through that again.'

'I love you, Cat, I really love you.' His voice held a ring of despair, he was defeated and he knew it.

'Accept it, Boyo, I'm going to marry Liam, I'll be leaving Wales for good then. I shall be living in Ireland with my husband and his family. You and I must never see each other again, I think that's for the best.'

She closed the door and he heard the bolt being shot home. He stood for a long time staring at the painted woodwork, peeling and shabby, at the empty window, curtained against the night. Slowly, he turned away.

The next morning, before he was dressed, the maid came to tell him there was a woman waiting for him in the back hallway. With a sigh, Boyo glanced at the dining table laden with breakfast food he could not eat and went towards the back of the house.

'Cara, what on earth are you doing here?' He wasn't pleased, he wanted nothing to do with Bethan, so why was she sending her maid to see him? The girl bobbed a curtsey and when she looked up, Boyo saw that her face was white and strained.

'Cara, is anything wrong?'

'It's the missis, sir, she's sort of sick.'

'What, again?' Boyo led the trembling girl into the drawing-room where a cheerful fire burned in the grate. He could hardly take her into the kitchen where the servants would listen to every word that was being said.

'It's true, she really is bad, sir.'

'All right, tell me calmly what's happened.'

'At night she's funny-like, it's happening more and more.' The girl seemed incoherent with fear. 'She moans and cries out your name, I think she's very sick sir. In the head, begging your pardon.'

Boyo looked closely at the maid, trying to gauge if the girl's concern was genuine or if she was simply carrying out one of Bethan's convoluted schemes. But her distress was real enough, the maid would have to be an actress of the first order to feign the fear he saw in her face as she tried to explain.

'Cook thinks Mrs Hopkins is possessed, sir, we both feel we can't carry on working at Ty Craig unless something is done.'

'What do you want me to do?' Boyo asked.

'Come over with me now, sir, stay outside the missis's rooms tonight, listen to the goings on and see for yourself. Then, sir, you can send her into some sort of hospital, like.'

For a moment, Boyo was angry. Why should he concern himself yet again with Bethan's problems? 'If she's sick let her see a doctor.' His voice had an edge to it and Cara burst into tears.

'She won't have it, sir, she says there is nothing wrong

336

with her, she has never been happier in her life, she says. But she's acting so funny, Mr Hopkins and me and Cook don't know what to do. Cook says we are only servants, we can't be responsible for what happens if you don't come.'

Boyo sighed. 'All right, I'll come over sometime in the next few days, will that do?'

She shook her head. 'Please sir, you got to come tonight, me and Cook will be packing our bags and getting out of that house in the morning if nothing's done.' The girl was terrified, this was no ploy, there was something very wrong going on at Bethan's house.

He had felt the chill of it often and he shivered now with superstitious fear. He rose abruptly, was he a man or a cowering mouse? 'All right, I'll come later tonight. Now go home and try not to worry, I'm sure everything will be all right.' As he crossed the hallway towards the door to see Cara out, Boyo wondered just what he was getting himself into. When he saw Bethan he would make it clear to her once and for all that her problems were her own, she could not drag him back into her web, whatever tricks she tried.

'So you sent him away then?' Doreen nodded her approval. 'It's the only sensible thing to do, love, so don't look so down in the mouth. Your Liam is a lovely man, if I wasn't spoken for I'd go after him myself.'

'I can't help it, Doreen, Boyo is under my skin, there's nothing I can do to change that.'

'Well, a few weeks with young Liam Cullen and you'll feel different, I just know you will. He's a fine, strapping man, a good man and he loves you to bits.'

'I know. I am going to marry him, I've given my word but that doesn't help me to forget Boyo.'

'Well, I'm missing Liam already,' Doreen said quietly. 'He's the sort who makes a girl feel safe and yet beautiful, all in one, know what I mean?'

Catherine's face softened. 'I know. I'm very fond of him. It's just a great pity that I'm in love with someone else.'

'You could well be fooling yourself about that,' Doreen said briskly. 'And think of this, you won't be getting a bastard like the one I've had to put up with all these years, so thank your lucky stars, my girl.'

In bed that night, Catherine could not sleep. She thought about Boyo, felt his nearness, the power of him, the tension that flared between them whenever they were together. She remembered his face, shadowed, strained, and it struck her that he had not seemed well. A shiver of fear ran through her. What if he was sickening for something, what if he died, how could she bear to live knowing that Boyo was no longer there in the same world as she was? She put her hands over her eyes. 'Stop it!' she whispered fiercely to herself. But it was a long time before she slept.

At work the next morning, the staff were called into the office upstairs. Catherine looked at the fine polished banister, admiring the craftsmanship in the curving wood. Summer Lodge was a fine house, the house of a rich man and now it served as a shop where anyone could walk if they wished to buy the goods on sale.

And yet this part of the house was sacrosanct, set apart, the landing large and airy; the carpet rich red, thick, deep pile. The doors were enormous, leading into bedrooms big enough to contain a whole family.

At the end of the landing was the office, converted from a smaller bedroom. It was functional, furnished with a large polished oak desk, the leather top stained with ink. A fire burned in the grate, a splendid, carved mantel surrounding the black cast iron, the only remainder of the elegance the room once possessed.

Seated behind the desk was Hari Grenfell, her face rosy with excitement. 'I won't keep you long, girls.' She smiled. 'Don't be alarmed, I have good news for us all: the business is saved, we have been given the chance to clear all our debts.' She glanced at Catherine and smiled. 'So we are not obligated to anyone.'

She took a deep breath. 'From now on, every penny we make will go to building the emporium into a thriving industry.' She held up a piece of paper. 'This is our salvation, it is an order for a whole range of boots, shoes and gloves in the finest leather money can buy. There'll be plenty of work for everyone for as many hours as you chose to put in.'

Doreen pinched Catherine's arm and winked. 'You'll be able to earn plenty of money for your bottom drawer,' she whispered.

'I've looked into the background of the company which is called the Llewellyn Company.' Hari continued. 'They are brand-new but with very strong financial backing behind them. They intend to buy our handmade products at wholesale prices and sell them in North Wales, as well as in England and Scotland.'

'Won't that harm our own sales?' Catherine ventured timidly.

'That's a very good question,' Hari smiled. 'It's one that occurred to me, too. The conclusion I came to after much thought was that even if we didn't sell so many of our goods locally, we would have our hands full with the orders from the Llewellyn Company. The loss of a few home sales would make little if any difference.' She paused and looked at Catherine. 'I can see another question is hovering on your lips,' she smiled encouragingly. 'Please, speak up.'

After a moment, Catherine shook her head, how could she put into words the unease she felt about the scheme? It was something that lay heavily in the pit of her stomach, a premonition, but of what?

'No, it's nothing Mrs Grenfell,' she said and even to her own ears it sounded as if she hadn't the courage to voice her own ideas.

'Well, has anyone else got any questions?'

'What about hats, Mrs Grenfell?' Doreen asked. 'I won't be done out of a job by all this, will I?'

Hari shook her head. 'Not a chance! I should think you would be even busier, I might even need to take on an apprentice to help you.'

'What about Cath?' Doreen plunged in and Catherine

looked at her in surprise. 'Well,' Doreen said quickly, 'she's already helped me at home, she's deft with those little fingers of hers, she might make a good milliner one day if she listens to me.'

'It's up to you, Catherine,' Hari Grenfell said. 'I am happy to have you in my employ whatever you do.'

'I'd like to learn the trade if Doreen is willing to teach me,' Catherine said quickly. She knew she was distancing herself from the business of leather goods, frightened that something very wrong was going to happen.

'Right then, that's settled. Now, back to the shop floor with you, girls,' Hari rose to her feet, 'it's time the shop doors were opened. Mustn't keep our customers waiting, must we?'

Over the next few days, Catherine's uneasiness increased as additional machinery was shipped in to cope with the expected rush orders. Extra leather was brought over from France and some from the Welsh valleys. The machinery was costly and so was the best leather, the entire project was doubtless putting Mrs Grenfell into debt once more. Still, that was her business, Catherine reasoned, Mrs Grenfell must be sure of herself to take such steps.

Some of the outbuildings were converted into storerooms; workmen did repairs, built up sagging walls and whitewashed the exteriors so that the buildings were fresh and clean and most of all weatherproof.

In the small part of the shop set aside for Doreen's millinery work, odd pieces of leather were utilized for the decoration of straw and felt hats. Doreen used the softest leather for edging the crown and feathered some pieces of calf as though the hat wore dancing plumes.

'I don't know what's the matter with you lately,' Doreen grumbled one afternoon when Catherine had been working in silence, lost in thought. 'You're as grumpy as a ram with no ewes to tupp.' She smiled. 'Missing being bedded, that's your trouble.'

'Shut up!' Catherine said good-naturedly. 'That's all you seem to think of, you and your Jerry and me sitting downstairs in front of the fire like an old maid. Do you wonder I'm grumpy?'

'No, but it's more than that, isn't it, love? I know you are troubled about your marriage an' all that and still pining for Boyo but there's something else nagging at you, come on, tell me.'

'I don't know,' Catherine said slowly, 'it sounds daft but I feel somehow things are going to go wrong at work. This big order, I can't believe it's real, don't ask me why.'

'Well, I wouldn't give it no more thought, if I was you,' Doreen said firmly. 'Mrs Grenfell is a sensible lady, she looked into this business and they got plenty of money so what could go wrong? In any case, it's not our worry, is it?'

'It would be if we lost our jobs,' Catherine said quietly.

Doreen shook her head at her in reproof. 'For Gawd's sake, haven't you heard the saying "never trouble trouble, till trouble troubles you"?'

Catherine laughed out loud. 'Well, I have now! You're right, it's not my worry, I'll do my best to put it all out of my mind. Come on, now, Dor, show me how to shape this damn straw over the head of this awkward model that keeps trying to get away from me.'

'Right, now you are talking.' Doreen glanced at the clock, 'It'll soon be time to go home, mind, so pay attention 'cos I'm not staying here late for anyone.'

'Don't tell me,' Catherine said in mock resignation, 'Jerry Danby is coming over again.'

'Dead right!' Doreen said and deftly shaped the straw into place so that, at once, it looked like the crown of a hat.

Boyo arrived at Ty Craig just as the moon slid between the clouds, obscuring for a moment the outline of the folding hills and the dark outcrop of rocks that hovered over the building. He moved round to the back of the house and tried to see above the high windows into the kitchens. He could just make out the large hams hanging from the beams and bunches of dried herbs but he

341

could not see any sign of the young maid or of the cook.

His gentle rapping at the door, however, elicited a swift response. Cara stood looking out at him, her eyes over-large in her small white face. 'She's very quiet up there, the missis, I mean, hope she's all right.'

'I'm sure Mrs Hopkins is fine, I don't know why you are making so much fuss.'

'The place is haunted, sir, I just know it.' Cara shivered. 'I hate going to that bedroom, it's always cold, however high I bank the fire and those rocks outside, well, I don't wonder Mrs Hopkins is going funny-like.'

In the kitchen the cook was seated in a rocking-chair, her hands on her lap, her eyes closed. She was breathing heavily, almost snoring and Boyo felt a dart of pity for the old woman, she should not have to work, not at her age. No wonder she was staying here at Ty Craig, no-one else would take her on.

'I've done a drink ready to take up to Mrs Hopkins,' Cara said. 'I've put an extra cup of hot milk for you too, sir, thought you could do with it on such a cold night.'

It was cold, Boyo had not realized it while he had been riding from town but a sharp easterly wind seemed to have blown up and now the trees outside were swaying, the branches moaning like distraught spirits. He was being absurd, he was allowing the atmosphere of the house to affect him as badly as it did the young maid.

'Give me the tray.' He took the stairs two at a time, the draught in the hallway was lifting the door knocker, rattling brass against the wood with an insistent beat. He glanced over his shoulder and looked at the paintings of some of Bethan's ancestors and for a split second, the eyes seemed to be alive and following him.

It was cold in the bedroom, Bethan, it seemed, was soundly asleep. Just as he thought, the maid was making a fuss about nothing. Boyo put the tray onto the small bedside table, noticing the array of coloured glass bottles. They were unmarked and he wondered what sort of rubbish Bethan was pouring into herself.

As quietly as he could, he placed coals onto the fire so that the flames shot anew up into the draughty chimney. Even the leaping flames offered little comfort and Boyo rubbed his fingers, trying to bring some warmth into them.

He thought he heard a sound behind him but when he turned, Bethan was still lying quietly against the pillow, her hair spread out around her. In the firelight, it seemed to glow red, almost as red as Catherine's.

He dusted his hands and moved into the dressing-room to wash the grime from his fingers. When he returned to the bedroom, the fire looked dull and lifeless and with a sigh, Boyo took up the glass of hot milk, forcing himself to think clearly. He was here to watch Bethan as she slept, to make sure she was not subject to strange fits, as Cara had claimed.

He sank into a rocking-chair and finished off the milk, the warmth of it was comforting. He closed his eyes, suddenly weary, he was too tired to think anymore. He had failed in his attempt to win Catherine over and nothing else seemed important, not even the wife who was the one obstacle standing in the way of his happiness.

His thoughts became hazy, he tried to drag himself to full wakefulness but he was fighting a losing battle. He saw himself rise from the chair as if watching an apparition. He saw white arms reach up for him, saw firelight gleam on red hair, felt the smoothness of skin beneath his touch. Desire surged through him. He was plunging into the softness beneath him, arms were clinging to him, breasts were pressing against his chest. The act seemed to go on and on. It was as if the life was being drained from him as a hotness surged through his loins. He fell gasping, his senses reeling and then his mind was blank, he was being plunged into a deep darkness.

When he awoke, he was sitting in the rocking-chair, fully dressed. The bed was empty. Of Bethan there was no sign.

Boyo rubbed his eyes, had he had a weird, fantastic

dream? He rose to his feet, his limbs felt heavy. He went into the dressing-room, he would wash his face in cold water, splash away the foolish illusions of the night, for illusions they must be, there was no other explanation.

Downstairs, a calm, collected Bethan greeted him with a smile. She looked perfectly normal, as though she had slept peaceful as a baby throughout the night, which was more than he had done. Boyo wondered at the vividness of his dream, if that was indeed what it was.

'Good morning, nice to see your face when I woke this morning.' Bethan handed him some tea. 'To what do I owe the honour of your visit?'

He was thrown into confusion, what could he say? That the maid suspected Bethan either of having fits or of consorting with the spirit world. 'I came over to talk, I came up to your room, it was late, I should have known you would be asleep. I sat in the chair for a moment and I must have dozed off.'

'Well, whatever, it's wonderful to see you.' She studied him carefully. 'You look rather tired, perhaps you did not sleep too well in that uncomfortable chair.'

'Probably not.' He drank the tea thirstily and then rose to his feet. 'I must go.' He moved to the door and let himself out into the hallway. Cara hovered beside him and he drew her outside.

'I'm afraid I've nothing to report, I fell asleep. Did you hear anything in the night?'

The girl looked uncomfortable. 'I don't know, sir, I think I just left it all to you to sort out.'

'I see.' He felt she was not telling him the truth but there was no way he could force her to speak.

As he rode home, he felt tiredness sweep over him, he was drained, as though he had moved mountains during the night. He was getting as fanciful as that silly maid, it was about time he snapped out of this nonsensical way of thinking.

Once home, he went to his bedroom and pulled off his clothes, they smelt of Ty Craig and Bethan. Naked, he stood before the mirror. Quite what he expected to see he did not know. He turned from the waist and his breath hissed sharply between his teeth. There, scarring the whiteness of his skin, were the livid marks of a woman's nails.

CHAPTER TWENTY-SEVEN

The hills outside Cork were verdant, lush, the breezes from the sea were balmy. As Catherine climbed down from the cart and stared up at the largeness of the convent rearing upwards against the sky, she knew she could love this country, love Ireland more than she could ever love the man she was going to marry; and she would marry Liam. One day, one day, but not yet, a small voice inside her head said.

She thought of Boyo with a sense of pain, it was rumoured that he was back with his wife. He was not hers, had never been hers and yet she could not regret the times she had spent in his arms. She had known love, the singing, passionate kind of love that only comes once in a lifetime. The sort of love that makes the touch of a hand, a glance, a magical moment to remember.

Now she was back in Ireland, the country of her ancestors, at least on her father's side. The country of her husband-to-be and she'd never felt more miserable and unsettled in the whole of her life.

Her mother had asked her to come, she had wonderful news to impart. Catherine could guess what it was and as she entered the portals of the convent, she made an effort to appear relaxed and happy.

Fon came across the great hallway, arms outstretched, she was looking brown and happy, her hair completely grey now. 'I have asked to be received into holy orders, Cath.' Fon took her daughter in her arms and hugged her. 'As soon as I'm able, I'll start my novitiate.'

Catherine knew it had to come and yet she felt abandoned, as though her last link with the security of her childhood had been severed. She looked at her mother's arms, brown under the rolled-up sleeves and the hands ingrained with earth and knew she should be happy for her.

'You look as though it suits you, Mam.' She tried to inject warmth into her tone but Fon was looking at her quizzically.

'I'm still your mother, Cath, I will always be here for you if you want to talk anything over with me, mind.'

Catherine remembered the last time she had 'talked things over' with Fon. Then, her mother had been impatient, telling Catherine what to do with her life rather than listening to her unhappiness.

'Is anything wrong, Catherine? You seem a little on the edgy side.'

'I'm getting along just fine, Mam,' Catherine said. 'I've got a new job now, I'm training to be a hatter, getting quite good at it, I am.'

Fon took her daughter's hand and looked at the ring glinting there. 'And when are you going to marry and give me grandchildren? Don't leave it too long, love, I'm not getting any younger, remember.'

'That's silly talk, Mam,' Catherine said quickly. 'You are the picture of health, you'll live to be a hundred.'

'Don't avoid the question, have you named the day?'

Catherine thought of Liam, waiting for her in the old farmhouse and Patricia, his sister, scorned by her lover. A mother now but not changed for the better by her experiences. She sighed, 'I will do, quite soon.'

'Come along,' Fon said, suddenly brisk, 'the sisters have requested that you eat with them. Later, we will pray together for God to give you guidance.'

It was cool within the walls of the convent and strangely peaceful. The supper was a simple affair of soup and bread and fruit piled in huge earthenware bowls.

Later, she talked with Fon but it was mostly about the convent, about the peace of mind Fon had gained from being there. And, at last, when Catherine took her leave, she hugged her mother as though she was saying goodbye to her for ever.

As Catherine guided the pony and trap along the

347

craggy hillside, the verdant grass interspersed with out-crops of rock looked cool, silvered by the moonlight.

She felt as if the power of her mother's prayers was with her and she envied Fon her tranquillity. Fon had so much more strength of mind, of purpose, than Catherine ever had. So far, Catherine knew, she had been swaying in the breeze like a fallen leaf. It was high time she took her fate in her own hands and shaped her future the way she wanted it.

She felt filled with energy as she breathed in the soft Irish air and felt the first small drops of gentle rain. She was young, she had her health and strength, she had her whole life before her. What was she going to do with it?

She drove the cart over the brow of the hill, before her was spread the sea. It stretched calm and serene, as far as the eye could see. From this distant vantage point, the waves breaking on the shore made little sound, little movement in the still of the night.

So what did she really want? Catherine asked herself and the answer was there, in her heart, her mind, in the base of her being: she wanted Boyo, she longed to be in his arms.

'Then for heaven's sake go out and get him!' Her voice drifted away on the breeze carried like a leaf towards the sea. Would it breach the gulf of the distance between her-self and the man she loved? Would he know, somewhere in the core of him, that she was coming home to him?

She had wanted life to be easy but did she think of her parents wresting a living out of the bleak hill farmlands? Jamie had proved he had courage, surely she had some of the spirit of her father in her?

She jerked the reins, her progress more purposeful now as she turned back towards the farmstead. She would tell Liam face to face, that she could never marry him. In spite of herself, doubts about her feelings surfaced; she liked being with Liam, would miss him when she returned home but surely that was friendship, not love?

This was a new era, a time when women were finding

a voice, when she herself was learning a trade that could take her anywhere she wanted to go.

She arrived at the farmhouse with a sense of relief. Through the windows gleamed the lights of the lamps and as Catherine entered the kitchen, Patricia turned, her face a mask of dislike and Catherine wondered what there was about her that evoked lust in men and hatred in women.

'He's still out in the fields working, there's a lot to be done and I can't help him, not with the baby to look after,' Patricia said. Her tone implying that Catherine was neglecting to do her duty. Catherine picked up the kettle and Patricia moved forward to intervene. 'I'll do that.' Her tone was hostile.

'No need.' Normally Catherine would have allowed Patricia to have her way but now a sense of rebelliousness was rioting through her; she had been quiet for long enough. 'I'm not helpless, I can make myself a cup of tea.' She turned to look at Patricia, the girl's mouth was drawn downwards, sullen, mutinous. 'If Liam had his way, I would be mistress here, you would have to do what I said or leave, it would be as simple as that.'

Patricia was silent, staring at her as though Catherine had suddenly grown two heads. She moved away from the fire and sat near the crib where her baby lay. After the first feeling of triumph, a sense of pity took its place. Catherine realized how easy it would be to assert her power over the other girl, the thought gave her no pleasure.

'You needn't worry,' she said, 'you will always have a place here.'

'I don't believe you, you want me out, I know you do.'

'Please, there's no need to worry, I mean it.' She poured tea for both of them and sat at the table, her face in her hands.

'What's wrong, is your mother sick again?' Patricia was making an effort to be nice and Catherine felt a pinch of guilt at her own spiteful outburst.

'My mother is looking better than I've seen her for many a month.'

'What is it then, you look different?'

'You'll know soon enough. Now, what are we going to give Liam when he comes in from the fields?'

Patricia smiled, 'So you do find me useful for something then, even if it's only as head cook and bottle washer.'

Catherine looked at her levelly, 'It didn't take you long to revert to your old self, did it? If you wish, I can make the food myself, I was brought up on a farm, I know how to cook a meal for a man, never doubt it.'

Patricia seemed to have regained some of her spirit. 'Not very good at business though, were you? Let your farm run into debt and lost it, that wasn't very clever, was it?'

'No,' Catherine agreed solemnly, 'it wasn't clever at all.' She lifted her head. 'But I have learned a valuable lesson from it which is only just becoming clear to me: in this world you fight for what you want, fight any way you can, with any weapon at your disposal.' She leaned forward in her chair. 'My weapons are my strong spirit, and my determination. What are yours, Patricia, a spiteful tongue and a shrivelled soul?'

Patricia began to cry so quietly that at first Catherine didn't realize what was happening. Patricia's face crumpled slowly, like paper screwed into a ball, and tears ran unchecked down her face splashing onto the inert hands in her lap.

On an impulse, Catherine moved towards her, awkwardly, she took Patricia in her arms and cradled her. 'There, there, I'm sorry, I didn't mean to be so cruel.'

Patricia clung to her like a lost soul. 'I'm so unhappy, Catherine, so unhappy.' She gulped. 'You're right, I am spiteful. 'Tis because I'm jealous of you. I'm plain, no man fancies me and you are so beautiful with your red hair and your pale skin, sure, can you wonder that I am nasty to you?'

'Hush, don't cry, everything is going to be all right, you'll see.'

Patricia rubbed at her eyes. 'You keep hinting at some-

350

thing, Catherine, what is it? By the name of our Virgin, put me out of my misery.'

Catherine knew that she should first tell Liam of her decision not to marry him face to face and yet she found it difficult to resist the entreaty in Patricia's reddened eyes.

'I'll be leaving Ireland soon and I won't be coming back.'

'You mean you are not going to . . .' Patricia's words trailed away as Catherine put her finger to her lips.

'Hush, now, I will talk to Liam, later. For now, let's see what we can cook for his supper, he'll be starving by the time he comes in.'

It was less than an hour later when Liam came into the kitchen, his face weary, his hair ruffled by the cold wind that had blown up. Catherine looked up with a dart of pity and pain, this was how her father had looked when the work on the farm drained the strength from him.

'Go and wash,' she said softly, 'your meal is almost ready.'

He bent and kissed her nose and she smelt the sweat on him, mingled with the heady scent of ripe corn. 'So, bossing me about already is it?' He laughed and the lines of weariness eased from his eyes. 'Not even married and you got a ring through my nose right enough.'

Patricia emerged from the shadows against the wall and Catherine froze when she saw the expression on the other girl's face. She knew at once what Patricia intended to do.

'She'll never marry you,' Patricia said harshly. 'She's going home to Wales, crossing the Irish Sea for ever, go on, ask her if it isn't the truth.'

'Patricia!' Catherine could not believe that this harpy was the same woman she had cradled and comforted a short time earlier. She was turning and rending Catherine, cruelly forcing the truth on her brother with thoughts only of revenge, uncaring that she was hurting him with her words.

'Liam, I wanted to talk to you sensibly, we should

discuss this thing calmly and carefully, I don't want anyone hurt.'

'Is it the truth?' He looked at her, his eyes hot and angry. 'Come on, Catherine, you've told my sister and God knows who else, had you not better tell me, the man who you are supposed to marry?'

She could see there was no point in denying it. She lifted her head high and stared into his eyes. 'I can't marry you, Liam, I don't love you. It would not be fair to either of us, you must see that.'

'I see only a fickle woman, a woman I thought I loved.' He turned and strode out of the kitchen, slamming the door shut behind him.

'Are you pleased with what you have done?' Catherine stared at Patricia, more in sadness than in anger. 'You have hurt Liam and you have betrayed my trust in you. I doubt that any of it will bring you happiness, you don't deserve to be happy, do you?'

Patricia's smile was triumphant. 'You are a fool, Catherine, you put your silly feelings for a married man before your own interests. You could have been happy here with Liam, he is a fine man, he could have given you strong sons to carry on working the land. Now he will turn to a local girl, a respectable girl who has kept her virginity for her husband.'

'I don't think you have any right to cast the first stone, do you, Patricia?' Catherine stared at her dispassionately. 'You grasped at a man, any man, anxious to lose that precious virginity you talk of before it was too late. Well, you have taught me a harsh lesson today: not to trust anyone, anyone at all.'

She moved towards the stairs and paused. 'I shall be leaving first thing in the morning.' She smiled. 'Have you thought that my replacement might not want a bitch like you under her roof? Where will you be then, Patricia?'

She hurried up the stairs into the room, the darkness streaked with moonlight. Ireland was a beautiful place, a lovely place, but it was not home. Suddenly her heart lifted, she was doing the right thing, she was going back to Wales, to carve out her own destiny instead of following wherever the winds of fate took her.

'I can't understand it,' Hari was looking down at her books. 'Sales figures are down, we are sinking back into debt and I don't know why.'

'There are bound to be fluctuations, my love,' Craig said lazily, folding *The Swansea Times* so that he could read it more comfortably.

'I know, but this drop in income has continued for some weeks now, I don't like it. It is almost as though someone was working against us, driving our customers elsewhere. I only hope the Llewellyn Company arranges to collect the stock they ordered before too long, we need the money badly.'

Craig sat up straighter. 'Are you serious, Hari?'

'How are sales of the leather doing? Are they buoyant?' Hari said in reply.

Craig shook his head. 'No, as a matter of fact I have a large stock on my hands. I have cancelled an order for more calf, there is plenty in stock to see us through a few more months but this sort of thing has happened before.'

'Not on this scale,' Hari said. 'I have this feeling in my gut that we are being undermined and I have a fair idea who is doing it.' She paused, 'It has to be Bethan Hopkins.'

'I don't know how,' Craig sounded doubtful, 'it seems a bit far-fetched to me, why should she bother herself about us? I hear she's dripping with money.'

'You didn't see her face when I refused to get rid of Catherine O'Conner.' Hari bit her lip. 'I knew the woman was dangerous, she forced the sale of Honey's Farm, took Catherine's home away from her; she is not only a ruthless woman but a little deranged too, if you ask me.'

'I can understand the woman buying the farm,' Craig said reasonably. 'It went for a very good price and it's prime land for building on. That's what's taking off right now, houses, property, somewhere near the sea. And you

353

must admit that Honey's Farm has all that.'

'I know but then the land is over to the east of the town, it's not where the rich want to live, is it?'

'No, but haven't you heard that houses are going to be built there for the workers, the rent will be cheap and the slums of the town can be cleared away. I expect Mrs Hopkins got wind of the scheme and got her bid in early for the land. A shrewd move, I wish I'd thought of it.' He paused thoughtfully. 'If business doesn't pick up in a few weeks' time then I'll seriously consider what you've said. Until then, Hari, let's just get on with our lives, shall we?'

He sounded a little impatient. Hari took a deep breath, it was pointless to say anything more at this stage, Craig, being a man couldn't believe a woman could be so devious, so vengeful.

'By the way, where is that young girl, Catherine, isn't it? I haven't seen her around lately,' Craig said cheerfully steering the subject away from business matters.

'She went to Ireland to see her mother, she's coming back to work tomorrow.'

'She's a pretty little thing.' Craig looked at his wife with a gleam in his eye. 'But not half as lovely as my own little woman.'

'Your wife, if you don't mind.' Hari tried to respond lightly but she was worried about the business, more worried than she should be at this stage. So sales were down, it was nothing crucial and yet she had the strangest feeling that things could only get worse.

'Thank goodness you're back.' Doreen looked up from her chair with a smile as Catherine entered the kitchen and dumped her bag on the table. 'It's been like the grave by 'ere without you.'

'I'm sure!' Catherine hugged Doreen tightly. 'Don't tell me you haven't had Jerry Danby round here every night keeping you company.'

Doreen drew away frowning. 'We've had to be careful, mind, can't have Meadows finding out what's going on. Now you are back Jerry can call any time he likes.'

'I see!' Catherine placed her hands on her hips. 'That's why you're so glad to see me home again, is it?'

'Pipe down, for Gawd's sake, and get a cup of tea inside you, just made a fresh pot. I got a pie baked for you and some crusty bread, as well. Should have been making hats, mind, and if that's not a welcome then I don't know what is.'

With a sigh of contentment, Catherine sat at the table, the tea was hot and sweet, the aroma of the bread rose invitingly. 'It's good to be back.'

Doreen was looking at her quizzically. 'No ring, I see, is it all over then?'

'It's all off. I've told Liam I can't marry him.'

'Are you sure?'

'Sure as I'll ever be about anything.' Catherine took a gulp of her tea.

'In other words, you are not sure at all?'

'I know I don't love Liam the way a woman should love the man she means to marry.'

'But you can't settle for being a fancy piece to that Boyo Hopkins, Cath, you are too good for that. Anyway, it seems sure now that he's gone back to his wife.'

'It's only gossip, though, isn't it? Boyo is kind, he would not turn his back on his responsibilities, I know that. It doesn't mean he is living with her again.'

'Sorry to tell you this, love,' Doreen said, 'but talk is, she's fallen for a baby again. I can't believe it but there, nature is a funny thing.'

Catherine rubbed at her eyes, suddenly weary. Pain and shock ebbed and flowed like a tide through her veins and it took all her control not to rant and rave and cry that Boyo was hers, he would not go back to his wife, he would not go to her bed, she would not believe it.

'You'll get over him, love, you know you will.'

'Perhaps I will. All I know right now is that I can't marry Liam and go to live in Ireland.' Catherine's voice was hoarse.

'Well, you're young yet, there's time enough for you to meet some nice boy.' Doreen spoke comfortingly. 'I made the mistake myself of rushing into marriage, I thought Meadows was the cat's whiskers but I soon found out that the old bastard had claws.' Doreen smiled. 'Still, I'm happy enough now. Come on, eat your supper while it's hot. I can fill you in on all the gossip later.'

Catherine made a pretence of eating, her mind was numbed, her journey had been more tiring than she realized. Soon, she would fall into bed and sleep and try for a few hours to forget how unhappy she was.

As the days passed, Catherine settled into the routine of the emporium working in the millinery department with Doreen and soon it was as if the few days she'd spent in Ireland had never been. She tried to erase from her memory the sight of Liam's face, white, drawn with pain, telling herself it would never have worked, such a marriage could only fail in the end.

She was becoming adept at fashioning the headgear for the smart ladies of the town, adding touches of ostrich feather set at unusual angles, tying a length of chiffon around the brim, making each design a little different from the last.

In Catherine's absence, a larger room to the side of the house had been designated the millinery room where she and Doreen could work in comfort. A large window faced the sea and Doreen had placed a fine array of millinery on blocks that could readily be seen by the public.

There was plenty of work, indeed, the millinery department seemed to be doing more trade than the shoe shop. There, the stock grew dusty, standing on shelves far too long, even the sale of leather gloves was down, with only the fine cotton and velvet gloves selling at all.

'Things are getting bad, by here, you know, Cath.' Doreen was sitting before a block, shaping a piece of felt with energetic fingers, 'I don't like it, don't like it at all, I think someone is out to ruin Mrs Grenfell.'

Catherine was suddenly cold. 'Why, what makes you think that?'

'I got eyes in my head, love. The leather goods are getting out of fashion, shoe styles are changing and we still have all our last season's stuff. Aye, there's something going on, I can smell it.' She tapped her nose. 'I got a smell for dirty tricks and there's one going on here all right.'

Catherine studied her friend in silence. 'You know I had a bad feeling about this Llewellyn Company, could they be letting Mrs Grenfell down do you think?'

'I don't know. More competition could have sprung up from somewhere, I suppose. Anyway up, if things don't get better round here, some of the girls will soon be out of work, you mark my words.'

Catherine wondered briefly if Bethan Hopkins could somehow be influencing the leather market and yet it seemed such a far-fetched idea. Bethan was a vindictive woman, an evil woman but surely she was not that powerful or that vindictive that she would turn against Mrs Grenfell just because she was giving Catherine employment?

'Excuse me a minute, Doreen, I need to talk to Mrs Grenfell, I won't be long.'

Doreen looked at her questioningly but Catherine hurried from the room afraid that her courage would fail her, that she might seem foolish and hysterical.

Hari Grenfell was standing in the doorway of the main part of the emporium, Catherine could see her slender figure silhouetted against the sunshine. There were no customers, the girls stood about indecisively and Catherine realized that something was indeed very wrong.

'Mrs Grenfell,' she heard her voice tremble a little but she plunged on. 'I think I know who is behind all this.'

As Hari Grenfell turned to her, Catherine indicated the silent shop floor. 'I think it's Mrs Hopkins, she hates me and she seems to hate anyone who helps me in any way. I know it sounds absurd saying it like that but I . . .' her words trailed away as Hari nodded.

'I think you are right, Catherine, it is a conclusion I have been forced to come to myself.' She held out a letter. 'The Llewellyn Company ordered a great deal of stock, the order has now been cancelled.' She smiled wryly. 'I have just learnt, a bit late in the day, that Bethan Hopkins's maiden name was Llewellyn and she is listed at the head of the directors of the so-called Llewellyn Company.'

'I knew there was something suspicious about that company,' Catherine said. 'The trouble was, it was just a feeling, there was no sense to it.'

'Well, it makes sense to me now, I should have realized that when Bethan Hopkins threatened me, she meant every word she said. She is a very powerful woman and I underestimated her.'

'I must leave at once,' Catherine said quickly. 'Perhaps if she thinks you have dismissed me Mrs Hopkins will leave your business alone.'

'No!' Hari's tone was firm, controlled. 'No, I will not have anyone dictate to me how I should run my own affairs. This is nothing short of blackmail and I will not submit to it.'

'But, Mrs Grenfell, it would be better if I went.'

'I don't think so.' Hari Grenfell shook her head. 'I don't think it is as simple as that. Bethan Hopkins has me in her sights, whatever I do now, she is determined to bring me down. Well, I have no intention of allowing it.'

She smiled and placed her hand on Catherine's arm. 'Don't worry, I mean to ship the old stock of leather goods to Bristol. Clarks have planned a big shoe fair in Somerset, they have invited shoemakers from all over the country to bring stock. At least it's a chance to recoup some of the losses. Go back to work, Catherine, and let me worry about the business.'

Reluctantly, Catherine returned to the millinery room. She did not see the pieces of velvet, the floor strewn with discarded feathers, the blocks that stood like disembodied heads upon the shelves, she was thinking about Bethan Hopkins, wondering at the woman's capacity to hate.

'What's wrong, then, Cath? Come on, out with it, you can tell Doreen anything, you know that.'

Catherine sank into a chair and idly picked at a piece of straw that had come away from the crown of one of the hats. 'I know who is doing this to Mrs Grenfell and it's all my fault.'

'What are you on about, how can this be your fault?'

'It's Bethan Hopkins, she hates me, she'll stop at nothing to hurt me. Anyone who helps me gets into trouble, can't you see it?'

'Oh come on, love, it sounds a bit daft doesn't it?' Doreen had plenty of common sense but very little imagination.

'Mrs Hopkins is behind the Llewellyn Company, she used the name to ruin Mrs Grenfell.' She rubbed her eyes tiredly. 'She took my lands away from me, she had Liam arrested for theft. Then, to cap it all, Liam's farm was poisoned, the land ruined. What will she do next?'

'Well, it do sound a funny business put like that.' Doreen chewed her lip. 'But don't worry, now that you and Boyo Hopkins don't see each other any more Mrs Hopkins will try to put it out of her mind, forget it happened, make her marriage work. I don't want to rub it in, Cath, but if Mrs Hopkins *is* having a kid she got more important things to think about now, hasn't she?'

Catherine felt a pain that began low in her stomach and rose to her throat as if to choke her. For a moment, she could not speak. It made her sick to think of Boyo going to his wife's bed.

'Look, love,' Doreen spoke softly, 'this is all beyond you and me; if this Mrs Hopkins is out to get at Hari Grenfell then it's up to them to sort it out between them. The old witch will have met her match in Mrs Grenfell, I'm telling you.'

'Perhaps so.' Catherine picked up a hat in dark velvet, the material shimmered as she turned it in the light and she knew it would need very little decoration. 'I'd better do some work, I suppose. As you say, if I try to interfere, I might only make things worse.'

Over the next few days, Catherine tried to clear her mind. To forget about Bethan Hopkins, even to forget about Boyo. If he had gone back to his wife, then Catherine would have no place in his life. Then Hari

Grenfell called her to her office and her fears and suspicions surfaced again.

She was not the only one waiting to see Mrs Grenfell, two of the younger girls were there too, standing edgily outside the door. 'We're getting the boot.' One of the girls looked glumly towards Catherine. 'She don't want to let us go but she has to, there's no work for us, it's as plain as the nose on my face.'

Hari looked pinched and drawn when the three girls entered the office. She fiddled with a pen for a moment and then took a deep breath. 'I have bad news, I'm sorry but I will have to let you three go. You came into the firm after the others and you are the three who will most likely find work elsewhere. I have made up your wages and all I can promise is that if . . . when things improve, I'll take you back, if you still want to come and work for me.' She did not look at Catherine as the girls filed out of the office.

As she made her way back to the millinery room, Catherine knew that in spite of what she'd said to Doreen about not interfering, she must face Bethan Hopkins, ask her to stop punishing everyone else for what Catherine and Boyo had done. Her heart contracted for a moment in pain, how could she bear to see Boyo living with his wife, a happy couple about to have a child? She swallowed her tears, she was alone, unloved and it was her own fault. Well, she would just have to stop feeling sorry for herself and get on with her life. But first she must eat humble pie, beg Bethan Hopkins to forgive her. It would be difficult but somehow she must find the strength to go through with it.

CHAPTER TWENTY-EIGHT

Boyo sat near his wife's bedside, a feeling of unease tingling along his spine, making his hair stand on end. Something was very wrong with Bethan, she was either very sick or she was, as Cara the maid insisted, possessed.

Possessed, what a foolish idea, she was ill, she was overwrought, she needed to rest, that was all; and yet he failed to convince himself. He had felt a presence in the house that was almost tangible. It was a coldness, a sensation that someone else inhabited the place and that he was unwelcome. It was not that Bethan did not want him, oh, she wanted him all right but it was almost as though the house did not want him.

Bethan opened her eyes, suddenly. Eerily they looked through him, then her gaze seemed to focus on his face. A light warmed her face, she smiled at him and held out her hand. He took it reluctantly. 'I'm not very well, am I?'

'You seem a little better this morning, Bethan.' He spoke unconvincingly.

'I didn't sleep very well.' She sat up and Boyo plumped up the pillows, adding an extra one to support her.

She had dark circles beneath her eyes and her skin was pale, with a sheen of sweat glazing her hollow cheeks. He felt pity tug at him; pity but no other emotion, not love, not even affection. Bethan had changed, she was no longer the woman he had married and he was entirely to blame for that change. And so her helplessness bound him to her, forced him to stay in the house that he hated. But today he felt he must get out of Ty Craig, if only for a little while or he would go mad.

'I have to ride into Swansea today, business matters,' he said evenly. Instead of the rebuke he thought would be forthcoming, Bethan smiled.

'I know you have other things to do than look after a sick wife. Of course you must go, see to your business matters.'

He examined her face for traces of sarcasm but there were none. He felt guilt pour through him and was irritated, why did he allow Bethan to have this effect on him? She had money, resources, she could buy all the help she needed and yet he stayed. He was worried by her thinness, by the way she seemed diminished, shrunken from the fine, humorous woman she had been to a timid dormouse of a person. Had he done this to her with his coldness?

'I'll have some breakfast sent up to you.' He forced himself to speak pleasantly. 'You must try to eat a little, just to please me. I believe the doctor is going to call later today.'

She nodded. 'All right. In the meantime, I'll try to rest, my love, just to please you.'

He left the room with a sense of relief that was almost physical and hurried down into the gloomy hallway. There was no light in this house, no sunshine, the overwhelming feeling of claustrophobia he felt must be due to the overhanging rocks that perpetually dripped with water, whatever the weather.

A few minutes later, he left the house and moved round to the stables. At least, here, there was some relief from the towering hillside, there was an opening through the rock leading away from the house and Boyo could not wait to ride through it.

The breeze was chill but welcome as he guided the horse and trap cautiously through the outcrop of rocks over the rugged ground, he did not relish losing a wheel and being stuck for hours on the bleak hillside.

While he was in town, he would fetch some supplies, replenish the shelves in the pantry which were becoming bare. It was as though Bethan had no intention of providing sustenance for herself, almost as though she wanted to die, to join the other ghosts that inhabited the house. He repressed a shudder and glanced back over his shoulder, cursing himself for indulging in superstitious nonsense.

Once on the open road, he allowed the animal free rein and as he drew further from Ty Craig, his spirits lightened. Away from the oppressive atmosphere of the house, he was a different man. The situation was becoming intolerable, he could not stay at the house indefinitely nursing an unresponsive Bethan. Perhaps he should find a specialist doctor for her, or a priest who would exorcize the ghosts from the house. He smiled without humour, no self-respecting priest would set foot in Ty Craig.

The streets of Swansea were unusually busy for the middle of the day. He drew the animal to a halt outside Taylor's Grocery Store, smelling the heady aroma of coffee grounds, knowing suddenly that he needed some breakfast.

He would leave the horse at the stables in Gower Place and take a walk around the town, stop at the Mackworth for something to eat and then later, much later, buy the provisions that Bethan needed.

The ostler unhitched the animal and began to rub the horse down with long easy strokes of his brush. Boyo left the stables and made his way out along the road, a sense of freedom as heady as wine in his head.

He caught a glimpse of a slender figure, red hair piled upwards in a coil and his heart jolted within him. For a moment he thought it was Catherine and then she turned and he could see by her profile that the woman was a stranger.

He no longer felt hungry, he no longer felt light-hearted, he was dragged down by longing, his loins ached for her; Catherine, the only woman he could ever love.

But she was lost to him. She would marry her cousin, move to Ireland, forget all about the nights of passion she had shared with him. He sank down onto the edge of a horse trough and stared around him as though, by his will, he could conjure Catherine out of thin air. The people who passed him were strangers, women there were aplenty but not the one woman he longed to see, not Catherine O'Conner.

Once Boyo had left the house, Bethan's attitude changed. She sat up in bed and rang the bell non-stop until the maid bobbed into the room, her face white.

'I want some fresh toast,' she said, 'and another pot of tea. No, don't take the tray away, leave it where it is.'

Bethan stared with distaste at the toast with butter congealed upon it, at the cup full of cold tea; it would be there when Boyo returned, he would believe that she was still sick, could not eat and needed him with her. It was only by using moral blackmail that she could make him stay and the knowledge was like a bitter pill stuck in her throat.

After she had eaten, she dressed and moved to her study. There she examined pages of figures, studying them intently and then, satisfied at last, she smiled.

Hari Grenfell was losing her touch, the business was slipping away from her. The setting up of the so-called Llewellyn Company had been an inspiration and Hari Grenfell had fallen for the trick as Bethan had known she would.

The order Bethan had placed for a very large amount of stock had forced Mrs Grenfell into further expense, expense she could not afford. Now, with the Llewellyn Company abruptly cancelling the order and ceasing to trade, the Grenfells found themselves with machinery they could not pay for and a massive accumulation of stock that would gather dust on the shelves.

Bethan had not let the matter rest there. Posted on the roadway leading to the emporium were men who worked for Bethan. They discouraged would-be customers from visiting the Grenfell establishment. Not only that but Bethan had hired door-to-door salesmen who took goods direct from Clarks' in Somerset to the householder. It was not a new idea, it had been done before, tallymen were to be seen all over the valleys but never had it been done with such determination. Bethan could and did pay over-the-odds wages to the men who worked for her, encouraging them to greater efforts by offering a huge bonus to the salesman with the largest order.

Bethan had fitted out the large vans with shelves full of samples. Lasts in many sizes were at the ready so that any type of shoe could be made on the spot should the customer not require bespoke boots.

That Bethan's plan was working became evident when Mrs Grenfell began laying off her staff. Three of the salesladies had been dismissed and that O'Conner slut had been one of them. Bethan smiled, she had achieved exactly what she had wanted all along and Hari Grenfell had been too stupid to see it. Well, Mrs Grenfell was all but finished, at least in Swansea.

Bethan's own fortune was growing, she had always had a way with business, a gift for making money and it did not fail her now. What had begun as an act of revenge was turning out to be very lucrative. And of course, she had help, Elizabeth Llewellyn was beside her at all times, advising, informing, encouraging.

Bethan no longer thought of Elizabeth as a ghost from the past, she was as real as Boyo and almost as dear. When Boyo urged Bethan to leave the house, to move to a house where the sun shone in and where the aspect was open and pleasant, he did not know that to move would be to leave behind her best friend, the best friend Bethan had ever had.

She rose, it was about time for their morning talk, she and Elizabeth would have a great deal to discuss. And then, before Boyo returned, Bethan would don her night-gown, rub some powder into her face to hide the healthy colour and take to her bed. One day, one day soon, she promised herself, Boyo would be joining her in that bed. Her face softened, once she had the child, a daughter it would be this time, Boyo would have to stay with her. She hugged the knowledge to her, Boyo did not know of her condition, she was keeping that little secret until the appropriate time. And when that moment came, her triumph would be complete.

*

Catherine looked into the hot coals, feeling the warmth of the flames leaping from the hearth, feeling like a drowning man clutching at straws. 'I'm going up there, after supper. Mrs Bethan Hopkins is going to have a piece of my mind.' She sank into a chair, wishing she felt as confident as she sounded. She looked down at her hands, her fingers were sore from fashioning the brim of a straw hat which lay now, like a misshapen beast, against the chenille of the tablecloth.

Doreen picked up the hat and looked at it with raised eyebrows. 'Not doing very well today, are you, love? Don't try so hard, work on the felt hats, you'll find those easier.'

'I must try to do it all. If Mrs Grenfell is good enough to pay me for doing work at home then I must do it. I can't expect you to come to my rescue all the time, you've enough to do in the shop.'

Doreen did not meet Catherine's eyes, how could she tell her there was no pay for home work? All that was extra was Doreen's pay for overtime, some of which she transferred to a fresh envelope and gave to Catherine. It was some salve to the girl's pride, it gave her the chance to believe she was paying for her bed and board at Doreen's house.

'As for going up there to Ty Craig,' Doreen said, steering the conversation onto safer ground, 'forget it! That cow will have the servants throw you off the place, she won't listen to a word you have to say.'

'I have to try,' Catherine said quietly. 'You know as well as I do that she's selling good stuff from Clarks at cut-price. Mrs Grenfell doesn't stand a chance against that kind of competition. If I don't at least try then the emporium will close down, Mrs Grenfell will be ruined and all because of me.'

'I told you before, keep out of it, leave it to the big girls. Mrs Grenfell can hold her own, once she gets her fighting spirit roused there will be no stopping her.'

Catherine sighed, 'I hope you're right but I'll have to say my piece anyway.'

It was a cool evening with the sun setting in splashes of

red and gold behind the silhouette of the hill when Catherine began her long walk from Watkin Street to Ty Craig. Ruefully, she sucked at her finger where a needle had jabbed at her, drawing blood. She tried her best with the hats, conscious of Doreen's praise and help but in her heart she knew she would never make a first-class milliner.

The street out of town was busy with traffic: vans returning to depots, dray-horses, tails flying, freed of the burden of heavy carts laden with beer barrels, travelling now at a trot. A messenger boy on a cycle, basket jutting forward empty of goods, was whistling cheerfully as he rode past her. He winked saucily. 'Lovely day, miss, feel like a ride on my crossbar?'

'Cheeky brat!' Catherine said trying not to smile. As she left the main roadways and began to ascend the narrow lane leading away from town, Catherine paused and looked for somewhere to rest. The terrain was becoming rockier, more rugged and she chose a flat piece of grass and sank down gratefully. In her pocket, a letter crackled and she took it out and read it again; it was from Liam. It began without preamble:

'I miss you, Catherine, I want to be with you more than ever now. I will have you on any terms you choose, I will come to live in your country, if that is what you wish. I long to hold you in my arms once more, to taste your sweetness. How could I ever want another woman now that I have possessed you?

Please, Catherine, forgive me for my anger, let me back into your life.

Yours as ever,
Liam.

Catherine folded the letter and replaced it in her pocket, wondering what she could say to Liam. Could she tell him there was no hope of them being together, she had merely encouraged him to buoy her own faltering pride? She could not flatly reject him, she cared too much for him for that. And she missed him, she realized with a sense of wonder, she really had missed him.

She rose to her feet and began to walk briskly up the hill, pushing away the unwelcome thoughts. She had not realized how far away Ty Craig was. The darkness was closing in now, the rocky outcrops becoming larger and more numerous. Catherine looked up, almost willing the moon to appear between the clouds, but the skies remained overcast.

At last, the house came into view, the tall gables disappeared into the night sky but the windows of the lower floors were lit with lamplight. Catherine paused at the large wrought-iron gates and looked with a sense of sudden apprehension at the twisted dragons frozen in metal, heads turned, tongues protruding, as though to dart towards her at any moment.

She tried to laugh at her own foolishness and began the walk along the rutted driveway. The large house seemed part of the rocks that reared around it, the walls stood fortress-like against the backdrop of the sheer cliff face. She wondered how anyone could bear to live in so dismal a house but then Bethan Hopkins was a woman of mystery, a woman of darkness.

She paused near the arched doorway, wondering if she should go to the back of the house, but no, she would ring the bell, she was a visitor not a servant or a tradesman.

After a time, a white-faced maid opened the door and Catherine was relieved, she had been expecting a sour-faced butler who would give her short shrift. This nervous young girl would be much kinder.

'I've come to see Mrs Hopkins.' She spoke firmly and the maid looked at her with surprise, unable to decide how to treat the unexpected caller.

'Mrs Hopkins don't have visitors, she don't like 'em,' she said at last. She made to close the door but Catherine stepped forward into the hallway and the maid looked at her open-mouthed, wondering what to do next.

'Please let Mrs Hopkins know I'm here. I'm Catherine O'Conner, she will see me.'

The maid looked sulkily down at her boots, still

uncertain, wondering how to deal with such persistence. At last, she nodded sulkily. 'I'll tell Mrs Hopkins but you'll get me into trouble, I'm warning you.'

'No, I won't get you into trouble,' Catherine's tone was soft, reassuring, 'you would get into trouble if you sent me away.'

Catherine watched as the maid mounted the stairs reluctantly, lifting her skirts away from the rich carpet, stepping gingerly as though complete silence was required of her. Poor girl, she seemed terrified of Bethan Hopkins, probably with good cause.

The maid returned almost immediately and nodded to Catherine. 'You can go up, Mrs Hopkins will see you. Her room is the first one on the left of the corridor.'

Catherine mounted the stairs, feeling nervous now that she had accomplished her wish. What if Bethan railed at her, or worse, threatened her with violence? At the door, she took a deep breath and then rapped loudly.

The voice that bade her enter was neither angry nor pleading but low, almost sleepy. Catherine entered the bedchamber and blinked at the gloom; the curtains were partly drawn, the dark, heavy furniture crouched in shadow against the wall. The bed stood near the largest window and outside loomed the grey mass of the cliff face.

Bethan was lying against the pillows, her hair spread around her. Strangely, she looked younger than Catherine remembered, her eyes were large, luminous, her skin, though pale, glowed with inner light. She looked like a woman sated by love.

Catherine felt a dart of anger and pain, it seemed that Boyo and his wife had made up their differences in no uncertain terms.

'I want to know why you've come.' Bethan spoke quietly, without hostility and if Catherine had not known better, she would have felt that here was a reasonable, almost kindly human being.

'I'm here to say I'm sorry for the hurt I've caused you. Please, will you leave Hari Grenfell alone, none of this is

369

her fault.' The words fell into the silence, they sounded hysterical, absurd. Bethan's eyebrows lifted.

'I don't understand you.' She seemed to be enjoying herself, playing a game of cat and mouse and Catherine repressed a shiver. What other schemes did this strange woman have on her mind?

'Of course you do,' Catherine said quietly.

'But why should I harass Mrs Grenfell? You are ill informed, girl, I once invested a great deal of money in her business. Not that it is any concern of yours.'

'Then why did you try to force her to dismiss me and why are you taking away her best trade?'

'I have no interest at all in where you are employed, I think you flatter yourself that I should take such trouble over you. As to taking away trade, if you are referring to my new venture, selling shoes directly to the public, then I can only conclude you have no sense of business. Competition is healthy, it is also inevitable, as I'm sure Mrs Grenfell will appreciate.'

Catherine was getting nowhere, Bethan Hopkins was adept at deflecting questions and accusations, she was a very clever woman.

'Tell me why there are a gang of louts on the road barring the way to the emporium, then?' Catherine felt she was losing grip of the conversation; put into words she could see that she had flimsy evidence to support her arguments.

'Are we talking here about thugs on the roadways of Swansea? If so, my dear child, this is none of my doing, I cannot be held responsible for all the ills that befall Swansea or the inhabitants thereof.'

'Look,' Catherine made a last desperate attempt, 'I am no longer involved with Boyo . . . Mr Hopkins, it's over and done with, you have nothing to fear from me.'

'Oh, I know that,' Bethan smiled. 'A wife knows these things, you see. What my husband did with you was to amuse himself for a short time. It is not unusual for a husband to seek a particular sort of gratification else-where, it's the way of mankind.'

Catherine was speechless, Bethan Hopkins had twisted the whole thing, her affair with Boyo had been based on love, or had it?

'Have you said what you came to say?' Bethan lay back against the pillows. 'I'm tired, I must rest, you see.' She smiled brightly. 'This very afternoon I saw the doctor, he confirmed what I suspected, that I'm pregnant again. This time I will allow nothing to upset me, do you understand?'

Catherine's mouth was dry, so the rumours were true. She could not speak, she saw the look of triumph come into Bethan's face and she turned away to hide the rush of tears. As she left the room, Bethan's voice carried towards her.

'If my husband *should* seek solace with you this time, I trust you will do the honourable thing and send him back to me. You caused the death of my first baby, I don't know how women of your kind can sleep at nights.'

Catherine hesitated, battling with anger and guilt. 'I will have nothing to do with Boyo ever again but that is my own choice, not yours.'

She left the room and hurried down the stairs feeling as though dragons were at her heels, as though unseen eyes were watching her. She had come here to reason with Bethan Hopkins and instead she was running away like a whipped dog.

Outside, it had grown dark, the feeling that eyes were following her flight persisted and she realized she was frightened, but of what? Bethan Hopkins was inside, in her bed, a delicate woman, a pregnant woman.

The knowledge brought a bitter taste to her mouth but whatever she was, Bethan Hopkins was not a witch. She had no supernatural powers, she could not reach into the past or the future, she was an ordinary mortal like any other. Then why did the feeling persist that Bethan was all-powerful, that she could accomplish anything she wished?

Catherine hurried through the wrought-iron gates, her vision blurred, her throat aching with unshed tears.

Ahead of her, the roadway was shadowed by overhanging trees. She stopped suddenly as she saw a huge, dark shape bearing down on her. She half screamed as she darted into the hedge, the sharp twigs catching on her clothing. She tripped and fell headlong, her head hitting the pitted roadway.

'Catherine!' The voice was achingly familiar. 'Catherine, what are you doing on this road in the darkness? You could have been killed.'

'Boyo . . . I . . .' She stopped speaking, his arms were around her lifting her to her feet. For a moment she was dazed, she lay against his shoulder, breathing him in, love and hate twisting inside her like the iron dragons on the gate.

'Catherine . . .' his voice had softened, he was trembling. He touched her hair with his lips, his arms were around her and for a moment she revelled in the feeling of coming home being with him always gave her.

Bethan's words reverberated in her mind and she drew away from him, clasping her hands together tightly.

'Catherine, I love you, God help me, I love you, I want you so much it's like a physical wound inside me day and night.'

She took a deep, ragged breath. 'Oh, yes, you want me so much, you miss me, you love me, those are empty words, Boyo. Your wife has just told me that she is pregnant again.'

She heard him gasp in the darkness, he lifted his hand and brushed away a lock of hair and for an endless moment, he was silent.

'That cannot be,' he said at last. 'I have not . . . no, Bethan can't be pregnant, it just is not possible.'

'I have just spoken to her, why should she lie?' Catherine said quickly. But perhaps she had been lying; desperate women took desperate measures. And yet there had been the ring of truth in her voice when Bethan Hopkins had told her the news.

'Pregnancy is not something a woman can hide for long, the truth will out, Boyo. Whatever the truth of the matter, it means nothing to me, you and I are through, we have been for a long time.'

He sighed heavily, 'Catherine, I can't be responsible for what Bethan has been telling you. I know I have no rights over you but I want you to believe me when I say from the first moment we met, I've loved you. If I had been free . . .'

'But you weren't free.' Catherine looked up at him trying to see his expression in the darkness. 'And we should have known better than to start something that could only lead to disaster.'

She began to walk away. There was a chill in the air and the scents of the night were all around her, the salt of the breeze blowing in from the sea, hidden from sight by the folding hills. An owl hooted, a small creature scuttled through the grass.

'I'm taking you home.' He spoke heavily, he was defeated and Catherine felt her throat constrict. 'I will take no arguments, it is not safe for a young woman to walk in these deserted hills alone.'

He took the reins of the horse and drew the creature closer. He lifted Catherine into the saddle and swung himself up behind her. They were so close, the warmth of his thighs pressed against her body, his face against her hair. She closed her eyes in pain; she loved him so much.

The moon slid from between the clouds and the roadway shone silver, a ribbon leading through the hills. Catherine wanted the journey to go on for ever and yet she knew that if she stayed this way, in Boyo's arms, she would not be able to stand the torture of being so close to him without possessing him.

He was breathing heavily close to her ear and she knew that he too felt the heat between them. His arms tightened around her, drawing her back against him. She felt his body hard, aroused, and triumph flared through her. It was moonlight madness and it was so sweet, so tantalizing.

'You are like a pale moon goddess, Catherine, even your hair is silvered by the moonlight.'

'Stop talking like that, let me down, I can walk from here and you can run back to your little wife.'

'It is you I love, Catherine.'

She pushed his arms away and slid down from the saddle. 'I'm tired of hearing the same refrain: love, love, love. It's an easy word to say but what you really mean is lust, you lust after me, that is not the same thing as love. Goodbye, Boyo.'

She walked away, her head high, her back stiff, tears running down her cheeks. She wondered if he would come after her but Boyo had already mounted his horse and was galloping away as though the hounds of hell were in pursuit.

Catherine's whole body ached by the time she reached Watkin Street. Doreen looked up as Catherine entered the kitchen, her shrewd eyes showing her concern as Catherine slumped into one of the kitchen chairs.

'Want to talk about it?' She made tea, deftly bringing the cups to the table. 'I see the big bad witch didn't turn you into a frog then.'

'I've been such a fool,' Catherine said. 'I wanted Boyo so badly. I wanted him to make love to me again, in spite of everything.'

'Is that all.' Doreen pushed a cup towards her. 'I feel like that every night.'

'The difference is, Jerry Danby would marry you, if he could,' Catherine said, taking the cup in both hands, the warmth soothing her.

'And I suppose you think Boyo Hopkins wouldn't marry you if he had the chance?'

'He lies through his teeth when he says he loves me, it's his wife he's with isn't it?' She paused, taking a deep breath. 'It's true, she's pregnant again.' The words fell into the silence and Doreen sniffed.

'Maybe, maybe not. That one would say anything if it would hurt someone else. Anyway I didn't want you to go up there, did I? I warned you no good would come of it.'

'You were right, she denied everything, lied to my face.'

374

'There we are then, I 'spects she was lying about the other thing too; the baby she's supposed to be carrying.'

'I don't think so. She made me feel so cheap, Dor.'

'You only live once, grab what you can from life, that's what I say.' Doreen put some coals on the fire, rubbing her hands together to shake off the dust.

'I still want him,' Catherine said softly, 'damn him!'

'What did this Mrs Hopkins have to say, then, apart from the far-fetched story that she's expecting, I mean?' The sarcasm was evident in Doreen's voice and Catherine smiled, knowing that Doreen would take her part, even if she was in the wrong.

'Oh, she said men chase after other women when the wife is pregnant, it's only a release for their natural tension, sort of thing. In other words, it means nothing to them.'

'Well, sorry to be cruel, love, but from my experience, she's right. A married man will go with anything in a skirt, at least that's what Meadows did when he was younger. Can't get anybody now, the old sod.'

Catherine rose from the chair, a bitter taste in her mouth. 'I'm going to wash and get into my nightie, I'm worn out.'

Doreen rose to her feet. 'If I was you, I'd forget Boyo Hopkins ever crept into your bed. Get some sleep, there's shadows under your eyes big as saucers. Good night, love, I'll leave you to wash in peace.'

Later, lying huddled beneath the blankets in her narrow bed, Catherine's mind was racing, there was no hope of falling asleep. She found herself going over and over the way Bethan had told her she was pregnant. The shine in her eyes, the triumph on her face, convinced Catherine that Boyo's wife was telling the truth.

'Oh, Boyo!' She felt his arms around her again as they rode together through the darkness, felt the heat of his thighs, the warmth of his arms beneath her breasts.

'You fool!' she said out loud and turning her face into the pillow, she wept.

CHAPTER TWENTY-NINE

Hari sat in the office staring out of the window. The view from her room, indeed from most of the rooms at Summer Lodge, was breathtaking. The wide curve of the bay was spread out below and cutting a path into the sea was the promontory of Mumbles with the two hills sitting like breasts upon the water. And in the distance was the faint tracery of the fields of Devon. But Hari was, for once, unaware of the view.

She felt dragged down by fatigue, her head ached, her mind was racing, going over and over her problems without coming any nearer to a solution. She had travelled miles in the last few weeks, talking to Mr Clark of Somerset, seeking his advice.

He had been kind, telling her there was nothing he could do about a competitor who was taking Hari's trade. What he could do was to arrange, as he had done in the past, for Hari to take a stock of his boots and shoes home to Swansea on approval. That meant she did not have to pay him a penny piece until some sales had been made.

Her decision to join the strong Union of Boot and Shoemakers, Mr Clark warmly endorsed. She did not tell him that some of the more militant trade-unionists had voted to take strong action against Bethan Hopkins and her cut-price trading should lawful methods fail. No-one, it seemed, condoned the very rich buying into trade and taking the cream.

Now, back home, Hari felt drained but at least there was a glimmer of hope, a possible way out of her troubles.

'Morning, Mrs Grenfell, you wanted to see me?' Doreen stood in the doorway, her face pinched with worry and Hari's heart contracted with sympathy, she knew that Doreen feared she was about to be dismissed.

'No problems, Doreen, just a request from Mrs Charles that you go over to her house.' Hari smiled. 'Since you made her that wedding hat, she has had great faith in your taste and skill.'

'Right, Mrs Grenfell, I'll be glad to go over there, shall I go now?' Doreen's relief was evident and Hari swallowed hard, so much responsibility, such a heavy load to carry, her own and other people's future in her hands.

'If you wouldn't mind, perhaps you could take some samples with you. Mrs Charles lives over on the other side of Mount Pleasant. I've written the address down for you, do you think you can find the place?'

'*Duw*, course I can. It's a nice day and a walk won't do me any harm.'

'No need to walk, I've had the pony and trap made ready for you.' Hari smiled. 'Just load up the materials you need and enjoy the sun. And Doreen, after you bring the cart back, take the rest of the day off.'

She heard Doreen hurry along the corridor, her footsteps quick and eager and Hari shook her head, wondering how long she could keep her in employment. Doreen was a good worker and a talented milliner and without her there would have been no trade at all these past weeks. Hopefully, that would soon change.

Hari rose from her desk and went downstairs to the front of the building, the large, airy showrooms were practically empty, even though *The Swansea Times* had advertised Hari's half-price sale of boots and shoes. One or two desultory buyers from further up the hill on the land above Honey's Farm prodded the stock on the shelves and Hari wondered where the customers from town were. Usually news of a sale brought the people of Swansea flocking to buy the Grenfell's quality stock.

Hari felt despair grip her, she was going to fail; after all that had happened, after the success she had made of her business through sheer hard work and enterprise, it was all going to disappear before her eyes. She spent some time rearranging display stands but her heart was heavy; it would take a miracle to pull her out of the mess she was in.

She looked along the length of the shop, the room was silent, growing dusty from neglect and in a frenzy of activity, Hari found herself dusting and polishing as though her life depended upon it.

At last, worn out and breathless, she made her way through the hallway and outside into the fresh air, taking deep gulping breaths, trying to calm herself, trying to face the facts rationally. If matters did not improve over the next three months, she would lose everything, the business, the house, her livelihood.

Hari felt sure she could survive with very little money, she had endured enough poverty in her lifetime to know she could live in the poorest conditions but what about Craig? He was used to riches, to a fine house, good food, servants to wait on him. These were things he had taken for granted from birth.

It must not be allowed to happen, she would not be ruined, she would fight tooth and nail to keep her business going. And yet had her fighting spirit gone? The surge of optimism, all too easy when she was young, seemed to be missing now.

She was about to turn back to the house when she saw the pony and cart in which Doreen had left for Swansea careering towards her, blocks rolling to and fro across the base of the cart and materials flying out onto the roadway. Of Doreen there was no sign.

The animal came towards her, eyes rolling, the cart bumping over the loose stones. Hari had no hope of stopping the creature so she stepped hastily aside. Once on home ground, the pony was quieter. Hari approached the animal, speaking softly. 'Come on, there's a good boy, quiet now, what's frightened you then?' She rubbed the soft neck of the animal making soothing sounds though her heart was in her mouth. There must have been an accident, Doreen had been thrown out of the cart, she might be injured, lying in the road somewhere. Perhaps she had been set on by thieves, there had been reports of a gang of thugs roaming the roads into town. Hari felt chilled, she must do something, quickly.

She strode back to the house, selected a gun from the case in the armoury and picked up a box of shells. She loaded the gun expertly and took it outside and lifting her skirts climbed up into the cart, settling herself in the driving seat. She clucked softly to the pony urging the creature forward.

She rode out through the wide gates, eyes looking ahead, expecting any moment to see Doreen's crumpled figure lying on the ground.

She should not have sent her on an errand alone, Doreen was not used to the pony and trap, she held no truck with animals and usually kept well away from them. It was only fear of losing her job that made Doreen agree to the trip, Hari felt sure of it.

As she rode over the crest of the hill, the pony whinnied nervously. Hari drew the animal to a halt beneath the shelter of a group of trees. She peered ahead and saw a band of men standing in a circle jeering loudly.

Hari climbed down from the driving seat, picked up the gun and moved forward quietly. No-one noticed her approach, the men were too busy watching the spectacle on the ground before them.

She peered between the shifting bodies and caught sight of Doreen, her skirts above her knees, a man astride her and she swallowed her fear with difficulty, resisting the urge to run.

Hari lifted the gun and through the moving men, she saw Doreen's attacker rise and fasten his flies, a sneer on his face as he looked down at the beaten woman at his feet.

Hari felt a surge of fierce anger as she saw Doreen's pathetic attempts to cover herself. Lifting the gun, she fired a shot over the heads of the men and they froze for a moment in utter silence. The crowd moved apart then, the men turning to stare at her. Hari recognized Sergeant Meadows, he stood arms akimbo, looking at her with contempt in his eyes.

Doreen scrambled to her feet and ran to Hari's side, she was bruised and trembling, there were tears of pain

379

and humiliation mingled with the dust on her cheeks.

'I would advise you to lower your gun, madam,' Meadows said heavily. 'It might go off again and that could be dangerous.' He stepped closer but Hari held firm.

'Come any nearer and I'll shoot you,' she said in a hard voice. 'And you lot, you rabble, get away from here, clear off, do you understand?'

Meadows ignored her remarks, he brushed them aside as he might a fly that was irritating him. 'You'd better listen to me before you get what she just got,' he said. The anger building in his face was reflected in his voice.

He made a sudden rush and knocked the gun from Hari's hand. She staggered backwards and then Meadows was on top of her, his foul breath in her face.

'You play with fire, you get burnt,' he said, lifting her skirts with one hand, holding her down with the other.

'Get off, Peter, for Gawd's sake, that's Mrs Grenfell you got there, don't be a fool.' Doreen was pulling at his arm. Meadows reached out and pushed her away so violently that she went sprawling in the dust.

'She's nothing in this town now, it's about time she realized that. Can't take to be told, this one, won't keep her nose out of other folks' business.'

Hari scratched at his face, her nails raking channels along his cheeks. He slapped her hard. 'You are asking for it and you are going to get it.' He pushed her skirts higher and one of the men whistled at the sight of her silk-clad leg.

Hari panicked, bucking like a startled pony, trying to shake herself free of the intolerable weight of the man upon her. She slapped out at him and then she felt a hand at her throat. She gasped, sucking what small amount of air she could into her lungs, afraid she was going to die.

The men were gathering round now, one of them called out in a coarse voice, 'Go on, Meadows, give it to her, show her what a real man's like.' Meadows laughed, his hand on his buttons. Darkness was crowding in on her, she would be raped and then she would die.

A shot rang out. Above her, Meadows gasped as if

reeling from a sudden punch. His eyes were suddenly wide as a dark stain of blood formed on his jacket. The hand at her throat fell away and Hari dragged air into her lungs gratefully.

Slowly, Meadows toppled over, his mouth open, the light of anger dying out of his glazed eyes. Hari sat up, gagging, her head reeling. Dimly, she saw Doreen standing a few paces away, her face was white but the gun was held tightly in her hands. Meadows tried to rise but he was a dead man even before Doreen aimed and fired once more, shattering his jaw, sending blood flying in all directions.

Hari scrambled to her feet as Doreen turned the gun on the now silent band of men. 'Piss off out of 'ere before you gets the same.'

The men melted away like shadows and Doreen, her eyes huge, sank to the ground, the gun falling from her hands. She looked up at Hari. 'I had to do it, he would have had you, no bother. He don't care who he soils, the bastard!'

She was quite calm as she pushed herself to her knees. 'Go, Mrs Grenfell, send someone to get Constable Danby, he's an honest policeman, he'll do what is right.' Suddenly, Doreen was crying, great gulping sobs shook her thin frame. Her eye was black now, her mouth swollen so that it was difficult for her to talk. Hari took the trembling woman in her arms.

'Don't cry, everything will be all right, you were defending me, there was no other way of stopping the man.'

The two women knelt together in the roadway, the body of Doreen's husband lying a few feet away from them, head twisted at a grotesque angle.

At last, Doreen stopped crying, she leaned wearily against Hari's shoulder, her energy sapped, reaction was setting in and she began to tremble violently.

Hari helped her to her feet. 'Come on, you are coming with me.' She looked round for the horse and trap, she was afraid that the sound of the gun would have made the animal bolt but he was beneath the trees, head down, chewing the grass.

Hari helped Doreen into the cart and climbed into the driving seat. 'Try to be calm,' she said over her shoulder. 'You did what you had to do, there was no other way, just remember that.'

But as she drove towards home, Hari was swallowing hard, her throat still ached from the grip of Meadows's fingers. Surely the state that they were both in would convince anyone that Doreen's action was justified, but the law was sometimes the ass that people claimed it to be. Who knew what the opinion of some ancient judge in a dusty wig, with even dustier ideas of womanly duties, might be?

She closed her eyes for a moment and then, with an air of determination, urged the horse to a faster pace; the sooner she got home, within the boundaries of Summer Lodge, the happier she would be.

'Doreen, how are you feeling now?' Catherine opened the door to the small room in the hospital where the curtains were drawn against the daylight. Quietly, she moved towards the still figure in the bed.

Doreen stirred and opened her eyes. 'I hurt, I hurt all over, love, but then I've hurt like this many times before when that bastard has had his way with me.'

It had been Jerry Danby who had advised that Doreen went into the hospital. That way, he explained, he would not have to lock her in a cell. He was not entirely sure what he should do with a murderer but it had been clear to him that Doreen needed care and attention, not locking away.

'Know something awful, Cath?' Doreen said, her voice hoarse. 'I'm glad he's dead, glad he can't hurt me nor anyone else ever again. I know it's a sin to kill, the Bible tells you that, but there was nothing else I could do. He'd had his way with me, beating me, shaming me in front of all those men and then he was going to do the same to Mrs Grenfell. I couldn't let him do that, could I?' She was crying, tears running down her cheeks unchecked.

Catherine sat beside her and held her hand.

'Anyone with guts would have done the same as you,' she said. 'Don't you think about it, you just rest and get better, right?'

'And when I get better, what then; prison?' Doreen's eyes were anguished. 'I don't think I could stand it, not being shut away in a jail.'

'It won't come to that, Mrs Grenfell has got the best lawyer she can from London, you'll be all right, you'll see.'

She did not care to tell Doreen of the rumours that were rife in the town, rumours that Bethan Hopkins had hired the best prosecuting counsel she could find, a man of grim determination and with a hatred of the lower orders from which he himself had risen.

Julian Fitzgibbon had been seen riding through town with his nose high, as though the stink from the works along the river bank was a personal affront. He was determined to prove that Hari Grenfell was involved in the murder of Sergeant Meadows, influenced, no doubt, by the very large amount of money Mrs Hopkins was able to pay him.

The door opened and Catherine looked up. Her hands were suddenly cold, her face drained of colour. 'What are you doing here?'

Boyo Hopkins entered the room quietly, he was carrying a basket of fruit and a huge bouquet of flowers. He looked pale and drawn. 'I don't know how but my wife is involved in this mess in some way.'

Catherine fought the mingling of pity and love that rushed into her blood and moved to the window. Boyo must solve his own problems, if his wife was acting like a mad woman then it was up to him to sort it out.

The silence stretched endlessly but Catherine forced herself not to look round. Finally Boyo spoke again. 'I came to offer my help, it looks as if you might need it, Doreen,' he said quietly.

'Why should you want to help me?' Doreen asked in genuine surprise.

'Just say I do not like to see any injustice being done.'

'What injustice?' Doreen struggled to sit up against the pillows. 'What do you mean, do you know something I don't know?'

Catherine turned sharply, willing Boyo to look at her, when he did, she shook her head warningly. He read her well and she could see him searching his mind for the right thing to say. 'Usually women come out of such a situation as this badly. Judges do not take account of the ill-treatment meted out by a husband to his wife, I am afraid the odds are nearly always stacked in favour of the man. Money and influence always helps.'

'I don't want your charity, though it's kind of you to offer, I'm sure.' Doreen lifted her chin. 'I did what was right, I did the only thing I could do. They was all going to watch while Mrs Grenfell was . . . well, you know what I mean.'

Catherine could see by the tightening of Boyo's lips that he knew all too well what Doreen meant. 'Well, my offer stands,' he said at last; 'you just have to send for me and I'll be there.'

Catherine walked with him to the door and closed it behind her. 'Thank you, Boyo, for not telling Doreen about the lawyer your wife has hired, she's worried enough as it is.' She suddenly felt awkward being with him.

'Bethan has changed,' he said, 'she is like a woman possessed, there is no reasoning with her, I can't even talk to her any more.'

'Then it's not true that she's having your child?'

He frowned, 'I told you once, it's just not possible. Why won't you believe me, Catherine?'

'How can you not know!' Catherine heard the anger in her voice and changed the subject abruptly. 'Look, thank you for your offer of help, we might have to accept it. Doreen has no money and Mrs Grenfell is not very rich, not any more, thanks to your wife.'

Boyo sighed heavily. 'I'm sorry for all that Bethan has

done, I don't know how to deal with her strangeness, sometimes I fear for her sanity.'

He was suddenly vulnerable and Catherine could not bear it. She began to walk away from him but he caught her in his arms, holding her close. She clung to him for a moment as he smoothed back her hair, 'Catherine, what a mess I've made of things.'

She pulled away from him abruptly. 'You made your bed, as they say.' She turned and went back into Doreen's room, closing the door firmly behind her.

'The bastards!' Craig was pacing the room, he had been unable to relax ever since Hari had returned home, her face white, her clothes covered in blood. 'If I had been there I would have shot the lot of them. Worse than animals, don't deserve to live, not men like that.'

'Hush, love, it was days ago, now, it doesn't help to go on about it.' Hari rubbed at her eyes, she wished he would calm down, it was over, Meadows was dead.

'To think that man put his hands on you, I can't bear it.'

'Look, Craig, he paid for what he did with his life. I came to no real harm, not like poor Doreen who was hurt and humiliated before all those louts.'

'But it's not over, is it?' Craig sank into a chair. 'There will be the ordeal of going into court, telling all who wish to hear what happened out there, it's going to give you so much pain.'

'I did no wrong.' Hari was suddenly angry. 'For heaven's sake, Craig, stop this before you drive me mad.'

He looked at her. 'I'm angry for your sake, love, can't you see that? My job is to protect you and I was not there to do it.'

'There, you see? It's your masculine pride that's hurt most, your sense of honour, you can't take your revenge on Meadows so in a subtle way you are taking it out on me.'

'Rubbish!' Craig leant forward in his chair. 'That's just arrant nonsense.'

'Is it?' Hari suddenly felt too weary to argue any more.

385

'Let's not quarrel over it, Craig, please. Every time you speak of it you remind me of how frightened I was, can't you see that?'

He was silent for a moment and then he moved across the room and knelt before her, his head in her lap, his arms around her waist. 'I'm sorry, Hari, I'm a thoughtless fool! You're right of course, I want to batter someone into the ground and I can't.'

She smoothed his greying hair. 'Don't let this hurt us any more than it has already, Craig, we are both going to need all our patience and strength to face the gossips in the weeks to come.'

'Come on, Hari, I want to make love to you, I want my wife in my arms, I want to kiss those wonderful lips of yours.'

Hari allowed him to lead her to their bedroom and when they were both naked beneath the sheets, she clung to his broad shoulders with an urgency she had forgotten she possessed. As her husband made love to her, she knew that in some strange way they were renewing their vows, declaring their love afresh. She realized then that the ordeal she had faced would not drive them apart but would bring them closer than they had ever been before.

As Boyo Hopkins rode across the rocky ground towards Ty Craig, his shoulders were slumped, his spirits low. He would try to reason with Bethan once more, tell her to drop the whole matter of Meadows's death, it had nothing to do with her.

With a little planning, a little discussion with the right people, the whole tragic incident could be dealt with quickly. What had happened was a clear-cut case of self-defence and Boyo was confident he could find the men who had been present at the shooting and persuade them to tell the truth.

He reined his animal to a halt some distance away from the grim, grey stone of the house, trying to marshal his thoughts. If he could convince Bethan that she should not be taking this course of action it would make things so much easier.

With the weasel of a man she had brought in to act posthumously in Meadows's defence, the case would be a long, drawn-out affair. Julian Fitzgibbon would produce witnesses who would lie, or at best bend the truth. He knew that a case could go either way, it was a matter of who the judge chose to believe and what chance would Doreen Meadows have against a man like Fitzgibbon?

He jerked the reins and the animal moved forward slowly, as though reluctant to proceed to the shadowed walls of Ty Craig.

The groom appeared quickly at his side and took the horse, leading the animal towards the stables. Boyo took a deep breath and moved under the arched doorway and into the house.

Bethan was sitting in a chair, some papers in her hand, she looked more animated than Boyo had seen her in a long time. 'Boyo, you're home. Come here, darling, I want to talk to you about this Meadows business. Isn't it too bad when a member of the police force, going about his lawful duty, trying to relieve an overheated woman of a dangerous weapon, gets himself killed?'

So that was the way the prosecution meant to go and such an argument might well work if witnesses could be brought who were not above perjuring themselves.

'I want to talk to you about that very subject, as it happens,' Boyo said quietly, taking a chair opposite his wife.

'Oh? Why am I not surprised by that?' Bethan's pale eyes clouded so that he could not read her expression. 'What does this mean to you, what do you care about Hari Grenfell or this Meadows woman?'

'I could ask you the same question,' Boyo said quietly. 'Let it go, Bethan, it does not concern you any more than it concerns me.'

'Oh, but it does concern me,' Bethan said at once. 'Meadows was helping me out, he was at the spot near the so-called emporium on my business; of course I should concern myself with his death.'

She stared at him for a long moment before speaking. 'Is this going to affect your little fancy piece by any chance?'

Boyo ignored her words. 'Haven't you exacted enough revenge?' he said. 'Hari Grenfell is all but ruined, Catherine has lost her farm, her home and is out of a job. Her cousin's land is useless. How far do you intend to go before you satisfy your lust for punishment?'

Bethan looked at him, her head on one side. 'There is only one thing that will persuade me to let this matter drop.' She waited until she was sure she had his full attention. 'I have not told you the wonderful news yet, Boyo: I am expecting our child.'

'Rubbish!' Boyo was on his feet. 'Bethan, see sense, I have not slept with you, how can you be pregnant?'

'But you did sleep with me,' Bethan said, 'one night when I was not feeling very well. Remember you sat by my bed, we drank a hot drink together?' She smiled. 'You did not stay in your chair all night, of course.'

Boyo remembered, with a feeling of ice running down his spine, the scratches on his back, marks like those of a woman's nails. He had put it out of his mind, convincing himself there must have been a rational explanation for the marks. He looked at his wife and she nodded.

'Yes, I am expecting our baby, the doctor has confirmed it. Go to him, ask him if you don't believe me.' She took a deep breath. 'Say you'll come back to me, live with me here at Ty Craig and I will drop this case at once.'

Boyo sighed and rubbed his hand through his hair. He must agree to her terms, at least for the moment. Lull her into a false sense of security. 'Bethan, I am back, to all intents and purposes,' Boyo said. 'As you point out, I came to look after you because you weren't well and most nights I have stayed, what more can I do?'

'You can be a proper husband again, Boyo, that's my price.'

He knew what she meant, she wanted him in her bed, in her clutches, a man chained for ever. 'You are asking a great deal,' he said and he saw Bethan flinch. She paled and then the rich colour flooded her face as she grew angry.

'Very well, I shall take this matter all the way, I will not rest until I see the lot of them pay for what they have done to me. Don't think I have played my final card, Boyo, I have much more ammunition and I am ready to use it, your precious fancy piece will rue the day she tried to take you away from me.'

Boyo had risen to his feet but now he sank into his chair. There was a crazy look in his wife's eyes, a look that boded ill for Catherine. He felt instinctively that, so far, Bethan had only been playing with revenge; now, she was mad enough to do anything.

'All right,' he said, 'I'll do anything you want, Bethan, anything.'

He saw her settle back into her chair with a smug smile on her face and in that moment, he felt he could take her by the throat and throttle the life from her.

'That's good,' she was magnanimous now, 'I'll write a note dismissing Fitzgibbon . . . I'll write it tomorrow.' She was simpering like a young girl. 'For tonight, there are matters of far greater importance to deal with and I am looking forward to our second honeymoon with great anticipation. Now, Boyo, ring the bell, we shall have a drink of porter to celebrate the occasion.'

Controlling his anger, Boyo rose to his feet and pulled the bell-cord, he was putting on the greatest act of his life and he was not sure he could sustain it for very long. When the nervous little maid brought the wine, he managed to smile as he raised his glass. 'To you, Bethan,' he said softly.

CHAPTER THIRTY

Liam climbed from the train at Swansea Station and looked around him, taking in the dingy buildings that sprawled along the track. He had become used to making the journey from Ireland across the sea to Wales and each time he hoped that he would be able to persuade Catherine to return to Ireland with him. When he told her what had happened back home she would agree to making the trip, he was sure of it.

He began to walk towards Watkin Street, a mixture of anticipation at seeing Catherine again mingled with a sense of apprehension. There, hidden below the surface, was the fear that she would have gone back to Boyo Hopkins, a fear he could never quite conquer.

The house was one of a terrace, tall houses built about fifty years earlier, grimed now with dust and smoke, the stone changed from mellow warmth to a dingy grey. The curtains fluttered in the breeze, they were worn but clean, the flowery pattern almost lost by much washing. He knocked on the door and waited in a fever of impatience for someone to answer.

'Catherine.' She looked pale and there were dark shadows beneath her eyes. 'Catherine, are you all right colleen?'

'Liam, I didn't expect to see you.' Was there a tinge of disappointment in her tone. 'You look beat, you shouldn't be making the long journey so often just to see me.'

'I wanted to see you, I needed to see you, Cath, I want you to come home with me to Ireland.'

'I can't, Liam, don't let's go through all that again.' Catherine spoke quickly.

'Can I come in or do I have to stand out here on the

step?' Liam tried to force a smile.

'Doreen is in bed, she's not well, she . . . well, it's a long story.'

'Has something happened to her?' Liam asked, forcing himself to sound calm. He wanted to take Catherine and shake some sense into her.

She led the way into the kitchen and without asking poured him a glass of lemon water. 'There's no tea left, sorry.' She sat down opposite him and cupped her chin in her hands. She was thinner than when he'd seen her last but achingly beautiful with her red-gold hair coming loose from the pins.

'Tell me this long story, from the beginning, Catherine.' He realized that something was very wrong. He saw her look down at her hands. Her face was crumpled as though she was going to cry.

'Sure now don't go upsetting yourself, however bad it is, we can sort it out, I'm sure.'

'Doreen shot her husband. Meadows is dead.' Her voice was muffled.

Liam felt a shock of anger. 'It's probably what the old bastard deserved.'

He listened to Catherine's account of the scene up on the hill near Summer Lodge. His fists bunched, it could just as well have been Catherine with Doreen that day.

'You should have sent for me at once,' he said when she had subsided into silence. 'What's happening now, is Doreen being charged with murder?'

Catherine shook her head. 'That's the funny thing, it's all gone very quiet.'

'Go on,' Liam said.

'Well, Mrs Hopkins got the best lawyers down from London, we thought Doreen would be convicted for sure and then, suddenly, the whole thing was hushed up. Doreen got off with a plea of self-defence. Even the judge could see that Doreen had been beaten to within an inch of her life but we all expected this London man to get a conviction for murder.'

'Did Hopkins have a hand in this?'

'I don't know.' Catherine shook her head. 'I just don't know what happened. All I'm glad about is it's over, Doreen is free.'

'How is Doreen?'

'Not too bad, her wounds have healed but she's not getting the nourishment she needs to get her strength back. We are both out of work. We have no money left and Mrs Grenfell can't help, she is practically ruined.'

'So Mrs Hopkins got what she wanted then by the look of it.' Liam shook his head. 'The woman is insane.'

'It's not fair!' Catherine said hotly. 'This all happened because Mrs Grenfell wouldn't sack me. Now her name is being bandied about town, people are saying she is the one who pulled the trigger, it was her gun that was used to shoot Meadows. Folks won't shop with her any more.'

'Bethan Hopkins is dangerous,' Liam said heavily. 'Catherine, you'd better stay out of her way, she wants revenge, she hates you, she won't let it rest, not if she lives to be a hundred.'

'Well, if she wants me dead she needn't stir a finger to do it, I'll starve to death if I don't find work soon.'

'And Hopkins, what does he have to say, I expect he's been round here?'

Catherine shook her head. 'No, I haven't seen him, not for a few weeks.'

So that was the real reason for her distress: she was hungry, she was afraid, but most of all Catherine was longing to be with Boyo Hopkins.

'I'm sorry, Liam,' she said after a moment. 'I'm sure you haven't trudged all this way just to listen to my problems. Is everything all right back home?'

Liam forced a smile. 'Aye, your mammy is fine, sends her love,' he said. He looked down at his hands.

'Liam, what is it?' Catherine asked. 'There's something wrong back in Ireland and I've been prattling away about my problems.'

'It's Patricia,' Liam said. 'The baby is fine but . . .' He paused.

'Your sister, is she sick?'

'Patricia began to bleed . . . we . . . no-one could do anything.' He swallowed hard. 'She's gone, God rest her.'

'Liam, I'm so sorry.' Catherine touched his hand and he curled his fingers around hers.

'I want you to come back with me, Cath, to look after the child just for the time being.'

He saw Catherine's eyes grow large, her face was drained of colour. He could see the thread of a blue vein beneath her eye and he knew he was asking too much of her.

He thought Catherine would protest that she could not leave Swansea but she just sat there, cold and pale, her hands listless in her lap.

'Catherine, Maeve is managing the baby fine, I can't expect you to live in Ireland, not when I said I'd stay here with you.'

She rose and stood near the table as though uncertain what she should do next. 'I can't think.' She rubbed her eyes. 'I can't offer you anything to eat, Liam, I'm sorry but there is nothing in the house.'

He could see that, the fire was dead in the grate, no water could be boiled, even if there had been food in the pantry to cook.

'Will you put me up for the night, Catherine? I can't stay more than a day or two, I'm needed back home. Maeve is too old to chase round after a young baby and I'm not needed here, am I?' He looked at her questioningly, 'Am I?'

'You can stay,' she said quickly, 'of course you can, if you can manage on the old sofa in the parlour.'

'That will be fine.' He rose to his feet and moved closer, though he did not touch her. 'I couldn't bear it if anything happened to you.'

Catherine did not look at him. 'I know, Liam, I know.' She lifted her hands as if to ward him off and he took a pace back.

'I have some errands to do,' he said briskly, 'some business in town. I'll be back later.'

Catherine did not look up as he left the room, it was as though he had ceased to exist for her. Had he really held her in his arms? Made love to her? It was like a lost dream now. He felt, with a heaviness in his heart, that she would not come with him to Ireland, not even now when he needed her so badly.

Still, he must put his own feelings aside, there were things he could and must do for her, practical things like stocking the larder and getting in coal. He must insist that she took some money from him, otherwise she would not live to see another summer.

As he left the house, Liam saw Danby coming towards him, a bag in his hand. There was something furtive about the way he looked over his shoulder as though he was afraid he was being followed.

'Jerry, how are you?'

The policeman's eyes flickered away. 'I'm fine, aye, fine. I've plucked up courage to come and see Doreen. Been too scared of losing my job to come here before.'

'It looks as if Meadows got what was coming to him from what I've just heard.' Liam's voice was hard.

'That's as maybe, I could have killed him myself for what he did to Doreen but he was a copper after all and coppers stick together.'

'The man was corrupt, you know it and I know it.'

Jerry nodded. 'Most of my colleagues thought Peter Meadows was a bastard when he was alive but you'd think he was their bosom pal now that he's dead.'

'From what I heard, Doreen had no choice but to shoot the man,' Liam said. 'Surely even his fellow coppers could see that?'

'I expect they can but speaking for myself, I'm keeping my mouth shut. It's no good me being all heated about it and getting the sack. The way things are, at least I can bring a bit of bread and cheese to the girls when I get the chance.'

'Well, you haven't had much chance so far because, from what I can see, they are near starving to death.'

'Look, it's not my fault, man, I can't be responsible for

all the bad things that happen, at least I was here in Swansea.'

'I know.' Liam was suddenly ashamed of his anger, Jerry Danby was right, Liam had no room to criticize when he had been far away in Ireland.

'Anyway, what my mam always says is that if you see your best friend falling in a pond, you don't jump in after him unless you got a stout rope around your waist.'

'I get the point.' Liam smiled for the first time. 'What have you got there?'

'I got some bread and a bit of beef and some veggies, it'll help a bit anyway.'

'It certainly will, especially when I get them some coal to light the fire.' Liam smiled at the chagrin on Jerry's face. '*Duw*, I never thought of that and me a bobbie, not very bright, am I?'

'Don't worry, you go on in, I'm sure seeing you will cheer Doreen up a bit.'

'How is she?' Jerry was already moving towards the door.

'Don't know, didn't see her but I bet she'll see you all right.'

As he walked away towards the town, Liam felt pain and disappointment rise like a lump in his throat. What he had hoped for was that Catherine would fall into his arms, agree at once to go with him back to Ireland. But Catherine was still besotted with Hopkins, probably always would be. As the breeze blew into his face it was salt from the sea, salt that tasted like tears.

To Bethan's bitter disappointment, Boyo was still distant from her. Not even the knowledge that she was pregnant again with his child seemed to matter to him. Indeed, he felt she had tricked him into her bed. Well, so she had in a way, a small potion in his milk had made him so easy to manipulate.

Lately, though, she was not herself, she stayed in bed, eating little, feeling aggrieved at what she felt was Boyo's failure to keep his side of the bargain.

She recognized all too easily that Boyo was happy about her indisposition, it put off the day when he would have to come to her bed and prove himself.

Today, she had ventured downstairs, tired of being alone. She looked at him now, sitting a short distance away from her, his feet stretched towards the fire, a book in his hand. To an outsider, they would appear as any normal married couple, used to each other, slightly bored from familiarity, but no-one could see the storm that was building within her.

She was bitter about the way she had needed to bargain with him in order to bring him back to her. Boyo could be bought, oh, not with money, but with promises that involved that bitch of a girl.

There was some comfort in the fact that the girl was half starved and beaten down by poverty. There was no way out for Catherine O'Conner, Bethan had seen to that. Now that Hari Grenfell had been brought to her knees, there was no work and no money.

Following the scandal involving the shooting of Sergeant Meadows, no other inducement was needed to keep the affluent folk of the town clear of Hari Grenfell and her so-called emporium. Well, the woman knew her place now, knew that it did not pay to cross Bethan Hopkins.

As for the lawyer, she had paid him off and sent him back to London with a heavy pocket. He had assured her of his best services any time she should need them.

Now, looking at her husband, she was not so sure that she had done the right thing in acting so precipitously. Since Boyo had been back with her, he had been moody, morose even. He was acting like a sulky schoolboy and she was fast losing patience with him.

Apart from anything else, he was driving Elizabeth away from her. She did not come so often now and when she did, it was but for a brief visit. No, things were not working out as Bethan had planned, not at all.

She studied Boyo; his hair was crisp and curling, his frame lean and spare, there was a frown between his brows and suddenly her heart ached for the man he had once been, the affectionate husband, the friend she could laugh with. It had all been spoiled by Catherine O'Conner, how Bethan hated her.

Still, Bethan would only have to bide her time, she and Boyo would become lovers again, one day. She would be patient now until her child was safely born then she would win Boyo back, she was sure. He would come to see that his wife was worth ten of that stupid, insignificant girl.

He looked up, sensing her scrutiny, and when she smiled at him, he responded but his eyes did not warm. He rose to his feet. 'I think I will take a ride into town, have a drink in one of the hotels. I feel the lack of male company, Bethan, you know how it is?'

'I do not know how it is, at all, Boyo, you were never one for male company. Are you sure you are not seeing that bitch?'

'I am sure.' He emphasized the words. 'I have not seen her since . . . since we made our agreement.'

Jealousy swamped her, he had lied to her and cheated her once, how could she ever trust him again? 'I don't want you to go out.' She failed to realize how petulant she sounded until Boyo shook his head.

'You are acting like a child. I never agreed to be a prisoner in this house.' He sounded cold. Bethan saw now that she was pushing him too hard, she must tread more softly.

'You are right, of course.' She knew with a sense of triumph that she had said exactly the right thing.

'That's my girl, you sound more like my old Bethan now.'

She rose and hugged him, as though on an impulse. She looked up into his face. 'We were good friends once, we can mend fences, we can be friends again, can't we? Am I unreasonable in wanting you back?'

'You are unreasonable in the way you go about it, hurting people, destroying lives, it's so unlike the woman I married.'

'I know,' she said in a self-deprecating tone. 'I honestly

think that, for a time, I was quite out of my mind. First, losing the baby, then you leaving me, it was too much to bear. But we can be happy again, we will have a fine daughter this time and I shall call her Elizabeth.'

As she knew she would, she touched a soft spot in him. He held her in his arms, not like a lover but at least it was a start. She smiled into his shoulder, she knew how to play it, knew that she must appear to be repentant, to be the same gullible fool she had been before he had abused her trust.

'You are a kind man, Boyo.' She moved from his arms. 'I know I've been all sorts of a bitch but with your help, I can be better, I know I can.'

He sighed. 'I'll stay in, if that's what you really want.' He looked down at her, a worried frown on his face and she felt it was the moment to be magnanimous.

'No, you go out, it is only reasonable for a man to want to share a drink and a laugh with his own kind.'

He smiled then, really smiled for the first time since they had been back together. He moved to the door, his step lighter and Bethan knew with a sinking of her heart that he could not wait to be away from her.

'I won't be late,' he said and she lifted her hand to him, a smile fixed on her face.

'Be as late as you like, I must trust you, I do trust you. Go on, my love, enjoy yourself, I won't wait up for you.'

She heard the outer door slam and then the sound of hoof-beats fading into the distance. She felt empty and relieved at the same time, now she could talk, really talk, to Elizabeth, tell her the triumphant news that she was winning back the husband she loved.

Hari stood in the window looking out at the boiling seas far below. 'It was a good move to join the Union of Boot and Shoemakers.' A huge wave crashed against the rocks sending up a shower of foam. The weather was stormy, in keeping with her mood. 'They will help me get back on my feet again, give the firm respectability, substance. I've always wanted to be free of any unions, to be independent but now the time has come when I need the strength of others behind me. Whatever happens, there is no way I am going to allow that woman to ruin us.'

'My love,' Craig came and stood behind her, 'be sensible, let's cut our losses, give up the business. We will have enough to live on for years if we sell Summer Lodge.'

'We won't, you know,' Hari said shaking her head. 'The house is mortgaged to the hilt. Even if we could sell it there would be little in it for us.' Hari turned into his arms, 'If I let the business go, we shall have nothing.'

'We will manage.' He kissed her mouth tenderly. 'Look, I've got something to tell you.' He paused and took a deep breath. 'I've managed to find myself a position in the accounting offices of *The Swansea Times*.'

'Arian Smale gave you a job?'

'Well, don't sound so surprised, I am used to accounts, I am sound in mind and limb and what's more, I won't be the oldest employee working there; there's Mac, he's a fine reporter and he's actually longer in the tooth than I am.'

'Oh?' Hari was at a loss, she did not know if she should congratulate Craig on his enterprise or be angry with him for making such a move without consulting her.

He hugged Hari to him. 'Don't worry, we will survive this as we've survived so many things – together.'

'I don't want to lose Summer Lodge,' Hari said, moving away from Craig and sitting in a chair. 'I suggest we let it out for a time, perhaps a year or two just until we get on our feet again.'

'Who around here will want to rent this barn of a place?' Craig said reasonably.

'Think, Craig, think,' Hari said, tapping her forehead. 'You are right, no-one around *here* will want to rent the house but if we put a notice in the London *Times*, advertise the place as an ideal summer retreat near the sea, it might possibly attract some interest. At least it's worth a try.'

'It costs a great deal more money than we have to

advertise properly in a London newspaper.'

'Well then, we'll sell something, one of the paintings perhaps. Better to lose some of the possessions we've accumulated over the good years than to lose everything.'

'You might be right. I suppose it's worth a try,' Craig said kissing her, his hand straying to her breast.

'You are incorrigible, and you an old man.' She laughed up at him, not believing her words. He would never be old, not to her. Craig was her love, her life and as long as she had him, she had all that she could ever want in life – almost.

Suddenly, Hari felt close to tears. Because of Bethan Hopkins, because of one woman's wicked obsession, she had been brought to near bankruptcy.

Later, in bed, Hari lay wide-eyed, her mind racing over and over the problems of finance. After a while she rose, careful not to wake her husband and by the time she had bathed and dressed and made her way downstairs, she knew what she was going to do.

A few copies of the London *Times* needed to be bought, that was the first part of her plan. She would do work on some figures, try to assess how much a year could be earned by letting out Summer Lodge. Then she would follow Craig's lead, she would find a job. She would work as a cobbler as she'd done when she was young.

Ruefully she looked down at her hands, softened now by easy living. Surely she could resurrect skills they had once had? She would cut and stitch and tap working-men's boots as she used to, it was a beginning, a way back to solvency.

She had not wanted to join the Union of Boot and Shoemakers, not at first, but now she would need the might of the union behind her. There was strength in the unity of fellow tradesmen and women. She would attend meetings, fight for the rights of the working people. She had been complacent too long, rich too long, she had forgotten her roots. But now she would just have to get used to them again.

She would rent a place, a small, cheap house somewhere in the poorer quarter of the town. She had been born in the slums of World's End, she would easily adapt to the life again. For a moment her resolve weakened. Could Craig cope with it? Working in a stuffy office all day, adding figures instead of organizing the shifting of skins, would need a great deal of will power.

That he had the necessary ability for the job she had no doubt, Craig had been the one to buy in stocks, see that the goods were always available to put on the shelves. He had a good head for figures, he had learnt a great deal about trade over the years. He would be fine.

Hari made her way to the workroom and sat at the bench. Few repairs had been done here of late, very little shoemaking of any kind, come to that. Folk preferred to keep away from a woman involved in murder. Even the more tolerant of citizens preferred to buy stout, ready-made shoes at the respectable establishments in town. Why walk all the way to Summer Lodge when there were cobblers in every other street?

She picked up a dog, the implement used for holding the upper to the sole, and wondered if she had the energy for her new enterprise. Years ago, it had all seemed so easy, she had the optimism of youth then, the certainty that what she did would succeed. Well, she must find that optimism once again, for the alternative might just be the workhouse.

CHAPTER THIRTY-ONE

Catherine stared at Doreen in astonishment. 'Won't people talk if you marry Jerry so soon after . . . after?'

'After I shot that bastard of a husband you mean? What the hell do you think they're doing now, girl? My name is mud round here. Half the town believe I killed Meadows out of revenge and the other half think poor Mrs Grenfell pulled the trigger. No, love, no future in Swansea for me, not any more, who would employ a murderess?'

She shook her head and there was a glint of tears in her eyes. 'There's nothing for me here, not now. Anyway, Jerry's got promotion, they want him in Cardiff. It couldn't have worked out better really, could it, love?' She smiled wanly at Catherine. 'Sorry, love, I'm going to leave you in the lurch, so to speak, but it's better you know now when Liam is here to stand by you.'

'You mustn't worry about me, Dor,' Catherine spoke with an effort, she felt lost and alone. 'You have your own life to lead. I'll manage fine.'

'At least you got a roof over your head, old Lou won't chuck you out, he's a good sort as landlords go.'

'I'll be all right, stop being such a worry-guts.' Catherine smiled. 'Hey, your colourful way of putting things is rubbing off on me. I'll be swearing next, you are leaving just in time, girl.'

'What you mean?' Doreen pretended to be indignant. 'I don't curse, well, not much anyway.' She brightened. 'You'll soon have company; Mrs Grenfell said she was desperate for somewhere cheap to live, so I told her about the rooms upstairs. Since that funny old woman was carted away the place has been empty. Don't know if this dump would be good enough for our boss but then she did say she was desperate.' If she had expected a reaction from Catherine she was disappointed, Catherine was hardly listening. She watched with dull eyes as Doreen went into the back room. Drawers were being opened and closed again, Doreen was packing, she really was going to leave.

Catherine suddenly felt weary. What was happening in her life? Was she cursed? Had Bethan Hopkins put an evil spell on her? Whatever she did, whatever avenue she walked along, she always seemed to find failure and disappointment at the end of it.

It was all very well for Doreen to tell her she had a home. How long would the landlord tolerate a lodger who could not pay the rent? As for Hari Grenfell coming to live in Watkin Street, Catherine would believe it when she saw it.

Doreen came back into the room and put her bag on the floor. It was not a very big bag, she had little to show for her years in Swansea. 'Don't look so glum. Come on, let's have some of that tea Liam brought us, say goodbye properly, eh?'

Absent-mindedly, Catherine scooped the meagre leaves from the bottom of the tin into the teapot. She knew with her mind that Doreen was right, she had to leave Swansea, she had no choice and yet Catherine was afraid of suddenly being alone in the world.

'Look, love, why not marry Liam, he loves you like mad,' Doreen said. 'You're half in love with the boy already, if you ask me.'

Catherine poured the tea in silence and Doreen rushed into speech again. 'You want to be with Boyo and you can't, seems he's tucked his feet under the table up at that haunted house, gone back to his wife, hasn't he? So forget him, he's no good for you. At least with Liam you won't have to starve. Say you'll think about it, love, for my sake.'

'Aye, I'll think about it,' Catherine said. But she had thought about it, thought long and hard, far into the night and had found no answers. Yet Doreen's words made sense, they hurt, oh yes, they hurt badly but then the truth sometimes did. There was no getting away from it, Boyo had gone back to his wife, he no longer wanted anything to do with Catherine, that much was clear. So, was she going to go under, let herself be beaten, surely she had some fight left in her? And yet the prospect of poverty, hunger and homelessness loomed like a spectre before her.

'Well, it's your life, I can't live it for you.' Doreen drained her cup and lifted her bag onto the table, delving into its depths. Fumbling among her pitifully few possessions she drew out a purse. 'Have this, love; Jerry gave me money to get to Cardiff, it's too much, I won't need it all. He'll be following me up there as soon as he can.' She moved round the table and hugged Catherine tightly in an uncharacteristic show of affection. 'I'll send you my address when I know it.' Doreen's voice was muffled. 'You can come to me then if times get really bad.'

Without looking back, Doreen hurried along the dingy passageway. Catherine felt a small breeze of air as the front door opened and closed and then she was alone in the silent room. She sank down into her chair and looked at the small amount of money on the table. Suddenly, she was crying.

'I can't pay you a month's rent in advance, not right now.' Hari faced the landlord of the dingy house in Watkin Street, the stairs had creaked ominously as she climbed them and the smell of cats hung around the upper rooms. The last tenant of the first-floor rooms had not been too particular by the look of it. 'But you have my word on it that I am good for it, whatever you might have heard.' Hari wondered why she was trying so hard to rent the rooms, they were in a narrow street, back to back with other houses, with no green spaces or sea view, just the walls of other similar houses.

'Well, I've heard quite a few things, Mrs Grenfell, but I don't 'spects you carries a gun with you very often,' Luther Rees said. 'So I suppose you'll do as good as the next person.' He looked down at her, a tall man with a great belly but with a twinkle of humour in his deep-set eyes. Hari relaxed.

'It will be extra for the shed out the back, mind,' he added. 'Never had a shop here before, should be special rent for business premises but as it's you, I'll charge you the going rate, right oh?'

Hari felt a moment of panic, the money she had raised from selling some of the good pieces up at Summer Lodge was disappearing at an alarming rate. She would be picking up the proceeds from the latest piece of furniture on her way home. The money would just about cover a month's rent on the first-floor rooms. The shed outside she would use for storing boots and shoes. She would put a bench in there to work on, it would not be ideal but it would have to do.

She agreed to the landlord's terms, worrying what Craig's reaction would be. What would he feel about living in such appalling circumstances?

'I'll bring you the advance rent first thing in the morning. I'm sorry, I didn't realize you would want it right away.'

'That's the way business is done round these parts,' Lou said. 'Once the rent is paid up, you can move in right away, Mrs Grenfell.'

'You'll have your rent, don't you worry,' Hari said quickly. Lou nodded and handed her two keys. 'One for the front door, but it's never locked and this other one is for your own door.' He left her then and she heard his heavy footsteps on the uncarpeted stairs.

She looked round, the living-room was fairly large with two windows facing the street. A cast-iron fireplace was set in the wall, the surrounding tiles chipped and stained. Worn rugs, grey with dirt, covered the wooden floorboards. It was a far cry from Summer Lodge. Hari opened a window with difficulty, it had not been opened in a long time judging by the state of it.

She crossed the long landing, down three stairs and up three at the back of the house. Several doors led off the landing: the bedroom, quite large and bare, a spare room and an ill-equipped kitchen. Hari felt, with a sense of despair, that she had come full circle; she was back now in the slums where she was born.

She wandered aimlessly around her new home noting that the place would need to be scrubbed from top to bottom before she could live in it. The smell of cats permeated every room and even the breeze from the windows did not bring any freshness into the house.

For a moment Hari almost gave up, almost sank down on the bare boards and gave in to the weeping that was going on inside her. And then anger blossomed, anger against the woman who had done this to her, 'Blast Bethan Hopkins!'

Hari lifted her chin, she would not be beaten, she would not sink under the blow, she was born a fighter and she would die a fighter.

She left the rooms not bothering to lock the door, there was nothing to steal, and made her way back down the gloomy stairs. A figure was standing in the passageway looking up at her.

'Would you like to come in to my place, Mrs Grenfell? I can't offer you tea, I haven't any, but there's a little drop of dandelion and burdock left if you feel like it.'

'Catherine, that's very kind of you.' She followed the flame-haired girl into the room, similar to her own. The front room was clean but the all-pervasive smell of cats filtered down, even to here.

Catherine brought her a glass containing a brown liquid and indicated a chair. 'Please sit down, Mrs Grenfell. You can make these rooms quite comfortable if you try really hard.' Hari knew the girl was trying to be encouraging.

She looked around at the faded but clean curtains, at the logs glowing in the grate, the multicoloured rag mats on the clean, washed floor and her heart contracted within her. How could she bear it. She had faced grinding poverty before but then she had been young and strong, like Catherine. Now she was growing older, her children were adults, soon she would be a grandmother.

'I don't know how long I'll be able to stay here,' Catherine was saying. 'I must find a job or I'll be out on my ear, old Lou is a good landlord but he likes to get his rent on time.'

Hari smiled, though she could feel lines of tension around her eyes. 'I'm in the same boat as you, Catherine,' she said. 'I have to get in some work, I need boots and shoes to tap and plenty of them if I'm to survive.'

Catherine smiled, 'You'll do it, Mrs Grenfell, you are so clever, I can't see you being here for long. You watch, you'll be rich again before you know it, you were born under a lucky star.'

Catherine's face was that of a madonna, beautiful, with that wonderful bloom that was the gift of youth. As well as being beautiful, she was charming and had a kind and generous spirit.

'Well, if what you say is true then you'll be up there with me, Catherine. When I can afford to pay wages again, you will be the first one to have a job, believe me.' Hari rose to her feet. 'Well, I'd better go and break the news about our new home to my husband.' Her spirits lifted at the thought of being with Craig, safe in Summer Lodge, even if it was for this one night. Still they had each other, both of them enjoyed good health and they were in love, that was a blessing not given to many.

'You are so lucky, Mrs Grenfell. I've seen you and Mr Grenfell together, you are so close, I envy you.'

'I think you've been reading my mind,' Hari said. 'I was just thinking along the same lines.'

She moved to the door. 'Thank you for the refreshment, I'll be seeing you soon.'

As she walked along the dim passageway, Hari paused to look back up the stairs, thinking of the empty rooms that were to be her new home, and she was filled with doubt and fear.

Out in the street, she stared around her. It was growing dark, the late-afternoon sun was sinking lower in the sky and the trees were beginning to bend in the rising wind. Suddenly feeling the bite of the cold, Hari forced herself to hurry along the streets towards the shop where her beautiful hall table now stood with a sale ticket hanging from one of its elegant legs.

The door of the elegant shop was closed, it was dark inside and for a moment Hari panicked, thinking the proprietor had gone home. She knocked loudly and when there was no response, she knocked again, harder.

A light came on somewhere at the back of the building and Mr Compton, glasses held in his hand, came through the shop. When he saw her, he doubled back, reappearing, a few moments later, with a thick envelope in his hand.

'Mrs Grenfell, I have been expecting you.' She could hear the sound of voices from one of the back rooms.

'I'm sorry, Mr Compton, I didn't realize you had company, I shouldn't have left it so late.'

'No harm done, my dear.' Mr Compton was a lightly built man, with slicked-back hair and a thin mouth. There was something effete about him that made Hari uncomfortable.

She looked quickly in the envelope and then took a more careful look. 'Mr Compton, I think you have made a mistake, this is far less than the price we agreed on.'

'It's all I can offer, dear Mrs Grenfell, I am afraid trade is bad and the little table isn't as wonderful as I first thought it was. I am afraid that is the best I can do. You could always have the table back, of course.'

Hari knew he was trying her, he knew as well as she did that she could not afford to take the table back. She tucked the money into her bag and stood away from the door. 'Thank you, Mr Compton, and good night.'

'Good night, dear lady, it's a pleasure doing business with you. Any other little thing you want to sell, don't hesitate to knock on my door.'

He disappeared inside and Hari sighed heavily, turning up the collar of her coat, trying to force back the tears of disappointment and humiliation. It was bad enough to sell her lovely things without being cheated of a fair price.

She told herself to cheer up, she still had enough

money to rent the rooms she needed, it could be worse. With head high, she made towards the hill and home.

Her legs began to ache before she had travelled little over a mile, she was unused to walking, she had grown accustomed to riding in a plush carriage. But she had been poor before, she just had to find the old determination that had once burned so fiercely within her, but alone in the gathering dark, that was rather a tall order.

By the time she reached the top of the hill, she needed to pause for breath. She rested for a moment against a tree, wishing she had not left it so late to return home. The wind was growing fiercer, dark clouds were chasing across the sky. She shivered, she had yet to pass the spot where Doreen had shot her husband. It was foolish of her but she had a superstitious fear about the place ever since Meadows's death. The picture of him lying in a pool of his own blood, the fierce anger seeping out of his face as he died, would always be with her.

She realized full well that Doreen was forced into shooting Meadows, he had brutally raped and beaten her to within an inch of her life. He intended the same fate for Hari, he was an evil monster who did not deserve to live. Anyone would shoot in such circumstances. But would she? Hari was not sure at all. She might have turned and fled like a coward.

She shivered again. Standing there, thinking about the horror that had taken place on the spot was not helping at all. She must tell Craig about the wonders of their new home. She twisted her lips into a wry smile. One more night to enjoy Summer Lodge before it was let out to strangers, a few more precious hours to enjoy the comforts of home and here she was, wasting time dithering about on the road.

She walked on, head bent against the wind. It was rising now, sobbing in the trees with an almost human voice, tearing leaves from the branches, whipping them into Hari's face so that she could hardly see where she was going.

Hari longed for the sight of the house, of the lamplight

burning in the windows. She wanted to be safe in Craig's arms, to forget for a few hours that they were penniless and too old to be starting anew.

She hesitated as she saw the big twisted tree where Meadows had died. The hairs on the back of her neck prickled icily. There was a shadow among the bushes, was it human? She began to run, her breath tearing in her throat. She heard nothing behind her and when she risked a glance over her shoulder, she saw nothing but shadows. And then, there was a blinding pain in her temple and the earth was spinning away into deep darkness.

She did not know how long she lay there but Hari returned to consciousness with the rain falling onto her face. She struggled to sit up; what had happened, had the ghost of Peter Meadows been waiting to avenge himself?

She looked down, her bag was lying open on the ground, the white envelope had gone. It was not ghostly hands that had robbed her, whoever had taken her money had been all too human. She winced as she touched the back of her head and felt a lump the size of an egg.

She struggled to her feet and then the full import of what had happened flooded over her. The money was gone, now she had nothing, not a farthing, no money to pay the rent on the mean little rooms at Watkin Street. As she walked along the road, silent tears ran down her face, mingling with the spiteful darts of rain.

A sense of desperation filled her, she had done her best and she had been beaten, she could do no more. She would give up, forget about running a shoe shop, she would just have to manage on the wages Craig would earn at *The Swansea Times*, forget about living again at Summer Lodge one day.

But then, a small voice inside her said that then Bethan Hopkins would have won, she would have had her revenge. Anger and resentment began to pound in Hari's aching head, Bethan Hopkins had ground her into the dirt.

Hari shivered. If this was the punishment meted out just for refusing to do the woman's bidding what would happen to the girl who had taken her husband away from her? Catherine O'Conner would have to be warned that she was in great danger.

Hari's head ached intolerably, she longed to be home in Craig's arms, longed to feel his hand on her hair, hear his beautiful voice speaking soothing words. She sighed heavily, Craig was her one bright spot in a dark world. They loved each other, surely that was enough to see them through any disaster?

The rain ceased as suddenly as it had begun and Hari walked quickly as the gates of Summer Lodge came into view. The pitted drive had never seemed so long as the lights from the windows beckoned invitingly. Hari took a deep ragged breath, she had a pain in her side from walking too fast but she needed to be indoors, inside the safety of her own home with her husband's arms around her.

A carriage stood in the shadows of the trees but Hari did not notice, she was hurrying towards the open front door. The house was quiet, no sounds of servants working in the kitchen, no cheerful chatter of the shop girls, it was all gone, Summer Lodge seemed to be just an empty shell of a house.

'Craig!' She somehow sensed that Craig was not there but someone was, an unseen presence hovered around her and for the first time in her married life, Hari felt afraid in her own home. It was a big house, it would take her a long time to look through all the rooms but an urgency possessed her. Where was Craig? Was he safe? He surely would not have gone out this late in the evening.

An idea struck her, if Craig was out then he would have taken Brutus, the one horse they had kept when the stable had been sold. She hurried through the house and out to where the darkness of the stables loomed like shadows against the paler darkness of the sky.

She swung the stable door open and tasted the silence. There was no soft breathing of the sleeping animal to greet her, no restless hooves moving the straw. Brutus was gone.

Suddenly she was terrified, something had happened,

otherwise Craig would not ride out into the darkness. She ran back into the house and began to systematically search the rooms.

The workshop was dark and empty as she had expected and so was Craig's study. She hesitated at the foot of the stairs and then, head up, nerve ends tingling, she sensed that someone was in the sitting-room. Perhaps it was Craig after all, perhaps he had fallen asleep and had not heard her calling. Somehow she did not believe it.

As the door swung open, Hari made a small sound of surprise. Bethan Hopkins was sitting in a chair, leaning back comfortably as though she owned the place.

'I do own the place.' It was as though she was a witch and could read Hari's thoughts. 'At least for the time being; I am your new tenant.'

'Where is my husband?' Hari looked at the face of the woman who had done her so much harm, it was bland, ordinary, except for the burning light in the heavily lidded eyes.

'Summer Lodge is quite comfortable. I do not need it, of course, but it pleases me to take from you what you love most.' She paused for effect. 'Talking of what you love most, I think your husband might have . . .' she glanced up at the clock, maddening in her slowness, 'your husband might have met with some kind of accident. That horse, Brutus, he seemed like a devil to me, a creature with a most uncertain temper.'

Hari's mouth was dry. 'What have you done?'

Bethan smiled radiantly, as if she was a woman made happy by a skilful lover. 'I have punished you, Hari Grenfell, as I will punish all who oppose me.'

'You're mad!' Hari moved forward, incensed by the smugness in Bethan's face. The woman was taller than she, bigger boned, but fear and anger lent Hari strength. She hurled herself forward and as Bethan rose to face her, Hari bore her to the floor, her hands around the woman's throat. 'Tell me!' She shook hard and Bethan's head hit the carpet several times. 'Tell me what you have done with my husband before I kill you!'

412

Hari saw naked fear in the eyes that stared up at her and power surged through her; so Bethan Hopkins was not invincible after all.

'Elizabeth!' Bethan croaked the name. 'Help me, lend me your strength.'

Who was she talking to? Before the question had formed properly in Hari's mind, Bethan had jerked forward and then her hands were reaching out, claw-like, to fasten over Hari's nose and mouth, shutting off her air supply.

Hari fell back gasping, the room whirling in darkness as the hands held mercilessly until she thought her lungs were going to burst. She forced herself to relax, the only way out of this was to pretend she had lost consciousness. The hands held on for what seemed an eternity and then suddenly she was released.

Dimly she recognized the sound of running footsteps, she dragged air into her tortured lungs as she heard the crunch of carriage wheels and the drumming of horses' hooves. The sounds rocketed in her head, exploding in a whirl of noise and darkness.

She must have lost consciousness for a moment, in spite of her efforts, for when she opened her eyes and felt her face pressed against the deepness of the carpet, she knew that she was alone, the danger was past, Bethan Hopkins had gone.

She struggled to her feet and swayed for a moment, nausea and pain making her want to retch. She sank into a chair and put her head in her hands, trying to steady her senses. 'Think,' she told herself, she must think carefully over the words Bethan Hopkins had spoken so softly, so vindictively.

The woman had talked of the horse, Brutus, his ill temper. She had talked of punishment, she had said she would take away all that Hari loved most. A coldness pressed over her; Craig, where was he? What had Bethan Hopkins done to him?

She looked into the fire, it was dying low in the grate but it was alight. It was doubtful Bethan Hopkins would

413

have put on more coals, no, that would have been Craig's doing, so that meant he had not been out more than an hour.

Where had he gone, how had Bethan lured him out of the house when he would be waiting for Hari's return? She bit her lip. Bethan must have staged the robbery on the roadway, she would have let Craig know in her clever devious way that Hari was hurt, the victim of criminals. Craig would have mounted the horse without even pausing to saddle the animal. A trip wire across the roadway would unseat any rider, let alone one without saddle and stirrups.

Uncertainly, Hari rose to her feet, she felt sick and ill, she thought of the long dark road that led into town and wondered at the best spot for such a trap to be laid. The possibilities were endless.

She moved to the door, forgetting her pain and weariness, she would find Craig if it took her all night.

CHAPTER THIRTY-TWO

'Where on earth have you been, don't you realize how late it is?' Boyo looked closer at his wife, Bethan was white-faced, there were marks on her throat. 'Good God! What's happened to you?'

He led her to a chair, she was trembling and he felt pity well within him. He had never given her much of himself but at least he could offer her comfort and support. 'Who the hell attacked you? I'll kill him with my bare hands.'

'It was dark, I couldn't see. Don't worry, Boyo, I'm all right, just a bit shaken, that's all.'

'I think you should go to bed,' Boyo said softly. 'I'll get one of the servants to bring you a hot drink. In the morning, we'll have the doctor to see you.'

'Will you stay in my room with me tonight, Boyo?' Bethan looked at him pleadingly. 'Just hold me in case I have nightmares.' She rubbed at the bruises on her throat and he cursed the ever-present sense of guilt that Bethan aroused in him.

'All right, in the morning, it might be a good idea to notify the police. It's not good enough when a respectable woman can't ride out alone without being attacked by some cheap footpad or other.'

He took Bethan upstairs and helped her to undress. Her body was pale but with an unhealthily yellow tinge. He could not help but see the contrast between Bethan's paleness and the delicate alabaster of Catherine's young skin. He hid his thought by lowering his head and drawing back the sheets.

'Come on, get your nightgown on and then I'll fetch you something to soothe you.'

He tucked his wife into bed and she held out her hand and drew him down beside her. 'Boyo, I'm still trembling,

I am so afraid. The attack was somehow personal, as though someone set out to kill me.'

'Nonsense!' Boyo forced himself to be cheerful, he hated the way Bethan was clinging to him. What had happened to her spirit? Had Bethan's own poison destroyed her?

'Hold me close, Boyo, I feel so vulnerable, so alone. Especially now that I'm pregnant.' She could see he did not believe her and smiled secretly as he stretched out beside her.

'Don't talk now, you are overwrought, nervous, a good sleep will clear your mind.'

She curled towards him, her hair, sweet smelling and soft, brushed his cheek and he closed his eyes in pain; if only it could have been Catherine in his arms instead of Bethan.

As she always did, she guessed what he was thinking. 'You'll forget her, you'll see; soon that woman will be out of our lives, gone away for good.'

He was suddenly tense and he was too worried to conceal it. 'What do you mean, Bethan? What do you know that I don't know?' Maddeningly, she did not reply, she closed her eyes and feigned sleep and Boyo resisted the temptation to pull away from her, shake her eyes open and demand to know what she meant by her words. She was deranged, she was a dangerous woman, she would stop at nothing to get revenge, perhaps even murder.

He had an overwhelming need to see Catherine, to prove to himself that she was all right. He waited until he was sure Bethan was asleep and then he rose and left the bedroom and made his way downstairs.

Bethan knew he had gone and she knew where. She sat up in bed, frowning, so he was not keeping his side of the bargain, he was betraying her once again, how could he be so stupid? That Boyo had failed to make love to her hurt unbearably, the thought of his reluctance to take her in his arms was like a thorn in her flesh. She had given him time, a great deal too much time, and too many

416

chances to make amends. He had failed. How could she teach him that his best interests lay with her and her alone?

'I am angry with him, Elizabeth,' she said softly into the darkness. 'He has disappointed me yet again. All I find around me is hostility and betrayal. There is not one living person in this world who cares if I live or die. I am better off alone.'

She rose and drew on her warm robe. It was cold in the room with the pale moonlight silvering the furnishings but then it was always cold at Ty Craig, day or night, winter or summer, the temperature remained the same.

In the drawing-room, she took the decanter of port and poured a liberal measure. She thought of calling the maid to rebuild the fire but felt she could not stand Cara's pale, frightened face and her subservient manner. No, much better to be alone, not quite alone though, she would have Elizabeth, she would always have Elizabeth.

As though called from beyond the grave, the figure of Bethan's ancestor appeared in the room, but of course she was more than an ancestor. Elizabeth and Bethan were one, an incarnation of the same spirit that had gone down through the generations and would continue to be passed down when Bethan produced a child; a girl to carry on the work entrusted to the Llewellyns, the work of righting the wrongs in a wicked world.

Faintly at first and then growing in density, Elizabeth came to her, until a whole, vivid person stood in the room. Her dark hair was lustrous, her eyes deep with hidden secrets that only those who had passed through the barrier could know.

'Elizabeth, I'm glad you've come but then you always come when I need you.'

Bethan drank more port and she felt a little warmer. 'He's gone after that bitch, thinks I've murdered her or something. Murder, don't you think, might be a good idea? I've done it once so why not again?

'Oh, yes, Elizabeth, you did not think me so clever, did you?' Bethan took a seat and curled her feet under her. 'I have lured the husband of that awful woman, Hari Grenfell, into a trap. It was so easy, just a word from me that I had seen the bitch involved in a scuffle over on the other side of the woods. What? How will he die?' Bethan tapped her nose. 'You should know me as you know yourself, Elizabeth, we are from the same mould you and I. So what did I plan for him? I'll tell you, all in good time.'

She took a sip of her drink, triumph growing inside her at her own cleverness. 'I knew that fool Grenfell would ride hell for leather to save his precious little wife so I put a man in the woods, armed him with a gun. He has instructions to loose a shot, just as horse and rider reach the craggy rocks at the top of Rosehill, which will frighten the creature into bolting right over the edge and into the precipice below.'

Bethan felt a little giddy, no doubt the port was having an effect on her. Nevertheless she poured another full measure. 'Now I have to deal with the cause of all my trouble: Catherine O'Conner. I must get rid of her, I cannot let her get away with what she's done to me.

'Yes, you are right,' she nodded her head, 'she deserves to die, the whore. She tried to take the man I love, my husband, she made him betray me, humiliate me, it is she who has made me so unhappy.'

Bethan began to cry. 'I know, Elizabeth, he is not worthy of all the chances I gave him but I loved him, you see. I think I still do love him. Perhaps with her out of the way, he'll come back to me. It's worth a try isn't it, Elizabeth? When it is all over, we can live in peace, you and me and Boyo and our daughter.'

Bethan rose to her feet. 'You are right, I will go after him, the carriage is still outside. I will ride like the wind. You see, everything is working out for me. I'll fetch my husband back, convince him that his future is with me. I will deal with that woman, I will finish her, she will be no more.'

As Bethan left the house, she felt, for the first time, a sense of peace; justice was about to be done.'

'I don't know why you came here.' Catherine stood as far away from Boyo as she could. 'I am perfectly all right, as you can see.'

Boyo rubbed his eyes. 'I don't know what has come over me; it may be the atmosphere of that place getting me down but I feel, I *know,* that Bethan is up to something, something incredibly evil.' He rubbed his hand through his hair. 'Perhaps I *am* allowing my imagination to run away with me, I just don't know what to think any more.'

'Boyo, all this has nothing to do with me. You made your choice, you went back to your wife, so at least do the decent thing by all of us and be faithful to her, show her some loyalty.' She sank down into a chair. Suddenly she was pale, her mouth was trembling.

'Catherine, I had no choice but to go back to her,' Boyo said. 'Bethan promised to leave you alone providing we were reconciled. I thought I was protecting you by staying away. Now, I'm not so sure.'

'I realize that Bethan is a strange woman but even she would be afraid of going so far as to physically harm anyone.'

'I'm not so sure, Catherine, she's lost all sense of reality, she talks to herself and she seems to see things other people do not. She even believes she is pregnant again. Sometimes I'm afraid of my own wife.'

Catherine looked at Boyo, her mouth dry. 'Did you really go back to her for my sake, feeling as you do about her?'

'Catherine, I love you, God help me I'll always love you.' Boyo's hands were on her shoulders, drawing her to her feet, turning her to face him. She leaned against him.

'It's finished. This charade I've been playing can't go on.' Boyo's voice was firm. 'I must divorce Bethan, I must get out before she drives me as mad as she is.'

'Will Bethan agree to a divorce?' Catherine was doubtful.

'She will have no choice, I will have her committed to an institution if she won't see sense.'

Neither of them heard the small sound behind the doorway, or saw a shadowy figure retreating across the street to vanish into the shadows.

'Soon, Catherine, we will be together, then nothing will separate us ever again.'

CHAPTER THIRTY-THREE

Hari was exhausted. She had walked back to the spot where she had been attacked, that she felt was the most likely place for a trap to be laid for Craig. The roadway was empty, silent, the darkness was oppressive, but Hari forced herself to search among the shrubs for any sign of disturbance.

The moon had risen high, its silver glow illuminated the grass, glittering on the marshlands, so that they appeared to be lit by hundreds of fairy lights.

Hari felt helplessness sweep over her, there was so much ground to cover, so many places to search, how could she hope to find Craig by herself?

She paused, trying to think again of the words Bethan Hopkins had spoken so smugly. The woman had emphasized Brutus's evil temper, she meant Craig to have a riding accident, but if not on the roadway leading into town then where?

Hari froze. Over towards the other side of the hill was a deep woodland and beyond that a yawning precipice, a horse and rider might stumble over the edge in the darkness especially if some kind of trap had been laid. Hari bit her lip, imagining a nightmare vision of Craig, broken and injured, lying on the floor of the quarry.

She turned and made her way through the woods, she was weary, dispirited, but she could not return home to the empty house, she would search until she dropped if need be but she must find Craig. Alive or dead, she must find him.

It took her almost an hour to reach the copse. Here the moon could not penetrate because of the thickness of the trees; the darkness was intense. Beneath the trees it was cool, the rustle of small creatures in the grass was clearly audible in the silence. Hari shuddered, she was living in a nightmare because of the evil of Bethan Hopkins. The woman was not sane, she should be locked away, she was a danger to everyone.

Hari stood for a moment in silence, breathing in the night, listening, fully alert for any sound that might help her to find her husband. He was near by, she felt it in her bones. She strained to look through the blackness and towards her left, she heard the soft whinny of a horse.

'Brutus?' The animal came towards her, eyes rolling with fear. Hari patted his neck. 'It's all right, boy, it's all right.' Cautiously, she edged her way forward towards the edge of the rocky headland.

She lay flat on her stomach in the damp grass, peering downwards, willing the moon to shine, to illuminate the ground below her. She called Craig's name but her voice echoed distantly, lonely and lost among the rocks.

The sky to the east had begun to lighten, it was almost daybreak. Hari closed her eyes and prayed for the dawn, willing it to come more quickly.

She tensed, she thought she heard a sound of movement below in the quarry. She edged forward so that she was hanging over the cliff and, straining her eyes, she dimly made out a shape spread-eagled below on a flat surface of rock.

'Craig!' Her voice was urgent but there was no movement, no sound, and as her eyes misted over, she wondered if she was really seeing a figure among the rocks or if her senses were playing tricks on her.

Slowly, the day lightened, the trees that a few minutes ago were grey flattened shapes became solid trunks with thin branches whipped by the breeze.

Her grasping hands dug into the ground as she hung precariously over the rock-face. Yes! There was someone down there, it was a man. It was Craig.

'Craig!' She called his name but there was no movement, no sign that he was alive. 'Craig, answer me, please answer me.' She was sobbing, incoherent, and for a moment she rested her face against the cold grass straining for control.

She pushed herself back from the edge, she must be calm, she must do something positive; lying there crying would help no-one. She grasped at a tuft of coarse grass to give herself purchase and her hand encountered something metallic. She lifted it, stretching out her palm, knowing with a feeling of dread what she would see. It was a spent cartridge, someone had been shooting up here.

She closed her eyes against the sudden, overwhelming fear that Craig might be dead, shot through the heart, then pushed down into the quarry. She must get help but the nearest house was at least a mile away. Sobbing with exhaustion, she called to Brutus, he came at once, his soft nose nuzzling her hand. She climbed onto his back, praying the animal would not throw her and, slowly at first, began to make her way towards the town.

'I don't know what I am going to do, Elizabeth.' Bethan was back at Ty Craig. 'I heard him myself, telling the slut he would have me put away.' She sat in her chair before the grey of the rock, her face white with anger. 'They were so busy they didn't even hear me outside the door of that slum where she lives. I suppose even now he's having his way with the bitch!' Her lip curled disdainfully. 'Women of her sort are always ready to lie on their back for any man.

'Oh, he's clever, I'll give him that. With me in an asylum he could forget me and take charge of all my wealth. Well, I won't have it, I'll kill him and her both but I'll see them suffer the tortures of the damned before I send them to the hell where they belong.

'I know, Elizabeth, I must make a plan, a plan to get them both here together where I can deal with them. You will help me, Elizabeth. Talk to me, you are so wise, tell me what I must do.'

Bethan began to rock herself to and fro, nodding her head from time to time as though she was listening. At last, she leaned back and sighed with relief. 'You are right, that is a good plan. I'll tell Boyo that *I* want a divorce, that way I will put them off their guard.'

She rose and undressed and put on a fresh, clean night-gown, throwing her soiled shoes into the bottom of a cup-board. Boyo must never know she had been out, that she had spied on him and his whore, had listened to every-thing he had said. He might not come home until morn-ing but he would come, if only to gloat about bedding that bitch again. She had seen them in each other's arms, why had he never held her with such tenderness?

As she climbed into bed, anger bloomed like a rose within her, it was sharp and painful like thorns. She wanted to beat with her fists at those who had betrayed her but that was not the answer, other weapons must be used, such as subtlety and cunning.

She heard Boyo come in as dawn crept in through the window, she heard him climb the stairs and she lay back against the pillows, closing her eyes. He sat on the edge of the bed and she felt his breath as he leant towards her. 'Bethan, we have to talk.' He knew she was feigning sleep. She opened her eyes and pushed herself upright.

'Boyo, what is it, what's so important that it can't wait until a reasonable time? it's hardly daybreak.'

'I can't stand this situation any longer,' he said. 'I have to have a divorce, I can't live with you and all your ghosts or soon I'll be mad, too.'

'Mad, do you think me mad, Boyo?' She concealed her anger with admirable control and he looked at her care-fully, as if she was a cobra about to strike.

'Well, you need help, let's put it that way.'

'Why not put it this way: you want to get out of this marriage and any excuse will do, even to suggest there is something wrong with my mind, is that what you are say-ing?'

'I can't live with you, your threats, your tears, your strange ways. I've had as much as I can take of your whining and your selfishness, is that plain enough for you?'

'Oh, yes, I think so.' She smiled slowly, 'Strange, isn't it? If you had waited until I was up from bed and dressed, you would have heard my views first.'

She took a sip of water from the glass at her side. 'You see, Boyo, I have had enough of this charade too, I know you've been out all night and I can guess who you have been with. If you will do this to me when I am pregnant with your child, betray me in exactly the way you did before, then there is no future for us.'

She could see he was taken aback by her words, by her calmness. She pressed home her point. 'I want a divorce as badly as you do but there is one condition: that I talk to you both calmly about the division of our goods and chattels and of our joint wealth.'

'No need to discuss anything, you can have whatever you want. You have control of your own fortune, you have this house and I will make a generous settlement on you. There, see, it's done.'

She smiled thinly, he need not think he was getting away with things that easily. She shook her head, 'I insist that you bow to my one wish: to talk to you both together before we start proceedings. I feel such a discussion would prevent, shall we say, irregularities, arising later. I shall invite my solicitor to be present if you think I am out to cheat you.'

'No need for that,' Boyo said at once and Bethan knew she had shamed him. 'We can settle matters between us without interference from anyone else. Look, I will sign as much money over to you as you want.'

'Are you so anxious to be free, then?' For a moment, Bethan felt a pang of regret that their marriage was to end after all her hopes.

'It's over, Bethan, anything we had together is gone, you must feel that too if you want a divorce as much as I do.'

'Of course, you are right.' She had to be careful, she must not let him see the hate that was burning in her. He rose to his feet, he meant to leave at once, that much was obvious. He could not wait to get away from her.

He paused at the door. 'I really think you and I should settle this between us without bringing Catherine into it, what we have to discuss is nothing to do with her.'

'I will have my way on this,' Bethan forced a smile. 'Surely it is not much to ask that you both spare me half an hour of your time before you rush off to a wonderful new life together?' A new life in Hades, she thought balefully.

'I suppose not.' She could see he was not convinced. 'What harm could it do to talk?'

'None,' he replied, 'but I would rather the meeting take place on neutral ground.'

She hid her dismay. 'Where would you suggest?'

'The tearooms of the Mackworth Hotel perhaps.'

'That sounds very suitable.' It was not suitable at all but she would cross that bridge when she came to it, for now it was enough that Boyo was agreeing to bring that bitch to meet her. 'Shall we say a week today? We can have tea at the hotel.' She was playing for time and she wondered if he knew it.

She looked down at her hands. 'Last night, you said you would speak to the doctor, bring him to see if I was all right; you were anxious, angry that I had been attacked. Have you forgotten that so soon?'

She had touched a raw nerve, Bethan saw him flinch. 'I will send Cara for him at once and, if it means so much to you, I will wait to see what he has to say. In the meantime, I am going to bathe and shave and pack some clothes.'

She turned her face away as the door closed, she wanted to scream and rant and rage against him, she longed to plunge a knife into his black heart. After all they had been together, the pain they had endured, he meant to walk out of her life. Well, she would not let him walk away from her like that, she would wait and plan and then, when the time was right, she would spring her trap.

It was some time later that Boyo stood with the doctor at the curved doorway of Ty Craig. He watched the man climb onto his horse and canter away down the drive and his mind was whirling with confusion. Bethan had not been lying, she was expecting a child.

426

He remembered again the strange dream, the dream that he was making love, falling into a softness. He remembered with a thrill of horror the nail marks on his back. Somehow Bethan had tricked him, had put something in his drink. He lifted his head and stared up at the grey rock, his fists bunched. It made no difference, he intended to leave her and there was nothing she could do about it.

Hari rose to her feet as a white-coated doctor came along the corridor towards her. 'How is he?' Her mouth was dry with fear.

'Not too bad considering the fall and the hours of exposure to the cold and damp.' The doctor smiled reassuringly. 'He has a few cracked ribs but apart from that, he is remarkably fit.'

'When can I take him home?'

'You can take him home at once, nothing we can do here, it is up to nature now. Just let him rest, spoil him a little and in no time your husband will be as fit as a fiddle again.' He paused. 'He's been extremely lucky, a riding accident was it?'

Hari fingered the cartridge in her pocket and after a moment, nodded her head. 'It looks like it, perhaps when I speak to my husband he can tell me exactly what happened.'

'I expect so. Fortunate for him that you managed to find him in that God-forsaken place though.'

'I know.' How could Hari explain that a mixture of instinct and the putting together of the threats Bethan had made had led her to the spot where her husband was found? It all seemed too foolish for words.

'Right, then, I have work to do.' The doctor became brisk. 'I suggest you take a cab home, he's in no state to ride a horse or to walk far.'

Hari had thought of that, she could not afford a cab but she had appealed for help to Arian Smale. Arian had readily agreed to give her the use of a pony and trap.

Hari hurried towards the ward where her husband was

sitting on the edge of the bed. He smiled when he saw her, his old, teasing smile, and she leaned over him, kissing his face, his eyelids, his mouth with butterfly strokes.

'My love, thank God it wasn't worse. When I saw you lying there, I thought I'd lost you.'

'Can't kill a tough nut like me that easily,' he said and as he rose to his feet, she saw him wince.

'I've got a pony and trap to take us home.' Her lip trembled, home was not Summer Lodge, not now Bethan Hopkins had rented it for the duration. Home now was a dingy few rooms in the slum area of Swansea. But they would get used to it, they would have to.

'What happened, Craig?' Hari asked when at last she had managed to help him into the cart and had climbed up into the driving seat herself.

'I'm not sure, not even now when I have had time to think it over. I heard a noise, like a shot and then the horse went wild; next thing I knew, I was flying through the air into the quarry.'

'What were you doing there in the first place; looking for me, I suppose?'

'Now, how did you know that, you witch?'

'It was not witchcraft, Bethan Hopkins was sitting in our house when I got in. You must have seen her, she must have said something to worry you.'

Craig rubbed his eyes, 'It's coming back to me now, she came to tell me the same thing she told you, that she had rented the house. I thought she seemed sensible enough until she began to talk about you. She said that you had left Swansea hours ago, that there had been reports of footpads on the roads and why were you so late when she had an appointment with you at the house.'

'She had no appointment with me.' Hari did not choose to tell Craig how she and Bethan had rowed and wrestled like fishwives; no need to upset him, not when he was feeling bad enough already.

'Here we are, our new home, at least for the present.' Hari could sense Craig's dismay when she drew the pony to a halt outside the house in Watkin Street. It looked dingier than ever, the upstairs windows uncurtained, the paintwork peeling and dull.

'It won't be for ever, love.' She helped him down into the roadway and clung on to him, her eyes warm as they rested on him. 'You can take that as a promise for I intend to make us rich again, however long it takes.'

He kissed her hair. 'We are together and that is enough for me.'

As she helped Craig to walk along the dark passageway, Hari felt tears constrict her throat, the place smelt damp and she knew instinctively that they were alone in the house. There were no cheerful sounds from Catherine's rooms, the house was dark and deserted and so alien that Hari did not think she could bear to live there. But she had to live there, had to make the best of it for Craig's sake. He was sick, injured, he needed nursing. The last thing he needed was a snivelling wife.

Soon, he would regain his strength but until then, he could not work, not even at the offices of *The Swansea Times*. It was up to her to bring in the money or they would starve. For a moment, panic gripped her and then she squared her shoulders and lifted her chin high; she must not despair, she had skills, she had courage and somehow she would survive.

CHAPTER THIRTY-FOUR

Liam Cullen put down his glass of ale, and looked around him. The small back room of the George was crowded, filled with the smell of pipe smoke and he wondered why he was there. Outside, it was cold, the wind driving the rain in rivulets along the gutters; at least in the George it was warm and dry. He heard a voice, suddenly raised, and his attention was caught.

'Can't stand that Bethan Hopkins no longer, mind. Glad to get away from that morgue of a place, I am. I hated it at Ty Craig and hated *her*, Mrs Hopkins, as well. Right cow, she is, frightened me to death with her funny ways.'

He peered round cautiously and saw a young girl, with mousy hair and a complexion to match, elbows on table, hair dishevelled. She was obviously well into her cups by the look of the bottles on the table. Opposite her sat a man, dour and thin, his hand trailing beneath the table to touch the girl's leg. She seemed not to notice as she continued her complaints.

'Once the master left again, I knew I couldn't stay. Gone potty, she is, that Mrs Hopkins, talks to herself all the time, sees ghosts that are not there.' She smiled. 'The master now, Mr Hopkins, he's lovely. I don't blame him for getting out and taking up with that red-haired girl again, always had a soft spot for her, did Mr Hopkins.'

The pain was almost physical and Liam took a gulp of his drink, trying to dislodge the constriction in his throat. He thought of them together, Hopkins and Catherine, and he felt a knife turn in his gut. How he wanted her, he would have loved and revered her, put her on a pedestal. She could have borne him fine sons and daughters who would take over the farm. But it was no good thinking like that, Catherine was not in love with him, she would never be his, he might as well face it and go home to Ireland once and for all.

He rose abruptly and put down his glass. He would go to see Catherine one last time, say his goodbyes and then he would return to his lodgings and pack his few possessions. Tomorrow, he would sail for Ireland, try to find peace in the emerald hills and jewelled lakes of his homeland.

Some day, he might even forget Catherine, find another woman he could love. Somehow, he did not believe it. He walked out into the night and stared up for a moment at the clearing sky, the rain had stopped and the moon shone palely onto the wet streets. Liam breathed in the salt tang of the sea and knew he would miss Swansea, it had become part of him, in his blood, the way Catherine was.

He began to walk, turning uphill in the direction of Watkin Street. The sooner he severed all links with Catherine and Swansea, the better. A clean knife wound, it would hurt like hell but it was by far the best way.

Catherine was sitting huddled close to a fire that was burning low in the grate, she looked up at him, her face pale in the lamplight and he saw that she had been crying. His heart melted and he made a move towards her and then caught himself up.

'Liam!' She tried to smile but failed miserably. He sank into a seat, keeping his distance and cleared his throat.

'I'm going home to Ireland.' There it was said. He saw her eyes, unfathomable in the darkness, looking into him. 'It's no use pretending to myself any more that you'll marry me, is it?'

She shook her head slowly and the faint hope that had sprung within him died.

'When will you leave?' Her words were indistinct, he heard the hint of tears in her voice and he fought the urge to take her in his arms.

'As soon as I can get a boat. I have to get back to the farm too; I'm needed there, can't trust labourers to do the work properly without supervision. And there's Patricia's child to think of, I *have* to go home, Catherine.'

'I know.' She spoke softly. Her shoulders were slumped, she seemed lost and miserable. 'Catherine, what's wrong, what's troubling you?' Even as he asked the question, he cursed himself for not walking away.

'I thought making a decision about my future would be so easy but now I'm not so sure, about Boyo, about anything.'

'Have you told Hopkins how you feel?' Liam was unable to repress the surge of triumph the thought evoked in him.

'Not yet. His wife has told him she wants a divorce.'

'Well then?' Liam's tone was sharper than he had intended. 'Where's the problem?'

'Mrs Hopkins wants to have a meeting with us both, she wants to talk things over, she says.'

'Oh, and when and where is this meeting?' Liam asked flatly, as though the matter did not interest him at all.

'It was to be at the Mackworth but now she says she is sick, indisposed, we must go up to Ty Craig and meet with her there.' She paused and looked towards the dying embers of the fire. 'I know it sounds silly but I'm frightened. I don't know what I want any more. What if she has an attack of hysterics, I don't think I could face that.'

'Then don't go. Sure, I'm surprised at Hopkins for agreeing to such madness, the woman is not sane, in her own house she will be free to rant and rage against you all she wants.'

'It's not Boyo's fault, he was angry because I didn't want to talk to his wife. We quarrelled about it, he's gone, perhaps back to her, I don't know. The strain of it all is too much, it will destroy anything we once had between us.'

'Look, Cath, your future is doomed if you stay with Hopkins, you've had no luck since you took up with him, have you? You just think about it.'

It was unfair of him to pressurize her at this moment when she was so low but Liam felt a sense of dread at the

432

thought of leaving her at the mercy of Hopkins and his strange wife.

'What do you mean?' She was on the defensive and that made him angry.

'You broke your father's heart by the affair, your mother's too; and look at the string of ill luck you've had. He's no good for you, Catherine, he's weak, can't you see that?'

'I don't understand what you are trying to say,' Catherine's eyes searched his.

'I'm saying, think about others for a change. There's not just you and Hopkins to consider in all this, other people have been dragged into the mess, too; me and my family, have you forgotten that? And Mrs Grenfell, she's lost everything, her home her business and very nearly her husband. She's now reduced to living in this slum. If you are not convinced by all that, what of Doreen, involved in murder! What more do you want to happen before you see sense?'

Catherine was white-faced. 'I know you are right,' her voice was small, distant, 'but what can I do?'

'So you'll beard the lion in her den, walk into that creepy old house like a lamb to the slaughter? I never thought I'd say this but you are as big a fool as Hopkins.'

Liam rose from the chair so abruptly that it tipped over and crashed against the floor. Without waiting to straighten it, he strode to the door and let himself out without another word.

Catherine hurried to follow him, to call him back but he was storming along the road without a backward glance. 'Liam! Come back, I need you!' But he was gone out of sight, out of her life. What had she done? She felt she had lost the best friend she had ever had. Boyo Hopkins had given her passion, he had aroused the woman in her, brought her fulfilment, but he had never been a friend, he had not brought her happiness. It was Liam who had been there when she needed support.

She returned to the silent house, too weary and sick even to cry.

433

'It's so wonderful, I want to go down on my knees and thank God for answering my prayers.' Hari rose from the chair near the table where she had been sorting her mail, she glanced towards Craig, her eyes alight. He was reclining against the pillows, a copy of *The Swansea Times* in his hands. The morning light warmed the shabby furnishings, highlighting the grey in Craig's hair. The rooms were as comfortable as Hari could make them but the smell of cats still lingered in spite of all her efforts.

'Stop looking so smug and tell me what the un-restrained joy I see on your face is all about,' Craig said.

'Look,' Hari moved towards the bed, 'it's from Clark's in Somerset.' She sat on the edge of the bed. 'You know I wrote to the family a few weeks ago telling them of my situation and asking for their help and advice? Well, I have their answer.'

'And? You tantalizing woman!'

'And they are going to fund the business for a year to see if I can save it. Mr Clark Senior is warm in his praise for the way I have always conducted my business with him.' She smiled. 'He remembers my cheek in asking for a despatch of boots and shoes on the understanding that I make payment at a later date and admires me for my courage and enterprise.'

'So this means a new start, another shot at success,' Craig said, his eyes warm with pride as they rested on her. 'I knew that you, with your indomitable spirit and your ingenious mind, would find a way out of our troubles.'

He waved his hand to encompass the shabby room. 'It broke my heart to see you brought to this after all your years of hard work. I haven't been much help either, have I?'

She took his hand and held it to her cheek. 'Craig, I couldn't have done any of it without you.

'Another thing, we won't lose Summer Lodge, not now. We have only signed a short lease, soon Bethan Hopkins will have to get out of there. She might not be aware of that but she soon will be.'

'Hey, how much money do you think the Clarks are going to advance you?' Craig's voice held a note of caution.

'Enough,' Hari said. 'It makes better sense to utilize Summer Lodge than to try to rent and equip new premises. Until we can return we'll have to manage to work from here, of course.'

Craig nodded. 'I see the sense in that, yes. You are quite a wise old thing aren't you?'

Hari tapped his hand. 'Not so much of the "old" if you don't mind. This morning, I am eighteen again, just starting out on a new business enterprise and with the man I love at my side; what more could I want?'

Even as she leaned forward to kiss her husband's lips, Hari felt a shudder of fear as she thought of Bethan Hopkins, still out there, like a malevolent spirit just waiting for Hari to fall again.

'I'm sorry, I shouldn't have quarrelled with you, certainly not over Bethan and her foolish ideas.' Boyo made a move towards her and then hesitated, aware of Catherine's attitude of reserve.

'What I'm trying to say is, if you think it's the right thing to do then we'll go up to Ty Craig, have this sorted out with Bethan once and for all.' Catherine saw the distaste in his eyes as he looked around the dingy rooms.

'In the meantime, you are to move your stuff out of here, I won't see you starving and freezing in this hole any longer, not when I've money enough to make you comfortable.'

'Let's leave things as they are until we've spoken to your wife.' There was an uneasy note in Catherine's voice, Boyo's eyes were shrewd as they rested upon her.

'You are as reluctant to see her as I am, aren't you?' He regarded her steadily. 'Don't worry, I'll be there with you every moment, I won't leave your side, I promise.'

'I know. It's very silly of me but something Liam said . . .'

'Liam, he's been here?' Boyo heard the sharpness in his

voice and immediately regretted it.

Catherine's chin lifted. 'Yes, he's been here, to say goodbye, he's going back to Ireland.'

'I see,' Boyo's relief was evident in the easing of the tension around his eyes, 'but what has he been saying to make you so uneasy?'

'Oh, it's nothing,' Catherine waved the question aside, 'it's all too silly for words.' How could she tell Boyo that she did not really know what she wanted any more? She was no longer sure of what her feelings for him or for Liam were.

'But what did he say?' Boyo persisted.

Catherine sighed. 'How ill luck has dogged my heels since I took up with you. He made a list, like Dad dying; oh, you know, things like that.'

'But that's foolish, your father was a sick man, he would have died if you had never seen me again.'

'I know, I told you it was silly.' Catherine rubbed at her eyes. 'I just have a bad feeling, I can't explain it, Boyo.' She sighed. 'Perhaps we should call it off, we can speak to Bethan some other time.'

'No, let's just get on with it, the sooner we get this meeting over and done with, the better for all of us.' Boyo moved towards the door and after a moment, Catherine followed him, knowing it was the last thing she wanted to do.

When they arrived at Ty Craig the place was shrouded in mist, the grey walls appearing black in the strange light. A window, revealed by the ghostly vapour, shone dully, blank like a dead eye. Catherine shuddered, perhaps she was being absurd and fanciful but there was something evil about the house, she could feel it. She almost turned away but Boyo's hand was on her arm, guiding her towards the arched doorway.

Bethan opened the door herself and Catherine had the distinct feeling that Boyo's wife had been watching and waiting for them to arrive.

'Come in, do.' Her cool voice enunciated the words with precision, she was a woman held in check, the

436

knuckles of her hands gleamed white as she clutched her skirt.

Catherine glanced up at Boyo for reassurance, he was a big man, and yet she sensed an uncertainty in him. But that was foolish, nothing could go wrong so long as they were together.

Bethan led the way into the sitting-room, a fire burned in the grate and yet the room was chilly. There was a pungent smell in the air that Catherine identified as lamp oil. She glanced towards the fireplace again and saw a flame burn on the ornate bars of the grate. In spite of the fire, there was no warmth in the room.

Bethan had opened the door herself, it seemed there were no servants in the house and somehow that fact made Catherine more nervous than she was already.

'Please, sit down, I've put a tray of porter ready to welcome you, might as well make this meeting as civilized as possible, don't you agree?' She ignored Catherine and looked directly at Boyo.

'If you say so, Bethan.' He sounded noncommittal as he took a seat and waited for her to hand round the drinks. Catherine saw him shake his head slightly as she took a glass from the tray and, pointedly, he placed his own glass, untouched, on the table beside him.

Catherine's fear of Bethan was heightened; if Boyo did not trust his wife enough to drink from the glass she had handed him then he must believe her dangerous indeed.

'I want to know that you will make my husband happy.' Bethan addressed Catherine for the first time. 'I take it you are not just looking for rich pickings, or are you?'

Catherine sighed heavily. 'I think you are insulting me on purpose, Mrs Hopkins. Is this what you call a "civilized discussion"?'

Boyo made a move to rise but Bethan raised her hand. 'I'm sorry, I apologize, it's just that other women have made a play for Mr Hopkins, you see,' she smiled at Boyo indulgently, 'and I don't blame them, not any of them. I do realize that men, all red-blooded men at any rate, have needs that a wife may not entirely fulfil. Shall we say

437

"habits" that women of a lower order will not only tolerate but will enjoy; this is something I quite understand while I do not applaud it. Still, I have not heard you say anything yet. I apologize for talking so much, please, go ahead, state your case, Miss O'Conner.'

Catherine shook her head and looked towards Boyo. 'This is hopeless, I knew we shouldn't have come, she is just taunting us, well, me at least. She wants to see me humiliated.'

Boyo rose to his feet. 'Will you get to the point of this meeting, Bethan?'

'Very well,' Bethan was white-faced, completely calm but her eyes gleaming like those of a wounded animal. 'Boyo, I want to give you one last chance, will you give up this . . . this rubbish and come back to me?'

'Shut up, Bethan!' Boyo was flushed with anger, Catherine watched as he moved towards his wife and grasped her wrists. 'I was a fool to come here, you will never listen to reason, you are beyond reason, mad, insane. I do not love you, I never loved you, is that clear enough for you?'

Catherine remembered, quite suddenly, the way Boyo had held her by force, taking her on the floor like a harlot and she was frightened. Was she making the biggest mistake of her life?

'Please, let me go,' Bethan said quietly. Boyo released her at once. Catherine watched as Bethan moved carefully towards the ornate sideboard. She rummaged in a drawer, sniffing a little, as if she was crying. Catherine felt pity tug at her.

Bethan turned, she was pointing a gun at Catherine. 'If I can't have him then no-one shall have him.'

Catherine saw, with horror, Bethan's finger tighten around the trigger, and then she was hurled backwards as if struck by a giant blow. She was on the floor, head resting against the fireplace. She was conscious, she smelt the paraffin close to her face and heard the dull crackle of the fire.

'Oh, my God, what have I done!' Bethan's voice

seemed far away. 'You must get a doctor. I'm sorry, Boyo, I didn't mean to shoot, I just wanted to frighten her. The gun went off by accident, I swear it.'

'For God's sake, Bethan, send for the carriage, I'll take her to the hospital.'

'There is no-one here, no carriage, no groom, no animals. Take your own horse and ride into town; bring the doctor as quickly as you can, before she bleeds to death.'

Bethan's voice was closer, stronger. There was a creak as a door opened with a blast of air, cold and clammy, and it was then the pain struck. She bit her lip and in spite of herself, heard the moan that escaped from between her teeth.

Blades of fire were being thrust into her back and shoulder, she wanted it to stop and then, mercifully, she was tumbling downwards into darkness.

Bethan felt a deep satisfaction spread through her being, warming her heart, bringing a sense of power that cheered her. She concealed her feelings as she looked at Boyo. 'Don't stand there like a frightened child, go on, ride as fast as you can, into town. I'll take care of her. You must go, what other choice is there?'

She saw him hesitate. 'I could take her on the saddle with me.'

'She would never make it, there would be too much pain and too much loss of blood.'

'Blast you, Bethan! You make sure she does not die or by God I'll kill you with my bare hands.'

He hurried from the house and Bethan watched him ride away at breakneck speed along the drive. Ignoring the slumped figure in the sitting-room, she hurried upstairs to her bedroom. She felt cold, suddenly uncertain. It was all such a mess, she had meant to kill Catherine with the first shot and claim it had been an accident. She would have been believed, of course she would, whoever would think Bethan Hopkins, a frail, pregnant woman, could be capable of violence?

'I wish you had never been born, Catherine O'Conner,'

Bethan said bitterly. She placed some coals across the dying embers but that only seemed to dampen the faint glow into nothingness.

'Blast!' Bethan took up one of the oil-lamps and carried it towards the fireplace, removing the chimney and the wick, she tipped some of the paraffin into the fire.

The flame shot upwards, taking her unawares. The lamp became a fireball in seconds and with a shriek of pain, Bethan dropped it onto the carpet. The paraffin spread outwards, leaking towards where she stood, carrying with it a channel of fire. Backing away, her eyes on the sudden blaze, Bethan grasped the doorknob, it resisted, her hands were slipping, perhaps because of the paraffin on her fingers. She must get out! She jerked the handle hard and it came off in her hand. The curtains were alight now, she kicked at the door in fear and rage. She heard herself swear and curse like a sailor as the roaring behind her grew in intensity. She glanced over her shoulder, her eyes wide. The rug in front of the hearth was licked with flames. Bethan began to cough as the smoke reached her lungs.

'Elizabeth!' She thought she called the name but it was a mere croak. She saw her then, Elizabeth, from the rocks beyond the window, beckoning her, smiling at her, urging her to come with her so that they could be together for ever.

She flung open the window, feeling the heat from the blazing curtains, and stepped out onto the ledge. Elizabeth was on the rock outside, urging her onwards. Bethan did not dare to look down into the darkness below, she would need all her courage for what she must do. She hesitated only for a second.

'You will never have my husband, Catherine O'Conner!' she screamed. She reached out, took Elizabeth's hand and stepped into the abyss.

Liam had stared at the boat drawing away from the harbour and cursed himself for a fool. Why had he not boarded, why not shake the dust of this place from his

440

feet for ever? And yet he could not rid himself of the feeling that Catherine needed him, that she was in danger.
He knew she was going to see that Hopkins woman, the
mad, crazy woman who might do anything to get her
revenge. However foolish the idea, he had to find out for
himself if Catherine was all right before he turned his
back on her for ever.

Once back in Swansea, he had set out for the grey
house nestling in the folds of the hills. The place was difficult to find and he wasted valuable time, retracing his
steps and asking directions of a lone shepherd who,
having found an unexpected captive audience, wanted to
talk.

At last, rounding a bend in the road, he saw Ty Craig
looming up at him out of the mist. Liam stopped in his
tracks, fear clutching at him as he saw flames leaping
from one of the front windows. Even as he watched, a
pane of glass shattered outwards with an almighty
crash.

Liam's steps crunched on the gravel of the drive as he
pounded towards the front door. He pushed it open and
flames belched towards him. He slammed it shut and
hurried around the back. Somehow, he knew that
Catherine was inside the house and he knew he must find
her before it was too late.

'Catherine, for God's sake wake up!' She opened her eyes
and saw Boyo leaning over her, his face white and tense.
'Thank God I had second thoughts about leaving you and
turned back! We have to get out of here, the house is on
fire.'

She felt him lift her in his arms, felt the pain shudder
through her as he carried her towards the hall. There was
smoke everywhere, the west wing of the house was well
alight, Catherine could feel the scorching heat on her face
as Boyo negotiated the passage leading to the back of the
house.

Her arm was numb, her clothing soaked with blood but
at least she was still alive.

'Boyo,' she tried to speak but there was no strength in her voice.

'Don't try to talk.' He made his way through the hall and towards the back of the house along a dark passageway. The thick back door was locked, there was no key.

'The window,' Catherine whispered, 'there in the pantry, if you can break the glass you might be able to get us out.'

It was a slender hope but Boyo seized on the idea. He lowered Catherine gently to the floor and began to place boxes beneath the high window. The structure was frail, unstable, but Boyo did not seem to notice as he looked around for something to break the glass.

Catherine saw him tuck an iron bar into his belt and then he was clambering over the boxes and up towards the window. He was still a short distance away from the glass but by reaching upwards with the iron bar, he was able to smash through the small panes. The frame was rotten with damp and Boyo set about it with desperate strength. It broke easily, the timber was old, but the opening was still too small for them to get through. Boyo began to dig out the mortar between the stones surrounding the window.

Catherine saw a small trail of smoke appear beneath the door of the passage and snake its way towards where she lay. She began to cough.

Boyo glanced down at her and then renewed his efforts, hacking away with frenzied blows at the wall. One stone became dislodged and rolled downwards, crashing against the floor. And then the hole was suddenly yawning open, big enough for a man to climb through with ease.

He returned to where Catherine lay. 'I'm going to have to pick you up, I'll try not to hurt you but it's our only chance.'

She suppressed a moan as Boyo lifted her in his arms but as soon as he began to climb up on the boxes, they shifted beneath the extra weight.

Boyo paused and looked up, his face strained. Catherine

442

saw behind his shoulder, as if in a dream, that Liam was there, leaning into the opening, his big hands reaching towards her. 'Give her to me, for God's sake,' he said.

Catherine felt herself being lifted through the broken window, the pain in her upper body was so intense that she almost lost consciousness. Liam was holding her in his arms, the cool night air was on her face. 'Liam.' She wanted to tell him how happy she was to be held close to him in this way, that if she died in his arms she would be content, but she could not speak. Liam was looking at her wound, touching her shoulder tentatively.

'It's not too bad, my darlin', it will mend.' She must have lost consciousness then because when she opened her eyes she was lying against the damp grass, the scent of it clean and fresh in her nostrils.

She stared up at the darkness of the sky and saw the stars bright and clear and the acrid smell of smoke and the loud roar of flames encompassed her.

She lifted her head and saw Liam easing himself into the gaping wound in the wall where the window had been. Smoke billowed around him, enveloping him and she tried to call his name but her throat was on fire.

The back door of the house began to burn, the small licking flames quickly turning into a fierce blaze as the old timber caught light.

There was a crashing sound from within the house and Catherine realized the ceilings were caving in.

'Liam!' Her voice was a hoarse whisper. She crawled forward, inch by inch, pain engulfing her. 'Liam, come back, it's no use.' Her words were lost as a burst of fresh flames engulfed the house.

'Liam,' she whimpered, 'I don't want you to die, I love you, dammit!' It was true, why had she been so blind? Liam was in her heart, in her mind, in a way Boyo had never been. But the knowledge had come too late.

She fell back away from the heat, she was weak with fear and pain. Liam was going to die and it was all her fault. She felt blackness swirl around her and she gave herself up to the darkness.

She opened her eyes to the sound of a great roaring blast, the fire was engulfing the house now, a beast devouring its prey. Catherine struggled against the pain, trying to sit up, to see what was happening.

An indistinct shape was being thrust from the flying sparks and engulfing smoke and fell, sprawling on the ground. It was not Liam. Catherine stared down at the still face of Boyo Hopkins, his skin blackened by smoke. With the edge of her skirt, she wiped away the grime. His hair was singed and as she touched it, blackened pieces came away in her hand. His eyes were wide but they saw nothing.

Catherine wanted to cry for all the mistakes she had made in her life. Her mistakes had cost Boyo his life.

She held her head back and stared up through the smoke at the moon that was pale now, dying with the hint of morning. She raised her fist to the heavens.

'Give Liam back to me!' It was a feeble protest and one that went unnoticed as the clouds gathered once more. Catherine felt hopelessness engulf her. The upper part of the house was an inferno, flames leapt skyward, the heat was intolerable. She should try to move away from the house but what good was her life now when she would live it alone without Liam, without the man she loved. Why had she never realized it before? What sort of fool was she to have gone blindly through life throwing herself away on a man who was not fit to lick the boots of Liam Cullen?

The smoke cleared a little and dimly she saw the shape of a man, crawling on all fours towards her.

'Liam!' Gasping, she edged slowly to where he had fallen and now lay, spread-eagled on the grass. 'Please God don't let him be dead, too.'

He was quiet and still; fear lent Catherine strength and she leaned over him. 'Liam, I love you, don't leave me, not now.' She pressed her mouth to his, trying to breathe her own life into him. She fell against his chest, listening for his heartbeat.

So faintly that at first she did not know if she had

444

imagined it, a fluttering of breath whispered on Liam's lips. He opened his eyes and looked up at her. 'Hello, colleen.' His voice was hoarse but a glimmer of a smile lit up his eyes.

Catherine began to cry, tears ran down her cheeks onto his smoke-grimed face. 'Liam, my love.' She kissed his eyelids, his cheeks, his mouth. 'Thank God!'

The sound of the fire-brigade bell was faint at first against the roaring of the flames; it was growing louder, ringing inside Catherine's head. She felt as if the world was spinning away from her. She lay down beside Liam and closed her eyes.

'Hold on, help is here; we will be together always, I promise.' Liam's voice was so low she hardly heard the words. He spoke to her again, bringing her back from the edge of unconsciousness. 'Did you mean it, colleen? When you said you loved me?'

'I meant it,' Catherine whispered.

He sighed softly. 'That's what I thought. I knew a good Irish girl would see sense in the end.'

'Don't get too uppity.' Catherine tried to infuse some strength into her voice. 'There's enough Welsh in me to raise hell if I don't get my own way, mind.'

Above them, through the valley, between the sharp outline of the hills, a pale light was beginning to spread earthward, bringing the trees into relief. Dawn was driving away the darkness.

Liam reached out and took her hand, his fingers curling warmly around hers. Catherine knew then there would be no more darkness. For her and for Liam a new day was just beginning.